Love, Happiness and Other Lies My Mother Told Me

Love, Happiness and Other Lies My Mother Told Me

Krista Lee Woodman

iUniverse, Inc.
New York Lincoln Shanghai

Love, Happiness and Other Lies My Mother Told Me

Copyright © 2007 by Krista Lee Woodman

All rights reserved. No part of this book may be used or reproduced by any means, graphic, electronic, or mechanical, including photocopying, recording, taping or by any information storage retrieval system without the written permission of the publisher except in the case of brief quotations embodied in critical articles and reviews.

iUniverse books may be ordered through booksellers or by contacting:

iUniverse
2021 Pine Lake Road, Suite 100
Lincoln, NE 68512
www.iuniverse.com
1-800-Authors (1-800-288-4677)

This is a work of fiction. All of the characters, names, incidents, organizations, and dialogue in this novel are either the products of the author's imagination or are used fictitiously.

ISBN: 978-0-595-44331-4 (pbk)
ISBN: 978-0-595-88661-6 (ebk)

Printed in the United States of America

To my parents.

Acknowledgments

When I started working on this book back in the summer of 2001, I wasn't even sure if I'd finish it let alone publish it. I just wrote it because I wanted to get the story on paper. Without the encouragement and help of a few people, this never would have seen print.

First, I'd like to thank Brenda Neely for reading the final draft and finding any typos and spelling mistakes that had missed the cut. Any mistakes that remain are mine.

Second, I'd like to thank Lisa Avery for supporting my writing ever since we were kids. She was one of the first people to read this story, back in its earliest incarnation in 2002, and she encouraged me to publish it (and it only took me five years to listen to her).

Finally, I'd like to thank Kaitlyn Grasse and Jeff Woodman for assisting me with my punctuation problems (especially my aversion to commas). Their help was greatly appreciated.

Without these people, this story would have stayed safely tucked away in my computer.

Thank you.

Chapter One

I awoke to the sound of the phone ringing, loud and obnoxious and right next to my head. There were a few things I hated more than being woken up by the phone, but none of them were coming to mind. Ignoring it rarely worked; as soon as I tried to block it out, the sound only became more annoying.

At first I tried pulling a pillow over my head to block out the noise but it didn't work. All the pillow did was muffle the ringing, giving the sound a strange underwater quality while practically suffocating me.

How much longer until it went to my voice mail?

More importantly, who was calling me so early in the morning?

I finally jumped up to answer it, banging my elbow sharply on my bedside table for my troubles.

I glanced at the clock before picking up the receiver. It was only five after nine in the morning.

"'lo," I said groggily into the receiver, gingerly touching my elbow where I'd hit it against the table. It really hurt. I just *knew* I was going to have a huge bruise. I was already furious at the person on the other end of the phone, and I didn't even know who it was.

"Hello," a man's voice on the other end began, "May I please speak to Miss Abigail Shepherd?" He sounded very official, pompous and annoying.

I clenched my teeth in frustration. "Speaking." I had always hated the name Abigail. No one had called me Abigail since second grade and even then I didn't like it. I wasn't an Abigail. Or even an Abby, for that matter.

If this guy was someone from the phone company telling me how I could save money by switching my long-distance provider, I was going to lose it.

"Miss Shepherd, my name is Carter Stevens, and I represent your father."

Discussing my father. I almost wished it had been a telemarketer. I was seconds away from hanging up the phone.

I'd been awake for less than five minutes, and I'd already been injured, insulted and reminded about the sperm donation that had resulted in my birth. This day was not off to a great start.

"What do you mean 'represent'?"

"I'm your father's attorney."

"Good for you," I said, rubbing my eyes. "It's a little early to be talking about my father. How about calling back later? Like in about ten years." I had actually moved to put the receiver back on the cradle before I realized that he was still talking.

"Miss Shepherd, I'm calling because I have some bad news."

"What is it? Is he in jail?" I couldn't think of any other reason why my father would need a lawyer. And I really couldn't think of any reason why my father would be trying to contact me. It had to be jail.

"He's not in jail."

"Fine," I continued, "If you're calling because he owes you money, I can't help you." I was completely broke. My credit cards were maxed out and I only had a month's rent in my bank account.

"That's not why I'm calling."

"Why then?"

"I'm sorry to tell you that your father passed away about a week ago."

"Oh."

I wasn't sure what he expected me to say about that.

"I'm terribly sorry about your loss ..."

"What loss?" I said angrily, cutting him off. "Look, I haven't seen my father since I was eight, so it's really not much of a loss. This might sound insensitive, but his death doesn't mean anything to me. I don't have a clue where he's been for the last seventeen years. And I was perfectly happy with him out of the picture. I don't really need to have a reunion with him now that he's finally kicked it. So … Mr. Stevens is it? Unless you have something else to say, I'd like to get back to sleep."

"Actually, Miss Shepherd, there is something more. The reason I'm calling is because I'm the executor of your father's will. I need you to come to New Ferndale for the reading."

"Why?" This guy honestly didn't get the fact that I wanted to hang up on him. Completely clueless.

"You and your sister are both mentioned in the will."

"I don't really care." I didn't. It wasn't just a lie to get him to leave me alone. "I don't want anything from my father. Maxine can take care of it." Maxine thrived on this sort of stuff. She'd get to play the role of the good daughter and make me look like a deadbeat. "Just send me whatever forms will make it official, and I'll sign everything over to her." Maxine should be the one to inherit his beer mugs and old TV Guides. Let her deal with all his crap.

"Please Miss Shepherd, you and your sister are both mentioned separately. It's very important for you to come to the reading. Your father really wanted you both there. I promise it won't take very long. If you decide you still want to hand everything over to your sister, you can do it after the reading. You'll be back in the city before you know it."

"Fine." Anything to get him off the phone. "When do you need me?" I snuggled down deeper into my bed, pulling the duvet over my head. I hoped that I wouldn't have to deal with it for at least a few weeks. I needed time to build up my courage to face Maxine.

"The reading is at 11:00 AM tomorrow in my office. It's on the main street in New Ferndale."

I sat up again, giving him my full attention.

"Tomorrow? As in the day after today?"

"That's the traditional definition of 'tomorrow'."

"What's with the short notice?" I didn't own a car. How the hell was I supposed to even get up there?

"I had some trouble finding you," he said. "Your father didn't have your number and your sister only had an old one that was no longer in service. Are you in the witness protection program or something?"

I wish. Then no one could find me and wake me up before I was good and ready.

"How'd you manage to find me?"

"Bit of detective work. I'm sorry to spring this on you last minute, but please try to attend."

"Can't I just hand everything over to Maxine? I was serious when I said I didn't want anything from him." And then I wouldn't have to drive up there and risk seeing my sister.

"You can, but I still need you there tomorrow. The paperwork will be ready for you to sign when you get here."

His voice had a tone of finality in it. I guess he was done with his closing arguments and was sure that the verdict was going to be in his favour.

I sighed. "Fine. I'll be there." I didn't want to spend all morning arguing with the guy.

After getting directions from him I hung up the phone and sat up, running my fingers through my matted hair. I was wide-awake, which sucked. There was no point even trying to get back to bed. I'd had about five hours of sleep, and I wasn't pleased. I couldn't function properly with less than seven, although I preferred eight or nine. I was cranky and annoyed. I had a bad temper at the best of times, and it was even worse when I was tired. I half wished it had been a telemarketer calling so I could have at least vented some frustration.

How was I supposed to get up north for the will reading? I mean, honestly. My father could have been a little bit more considerate and died closer to where I lived.

I picked up the phone again and started dialing. It rang three times before it was answered.

"Dennis Wells speaking." I could hear papers being shuffled in the background.

"Hi Denny," I said. "You pretending to be busy in case it was the boss calling?"

"Kerri," he said in a surprised voice. "What's wrong? Why are you up?"

"There's a nine o'clock in the morning now. I'm calling everyone I know to spread the news."

"I'm at work. I've been up since six."

"I forgot that you were a sadist."

"Funny," he said, laughing. "Seriously though, something must be up."

I smiled to myself. Denny was one of my oldest and closest friends. He knew me better than anyone and he knew that I rarely got up before eleven.

As an accountant for the firm of Meyer & Tanenbaum, Denny worked long hours that started early and ended late. At thirty-three, he was a rising star on the fast track towards partnership. He wore a tie every day and had a tiny office the size of a broom closet with a view of the highway. I didn't know how he did it. I would have gone crazy after a month and started taking hostages.

I was the complete opposite of Denny. I was a somewhat self-employed, mostly unemployed, writer (and part time waitress). After having my first novel published three years earlier, I was working freelance for magazines and newspapers while living in Toronto. Presently I was working on a series of columns on the night scene in the city. The column was basically glorified advertising for nightclubs and restaurants. I was told by the paper which spots to write about (and sometimes whether or not to give a place a good review). It didn't even pay enough to cover my rent. It was boring and my articles were embarrassingly stupid. It wasn't unusual for me to be out on the town until three or four in the morning. I'd come home, completely wired and unable to sleep so I'd write until five or six and then go to bed. This was my routine at least three nights a week. The other four nights I worked as a waitress at a restaurant near my apartment. The two jobs combined meant that I was just able to scrape by each month.

At the age of twenty-five, I had hit the high point in my career three years earlier, and I was trying to convince myself that it wasn't all downhill from here. It was depressing. My jobs sucked, and the money sucked. I was writing crappy articles for a stupid section of the newspaper that no one ever read. Every word that I wrote for an article was another reminder that I still hadn't written a follow-up novel. Every article that I published was confirmation of my mother's repeated assurances that I'd never make anything of myself.

"I just got a call from some lawyer," I said to Denny.

"Are you being sued?"

"No. Apparently my father died. Why would you think I was being sued?"

"Maybe some club you gave a bad review to was suing you for slander."

"Thanks."

"Anyway, I thought your father was already dead."

"Wishful thinking. He is now, though. At least, that's what the lawyer said. Maybe I should demand to see the body as proof."

"What happened?" he asked. "How did he die?"

"I don't know," I replied, walking over to the mirror to look at my messy hair. There were still pillow marks on my face. "I forgot to ask. And I don't really care. I was woken up in the middle of the night, as I'm sure you remember me mentioning. How my father died is one of two things I don't ever need to learn."

"What's the other?"

"I never want to learn how hotdogs are made."

"Weren't you curious?" he asked, ignoring me. He always ignored me when I was being a smart ass. "About your father, not the hotdog thing. If it was my father, I'd at least be curious to know how he died."

"I wasn't, but now that you keep mentioning it I am getting curious. And annoyed at you."

"Didn't the lawyer tell you anything?"

"Yeah. I've got to go to the will reading tomorrow in New Ferndale. It's at 11:00 AM and I don't have a clue how I'm going to get there. Do you think he'd believe me if I called in sick?"

"Ferndale or New Ferndale?"

"Huh?"

"Well, there are two towns up north on Georgian Bay with similar names. One's Ferndale and the other is New Ferndale. They're about twenty minutes apart."

"Great," I said. "That's just what I need. I'm going to get lost in the middle of nowhere at eleven in the morning. That's really stupid."

"Plus it's at least a two hour drive up there."

"You're always so helpful."

"Which town do you think it is?"

"I'm pretty sure he said New Ferndale."

"How sure?" Denny knew I sucked when it came to directions. Especially in the morning.

"97% sure. Why would I add the word 'new' unless I'd heard it?"

"Good point."

"Why would there be two towns named almost the same? Was it done to intentionally screw up directionally-challenged people like me?"

"I don't know," he replied. "How are you getting up there?"

"I'm not sure. Want to drive me?"

"Can't. Working. Those of us with full-time jobs can't take off at a moment's notice."

Damn it. Why hadn't I thought to tell the lawyer that I had to work? It was a legitimate, believable excuse.

Unless he'd already spoken to Maxine, who would have been more than willing to tell him that I was pretty much unemployed.

"Can I borrow your car then?"

"God, Kerri," he said. "You know how I feel about you, but I'm not sure about your driving."

"Thanks."

"I mean, I like you a lot, but I love my car."

"I get the point."

"I've got other friends, but I've only got one SUV."

"Shut up."

"It's supposed to be really nice up there, though," he said, changing the subject. "A few of the partners have cottages up in that area. Maybe your father left you some property."

"I doubt it. He probably left me his bar tabs. Or his bill from the local brothel."

"I don't think a small town in Ontario is going to have a brothel."

"You never can tell. You said that area is a big tourist place. What says family vacation more than a brothel? I'm pretty sure that's what Disney wanted in the original plans for the Magic Kingdom."

"Are you all right?" he asked. As I said, he always ignored me when I was being a smart ass. "Do you want me to come over?" He was suddenly very serious. A very dangerous mood for Denny. It was always a sign that I should try to lighten things up a little.

"Yeah, I'm sure that Emily would love that." Emily was Denny's wife. She wasn't exactly my biggest fan, to put it lightly. She hated the fact that Denny and I were so close. And she pretty much just hated me. "Plus, don't you have to work? That seemed to be your reason for not driving me tomorrow."

"As long as you're sure you're fine. You free for dinner tonight? Emily's got a 'Mommy & me' class tonight and afterwards she's going to her mother's, so I was going to be eating alone. It would be nice to have some company."

"Sure. 8:00 PM?"

"I'll pick you up. And we can talk tonight about you borrowing my car. Bye, Kerri. I really am sorry about your dad."

After I hung up the phone I went into the kitchen. Since I was already up, I thought I might as well have something for breakfast. I was starving. The thought of eggs and toast made me feel slightly better about the day. I loved breakfast food, and normally I wasn't up early enough to enjoy it.

But who was I kidding. One look inside the refrigerator and I quickly changed my mind. The only things in there were two bottles of water, some baking soda, mustard and moldy cheese. I was hungry, but not that hungry.

Why did I always buy baking soda? I never baked, and I hardly ever had any food in the fridge. I certainly never had enough that it would start to stink. Yet I always had baking soda. I think I had elves in my apartment that stole my food and replaced it with baking soda. I had even eaten my emergency supply of canned soup and crackers, although I couldn't remember when.

My new goal for the day was to buy enough food to survive until tomorrow. My stomach growled, urging me to go out immediately and find food. But I couldn't leave the house until I looked somewhat presentable. Or at least didn't look like I'd spent the night sleeping in a wind tunnel.

I somewhat optimistically decided that since I'd had an early start to the day, I'd make the best of it. I made some terrific plans: a shower, a trip to the grocery store, a quick visit to the gym and even several hours of work before Denny came by at around eight. I was impressed with my own initiative.

I had a wonderful, leisurely shower. As I was towel drying my hair, I managed to find a rice cake in one of my kitchen cupboards. I think it might have been older than me (it had probably come with the apartment), but I was pretty desperate. It was stale and disgusting, but I ate it anyway. At least I wouldn't pass out on my way to the grocery store. I got dressed and headed to the grocery store at the corner of Yonge & Eglinton, a five minute walk from my apartment.

Unfortunately, on my way there I got side tracked. First Starbuck's tempted me with a coffee (it was only 10:30, and I'd been up for more than an hour already without the assistance of any chemical substances). And I had to have a muffin with my coffee; everyone knows you shouldn't buy groceries on an empty stomach. Then I popped into Indigo to see what was new on the best seller list (always a very depressing experience). The final distraction came when my cell phone rang.

It was my friend James, calling to see how my night had been. Tall, blonde and gorgeous, I'd have fallen madly in love with him years ago if he wasn't gay. He was the perfect date, since he never looked at another woman and always pointed out the good-looking men. After hearing my tale of woe (being woken up at a God-awful time of day; James kept my hours) he decided we had to meet for lunch. As a result, I abandoned my quest for groceries and headed directly for the subway.

James and I had met a few years earlier at a party held by the paper we were both working for at the time. We both came alone (to a party where everyone else was paired up) and spent most of the night at the bar. We hit it off immediately, bonding over our mutual love of tequila and our mutual hatred of happy couples. James wrote a syndicated fashion column that was published weekly in papers across the country. He was also in the process of developing a makeover show for the learning channel on TV.

James had picked his favourite restaurant for us to meet; a Sushi restaurant on Yonge near Bloor. I hated the place but it was always fun to hang out with James. When I arrived, James was sitting at a table near the window drinking a martini.

He'd already ordered us each a Sushi platter, even though he knew I hated raw fish. The texture made me gag.

Whenever we went out for Sushi, James did the same thing: he'd order me something I hated, pretend he forgot I didn't like it and then eat it himself. I made do with the miso soup and a salad.

"Kerrigan, sweetheart," he gushed, standing and greeting me with a kiss on each cheek. "You look fabulous. Even in the deepest mourning, I can't get over your hair."

I smiled at him, tossing my hair lightly. I could never decide whether I loved or hated my hair. Red, curly and down to the middle of my back, most days it was completely unmanageable. Today it was behaving.

"I'm not really in mourning," I said to him, sitting down at the table. "You know I haven't seen my father in years."

"That's too bad," he said, gesturing for the waiter. "I was hoping we could have a good old-fashioned Irish wake."

"Which one of us is supposed to be Irish?"

"Order something alcoholic, and we'll decide."

I ordered a beer and sat back to listen to James talk about his newest fling. Every week James claimed to have found the love of his life. But by Friday he had usually moved on to someone else. I rarely dated, so it was nice to be able to live vicariously through my friends. I didn't know how James did it, but he always managed to prove to me that the only good-looking, nice, single guys in Toronto were gay. Leaving me with a choice of trolls, jerks or married men.

"I've found the perfect guy for you, Kerri," James said suddenly, looking quite pleased with himself. He had no confidence in my ability to meet someone on my own. And as much as I hated to admit it, he was most likely right.

"Not again," I groaned.

"What is that supposed to mean?"

"You always claim to have found me the perfect guy and they always turn out to have something seriously wrong with them. Remember the last guy you fixed me up with? Tony Something?"

"I didn't know he'd just gotten out of prison," James protested quickly with a wave of his hand. "But this guy really is perfect. He's a dentist and has all his own hair. I think. I liked him for myself until I found out he was straight."

"No more fix-ups." I was seriously putting my foot down.

"You'll like this guy. I promise."

"No. You have no taste in straight men."

"Sure I do."

"Let's see. Before Tony there was Mike. Do you remember Mike?"

James' face darkened slightly. "Do you still have the restraining order out on him?"

"And before Mike there was Billy, who actually was gay."

"I didn't know that at first," James protested. "Honestly. But at least he was a nice, normal guy."

"No more."

"I hate to see you alone. You need to meet someone."

"No, I don't," I said firmly. "I'm an independent, completely modern woman. I don't need a man. I've got you. And besides I'm not going to meet Mr. Right on a blind date."

"Mr. Right? Have you been reading those romance novels again? I thought I'd confiscated all of them."

I scowled at him. "No. It's just that someday I'll meet that guy, that one perfect guy, who will give me goose bumps and make me dizzy." I saw the look of shock and horror on James' face, so I continued in a fake southern accent. "And then he'll sweep me off my feet onto his white horse, and we'll ride off into the sunset, and as God as my witness, I'll never go hungry again."

"Thank you, Scarlett O'Hara," James said in a relieved tone. "But I was being serious. I'd like to see you with someone nice."

"My answer is still no."

We sat in the restaurant for hours before moving to a nearby patio for more drinks. One of the many things I loved about Toronto was the fact that as soon as the temperature had inched past freezing all the bars and restaurants had their patios open. We sat enjoying the warm April sun while James supplied most of the conversation, forcing me to provide only the occasional nods and sounds of agreement.

James also paid for the drinks, and I was very happy to take advantage of him.

I headed home at six that evening (feeling slightly numb from too much alcohol) to get ready for dinner. I was in no shape to go out again. I hadn't accomplished anything on my 'to do' list. The day had been a write off, one of many lately. Why had I let James talk me into drinking so much (and so early in the day)? If Denny was late I thought I might have enough time to sober up. I considered fixing myself a cup of coffee before remembering my complete lack of food stuffs. I had to settle for multiple glasses of water.

And, unfortunately, Denny was on time as usual. At eight sharp the buzzer announced his arrival. I grabbed my purse and went down to the lobby to meet him.

"Hey," he said smiling when he saw me. "Chinese okay with you?"

"Anything, as long as it's greasy, and there's lots of it."

"So, what did you do today?" he asked as we got into his car.

"First, I solved the world's economic problems. After that, I cleaned up the environment before sitting down to a lovely afternoon tea with the Queen."

"You know, not every question requires a sarcastic answer."

"Aren't you impressed that I have the ability to answer everything sarcastically? It really is a gift."

"Just tell me what you did today," he said, scowling at me.

"I went out with James," I admitted somewhat sheepishly. Denny knew both of us well enough to know what an afternoon with James would entail.

"Kerri, you know I like James, but he's a bad influence on you."

"No, he's not. He's fun and sweet and bought me a lot of alcohol today. Plus, he's coming with me tomorrow. Actually, he's lending me his car, unlike some people who pretend to be my friend."

"I can't believe James is lending you his car."

"Well he is."

"He practically worships that car," Denny continued. "How drunk was he today?"

"Nice."

"No, seriously. He has seen you drive, hasn't he?"

"I'm a great driver."

Denny looked at me, one eyebrow raised.

"Okay, I'm not a great driver. I'm an adequate driver."

"James is going to drive, isn't he?"

"Yeah, but he's still a better friend than you are."

"Well then, I misjudged him," Denny said as he pulled into the parking lot of the restaurant. "He must be an absolute angel to put up with you for two hours in a car."

"Are you insinuating that there's something wrong with driving with me?"

"I'm sorry," he said. "I didn't mean to insinuate anything. I meant to say it out right. You're a horrible driver with no sense of direction and no taste in music. I mean, seriously, what twenty-five-year-old listens to ABBA all day?"

"Gee, Denny. Don't pull any punches. Tell me how you really feel."

"What are friends for?"

"I didn't realize we were friends. I just thought you were one of those groupies who hung around famous authors."

"There's a famous author here?" Denny asked, looking around.

"Thanks a lot." I punched him in the arm.

"And do authors actually have groupies? Aren't most writers weird hermits?"

"I'm starting to understand why someone might want to become a hermit."

"I'm just teasing you," he said, putting his arm around me and giving me a hug.

"And there's nothing wrong with ABBA."

"You're right; they're wonderful. And I'm starving. Are we going to eat tonight or not?"

As we walked into the restaurant, I could see Denny smiling flirtatiously at various women in the restaurant. He had his left hand in his pocket, keeping his wedding ring hidden from view. Women found him charming, even though he was a tease, a flirt and a womanizer. I would be the first to admit that Denny was gorgeous. Well, maybe the second, since Denny himself would probably admit it. But he was not to be trusted around women. He was always on the prowl.

"Were you this obvious when we dated?" I asked him as we sat down. "If you'd like, I can get their phone numbers for you."

"I don't know what you're talking about," he said innocently, smiling flirtatiously at some passing woman.

"You're terrible. Emily really should divorce you. If she had half a brain she would have left you years ago."

"Yeah, well Emily's not like you," he said, with what I thought was a trace of wistfulness in his voice. Warning bells were sounding in my head. Even though I was still half-drunk, I knew instinctively to change the topic of conversation. It was very sobering.

"I have a feeling I'm going to see my sister tomorrow," I said, leaning back in my chair. "All the traditional omens have presented themselves. Plagues of locusts, raining frogs, rivers of blood."

"That will be interesting," he said, spinning his wedding ring. It was a nervous habit, probably because he could never get used to wearing it. "God, do you remember how much she hated me?"

"Of course I do," I replied. Maxine was barely civil to Denny whenever she was near him. It was actually kind of funny. Maxine seemed to be the only woman in the world immune to Denny's charm.

"How long has it been since you've seen her?"

"Since Sebastian's funeral."

"That was more than two years ago," he replied. He looked very serious. "Are you going to be alright tomorrow? Maybe I can get out of my meetings and come with you. You could use the support. Christ, what if your mom's there too? You'll be eaten alive."

"It will be okay. I've got James coming with me, remember? He'll protect me from the big, bad Maxine. And I doubt my mom will be there." Shit, I hoped not. The thought of seeing both Maxine and my mother was enough to make me feel ill. I wouldn't have to fake sick at the will reading if they both showed up. My mother was the most terrifying person I'd ever known. I hated to admit the fact that at twenty-five I was scared to death of my mother, a woman who had to be in her early sixties.

"I'm being serious," he said, taking me by the hand. He looked deep into my eyes. "You think you're so tough and independent, but you're not. I know you, Kerri. Maxine and your mom scare the crap out of you. Let me help."

"Why do you always have to get serious?" I asked, quickly removing my hand from his. "I'm never serious."

"One of us has to be serious. Just say the word, and I'll come with you."

I looked at his earnest face and looked away quickly. It was easy to see why so many women fell madly in love with him. I really was no exception, much to my horror and disgrace. Looking at him sitting across from me made me feel exactly as I had the first time we'd met more than fifteen years earlier. He had been the love of my life when I was eighteen. I wasn't ready for the type of long-term relationship he wanted (I was only eighteen after all) so we split, and he had married Emily almost immediately. Emily could never forgive me for being involved with Denny before she'd met him. She hated me much more than Maxine hated Denny. Unfortunately, Emily had more reasons to hate me than she knew.

"I'll be fine. I'll sit through the will reading, and then James and I will come home. I'll be safe and sound in my apartment before the end of the day. If I'm lucky, I might not even have to talk to Maxine. Besides," I added cheerfully, "Maxine will be happy to see that you and I aren't dating anymore." That was an understatement.

"Alright," he said, sounding a little disappointed. I could tell that Denny had been picturing himself as my white knight, saving me from the clutches of my evil mother and sister. But I wasn't the type that needed rescuing, as I frequently reminded him. "Just promise me that you'll call the moment you get in."

"I promise," I replied. "Now can we please order something to eat? I'm starving. James took me out for sushi at lunch."

"In other words you had a liquid lunch today."

"I ate some soup."

"How much is this dinner going to cost me?"

"A lot," I said as the waiter arrived to take our orders. "I hope you brought more than one credit card."

Three hours and $150 worth of Chinese food later (of which at least $100 was entirely my fault), Denny dropped me off at my apartment. I was tempted to invite him upstairs for a drink, but I knew what would happen (and my new year's resolution was to avoid situations like that). Instead, I went upstairs alone and crawled straight into bed, falling asleep as soon as my head hit the pillow.

Chapter Two

My alarm went off at 8:30 the next morning. I was in the middle of a great dream (one where I'd finally gotten over my writers' block and was actually able to work again), and I did not want to get out of bed. I couldn't believe it. Two early mornings in a row and I was supposed to work the dinner shift that night when I got back into town. It was going to be a really long day.

Someone once told me that people actually get used to getting up early. I had always been sure that that was a load of crap, and now I had the proof. I was positive that it wasn't a good idea for me to go to the will reading. It would be horrible to run into Maxine on a day when I hadn't gotten enough sleep. Actually, it would be horrible to run into Maxine, period. The thought of my sister was enough to send me cowering under my covers. And still lingering at the back of my mind was the complete and utter terror at even the possibility of seeing my mother. I didn't know if I'd even be able to get out of bed. It would be much, much better if I just pulled the covers firmly over my head, shut my eyes tightly and pretended that I never even answered the phone the previous morning.

Unfortunately, it was too late to call James and cancel. He was going to be at my place by five to nine. And if I wasn't ready, James was going to be really pissed off.

I wavered between playing hooky and acting like an adult for about five minutes before getting out of bed. This left me very little time to actually get ready. I jumped into the shower and then quickly towel dried my hair after checking the clock. 8:45. James was going to be at my place in ten minutes. No time to do anything to my hair. I was glad that the only guy to see me was gay.

I dug around in my closet for something clean to wear to a will reading. One thing about working at home was that it didn't matter what I wore to work every day. It also meant that I didn't have a lot of clothes suitable for offices or funerals.

Why hadn't I had the sense to get some clothes ready the night before? I should have done laundry instead of drinking with James. My entire closet was empty. I didn't even know what a person was supposed to wear to a will reading, but it didn't really matter since I didn't have any choice. Grabbing the first clean outfit I could find, I threw it on and raced to the elevator.

I went down to the street to wait for James' car. The sun was shining, the birds were singing. It was a disgustingly beautiful day. I put my sunglasses on to shelter myself from the harmful UV rays. I was pale and sensitive to the sun—a result of late nights working (on my column and waiting tables) and a long winter of being indoors.

James drove up in the love of his life—a beautifully maintained 1960s Mustang convertible. The car was red, shiny and incredibly flashy. I knew he'd never let me drive.

And the top was down.

"Good morning, Sunshine," he said in a horribly cheerful voice as he pulled up to the curb. "Ready to head up north on this beautiful spring day?"

He was far too awake and cheerful for such an ungodly hour. If he was this happy for the entire drive, I would have to kill him.

"Shut up." I tipped my sunglasses down to glare at him, but I was wasting my time. He just smiled cheerfully and chuckled slightly.

"Not even your gloomy mood can bring me down on a day like today."

"Well, I'll try my best," I said darkly.

"And look at you. Not exactly dressed for a funeral, are we?"

I looked down for the first time at what I was wearing: a leather jacket, a white tank top with low-riding flare jeans and thick-soled boots. At least the clothes were clean and not overly revealing. Then I looked at James in his Armani suit and tie. He looked great. The jerk. I thought that maybe I could send James instead of me. I could pretend that he was my lawyer, and I was too prostrate with grief to go myself.

"It's not a funeral. It's a will reading. Besides, I didn't get a chance to do laundry yesterday. Instead I spent the entire afternoon getting drunk with you, remember?"

"Regardless, army-chique suits you. Nice tattoo."

I looked at my slightly exposed navel. My tattoo was visible, the result of an attempt at rebellious behaviour when I was fourteen. It, like everything else I did, went completely unnoticed by my mother. Maxine, on the other hand, had gone ballistic when she saw it. I pulled my shirt lower to cover the tattoo and got in the car.

"Thank you. Put up the top."

"No way."

"Yes," I replied. "We're driving on the highway, and I didn't do my hair." I was going to put my foot down; otherwise, I'd end up looking like the bride of Frankenstein.

"Just tie it back," he said with a grin. "It's too nice a day to have the top down. Get in."

I didn't have time to argue with him. Grumbling to myself, I tied my hair back from my face with an elastic band. James turned the music up loud and drove off at a break-neck pace. He sang along cheerfully to the radio while I sank lower in my seat in an unsuccessful attempt to get some sleep.

One hour and forty-five minutes later we arrived in New Ferndale. Population 1000, if the sign was to be believed. The town was tiny and quaint with one main street through the center. The place bugged me immediately. Christ, it was like driving into Mayberry. The buildings were too small (nothing over three stories), there weren't enough cars and there wasn't a single traffic light anywhere. How could anyone live in a place like this? What the hell did people do?

James found a parking space in front of the office of *L Carter Stevens, Attorney at Law*. We were fifteen minutes early, and I took the time to attempt a rescue mission on my hair. It was no use. It was going to be a big-hair kind of day. I'm talking 1980's-high school hair. Seriously big and seriously bad.

We popped into a coffee shop so I could get some caffeine into my system. It wasn't a Starbuck's or even a Tim Horton's, but it would have to do. It was a small bakery/coffee shop simply called *Mary's*. As soon as I entered the shop, the smell of fresh baking made me realize that I was starving. I hadn't had time for breakfast, and I knew it would be a while before I could have lunch. I walked up to the counter and ordered a blueberry muffin and an extra large coffee. If I could have, I would have asked them to hook the caffeine directly to a central line. While I drank, James picked up a brochure and began to read.

"This is very interesting, Kerri," he said to me after a few moments.

"What is?" I wasn't really paying attention to him; the coffee was really good and the muffin was the best I'd had in a long time.

"This town, if you can believe the local propaganda. Listen: 'Nestled on the shores of Georgian Bay, New Ferndale, originally dubbed Ferndale by the first European settlers in the early 1800s, was a town of great importance to the development of Canada. A town renowned for its logging and its natural port, New Ferndale has always been a beacon for the weary traveler.'"

"Good lord," I interrupted. "Who wrote that?"

"Quiet," he said, continuing. "'The introduction of a rail line from Toronto to New Ferndale and then further north at the end of the 1800s brought with it a new species of visitor: the summer cottager. Each year, for more than a century, people have been drawn to the town's rocky shores, crystal waters and friendly locals.'"

"Does it say why there's another place nearby named Ferndale?" I asked, in between bites of my muffin and sips of coffee.

James quickly scanned the rest of the brochure. "No, it doesn't. We'll have to ask someone." James stood, as if intending to start asking the patrons of the coffee shop.

"Later," I said to him, looking at my watch. "We've got to get to the lawyer's office. It's almost eleven."

We left the shop and crossed the street to the office. I didn't even have to look both ways before crossing the street. There was only one car driving on the road, and it was still a ways off. I thought that 1000 people as the population may have been a gross overstatement.

"Why do you think they even need a lawyer in a town like this?" James asked.

"I'm sure there's a great need for lawyers," I replied sarcastically. "Pig theft, jay walking. Big things like that."

"You know, you can get executed in Texas for pig theft," a voice behind me said, making me jump.

I turned around to see who it was. I hated it when people jumped into my conversations without being invited. It was incredibly annoying. "You know this personally?"

"Yes. I'm a notorious pig thief," he said. He was fairly good looking, in an annoying and goofy kind of way. Tall with dark, kind of floppy hair and clear, blue eyes. I was pretty sure he was mocking me, and I disliked him immediately.

"Well, Mr. Pig-thief," James said, turning on the charm. "What are you doing here on this fabulous day?"

"I heard there was a will reading today."

"Big fan of will readings?" I asked.

"Huge. Wills have big turnouts here. No cable." He flashed me a big grin.

I rolled my eyes.

"James Mason," James said, extending his hand to Mr. Pig-thief.

"Pleased to meet you."

"And this vision of beauty is Kerrigan Shepherd."

I shot James a dirty look while I shook the guy's hand.

"Nice to meet you," he said with a grin I didn't like. I knew he was laughing at my puffy hair. And possibly my outfit. The jerk.

"Yes, it's always a pleasure to meet me," I said, somewhat impatiently. "Look, I don't want to be here in this town, so I'd like to get this over with as soon as possible. I'm going in there to hear what the lawyer has to say, and then I'm getting back into this stupid convertible and going back to civilization."

I turned to enter the office and heard them whispering behind me.

"She's certainly a city girl, isn't she?"

"Definitely," James, my former friend, said behind my back. "She goes into withdrawal as soon as she passes the city limits. But she really is very sweet. And very single."

I shook my head and pushed open the door. I had decided not to let James bother me—after all, he had been nice enough to drive me. But it was difficult not to rush back there and throttle him with my bare hands. I tried instead to focus my attention on the onerous task ahead of me.

I stepped through the door and into the reception area. The office was surprisingly well decorated. It gave the impression of success without seeming too flashy. There were a few plants scattered around the room looking much healthier than any plants I'd ever owned (I wasn't very good at keeping things alive). The paintings on the walls were tasteful landscapes showing rocky shores of what I guessed was Georgian Bay. Most likely the wife's touch, I thought as I went up to the receptionist.

There were about five other people waiting in the lobby. They all looked up at me when I entered. Fortunately, my sister and mother weren't among them. And I couldn't smell the cloud of smoke and cheap perfume that usually accompanied my mother wherever she went. I was relieved; I was off the hook for a few minutes at least. Maybe I would be really lucky, and they wouldn't be able to make it at all. Maybe Maxine's daughter was sick, or she had to work (that is, if she even had a job—I didn't even know if my sister was employed or not). If the gods were on my side, she could have a flat tire or a dentist appointment. I wasn't too picky. It was never a good time to see my sister.

As for my mother, I kept saying a silent prayer over and over that she wouldn't be coming. Sebastian had been the only one of the three of us kids that Mom had even remotely liked. He used to tell me to go easy on the 'old girl,' as he affectionately called her. Our mother's dislike of both of us was the only thing Maxine and I had in common. If my mother was here today, I was honestly afraid of what would happen.

Shaking my head to clear it of any thoughts of my family, I faced the receptionist.

"Hi," I said to her. Her nameplate read *Charlotte Durand*. I forced a smile. I thought if I was nice maybe they'd let me out early for good behaviour. "Kerri Shepherd here to see Mr. Stevens."

"I'm sorry," she said, looking me up and down with barely-hidden disdain. I suddenly felt very conspicuous and very, very underdressed. "I don't have a Kerri Shepherd on the list."

I sighed. "How about Abigail Shepherd?" I asked. Again, she sneered at my appearance. She was one of those impeccably dressed thirty-something women who could have been a fashion model. Her suit looked like it cost more than a month of my rent. Her hair was long, blond and perfectly straight and smooth. I thought about my own wild red hair and white tank top with embarrassment. I felt myself turn pink under her critical gaze. "Look lady, I'm here for the reading of my father's will."

"You can wait in Mr. Steven's office," she said, pointing to the open office at the end of a short hallway. "He's just stepped out for a moment, but he'll be along shortly."

"Thanks," I said, walking towards the office.

I sat down in the chair opposite the desk and looked around the room. I looked at my reflection in a picture on the wall and attempted (with little success) to tame my hair. At least I looked slightly more presentable than I had when I came in.

Suddenly my mother's voice sounded in my head. I could hear her as clearly as if she was standing in the room with me. "Abigail, you got all that God-awful hair from your bastard father's side of the family. The Shepherd's were always one step above trash, but you look like you've just dragged yourself out of the gutter." In my head she pauses momentarily to take a long drag from her cigarette and to give me another look over. The expression on her face is as if she's just seen something incredibly distasteful. "I always knew you'd turn out this way."

Where the hell is James, I thought, desperately trying to banish thoughts of my mother from my head. Finally I heard Miss Personality talking to someone in the hall.

"I asked her to wait in your office, Mr. Stevens," Miss Durand said sweetly. "Just like you asked."

"Good morning, Miss Shepherd," a voice directly behind me said, making me jump. I hadn't expected him to walk so quickly down the hall.

I turned around. It was the guy from outside. "What are you doing here?" I asked tactlessly.

"I thought I'd come into my office," he replied with a smile. He placed a newspaper on the desk and sat down behind it. "If you don't mind."

"You're the lawyer?" I should have seen this coming. The day was playing like a poorly written soap opera. I'd had a mental image of the lawyer before I came here: a man in his fifties with graying hair and a potbelly. Probably with two or three kids he was supporting through university. Unsuccessful and not very happy with his life. I was reminded not to make assumptions about people before meeting them—it usually got me into trouble. I certainly wasn't expecting a thirty-something, good-looking (and annoying) guy.

He nodded.

"Figures," I said. "It was nice of you to introduce yourself when we were outside.

"I'm sorry, Miss Shepherd."

"It's Kerri."

"I thought your name was Abigail."

"I never once said my name was Abigail."

"Where does 'Kerri' come from?"

"My full name is Abigail Kerrigan Shepherd, but I only go by Kerri."

"I'm Carter Stevens. Pleased to meet you. I'm usually a little more forthcoming with my introductions."

"Except when you want to torment innocent people early in the morning."

"Exactly," he said with a grin, reaching for a file.

"Can we get on with this?" I was starting to really dislike him. It was rare for someone to annoy me this much on first meeting.

"Of course. You want to get home. Don't worry," he said, standing up, "we'll be done in plenty of time for you to miss rush hour." He walked towards the door. "Come on. We're doing the reading in the conference room. The rest of the people are waiting in there, including your sister."

Great, I thought. I was the last one to arrive. The only thing that made me feel slightly better about the day was the fact that he hadn't mentioned my mother.

I followed him into the boardroom. There were seven people already seated around the table. They were all dressed for a funeral, in outfits of somber black. I felt like a moron. An incredibly underdressed moron.

My sister was one of the many people that looked up as I entered the room. Maxine was dressed like the perfect wife and mother that she was. She was wearing a very appropriate navy blazer and matching skirt. She was the very picture of the mourning daughter.

I felt myself immediately go on the defensive as soon as our eyes met. I was surprised she didn't have a string of pearls around her neck—it would have completed her Jackie Kennedy-like appearance. She shook her head and her eyes darkened as she appraised my appearance. Red, unruly hair, a tight shirt and jeans. Great decision, Einstein, I thought to myself. It would have been better if I had worn something more appropriate, even if it had been dirty. I felt six-years-old again under her disapproving gaze. Maxine had red hair, a shade or two darker than mine, which had always been straight and manageable. She would never let anyone misbehave, let alone her hair. We hadn't even spoken yet, but I was already mad at her. I took a seat next to James and tried to become invisible by slouching deep into my chair.

All eyes stayed on me until Mr. Stevens began to speak.

"I'd like to thank everyone for coming today," he began. "Especially those of you who came from out of town today for the reading.

"I would first like to express my condolences to Mr. Shepherd's children, Maxine Shepherd-Holbrook and Abigail Shepherd. I'd like to thank you both for attending today.

"Peter Shepherd asked me to gather all of you here today in order to view his will." He looked to the door where the receptionist was entering, wheeling a television on a cart. "Thank you, Miss Durand. Peter recorded a living will a short time ago. It's under his direction that I'm going to show it to you."

He placed a tape in the VCR, pressed play and sat down.

There he was on the screen. My father. I hadn't seen him since I was eight. I'm sure some sound escaped my lips because heads turned in my direction and James squeezed my hand. I stared straight ahead, not noticing anything but the image on the screen. I had to keep reminding myself that I was an adult and not the little girl that he had abandoned.

My father looked different than I remembered him. When I was eight he seemed larger than life. The man on the screen seemed old and frail. But it was definitely my father. The first seconds of the video erased any of my doubt as to the identity of the deceased. Suddenly, he began to talk.

"I'd like to thank you all for coming today," he began. His voice was loud and clear, which seemed wrong to me somehow. I didn't expect a dead person to sound so alive. "I'm sure some of you traveled a long way to get here today, and I'm glad you're all here." He paused for a moment and then smiled slightly. "Of course, if you're watching this it, means I'm dead. So I guess I'm not that happy to be speaking to you today."

There was some soft laughter in the room and a few sniffles. I sat staring straight ahead motionless and I'm pretty sure Maxine did too.

"And now, down to business," the video continued. "I, Peter Matthew Shepherd, being of sound mind and somewhat sound body record this will on November 16, 2002. This will overrides any earlier will I may have written. Now onto the good stuff. I bequeath my worldly possessions in the following manner.

"To my friend Thomas Jenkins, $50,000 and my truck so he can plow the snow from my driveway this winter. To Mary Lufkin, $50,000 and my gardening books."

The tape went on like this with my father giving $50,000 to each of the five people present in the room. I couldn't believe it. My father died with at least $300,000, and he had never paid a penny of child support that I knew about. At least that's what my mother had always told me. I looked over at Maxine and saw that she was not very impressed either. I felt James' restraining hand on my arm.

I wanted to jump from my chair and smash the television. I wanted to tell these people exactly what kind of a man their good friend was. The type of man who would leave his three children to the care of a drunken harpy. A man who missed graduations, Maxine's wedding, the birth of his first grandchild, and, most importantly, the funeral of his only son. These good people had a right to know that they were taking money from the worst example of a human being I'd ever known. With the possible exception of my mother. But, of course, I didn't move.

"And finally to my daughters." I turned back to the television, trying to control my rage. "To my eldest daughter, Maxine Cassandra Shepherd-Holbrook, I leave $500,000 in cash and bonds and my sincere apologies. I know that after all these years, it is probably too late for you to forgive me. Everything we did was done with your best interest in mind, and I realize now how wrong we were. To my youngest child, Abigail Kerrigan Shepherd, I leave my house, its contents and the remainder of my money. You're probably not even here. I know I certainly don't deserve it. But if you are here, it's a credit to Carter's persuasiveness and tenacity. Kerri, I know I wasn't there for you while you were growing up. I hope that you will both somehow forgive me for the past and all the mistakes I made.

"And now I'll turn this event back to my good friend Carter. Thanks for taking the time to listen to a dead man."

The screen went black. The lawyer turned off the television and addressed the audience. I sat in my chair, seething with rage, staring blindly at the blank TV screen.

"Well, that's pretty much it. You'll each have some papers to sign, but those of you who are local can come by later this week to do that. At Peter's request, there will be no funeral service. Right now there'll be a reception for Peter over at *Patrick's* for those of you who are interested. I hope to see all of you there shortly." People began filing out of the room. I waited for a few minutes before standing to leave. I was shaking with suppressed rage. I had to get out of there before I said or did something I would regret. But I also didn't want there to be an audience for my departure. "Mrs. Holbrook and Miss Shepherd, can I speak to you both for a moment?"

"Sure," I replied through clenched teeth. "James, will you wait for me in the car?" My voice was dangerously calm. He nodded, squeezed my hand softly and left the room. James knew me well enough to stay out of the way when I was really angry.

Mr. Stevens turned his attention back to Maxine and me. "Now Miss Shepherd, if you'll just ..."

"Listen here," I said, barely containing my anger. My face was flushed, and my hands were shaking. "I told you on the phone that I didn't want anything from him. I don't want his house, and I don't want his money. Give it to her." I gestured to Maxine.

"I understand what you're feeling ..."

"You can't understand," I yelled, venting my anger on him. "You weren't eight when your father walked out on you."

"Kerrigan, quit being such a baby," Maxine said calmly from her seat at the other end of the table.

I was furious with my father, Mr. Stevens and now Maxine. How could she be so calm at a time like this? I nearly exploded with anger. "How do you think I feel about suddenly finding out he had a ton of money when we spent our lives just trying to make ends meet?"

I should have known Maxine would act like this. She never took my side, even when it came to our deadbeat father.

"You weren't the only one he abandoned," Maxine said standing up and finally sounding angry. "He left all of us. Sebastian, Mom and me included."

"Yeah, but you had already moved out by then. I was eight and you were twenty-three. There's a big difference."

"You were too young to know what was happening. I had to deal with Dad leaving and look after you and Sebastian. If you remember, Mom kind of flaked out when Dad left."

"Right," I said sarcastically. "Poor Maxine the martyr. It must have been just horrible for you." I was so sick of her and her insistence that she was the only one who had been wronged. This was why it had been two years since I'd had any contact with her. It was always like this when we met. She always managed to piss me off.

"God damn it, Kerri," she said angrily. "I'm not saying that I was the only one hurt. Just try and look at things from someone else's perspective for a change." She was really angry now. Maxine never swore.

"I could say the same to you." I crossed my arms over my chest stubbornly.

"Me? You're the one who's been acting like a spoiled brat for about twenty years. You never think of anyone but yourself. When was the last time you saw Mom? What's it been? Two years? You're not the only one who lost Sebastian, you know."

"Don't you dare bring him into this," I said in a low voice.

"Why not, Kerri? He's been dead for two years. You need to get over it."

"I don't want to get over it," I yelled, my voice shrill and bordering on hysteria. "Why should I get over it? Everyone keeps telling me to move on with my life but I don't want to. He was my brother and my best friend. I can't just forget about him."

"Of course you won't forget him," Maxine said, her tone slightly softer. "I don't expect you to. I don't want to forget Sebastian either."

"Did you know that Dad had all this money?" I asked, changing the topic to something I felt would be safer.

"How would I know?" she replied, throwing her hands up in frustration. "I haven't had any contact with him since before he left."

"Yeah, but you were older and can remember that time better than me."

"Well, I remember him having money. When I was younger. It was family money that he'd inherited from either his parents or his grandparents, I'm not exactly sure. But I thought he'd gone through it a long time ago."

"Or you'd have hit him up for a loan ages ago." I knew I was being deliberately bitchy, and I didn't even know why I said it. I just couldn't help myself. I liked to bait Maxine.

"What's wrong with you?" she yelled back, growing angry again. "Why can't we ever have a civil conversation without you acting like a child?"

"Can I please interrupt?" Carter asked, holding up his hands as if to ward off any sudden attack. He seemed embarrassed to be caught in the middle of a family battle, and it looked like he was ready to referee.

"No," Maxine said.

"Yes," I said. "I'm finished talking to her."

"I understand that neither of you may want to accept the inheritance …" he began.

"I don't have a problem with it," Maxine said.

"Figures," I said under my breath, just loud enough for both of them to hear me. Maxine shot me a dirty look. I really was acting like a child, but I didn't care.

"I think it would be good for you to at least take a look at the property, Miss Shepherd," he said to me. "If you don't like it, I'll help you sell it and you can give all the money to a home for cats."

"I hate cats."

"Fine. No cats."

I sighed. "Alright. I'll take a look at it."

"Great," he grinned. "We can drive out there right now. Mrs. Holbrook, I have a few papers for you to sign, and then you can be on your way."

"Thank you," Maxine said. I could feel her eyes on me, even though I was purposely not looking at her.

"I'll go grab James, and we'll wait outside," I said to Mr. Stevens. I turned to leave.

"Do you want me to say anything to Mom for you?" Maxine asked before I left.

"Nothing that can be repeated in a polite conversation." I continued to leave the room without looking back at her.

James was waiting for me on the sidewalk. He looked up when I approached.

"You done with your rant?"

"It wasn't a rant. I have a perfectly legitimate reason to be angry."

"I know you do, sweetheart. But you look so cute when you're angry. I'm sure that fabulous lawyer can't get enough of you. The flame-haired goddess with the volatile temper."

"Right," I said, rolling my eyes at him. "That's why I was angry. I'm trying to pick-up a guy at my father's will-reading."

"And how was your charming sister? She didn't seem quite as horrible as you always say she is. I noticed that you didn't bother to introduce me to her."

"I'm sure she was fine. I didn't have time to ask." And I didn't care either, but I didn't say that out loud.

"It's nice to see that you'll still be attractive when you're forty," he said.

"Maxine and I don't look anything alike," I said firmly.

"Except for the hair, you two could be sisters."

"Shut up, you clown."

"So, what are we doing now? Ready to go back into civilization again?"

"Yeah, but unfortunately first we have to take a look at the house. I've been bullied into checking it out before I can sell it."

"How are we getting there?" James asked nervously. I could see that the idea of driving his precious car all over the countryside on roads of questionable quality didn't exactly appeal to him.

"I'm driving," Carter said as he came outside. "My car is around back."

We followed Carter around to the back of the building. James grabbed my arm and pulled me close.

"Your own personal chauffer," he whispered in my ear. "He must like you."

"Give it a rest," I whispered back. James was always trying to push guys on me. That is, unless he decided he wanted the guy for himself. And since he had obviously decided that the lawyer would be good for me, there would definitely be something horribly wrong with Carter Stevens.

The three of us climbed into Carter's vehicle, a silver SUV. We drove for about five minutes before James started talking.

"Where are we going?" He leaned forward towards the front seat eagerly like a little boy.

"The house is about fifteen minutes outside of town," Carter said as he turned onto a gravel road. "It's right on Georgian Bay."

I was fighting a growing feeling of carsickness. He was taking the turns a little fast for my stomach. I was seconds away from telling him to slow down.

"What's it like?" James asked.

"We'll be there soon," Carter said. "Why don't we make it a surprise?"

I hated surprises.

"It's probably a shack," I said, trying desperately not to puke all over his dashboard. "Actually, I take that back. It's probably a mansion. Paid for with this mysterious fortune the deadbeat seemed to have."

"If there's a guest house, I'm moving in," James said.

About ten minutes later Carter pulled into a driveway. He parked the car, and we all got out.

"Here we are," he said to me. "What do you think?"

It was an old house high above the water. The view was amazing: the water below was clear and calm, and trees covered with spring buds surrounded the place. The paint on the house was faded and slightly chipped, but everything seemed to be in good condition from the outside. The building was large, much bigger than anywhere I'd lived growing up. There were cottages on either side. The one on the right was twice the size of my father's place and looked brand new. The one on the left was smaller and set further back into the trees.

"How much land does she own?" James asked.

"Five acres with about five-hundred feet of water front," Carter replied.

"Is that a lot?" I asked. I'd never owned any property so I didn't have a clue.

Carter nodded.

"If you sell, you'll get a bundle just for the land," James whispered to me.

"Can we go inside?" I asked. I was vaguely interested in seeing how my father had lived, although I wasn't about to admit it.

"Sure," Carter said, walking to the side door and taking out a key. "The place is in great condition. In-door plumbing, electricity and it's fully winterized. Plus, it's already been hooked up with satellite television."

"Wow. In-door plumbing. Is that a big deal around here?" James whispered to me.

I elbowed James before speaking to Carter.

"Are you sure you're not a real estate agent on the side?" I asked, raising an eyebrow.

We stepped inside into a large, open concept room. The front of the building was composed entirely of large windows overlooking the water. Despite a slightly musty smell (which James eloquently described as 'old people' smell) and a thin layer of dust on everything, the place really was in good shape. Something about the room seemed familiar, but I couldn't place what it was.

"What's wrong?" James asked, looking at me with concern.

I shook off the strange feeling and smiled at him. "It's nothing. Just a slight case of déjà vu. Those are great windows."

"The building faces west, so you get a terrific view of the sunset," Carter said, seeing my interest in the view. "There's also a large deck out front, complete with an awning and steps leading down to the dock."

"How the hell did my father get a place like this?" I asked bluntly.

"It belonged to his grandparents," Carter replied. "Apparently the land's been in your family since the 1900s. At one time your family owned pretty much the entire side of the lake for several miles. Your father sold all but this original building over the years. Aside from a few modifications, the cottage is pretty much the way it was when it was built. It was winterized back in the 1970s and the road gets plowed by the township so it can be used all year round. Your father showed me some old pictures of the place once. It looked pretty much the same, except there were more trees and fewer neighbours. He said there was a trunk full of old stuff in one of the rooms upstairs. Things that belonged to his parents and grandparents, I think."

"Did you know him very well?"

"Who?"

"My father."

"I've known him for awhile," Carter replied with a shrug.

"How long did he live here?"

"I think he moved back permanently about ten or twelve years ago. Before that he was here in the summers. I guess I've known him since I was a kid."

It was strange to think that Carter probably knew my father better than any of his children ever did. I had a million questions. What did my father do? What was he like as a person? Why did he abandon us? But I wasn't ready to ask any of them out loud.

"How many bedrooms are there?" James asked from the kitchen.

"Four," Carter replied. "There's one on the main level that your father used and three more, including the master bedroom, upstairs."

"This place is amazing, Kerri," James said. "All the kitchen appliances are brand-new and top-of-the-line. Not to mention that thirty-inch television in the sitting room. None of this stuff looks like its even been used." James walked over to the bookshelf to take a closer look at my father's books. "Honey, come here."

I wet over to see what James was looking at. He was holding a well-read copy of my book. I took it from James' hand and flipped though it slowly. Sections had been underlined in pencil and there were notes in the margins of some pages. Carter glanced over at what we were staring at.

"That was one of his favourite books," Carter said. "He must have read it a dozen times and he gave it to everyone he knew. He made me read it too."

"What did you think of it?" James asked. Since I'd used a pen name, I could tell that James was fishing to see if Carter knew I'd written it.

"It was pretty good,' Carter replied. "Well written but a little depressing."

I immediately felt my back go up. "What do you mean 'a little depressing'?" I didn't want to admit it, even to myself, but I was highly sensitive to any criticism of my work.

"I mean, the main character had quite possibly the worst life ever."

"That might have been the point," I said coolly.

"But something good had to happen to her eventually," Carter replied, not noticing my tone.

"Why?" I asked. "Not everyone lived like the Brady Bunch."

"Yeah," he replied, "but you've got to admit that it's a pretty depressing book."

"I realize that it might not be up to the standard of *Maxim* or whatever it is you usually read, but some people found it quite enjoyable."

"Sorry. I didn't realize you were such a fan of AK Sebastian."

"Carter," James said quietly, "she *is* AK Sebastian."

"Huh?"

"It's a pen name," I explained. "A as in Abigail and K as in Kerrigan. Sebastian was my brother's name."

"Why the hell wouldn't you publish under your own name?" He was embarrassed. Good.

"This way I can get honest feedback about my writing."

"Which you then take as a personal slight and get pissed off," Carter said. "Good plan."

"At least your father enjoyed it," James said to me.

"Do you think he knew you wrote it?" Carter asked.

"I don't know," I said. "He didn't tell you, so maybe he didn't. But it's quite a coincidence."

It really was strange that he had a copy. It had sold okay but it wasn't on everybody's shelf. Despite some good reviews, it had never really hit the mainstream market. In fact, up until this moment I was pretty sure I knew absolutely everyone who had read it.

"Maybe he just liked Canadian authors," James said, looking at the other books on the shelves. "Timothy Findley, Margaret Atwood, Mordachi Richler. Mostly Canadian fiction."

"Fine. If we're done analyzing my father's reading habits, can we continue the tour?"

Carter led us upstairs to the bedrooms. All the rooms had been recently refurnished and repainted. The master bedroom had an en-suite bathroom, complete with Jacuzzi tub, stand-alone shower and a skylight. The bathroom was probably the size of my entire apartment in Toronto. One of the smaller bedrooms had a set of bunk beds and the other had a double bed. These two rooms were attached by an adjoining bathroom.

"I'm pretty sure none of these rooms have been used since they were redone," Carter said. "Your father moved downstairs a few years ago and I don't think he went upstairs too often. I don't even know why he had so much work done on the place."

"Why?"

"Why what?"

"Why did he move downstairs?"

"He had a stroke a couple of years ago, and he wasn't very good at going up and down stairs."

"Oh." I guess that made sense. I knew my father had been in his late fifties when I was born, but it still seemed strange to think of him as a frail old man. I didn't want to let myself feel any sympathy for him.

James, sensing my discomfort, chimed into the conversation.

"Let's take a look outside," James suggested. I smiled at him in gratitude.

As Carter led the way back downstairs, James grabbed my arm and pulled me back a little.

"You can't sell this place," James said vehemently.

"Why not?"

"It's been in your family for almost a hundred years. There's too much of your family's history in this place."

"Yeah, but I don't want anything from my father," I protested. "I'll just sign it over to Maxine. Or maybe I should sell it. I could definitely use the money."

"True, but you'll regret selling it. Think of it in terms of child support payments. It's not a gift from your father. It's something he owed you. And you can't just give it to your sister without thinking it through first. Why should she get all of your father's money *and* the family home? I think you should move here. Sublet your apartment and spend the summer here. You could save money and it'd be a great place for you to write your next book. I'm sure you'll get tons of inspiration from a place as old as this."

"I can write in my apartment."

"I don't think you can."

"What do you mean?" I asked.

"Kerrigan, you're my friend, and I love you dearly, but ever since your brother died you haven't been able to write much of anything."

"I write all the time!"

"Maybe you've been able to write your column and a few other articles that you force yourself to finish. You know as well as I do that all those columns are crap. Sure you could stay where you are and keep doing what you're doing. But you're a novelist. You should be writing books. When I first met you, that's all you could talk about. You haven't done any serious writing in two years."

"Maybe I've grown up a little. Have you ever thought that I might be happy the way things are?"

"You're not happy, sweetie. And you can't give up yet. It's still in you somewhere. Maybe out here you'll be able to find it. Maybe this place will help you get back into the groove and start writing again for real again."

Just then Carter called to us from outside. "I thought you were coming out."

"We'll be right there," I said, heading down the stairs.

I didn't pay much attention to the rest of the tour. I was too busy thinking about what James had said. Maybe he was right. A change of scenery might be what I needed to complete my book. Or start my book.

The ride back to town was silent. We pulled into Carter's parking lot and got out. There was no sign of the other people who'd been at the will reading, including, thankfully, my sister. I was very happy not to see her again. I would be perfectly content to wait until Mom's funeral to see Maxine again.

"I need you to sign some papers before you leave," Carter said. "And we can draw up some forms if you still want to sign over the property to your sister."

"I think I might wait," I said. "Maybe I'll sell it later in the summer. I should probably think it over."

Chapter Three

On a Thursday afternoon two weeks later, Denny and James were helping me move into the cottage. The time had passed quickly, and it was all a blur. During the past two weeks, I'd managed to find someone to take over the lease on my apartment. It was going to be nice not to have to pay $1200 a month in rent during the summer. The only challenge would be keeping my sanity while way from the city for so long. In my entire life, I'd never lived anywhere but Toronto. In fact, I'd only been north of the 401 a handful of times. The city sights and sounds were comforting to me. I was never alone, because there were always a couple million other people nearby. I wasn't exactly sure what to expect from the country.

I gave notice at the paper, and, unfortunately for my ego, they didn't seem to care that I'd no longer be writing my column. I also quit my waitressing job, a somewhat cathartic experience. Maybe James was right. I'd be able to focus my full attention on my writing without any other distractions. If I ever hoped to write anything, it would be now or never.

My final step was buying a used car since I figured I would need a vehicle living in the middle of nowhere. It was small but seemed reliable. I was kind of excited since this was the first car I'd ever owned. I was now the owner of a car and property. It was like I was finally on the road to becoming an adult.

I put all my furniture into storage since the cottage had more than enough for me. James tried to convince me to just throw out all my furniture—he didn't appreciate my garage-sale furnishings, and he didn't understand that I, unlike him, did not have an endless supply of money. As a result I managed to fit all my stuff in my car and in the U-Haul trailer Denny was towing behind his van. It was strange to think that the entire contents of my life could fit into a storage locker, an old Civic and a U-Haul trailer.

The only piece of furniture I'd insisted on bringing was my old writing desk. Sebastian had bought it for me from an estate auction when I was sixteen. It was a beautiful antique desk that I had used when I wrote my first novel. It hadn't been very inspiring lately, but I couldn't bear to have it put into storage.

On the drive up north, I followed behind Denny and James so that I wouldn't get lost. Pulling into the cottage driveway, I saw a familiar vehicle already parked near the building. It was Carter's SUV. I saw the smug expression on James' face as I stepped out of my car, and I shot him a dirty look.

"Got the keys for you," Carter said, tossing them to me when I got out of the car.

"Thanks," I said, catching the keys awkwardly before they could hit me in the face.

"And I thought I'd see if you needed any help moving in."

"That won't be necessary …" I began. James cut me off.

"We could definitely use your help," he said. "Kerri has a lot of crap."

"Not true," I said. "It's all very valuable property."

"Right," Denny said. "It's all very valuable." He was holding up an extremely old rag doll. I grabbed it from him.

"It has sentimental value," I said quickly. "It helps me write."

"Sure it does," James said.

"Can we just move my stuff inside?"

"I brought an assistant," Carter said. "Alex!"

A woman came around from the front of the house. She had jaw-length brown hair and looked to be in her early thirties. I was glad that Carter had brought his girlfriend: it would shut James up.

"You bellowed?" she said.

"Kerri, this is Alex," Carter explained.

"Nice to meet you," I said, shaking her hand.

"Alex's the town's doctor," Carter added.

"Good to know," I replied.

"Hopefully you won't need to call on my services," Alex said.

I could hear Denny and James clearing their throats behind me.

"Sorry. I should introduce my friends, although they seem to have come down with colds. This is James, and this is Denny."

I could see Denny and Carter sizing each other up as they shook hands. It was like watching those nature shows where two gorillas face off. I honestly wouldn't have been surprised if they started grunting and banging on their chests. It looked like they were each trying to break the other's hand as they shook.

"Alright," I said, before violence broke out. "If you're all here to help, why don't you pick something up and carry it inside."

Everyone grabbed something from the U-Haul and carried it into the cottage. Denny, Alex and I were each carrying boxes for my office (I couldn't believe that I was actually going to have an office).

"I'm going to use the small upstairs bedroom as an office," I told them, leading them upstairs. "We'll put the books and the desk in there."

"Why do you have so many books?" Denny asked, scowling at me.

"Because."

"That's not an answer," he grumbled, struggling to carry a box up the stairs.

"If it's too heavy for you, I can probably take it," I said innocently. I knew Denny would stop complaining as soon as I threatened his masculinity.

"Don't bother. I'm fine," he said, carrying the box the rest of the way upstairs without a word of complaint.

"Thank you," I replied sweetly.

"So, how long have you been dating Carter?" Denny asked Alex. I rolled my eyes. Denny needed to have all women in love with him. And he apparently had set his sights set on Alex.

"We're not dating," she replied. "Carter's my brother."

"Oh," Denny said, looking at me. I rolled my eyes at him. I would have punched him but the box in my arms was too heavy.

"What? Did I miss something?" Alex asked, looking first at Denny and then at me.

"No," I said quickly.

"Actually," Denny began, "James thinks Carter would be great for Kerri. If he's single, that is."

"Shut up," I said under my breath. Why did I bring my friends anywhere?

"Well, he is single and I think he likes her," Alex replied, completely ignoring my frustration.

"How can you tell?" Denny asked.

"Why else would he have dragged us out here to help Kerri move in?"

"Enough!" I exclaimed. I knew my face was bright red. Denny and James were bad enough. I really didn't need Alex giving them any ideas. "I don't think Carter would like the two of you talking about him behind his back."

"He wouldn't care," Alex said with a shrug.

"We could always start talking about you," Denny added helpfully.

"That's it. I'm leaving." I went back downstairs to get more of my stuff, leaving the two of them to start unpacking (which I really doubted they'd do).

I grabbed a bag of clothes from the back of the trailer and turned to go back into the cottage.

"Want a hand?" a voice behind me asked, making me jump. It was Carter. "I had to escape James. He kept telling me what a terrific person you were, and how you were single. I think he was hinting at something." He grinned at me.

I felt myself blushing again, and I started plotting horrible revenge on James.

"I'll have a word with him. And with Denny. I don't know why I brought either of them with me. In fact, I'm not even sure why I'm friends with either of them." I passed him the bag of clothes and grabbed a box. "That goes in the master bedroom."

"Yes sir," he said with a fake salute, carrying the bag upstairs.

I wasn't sure what to make of the whole Carter situation. He seemed like a nice guy, and he was kind of cute. But despite James' insistence that I needed a man, I really didn't want to get involved with anyone. It wasn't a good time, and it really wasn't a good place. And the last thing I needed was to get involved with someone who'd been friends with my father.

Carter hadn't shown any interest in me other than as a friend, and I hoped things wouldn't change. I would definitely have to make sure that things didn't change.

Shaking off a slight feeling of foreboding, I followed Carter into the cottage.

About an hour later everything was inside and mostly unpacked. There were a few things that I was going to have to buy tomorrow (like some light bulbs and cleaning supplies), but the place was pretty well stocked.

Thankfully, Denny had had enough foresight to buy groceries before we left Toronto because I hadn't even thought about it. I graciously invited everyone to stay for dinner as a way of thanking them for helping me move. James and Denny were quick to say yes because they didn't want to rush back to the city, and I was pretty sure that Denny didn't really want to face his wife after spending a day with me. Alex and Carter didn't have any other plans, and so the five of us decided to christen my new place with a dinner party.

"I'll barbeque," Carter volunteered.

"That's okay," I said. "As the host it's my responsibility to cook for you. You all helped me move. It's the least I can do to thank you, even though Denny paid for the food."

"You'd better let him do it," Alex said, trying very hard to keep a straight face. "He gets kind of pissy if you don't let him be in charge of the barbeque. It's some sort of a throw back to the cave man."

"Yes. Me like fire," Carter added solemnly.

"Plus, remember that time you set your apartment on fire making garlic bread?" James added helpfully. "You're not the best cook, Kerri, and, although I'm sure Alex's a fabulous doctor, I don't feel like getting food poisoning this far from a hospital."

"Very funny," I replied sarcastically. "And it wasn't the entire apartment. I only set the oven mitt on fire."

I gladly relinquished my hold on the barbeque (I hadn't really wanted to cook; I was only being polite) and gave Carter full control of the grill and kitchen. James was right about my cooking ability. I was a fabulous re-heater. I could even make a bowl of canned tuna that was to die for. But I wasn't great using appliances other than the microwave.

After leaving Carter to sort out dinner, I grabbed a bottle of wine and some glasses from the kitchen and went out onto the patio with the others. Despite the fact that it was only the end of April, it was a surprisingly warm evening. It was still early but the sun was just beginning to set. Carter had been right about this place. It did have a spectacular view. The water was calm and glass-like, and the reflected sunset gave everything a pink hue.

"It's so quiet out here," James said. "No cars, no boats. No signs of life from any of the other buildings."

"It won't be like this for long," Carter said from behind the barbeque. "A few weeks into May there'll be so many boats on the lake, it will look like rush hour. And all these cottages will be packed on the long weekend in May." He turned on the grill and looked up at me. "Are the burgers in the freezer?"

"No," I said, "I put them in the fridge. I can get them for you."

"That's okay," he said. "I'm doing the cooking, so I'll get the hamburger patties. You sit down and enjoy yourself." He turned and went inside.

Denny was talking to Alex when I sat down next to him.

"How long have you lived here?" he was asking her.

"Practically my entire life," Alex replied, picking up a glass of wine. "Carter and I were both raised here. I came back a few years ago, but Carter's been back here since he finished law school."

"Where did you live before moving back here?" I asked her.

"I was working in Toronto at Sunnybrook Hospital, but I always wanted to get into my own practice. There's a real need for doctors in this area, so I came back here and took over my dad's practice when he retired."

"Was it hard moving back here after living in the city?" I asked her. "There can't be half as much to do here as in Toronto."

"I get to work better hours here than I did when I worked in the ER in Sunnybrook," she said. "When I was in Toronto, I didn't have time to do anything. I actually get to have a life here, despite having something like 5,000 patients. There's a serious lack of doctors in rural areas like this. It may not be exciting, but at least I know I'm needed."

"But being so close to your family can't be easy," I insisted.

Alex laughed. "Actually, I like living close to my family. Carter and I get along, and my parents don't drive me too crazy."

"Kerri just thinks that everyone is like her when it comes to family," Denny explained. "She's not too fond of hers."

"To put it lightly," I added.

"Kerri never speaks to her sister," James said. "It's just surprising to her that you and Carter get along so well."

"We weren't friends when we were kids," Alex explained. "Carter was always picking on me. But I can't really blame him. I was the annoying kid sister tagging after him all the time."

"How many years between you?" I asked.

"Four," Alex replied. "Still close enough in age to play together when we were kids, but too many for us to seriously fight."

"There are fifteen years between me and my sister," I said, trying to justify why I wasn't close to my family. "Far too many for us to have anything in common."

"So what sort of a husband will Carter be for our little Kerrigan?" James said with a smile.

"God damn it, James," I said in annoyed tone. "I'm sitting right here."

"We know that, Kerri," Denny replied. "You should be happy that we don't talk about you behind your back."

"Fine. But just so you're all clear about this, I'm up here to write not to catch myself a man. I *like* being single. Besides, I'm not interested in Carter that way. He seems like a very nice guy, but he's not my type."

"Right," James said. "He's tall, good-looking, smart, has a great job, his own car …"

"And his own house," Alex chimed in. "Plus he still has all his own hair and his original teeth."

"… why would you be interested in someone like that?" James concluded.

"You know Kerri's type," Denny added. "Dumb, good looking and blindly devoted to her. Someone she can lead around for a week or two before she dumps him and heads for the hills."

"Wow. You guys are really mean today. You must have had an extra dose of asshole with your cereal this morning. Try to remember that I'm the one with the cottage on the lake."

"You know we're just teasing you," James said. "You wouldn't hold that against your closest friends, trapped in the city all week, with the humidity, the smog and the air advisories? And Denny, you should be careful about what you say about Kerri's former boyfriends."

"Shut up, James," I said, feeling my face grow hot. I did not want to get into this right now, in front of strangers. This was not the time to bring up ancient history (and not-so-ancient history).

"What's going on out here?" Carter asked as he came outside carrying a tray of hamburger patties.

"Nothing," I said, hoping the subject of Denny and I would die if James' attention was diverted. "Do we have enough burgers?"

"We're just tormenting Kerri," James explained. Apparently James had fixated on something, and he was going to make sure I was humiliated.

"I think we've just learned that Kerri and Denny used to be a couple," Alex said to Carter.

"Really," Carter said, sounding interested as he put the burgers on the grill.

"I really don't think we need to get into this boring subject right now," I said.

"Why not?" James asked innocently. I shot him an angry look. James didn't know what he was getting into. He didn't know the whole story.

Denny and I had started dating back when I was eighteen. He was twenty-five at the time. I'd known him for a long time, and I'd had a crush on him from the moment we'd met. He was friends with my brother Sebastian from the day they started high school. I think I was about seven when I first met him. After Denny graduated from university he took a job in England. When he left I'd been the fifteen-year-old kid sister of his best friend. When he came back I was just starting my first year of university. Denny was (as Maxine constantly pointed out) far too old for me. Maxine would sometimes refer to him as the 'cradle-robbing pedophile', which only made me stick up for Denny even more. If she hadn't meddled I probably would have ended it much faster than I actually did. I never found out what Sebastian thought of the whole thing, but I don't think he was too pleased with his best friend dating his baby sister.

Denny and I had an incredible, horrible relationship that lasted about ten months (still the longest relationship I've ever had). We fought every day. He was ready to settle down, and I was like other eighteen-year-olds. Who wants to be tied down when they're eighteen? I think one of the biggest problems was that I'd finally gotten exactly what I'd wanted. Having Denny wasn't half as much fun as worshipping him from afar.

And on top of all that, we just weren't very compatible. Our breakup was horrible. Denny wouldn't even talk to me for more than a year after our relationship ended. That was the hardest part for me. I lost a boyfriend and a best friend in one single fight.

Five months after we broke up he married Emily. Unfortunately, Denny still claimed to be in love with me (something he confessed to my brother at the bachelor party and which Sebastian told me a few months later). And also unfortunately, Emily seemed to know this. Emily was Denny's attempt to show me and the world that he'd finally gotten over our breakup.

James knew all that. That part of the story was pretty much public knowledge. What he didn't know, what nobody knew, was that Denny and I had a little slip-up about two years ago after Sebastian's funeral.

It wasn't something I was proud of, but it happened. I was heartbroken after losing Sebastian, and Denny was the only one who understood. It was supposed to be a one-night thing. But it wasn't. It kept happening. I turned to Denny whenever something went wrong. Whenever I needed a reason for ending a relationship, I'd go back to Denny. It was an awful cycle and I hated myself and him for it. But I couldn't cut him out of my life. He was my last link to Sebastian. Denny was the only person who had known my brother as well as I did.

"Yes, Kerri appears to be uncomfortable talking about this," Denny said quickly. "I think we should change the subject."

Leave it to Denny to be a gentleman when he was covering his own ass. Not that I minded. It was nice to have one of them defending me rather than attacking me.

"That's fine with me," Carter said amicably. "I'm pretty sure I've missed most of the conversation anyway. And I don't think I really want to know what you've been talking about. So I'll just go and cook the burgers, and we can have dinner."

During dinner I discovered that my first impressions of Alex and Carter were right. They were really nice, fun people, and it seemed that we all had a lot in common. I found out that Alex, like me, had attended McMaster University. Carter and Denny had lived in the same dorm at U of T a few years apart. They actually had a few friends in common. We learned that Carter had been a water-skiing champion as a teenager and that Alex originally wanted to be a vet. Dinner was fun, and the conversation came easily without any awkward pauses.

Throughout dinner I noticed Denny spending an unusual amount of time staring at Alex. I wasn't really surprised that he was checking out a woman (Denny had cheated on Emily with women other than me), but Alex didn't strike me as his usual type. She was of medium height and had an appearance that would be best described as cute. She did, however, have blue eyes that were very striking. But she seemed to be immune to Denny's charm, or at least I hoped so for her sake. She seemed to have too much sense to fall for Denny's routine.

After we finished dinner, James and Denny headed back to Toronto, promising (or threatening) to return the following weekend. I think they were both a little worried about leaving me alone for an entire week. Carter and Alex left at the same time, heading back into town. That left me alone in the cottage for the first time.

I took the opportunity to wander around the cottage, moving some of my stuff to different rooms. I put fresh sheets on the bed and hung most of my clothes in the closet. But I didn't unpack everything. I still wasn't 100% sure that I'd even stay in the house for more than one night. I wanted to be able to make a quick escape if I needed to.

I'd noticed earlier that the house had lost most of its musty smell. Carter must have had someone in to clean before I moved in. I made a mental note to ask him about it so I could pay him back.

I'd never lived in a place this big before. I certainly wasn't used to having so much space to myself. It was incredible. I didn't think I'd even use half the rooms. I strolled from room to room, picking up knickknacks and looking around. I wandered over to the bookshelf, grabbing the first volume that touched my hand. I started absently thumbing through the book, glancing quickly at the notes in the margin. I think I was subconsciously trying to figure out who my father had been. I dropped the book I'd been holding, disgusted with myself. I didn't want to find out who he had been. If he hadn't wanted to learn about me, why should I care about him?

Before I could stop myself, I began to take a mental inventory of what I knew about the man. He was dead. He'd had a stroke. He had friends in town. He'd had money and property inherited from his family. He had read my book and wrote notes in the margins when reading. It was like I was doing a character sketch on my father and was coming up with only superficial traits. I was no closer to knowing my father than I had been a month ago. Except now I was beginning to be curious about him, which really annoyed me.

I tried to shake off the feeling of annoyance. How could I expect to live here if the first night bothered me so much? This was *my* house, filled with my things. I kept telling myself that, trying to remind myself that I was twenty-five, not eight. I decided that first thing in the morning I would pack up all of my father's stuff and put it in storage. I knew this would help, and I felt a little better immediately. Out of sight, out of mind.

As the darkness settled around the cottage, I grabbed the book I was reading and sat down in the main room, staring out onto the lake. I was re-reading *Wuthering Heights*, one of my favourite books. I curled up into a big easy chair and tried to lose myself on the moors. The darkness and isolation of the cottage made Emily Brontë very eerie. I was still at the beginning of the book, where the narrator is visited by the ghost of Catherine. I had never realized just how frightening that scene was. I knew that if I heard knocking at the window when I slept that night, I would have a heart attack. It was so dark outside, I could hardly see beyond the end of the patio.

But it was also incredibly peaceful. There weren't many other lights visible across the lake, making the sense of isolation complete. The moon was reflected on the glass-like water. I had never been in such a tranquil spot before. This is nice, I thought.

My sense of peace and tranquility lasted for about a second.

Suddenly every single horror movie that I'd ever seen came rushing back to me. An isolated cabin. No one around for miles. No one to hear me scream. I was pretty sure that 50% of all slasher films had this exact same plot. What if something happened in the night? I didn't know exactly what could happen, but it would be something horrible. I didn't even know my address. What if I had to call the police? I doubted that I'd even be able to give them adequate directions. My only hope would be to set the place on fire and pray that someone would see the flames.

Yeah, it was quiet alright. Too quiet. Eerily quiet. I hadn't spent a night away from the noise of the city for a long time (I couldn't even remember how long it had been). How did anyone sleep without the soothing sounds of traffic? Where were the sirens and car horns? I missed the sounds of bars and restaurants, the sounds of people out and about at all hours of the day and night. I looked at my watch. It wasn't even nine o'clock, and already everything was dead quiet. What exactly was I supposed to do?

And it was dark. Not a single building near me had any lights on. There were no traffic lights, no street lights. Not even the flashing light of a police car or ambulance. The only lights (other than the ones coming from my place) were the stars.

The darkness seemed to permeate every inch of the cottage. I had never seen darkness like this before. At home even on a cloudy night there were still lights coming from somewhere. Goosebumps formed on my arms. I quickly turned on every light in the room to make sure that there was nothing lingering in the corner, just waiting until I was sleeping to pull out its axe and chop me into a thousand pieces. How far was the closest mental hospital? Didn't people escape from those things on a daily basis?

I knew I was being ridiculous. Paranoid. I had lived in Toronto my entire life and was never afraid of walking home alone at night, but here, in the middle of nowhere, I was afraid of serial killers. I laughed at myself for being so stupid. The sound of my laughter echoed throughout the empty building, only serving to further scare the crap out of me.

It was ridiculous. *I* was ridiculous. There was nothing to be afraid of. Then why was the house making so much noise? It then occurred to me that I'd never found out where my father had died. For all I knew he could have died right here in the cottage. Maybe even in the chair I was sitting in. The thought was not a pleasant one, and I jumped quickly to my feet.

Stop it! I yelled at myself. I was acting like a four-year-old.

Making a mental note to stop watching horror movies and to only read nice, light, happy stories, I stepped out onto the porch to look at the stars. Without any lights around, I could see every star in the sky. It was amazing. I shivered as the warm evening turned into a cool spring night. The breeze from the lake was cold, so I pulled on a sweatshirt and snuggled deep into a deck chair. There were no bugs to drive me inside, and I sat on the deck to enjoy the peaceful evening. It was like I was the only person left on earth. It was kind of nice in an isolated way. This really would be an ideal place for me to turn into a hermit, I thought. I tried to relax and enjoy myself. The sound of the phone ringing brought me back to reality. I went back inside to answer it.

"Hello?" I said kind of confused. I wasn't sure who would have this number, since I didn't even know what it was yet. Setting up a phone line was something I'd forgotten to do before I left the city.

"Hi Kerri, it's Carter."

"Hi."

"I forgot to mention one thing while I was there, but I don't want you to get freaked out by it."

"Let me guess," I said, laughing nervously. "A serial killer has escaped from the mental institution just outside of town, and he used to be a counselor at an abandoned summer camp nearby." I looked around the room to see if anyone was lurking in the shadows. I wished that Denny and James hadn't gone back to the city. Why couldn't they have taken me with them? I was crazy to want to stay here. I was sure I wouldn't even survive the night.

"Close, but no." I could tell he was laughing at me, even though he was doing his best to hide it. I was not pleased, despite my terror. But I was still more afraid than I was angry, so I didn't hang up on him. "I was going to say that there's no spring bear hunt this year. There've been some bear sightings in the area in the past couple of weeks. Make sure you don't leave any garbage on your porch or anywhere near your screen doors, for that matter. Bears have been known to tear the screens off cottages."

"Thanks a lot," I said, my fear of being murdered quickly changing to a picture of me getting mauled in my sleep. "You couldn't have mentioned this a little earlier? Like when it wasn't too dark for me to get into my car and drive back to Toronto?" I was picturing huge dripping fangs and sharp claws ripping through the screen and a giant bear bursting into the cottage. There was no way I could head back to the city now. It was too dark. I'd never make it to my car before the bears got me.

"Don't worry. They generally don't start bothering cottagers until later in the season. I just wanted you to keep an eye out for them." His voice was calm and reassuring. "And they're just small brown bears. There's actually nothing for you to worry about. I just don't want you to freak out if you see anything tonight."

Unfortunately, I was well past the point for reassurance. I was already terrified and wasn't going to be easily calmed down. "What if the bears come by the cottage, don't see any garbage out on the deck and then get pissed off? What happens then? Are they going to break down the door and come after me?" I was sure my voice sounded shrill and bordering on hysterics.

"I don't think bears act like that," Carter replied in what I could tell was a forced-serious voice. He was definitely laughing at me now. "You really don't have anything to worry about."

"Then why did you call?"

"I just didn't want you to be surprised by anything."

"Thanks."

"Look, if you're that worried about it I can come back out there and double-check your doors."

That was the last thing I wanted, and it was enough to stop me from acting like a little chicken. I didn't need him coming out here and acting like the big manly man, protecting the helpless female. "I'm sure everything will be fine," I replied somewhat stiffly. I didn't need to be protected by a man, let alone some guy I hardly knew.

"Okay," he said in a cheerful voice. "But you have my number. If you need anything just give me a call."

"Alright." Even if a thousand bears broke into the house led by a group of axe-wielding maniacs, I wouldn't call him.

Great, I thought as I hung up the phone. Why the hell would anyone want to live in a town where bears could attack them? I had always considered myself to be something of an environmentalist, but now I wished that all bears were dead or in zoos. Bears didn't really have a place in the ecosystem, did they? If they were all gone, would we really notice?

The city was looking better and better with every passing minute. At least in Toronto you didn't have to worry about bears breaking into your apartment. Burglars, yes. But no bears. The only animals going through our trash were rats and raccoons (to be perfectly honest, some of the raccoons I'd seen in Toronto had been pretty vicious; they were probably worse than bears).

To get my mind off of bears and serial killers, I sat down and turned on the television, flipping through the channels mindlessly. It didn't distract me at all. Five hundred channels and nothing on that could help me to forget about bears. And one channel was showing a marathon of *Friday the 13th* movies, which I very quickly switched off. In the empty building, the sound from the television sounded magnified. I was sure that if there had been anyone in the cottages across the lake, they would have been able to hear what I was watching. I spent a few hours watching some mindless sitcoms before deciding to venture upstairs for bed. After checking to make sure all the doors were still securely locked, of course. And the windows. If I'd had a hammer and some nails I would have made absolutely sure that nothing could ever get into the building (of course then I'd be trapped inside with whatever bear or serial killer was already inside with me, and if the building caught on fire, I'd be pretty much screwed). I also tried to make sure that nothing was in the house with me already, by checking every single closet and under every bed.

Finally, I climbed into bed and shut off the light. I lay there for what seemed like hours but I couldn't sleep. Every sound outside made me jump. I swear there were at least a hundred raccoons climbing all over the front porch. Mostly, there were sounds I couldn't identify. And the building creaked. I was used to an apartment building. They rarely creak. I heard pipes clanging, wood squeaking and furniture moving (I swear) and each noise made me jump. I pulled the covers securely around my head and shut my eyes as tight as I could.

At around three in the morning, I finally felt myself starting to drift off. At first I slept peacefully. Then I started to dream. I dreamt that a bear had escaped from a near-by mental institution and had come looking for me. For some reason it looked like Smokey the Bear and he was wielding an axe that was dripping with blood. I tried to run but I couldn't. Everywhere I went I kept ending up back in the cottage with the bear inches from my face. I could feel its warm breath on my neck every time I tried to escape. Finally I ran into Carter who wouldn't help me because I had refused to call him.

I don't know how long I slept before I felt it and woke up. Something really was touching my face. I quickly reached over and groggily turned on the light. What I saw will be burned onto my brain for all eternity. There on the pillow next to me was a bat, wings flapping, looking at me with its incredibly beady eyes. I screamed like I'd never screamed before.

Chapter Four

I opened the door and let Carter into the cottage at about nine the next morning. I was tired and angry and in no mood to be hospitable.

"What?" I said in frustration.

"I know you're not a morning person," he said, cheerfully, "but I come bearing coffee and donuts." He stopped when he noticed my appearance. "Rough night?"

I shot him a dirty look. I knew I looked like crap, but I didn't need him to point it out to me. I'd gotten about fifteen minutes of sleep, and I was cranky and tired. After spending about an hour trying to kill that stupid bat (which involved me and a tennis racket chasing the bat around the cottage) and then trying to get rid of its corpse, I couldn't get back to sleep. Every time I closed my eyes, I just knew there would be another one of those awful flapping things next to me when I opened them again.

"I didn't really sleep," I snapped. I knew it wasn't his fault, but I wanted someone to blame. And I did kind of blame him for the whole bat-thing (I know that didn't make any sense but I needed someone to be mad at and Carter was standing right there on my doorstep).

"I'm sorry if what I said about the bears kept you awake."

"No, it wasn't the bears. I'm not such a girly girl that some stories about bears kept me awake." Okay, so that was a bit of a lie. "I woke up with a bat at about three this morning. You didn't say anything about bats last night. Did they call off the spring bat-hunt too?"

Carter threw back his head and laughed, stopping only when he saw the dangerous look on my face. "I'm sorry. I know it's not funny."

"You better watch it. That bat's not doing too much laughing this morning. I'm pretty handy with a tennis racket."

"I'll keep that in mind. Nice outfit." I was wearing a ratty old flannel housecoat and big floppy slippers.

"Thank you. It's what all the most glamorous people wear first thing in the morning when they want to look like crazy bag ladies."

"I think it's kind of cute."

I blushed lightly and changed the subject. "Why aren't you at work?"

"I was at work. I had to come out this way to visit a client, so I thought I'd drop by with some coffee. You strike me as the kind of person who can't survive without caffeine. And after our talk last night, I thought I'd better make sure you were still alive out here. I half expected you to be on your way back to Toronto. Plus Mr. Smith seemed anxious for a drive."

"Who's Mr. Smith?" I asked, looking around at his car, annoyed with him. I did not want to see anyone else while I was dressed like a slob. I tightened my housecoat around me and tried to smooth down my hair. I was going to kill Carter.

"My dog," he said with a grin. "Smitty!"

A big golden retriever came bounding towards me. He was carrying a large stick and looked incredibly pleased with himself. He dropped the stick at Carter's feet and looked up with a big dopey grin.

"Kerri, this is Mr. Smith."

"Nice to meet you," I said, bending down to pet the dog on the head.

I was definitely a dog person. Cats drove me around the bend. Mr. Smith seemed pleased with the attention I was giving him. His tongue was hanging out of his mouth and he kept knocking at me with one of his paws. I was hooked.

"Why did you name your dog Mr. Smith?" I asked, looking up at Carter while continuing to pet the dog.

"Because if I named him Mr. Stevens, our mail would get mixed up."

"The dog gets a lot of mail?"

"Tons. He's very popular with the ladies."

"I can see that," I said.

"Any big plans for the day?"

"I plan on spending my day writing. I'd like to get some work in on my novel. It's been a pain in my ass for the last couple of months," (that was the understatement of the century), "and I'm hoping that the change in scenery will help me get going again."

"What's it about?"

I stood up, trying to ignore the big brown eyes that were insisting I keep petting. "I don't generally like to tell people what I'm writing about. They always feel the need to give me advice and tell me how the plot should be changed." Translation: I hadn't started and didn't want anyone to know. I'd been struggling for months now to come up with a good idea. Nothing seemed to work, and I was growing increasingly frustrated. Everything I thought of had been done to death. I was seriously considering a change of occupation.

"Come on. I promise I won't tell anyone, and I won't say a word to you about it. Scout's honour." He put one hand on his heart and raised the other in a Boy Scout's salute. He grinned at me like a little kid.

Shit. "Fine. It's a psychological thriller about a woman whose husband has her committed to a mental institution against her will. She's trying to convince everyone that she's not crazy, but they keep her so drugged up that they don't believe her." Good idea. I was always good at thinking fast on my feet. When I was a kid and I had been out past curfew, I was usually able to make up a good story for Maxine or my mother when I got caught. I wondered if I'd actually be able to do anything with the idea.

"Interesting."

"What do you mean 'interesting'? Is that good-interesting or bad-interesting?"

"I'm not supposed to give you any comments, remember?"

"Fine. Forget I even asked."

"Okay, I will. If you get bored today, you should come into town and drop by. I could introduce you to some people. My schedule's not too full today, so I've got time to show you around. I could give you the grand tour. It should take about five minutes."

"That's okay. I'll be really busy here all day. I've still got a ton of unpacking and reorganizing to do. And I don't think I need to meet anyone in town. I don't even know how long I'll be here. After last night, I'm really tempted to sell the place right now."

"You should know that everyone is really curious about you and your sister. I think just about everyone in town knew your father. His family has been coming here for a really long time. They all want to meet you."

"Great. That's even more reason to sell the place. I don't want to get to know old friends of my father's. Maybe Maxine will come back and do the rounds."

"Okay, I can understand that. You might change your mind in a couple of weeks. But I'm going to insist that you at least come into town and have dinner with me."

God, is he asking me out? This could be bad, I thought. I had to set him straight. He wasn't my type. But he'd been really nice to me, and I didn't know anyone else in town, so I didn't want to crush him immediately. I would let him down as gently as possible.

"I don't know. I've got a lot of food here, and I should try to concentrate on my work."

"It'll just be the three of us. You, Alex and me. If you don't show up, I'll owe Alex $20." He grinned. "Plus, Mr. Smith will never let me hear the end of it."

"Fine. I'll come. But I don't want to be surprised into eating with my father's ex-girlfriend or an old high school acquaintance." Having his sister there would mean that it definitely wasn't a date.

"You've got a deal. Come by my office around six." He went over to the door. "I'll leave you the donuts. Maybe the sugar will help get your creative juices going. Come on, Smitty."

The dog stayed firmly rooted at my feet.

"We have to go," Carter said again, snapping his fingers.

Mr. Smith looked at me, and I swear he rolled his eyes. He was going to go when he was good and ready.

"I can see who's in charge in your household," I said wryly.

"I think he likes you," Carter said.

"I can look after him today if you'd like."

"I thought you said you had to work? He'd be a big distraction. I'll take him back to my place." He snapped his fingers again. "Come here," he said firmly.

Finally, the dog sighed (honestly, he did), shrugged in my direction and then followed Carter outside.

After they left, I wasn't sure what to do with myself. It was early, and I thought I probably should take advantage of the time and try to get to work. I grabbed my coffee and a donut, picked up my laptop and headed out onto the deck. I thought that the view of the water and the warm sunshine would help me think of what I wanted to write. It was a beautiful spring day. The sun was warm but the breeze off the lake was actually quite cold. I pulled my house coat tightly around me and curled my legs up into the chair. The view from the deck really was nice. The lake was perfectly calm, and I was pretty sure I was the only human around for miles. I watched a pair of loons swim past the end of the dock. A couple of chipmunks were chasing each other around a stump out front. It was kind of cool. I'd never had much exposure to nature and here it was frolicking in my front yard like a Disney movie. There had to be some inspiration in it, right?

I thought I'd try using the idea that I'd made up for Carter. It was better than nothing and I thought I might actually be able to get something out of it. I started writing an outline for the story. Surprisingly, I was actually progressing on it. It wasn't good, but there were words on the screen (something that hadn't happened in ages). For nearly an hour I typed happily before hitting a snag. I had my heroine strapped down in the hospital, but I couldn't figure out what to do from there. Initially, I thought about her picking the lock on her straps using a piece of metal she'd hid in her mouth, but then I realized that was a little too Linda Hamilton in *Terminator 2*. Maybe I needed to go back a little further. Before she was strapped down. Then I could figure out what needed to be done next.

Two hours later I hadn't written another word. I stared at the screen in dismay. I was so frustrated I felt like tearing out my hair or tossing the computer off the end of the dock. Maybe the whole thing needed to go. It was a stupid idea anyway, I thought to myself. I closed the file and put my computer down on the picnic table. I needed a new idea. A good idea. One that I could actually do something with for longer than a couple of hours. But not today. I knew that there was no point in continuing to bang my head against the wall today so I took off my housecoat and lay in the sun, attempting to get some colour in my pasty-white winter skin. Despite being red-headed, I tanned. Not like Maxine who always turned pink in the sun. Maxine also freckled (not that I was constantly trying to find imperfections in my sister).

At noon the phone rang. I ran inside to get it and was pleased to hear James' voice on the other end (talking to him was at least a legitimate excuse for not working). I had been feeling slightly isolated out in the middle of nowhere by myself all day and was glad to finally have someone to talk to.

"Hi sweetheart. Here's your wakeup call."
"I've been awake for hours, James," I said to him.
"Seriously?"
"Yeah, why?"

"Is everything alright? Are you sure you're feeling okay? I didn't know you had the ability to function during the daylight hours."

"Shut up, smart ass."

"I guess you're already becoming a country girl. Up at the crack of dawn to milk the cows and feed the chickens."

"Right. All those chickens that I've got here."

"You should look into getting some. They might help keep you company out there in the sticks."

"And they might keep me busy," I added.

"How's the writing coming?" James asked. "Is the change in scenery making it any easier for you? Any new ideas?"

"Oh, it's going fabulously. I've written at least three chapters. You wouldn't believe what a difference the change in scenery has made."

"You haven't written a thing, have you?"

"Not a single bloody word," I admitted with a sigh. "I don't know what's wrong with me. I've never had a block that's lasted so long. Maybe this is why Harper Lee never wrote again. Or Margaret Mitchell. Maybe I need to become a strange recluse and just accept the fact that I'll never write another word. I'm already beginning to feel like a hermit out here, and it has only been one night. Of course, my first book wasn't exactly 'To Kill a Mockingbird' or 'Gone with the Wind'."

"Or you could be overreacting again, and you just need to keep trying. It will come back to you eventually. You've only been up there for a day. I'd give it at least a week before you quit showering and hang up the 'No Trespassing' sign."

"Fine," I said sulkily.

"While I do enjoy talking about this, I did have a reason for calling you long distance in the middle of the day. I have some potentially good news for you. My paper wants you to do a series of articles on cottage life up north. Well, actually they asked for *someone* to do a series of articles, and I suggested you. I gave them some of your old work and a copy of your book, and they agreed that you'd be a good choice."

I felt a twinge of excitement. Finally, something to do other than staring at my blank computer screen. "What sort of things are they interested in?"

"They want articles on resorts, stores, bakeries ... anything that's quaint and of interest to those people trapped in the city five days a week. The cheesier the better. I'm not talking about high-quality literature here. I'm talking about mindless schlock to entertain the masses. However, the money will be pretty good, and I know you need it. They said they'll pay fifty cents a word."

"That's more than I was getting in the city." The last of my royalty money from my novel was drying up quickly. The articles I had been writing in Toronto were only paying twenty-five cents a word. A steady paycheck would be great this summer when my living expenses were so low. I would do my best to make the articles very long. "All right. Tell your editor that I'll do it. When does he want me to start?"

"He wants your first article to be published the Friday of Victoria Day weekend. He said it's up to you to pick what you want to write about. They'll decide how many more they want after they get the first one."

Sort of like an audition, I thought. I guess I couldn't really complain, since James had obviously worked really hard to get me the chance at the job. The fact that the editor had read my book and was still considering hiring me was a testament to James' persuasive abilities.

I thanked James and hung up the phone. Now I had something to occupy my time while I tried to work on that stupid novel. I was good with mindless. One of my English professors told me that I had a skill with bullshit that was unnerving. I was the queen of the last-minute essay. Plus, the money would be great. People didn't realize how hard it was to make a living as a writer. Unless you're John Grisham or Stephen King, it's hard to survive by publishing alone. And trying to work more than one job made it difficult to find the time to write. While I was in university I'd had a job writing the descriptions in catalogues. My crowning achievement was when they gave me the outer-wear section. I had dreams of Oprah's book club or movie rights catapulting me to the big time. I had no qualms at all with selling out. In fact, I eagerly waited for the day when I had a ton of yes-men telling me that I was the greatest thing in the known universe. Until then, I'd have to take what I could get. There were times when I seriously considered going back to school to become a teacher. At least I'd be able to get paid for doing something and then have the summers off to write. I was giving myself until my twenty-eighth birthday to make something of myself as an author. Then I would give up, throw in the towel, quit ...

After lunch, I started going stir crazy. Completely crazy. Trapped-in-an-isolated-lodge-all-winter-long crazy. I made up my mind to venture back outside. I changed into my bathing suit and walked down to the water. I stuck my toe in and immediately pulled it out again. The water was freezing. I was disappointed since it was so warm outside, and I loved to swim. I knew it was only April but it felt more like July. The ice had only been off the lake for a few weeks. I settled back into sunbathing on the dock, after slathering myself with sunscreen.

By the middle of the afternoon, the sun had moved off the deck, and I was starting to get a little cool. Rather than spend the rest of the day in front of the television, I thought I'd take another stab at writing. I met with the same success I'd had in the morning. Nothing. This was pathetic. Despite the fact that this was only my first day here, I was starting to feel a great deal of despair. I imagined the long summer days stretching out before me just as unproductive as this one. Giving up yet again (which was definitely becoming a theme with me), I decided to look around the house and rearrange my stuff.

I went into the room that I was going to use as an office and looked around with pleasure. It was the room with one double bed that had a view overlooking the lake. I pushed the bed up against the wall and set my desk up in the corner under the window. It was perfect.

I'd always wanted an office where I could work. Unfortunately, I could never afford the rent on a two bedroom place in Toronto. In the city I either wrote at my desk in my bedroom, at the kitchen table, or took my laptop down to a coffee shop and wrote there. An office had been my dream; my desk would face the window, and the bookshelves would be filled with my favourite authors. In this dream, I'd be able to work steadily and productively for eight hours a day.

I looked around the room to see what there was for me to do. Denny and Alex had cleared off the bookshelf for me, but they hadn't put any of my books away. Pleased at finally finding something to do, I took my time arranging my books neatly on the shelves. I was tempted to waste even more time by arranging them alphabetically (or chronologically or even thematically), but I resisted. I'd save that for another day when I had even less to occupy my time. I was putting the empty boxes in the closet when I found the trunk.

At the back of the closet was an old trunk covered by some blankets. I pulled it out to get a better look. It was heavy, but I managed to drag it across the floor into the center of the room. I sat cross-legged on the bed and stared at it. It was an old fashioned-style trunk, the kind you'd expect to see in an old movie, locked with a big padlock. I jiggled the lock, but it was still in good shape and wasn't going to be easy to open. I had a feeling I'd need a key if I wanted to get into it. I thought about going to the tool shed to grab a hammer, but then I noticed the time. It was already five and I needed to have a shower before I went into town. The trunk would have to wait until another time.

I arrived at Carter's office at ten minutes past six. He was standing outside with his arms crossed belligerently over his chest when he saw me drive up.

"You're late," he said as I stepped out of my car.

"No I'm not," I said. "It's only ten after. That's not late."

"Sure it is."

"If you want to see late, you need to spend time with James. I've seen him show up an hour after he was supposed to."

"Fine. You're not late. But Alex is already waiting in the restaurant, so you'll have to be the one to explain it to her."

"Okay," I said with a shrug. "Is Mr. Smith not joining us tonight?"

"No," Carter replied. "He had a previous engagement with the poodle down the street. He asked me to say 'hello' to you, though."

"Really. The dog can talk?"

"Sure. Well, actually he asked me to give you a big sloppy lick on the face, but I told him that since I'd only just met you, it probably wasn't appropriate." He grinned down at me.

I turned beet red and looked at the ground.

"Where are we going?" I asked trying to put an end to whatever kind of flirting that was going on between the two of us.

"Just a little place down the street. You can leave your car here, and we'll walk."

We walked about half a block to a small Irish pub. The sign read *Patrick's*. The place was pretty busy when we entered.

"This is where you held my father's wake," I said to him when we reached the door.

"Yeah."

"I'm not going in there," I said firmly.

"Why not?" he asked genuinely confused.

"This is a trap. I only agreed to come if you promised not to ambush me with scenes from my father's past."

"Honestly, it's nothing like that. It's just a great pub with good food. It's the best restaurant in town. Actually, it's the only restaurant in town. Unless you count Jerry's Chip Stand on the highway, but that won't open for another couple of weeks." He looked down at me and must have seen the doubt in my eyes, because he continued. "I have no ulterior motives. There's no one inside waiting to ambush you. I promise. Just Alex."

I sighed. "Fine. I'll go in. But if anyone so much as *mentions* my father I'm driving straight back to Toronto."

"You've got my word that I won't bring him up. And if Alex says anything, you have my permission to kick her ass." He opened the door and gestured for me to enter the restaurant.

"This is a really popular place in the summer," Carter explained to me as we entered, waving at several people that seemed to know him. "A lot of the cottagers in the area come here. They get live bands here throughout July and August, and they have a great patio out back. Every week from Thursday to Sunday, this place is packed." He caught a glimpse of Alex sitting at a table near the back and steered me over in that direction.

"Hi," I said as I sat down. "Sorry we're late. Carter needed to stop and fix his hair."

"Thanks," he said sarcastically.

"Well, you told me to tell Alex why we're late," I said innocently.

"I know all about his fixation with his hair," Alex said. "Remember, I had to share a house with him for the first eighteen years of my life."

"Something that will no doubt qualify you for sainthood," Carter replied. "Have you ordered?"

"No," she said. "I thought I'd wait for you. If I'd known I would have had to wait so long, I definitely would have ordered. I'm starving."

The waitress came over at Carter's signal. She looked at me with barely hidden curiosity before pulling out her order pad. I felt like I was on display. We ordered our drinks and meals and she left.

"We're under strict orders not to talk about Kerri's father," Carter said to Alex. "I think she has some issues. But we'll have to get into that at a later session."

I kicked him under the table.

"Did Carter tell you that this is quite a hot spot in the summer?" Alex asked.

"He mentioned something about it," I replied. "Maybe I should do an article on this place. I got a new job today." I announced with pride.

"That's great," Alex said. "Doing what?"

I told them about James' call and about the series of articles I'd be writing.

"I bet if you mentioned it to some of the people in town, they'd be more than willing to talk to you," Carter said. "It'd be free advertising for them. You should start talking to people on the main street."

"This isn't another ploy to get me to meet some of my father's old friends, is it?" I raised an eyebrow at him.

"No," Carter said innocently. "Why would I do a thing like that?"

"Don't trust him," Alex said. "He's a terrible liar. He starts to fidget and gets a weird look on his face. If you're ever playing poker with him, it's easy to clean him out."

"Thank you, again," Carter said. "This is why you're not supposed to be friends with your sister."

"At least I'm better than your ex-wife," Alex said.

This caught my attention. "You've been married?" I asked tactlessly.

"And here it is," Carter said. "I've been here less than five minutes and you're already bringing this up. Thanks a lot, Sis. I'll remember this for another time."

"Sure he has," Alex replied, ignoring him. "Straight out of law school. He fell for the first little blonde that looked his way. He always had a weakness for blondes. All through school. She's the worst one for trying to fix him up and embarrass him in public."

"Which is why you should never associate with your former wives after the papers have been signed," Carter said. I could tell he wasn't really enjoying this, and, for some reason, that pleased me. It was fun to torment him.

"You should keep that in mind for your next ex," I said.

"Good idea. I'll tell her on our first date that when we get divorced, I expect her to immediately leave town and never speak to me again."

"At least you're not jaded on the whole concept of marriage," I said sarcastically. "It's always good to go into a relationship knowing that you're doomed from the outset, don't you think?"

"I don't know. I've got a 100% marriage failure rate right now."

"True, but you've only tried it once. My mother tried it at least four times before she gave up. Or I think she gave up. I haven't really talked to her in a while."

"Your mother was married four times?" Carter asked, looking surprised.

"At least four," I replied as the waitress placed my drink in front of me. "She moved to Vegas for a few years when I was fifteen, and I don't know if she married anyone else when she was there. She might have even been married before she met my father. Maxine would probably know more about our mother than I do." I'd never really been interested enough to find out.

After my dad moved out, my mom had a series of relationships that frequently resulted in marriage. Each time, she married the guy, used up all his money and then kicked him out before moving on to her next victim. She was like a black widow spider (except I don't think she actually killed any of them).

"What did you do when she moved to Vegas?" Alex asked.

"I lived with my brother. He was in university, and we shared an apartment together."

"Nice brother," Alex said. "My brother used to swear at me for entering his room when we were growing up. What does your brother do now?"

Carter looked uncomfortable, since he already knew the answer.

"He's dead," I said, taking a big drink.

"I'm sorry," Alex said awkwardly. "I didn't know." She looked embarrassed. "Sometimes I like to eat dinner with my foot wedged firmly in my mouth."

"It's okay," I said honestly. "I really don't mind talking about him." It was just his death that I didn't like to discuss.

"Sounds like a good time to change the subject," Carter said.

"I agree," I replied. "Why'd you get a divorce?"

Carter groaned. "We're back to this?"

I nodded. "Just curious."

"She didn't want to live in a small town and I didn't want to move to the city," Carter replied.

"So if it wasn't for that, you'd still be married?"

Alex burst out laughing. "Not really. Tell her the rest of the story, or I will."

"What?" I asked, intrigued. "Was it an affair?" I didn't think it could be anything too painful or Alex wouldn't be making fun of her brother the way she was. I felt completely fine about digging deeper into Carter's sordid past.

Carter scowled at his sister. "Let's just say that my wife realized that she preferred the company of women."

"Oh …" I said, not sure how I should react. I looked at both of them to gauge their reactions.

Alex was still laughing. "She and Carter have been divorced for about seven years. It's funny now, but Mom and Dad didn't find it too funny then. Especially Mom."

"Mom still doesn't," Carter admitted. "I think she still believes that Marlie's just going through a phase and will come to her senses eventually. An incredibly long phase. Mom keeps giving me brochures to give Marlie about programs claiming to make people straight. Which I of course send to her with a big card from Mom." He laughed as he took a long drink from his beer.

"Is that why Mom didn't go to Marlie's wedding last year?" Alex asked him.

"My ex married her girlfriend last year," Carter explained. "It was very nice. They have two kids with a third on the way. None of them are mine," he added quickly. "If you're both done tormenting me, why don't we talk about something else?" He looked at me. "How did the writing go today?"

"Yeah, that's a great subject," I said sarcastically.

"What do you mean?" he asked.

"Everyone keeps asking me about my writing. To tell you the truth, I haven't written a single word all day. That novel hasn't had any work done on it for about half a year." I was going to continue and tell him that I didn't even have a solid plot idea, but I stopped myself.

"Maybe you need to get a new idea," Alex suggested.

"I was thinking about doing that, but I haven't been able to come up with anything new. Everything I think about has been done to death."

"I'm sure something will come to you," Alex said. "I read your first book. It was great."

Why were people always convinced that because I'd written before, I'd get another idea? It didn't always work like that, at least not for me. I was certain I'd never get another decent idea for the rest of my life. My throat closed slightly with desperation. I tried to shake off my worry and concentrate on my dinner companions.

"I'm glad some people enjoyed it," I said, shooting Carter a dirty look.

"I never said that I didn't enjoy it," Carter protested. "I just said it was depressing."

"Same thing," I insisted.

"No," he said. "Some people like to be depressed."

"Like my brother," Alex chimed in. "If he didn't like being depressed, he wouldn't have married a lesbian."

The waitress arrived with our meals just in time to stop Carter from killing Alex. I had decided to eat only healthy foods, so I'd ordered a big pile of chicken wings. Carter had a steak and Alex had a salad.

"You know you're going to have a heart attack before you're forty if you keep eating like that," Alex said to Carter, shaking her head.

"Then I've still got four years to enjoy myself. I'd starve to death if I ate like you do."

"There's nothing wrong with what I'm eating."

"If you're a rabbit."

"Not true," she said. "Some people just like to eat healthy."

"Kerri ordered wings," he said, pointing to my plate.

"Hey," I said. "Don't drag me into what is obviously a family argument."

"Kerri's still practically a child," Alex said, ignoring me. "Her metabolism is probably much faster than yours. And she has years and years before she's as old as you."

"I'm not a child," I grumbled.

"Compared to Carter you are," Alex said with a laugh.

"Ignore Alex," Carter said to me. "She loves to hear the sound of her own voice and she especially likes to pretend she's a real doctor. I'm not convinced she actually graduated medical school but she's always preaching at me."

"It's for your own good," she shot back. "You'll thank me when you're eighty and you still have all your own organs."

"Your parents must be really proud of both of you," I said suddenly, changing the subject. "The town's doctor and lawyer both from the same family."

"It's really not that impressive," Carter said, taking a wing off my plate. "There are only something like four distinct families in the town. And our father was the doctor here until he retired a couple of years ago. Alex played the role of the dutiful son and went into the family business."

"That's interesting," I said, slapping his hand away as he tried to steal another wing from my plate. "Eat your own food."

"I did. Now I'm helping you eat yours."

"Thank you, but I can manage fine on my own."

"I don't think you can. You're such a tiny thing; I thought you'd want my help." He flashed me a big, goofy grin.

I rolled my eyes at him as a response.

"You two are so cute," Alex said laughing.

"What are you talking about?" I asked.

"This. The way you two are flirting with each other. It's so cute."

"We're not flirting," I said firmly.

"Yeah," Carter agreed. "I don't know what you're talking about."

"Yes you do. Carter, you haven't been able to take your eyes off her since we got here. And Kerri, you love it when he baits you."

"You're being ridiculous," I said, feeling my face go red. "You're crazy."

"Why don't I leave you guys here and you can have your date without a third wheel." She moved to stand as if she was preparing to leave.

"No, that's okay," I said jumping to my feet. I pulled some money out of my wallet and put it in the center of the table. "I was just leaving anyway. Carter, you can finish the rest of my wings."

"Kerri, you don't need to go. I was just teasing," Alex began.

"No, honestly I've got work to do at home. Research. It was nice seeing you both again." I grabbed my coat and headed towards the door in a graceful retreat.

Of course, instead of disappearing gracefully, I backed into the table behind us knocking several drinks on the floor. And then, when I knelt to clean up the mess I'd made, I ended up tripping a waitress.

A waitress carrying a tray full of food.

The food went everywhere. Everyone within a ten-foot radius was splattered. The waitress looked like she wanted to kill me.

Alex was laughing so hard she had tears streaming down her face.

Carter jumped up to help me, which only made things worse. He knelt down next to me and started to pick up some of the broken glass. Then we both reached for a plate at the same time and our fingers touched. I pulled my hand back so fast I ended up throwing the plate across the room.

"I should get out of here before I do any more damage," I mumbled, trying to pick salad out of my hair.

"Let me help you with that," Carter said. He reached over to pull a leaf of lettuce out of my hair.

"I'm okay," I said, trying to regain some of my dignity. I stood and took one step away from Carter.

And I stepped directly onto a plate of spaghetti, falling promptly onto my ass.

More embarrassed than I'd ever been, I jumped to my feet and practically ran out the door. The last thing I heard as I finally managed to leave the restaurant was the sound of Alex laughing.

Chapter Five

It was the Thursday before the May long weekend. I had been at the cottage for more than two weeks; two very unproductive weeks. The novel was still a disaster but, thanks to James, I at least had something to do to keep me from completely losing my mind. I'd been hard at work researching my first article on cottage country.

Well, sort of hard at work.

Actually, to be perfectly honest, I was doing a half-assed job of it. But it wasn't entirely my fault. I was a city girl, and writing a story about country life was turning out to be a little more difficult than I had originally thought. I didn't even know where I should start. I'd been spending a lot of the time talking to local business owners about the effects of summer residents on the local economy, learning about local history and checking out some of the interesting spots in the area.

According to my notes, I'd learned the following things about New Ferndale:

1. The town's two oldest buildings were both churches

2. A mill fire in the 1900s killed fifteen people

3. They had a party-line phone system up until five years ago

Nothing I'd found out was even vaguely interesting for an article. I was clueless as to how to proceed.

Carter had been right about one thing. Everyone I talked to in town was more than willing to discuss their lives with me. Sometimes, a little too willing. Someone (my money was on Carter; Alex didn't seem to be quite as devious) had let it slip that I was writing an article and everyone had suggestions for me. I didn't even have to ask any questions before they gave me the whole song and dance.

Unfortunately, everyone was also more than willing to volunteer information about my father. He was usually the first thing anyone mentioned to me. Apparently, everyone had loved him. I didn't want to ruin my chances for future information by telling them what he was really like (a dead-beat was the description that sprung to mind most often), so I just plastered a fake smile on my face whenever I was in town. I swear, my cheeks felt like they were going to break if I smiled once more.

Mary at the bakery told me how she'd known my father since she was born. She was a few years younger, but mentioned that her brother Charlie had been good friends with my father. My father's family had apparently spent every summer at the cottage, and he had spent most of his time playing with the town kids. According to Mary, my father had been an only child raised by his mother and then his grandparents. She implied that my father's childhood hadn't been very happy after his mother left him with his grandparents. Mary didn't know much about my great-grandparents, since they hadn't liked the fact that my father socialized with the kids in town. They were old money and felt that the locals were beneath their social sphere.

At the grocery store I learned that for the last fifteen years my father had always had his groceries delivered right to the cottage. Near the end of his life he was too ill to come into town, but prior to that, he merely preferred to keep to himself.

The woman behind the desk at the post office told me I looked exactly like my father had when he was a boy, except for the eyes (I wasn't sure she actually knew my father when he was a boy since she didn't really look old enough, but I just played along).

It was enough to make me want to go even deeper into hiding. I already felt like I was stuck in the middle of nowhere in this stupid little town. If I went any deeper into hiding, I think I'd actually be living in a tent in the bush. But these people were driving me even more nuts than I already was. I was afraid I'd end up killing the next person who mentioned my father and then I'd be writing a series of articles on prison food or how to decorate a cell (but Martha Stewart would probably be able to do that better than me; maybe I could write articles about making a shank from a toothbrush).

Everyone in town also kept going on about what a great guy Carter was. He was always the second topic, right after some little tidbit about my father. I was pretty sure *this* was Alex's doing. It seemed like the entire town was conspiring to fix Carter and me up. Possibly it was some strange project for the New Ferndale Chamber of Commerce: find the local lawyer a date. It was unbelievably infuriating.

And they weren't exactly subtle about it either. I was given Carter's entire family tree, the tale of how he managed to overcome his painful divorce, and how he'd be a great father (I think if I'd lingered much longer in the camera shop the clerk would have given me mock pictures of Carter's and my future children).

At first I tried telling them that I wasn't looking to date anyone at the moment. That didn't seem to matter to them. They just insisted that I hadn't met the right guy yet. I tried saying that I had just ended a long-term relationship, but they didn't seem to care about that either. Finally, I gave up trying to shut them up and just ignored them. It was like a town full of Jameses. I wasn't sure if I could take all the pressure.

Despite all the extraneous information that I was bombarded with, I managed to get a ton of research done on my first column, as well as get some good ideas for future articles. If the editor wanted me to write any more articles, that is. I wasn't sure how he'd like my first one. I could be back to staring all day at my blank computer screen after he read the first article I sent him.

By noon Thursday I'd finished my article and was preparing to send it off. I gave the opening a quick read through before emailing it to the editor:

> *For most Canadians, Victoria Day Weekend signals the beginning of summer. For business owners in cottage country, it's the start of their busy season. Stores are eagerly anticipating an influx of countless visitors trying to escape the craziness of the city by heading up north.*
>
> *In New Ferndale* (I still hadn't found out anything about the name of the town) *a town like many others on the coast of Georgian Bay, shopkeepers have been anxiously awaiting the first signs of summer for months. An early warm spell can mean record-breaking profits for local businesses that depend mainly on the dollars brought by summer visitors to sustain them through the long cold winters. This picturesque town, complete with an award-winning bakery and an Irish pub (which, I'm told, is the single best night spot north of Toronto), will soon be crawling with outsiders—but these outsiders are welcomed with open arms.*

> *Along the main street of New Ferndale, Mary's Bakery has been serving the town and its summer residents for nearly 50 years. This place has become an institution: no respectable cottager would think of passing up a chance to buy one of Mary's famous butter tarts. And those Torontonians watching their weight will be happy to know that Mary has developed her own brand of sugar-free delights, which are indistinguishable from her original recipes.*

It was cheesy, but it was what James told me the editor wanted, loaded with schlock and bullshit. I hoped he'd be happy; it went on for another half a page in a similar vein. After I emailed it to the editor (which produced a huge feeling of satisfaction and accomplishment—it was the first completed writing I'd sent to anyone since I'd left the city), I decided to call Denny to see if he, Emily and James were still coming up for the weekend.

We'd made plans a few weeks earlier for them to spend the long weekend with me, and I was kind of regretting the invitation. I'd asked them when I'd been feeling lonely and depressed. I put the whole thing down to temporary insanity, but now I was going to be stuck with them. I wanted to see Denny and James; they weren't the problem. But I was definitely not looking forward to spending a weekend with Emily. I was struggling to come up with ways to have Denny come without bringing her, but none of my ideas were very good (they ranged from calling Denny and telling him to leave her at home to not answering the door when they arrived). At least I'd have James to help diffuse the situation if things got too tense.

Emily got under my skin faster than anyone I knew. She sucked the joy out of every event. Nothing was ever good enough for her. The temperature was always either too hot or too cold. Food was too spicy or too bland. And she always needed to be the centre of attention. She was one of those women who saw every other woman as competition. Emily was always sickeningly sweet around men, but in a crowd of women, it was another story. The teeth are bared, and the claws are out, ready for a fight.

And she was always nagging Denny whenever she was with him. It was no wonder he left her behind most of the time. He couldn't do anything to please her. I felt sorry for the poor guy, even if he had brought it on himself by marrying her. But the main reason why she bugged me so much was because she hated me. I mean she *really* hated me. She even went so far as to try and ban me from their house, something that Denny wouldn't stand for. Despite his efforts, I rarely went to their place. I just couldn't take Emily's attitude. She often insulted me to my face (comments about my clothes or hair) and behind my back (calling me 'the Red-Headed Whore' seemed to be her favourite—James always loved that one and eagerly recounted it to me whenever she used it). Denny threatened her with a divorce if she didn't start acting more civil to me. Of course, my conscience kept reminding me, I guess she did have a reason to hate me.

I picked up the phone and dialed Denny's office number.

"Dennis Wells," he said in a brusque voice when he answered the phone.

"You sound busy."

"Never too busy to talk to you, Kerri. What's up?"

"Just calling to see when you guys are going to get here this weekend. If you're still coming, that is."

"We're coming tomorrow. We should be there in the early afternoon. I'm taking the afternoon off to miss traffic."

"Are you all coming?" I crossed my fingers.

"Yes, even Emily."

"Great," I said, even though I didn't mean it. I tried to make my voice sound cheerful so that Denny wouldn't feel bad. "We've been invited to a barbeque at Carter's place on Saturday night. He and Alex are holding it together. I told them we'd all come, but I can cancel pretty easily if you don't want to go." I actually thought the party might be a good idea. With so many other people around, I wouldn't have to spend my day entertaining Emily. Or hiding from her, which was probably the more likely scenario.

"No, that's great. It sounds like fun."

"Oh, I doubt it will be fun. He's invited half the town from the sounds of things. I'm sure we'll be the only people there under fifty, and most of them will spend the evening staring at me to figure out how much I look like my father."

"At least you've developed an interesting new complex while you've been there. How are things going with you and Carter?"

"What do you mean?"

"I mean, how often does the good lawyer come a callin'?"

"Nothing is happening with Carter," I replied in an annoyed tone. "He's a nice guy and we're friends. That's it. Besides him and Alex, I don't know anyone else in town."

"I think he has a thing for red heads."

"Ha, ha. Very funny. Actually, I've been told he has a thing for blondes. Why can't you just drop it? He's not interested in me, and I'm not interested in him. We're just going to be friends."

"Did he tell you that?"

"No, but I'm sure it's true."

"You're just saying that because he hasn't tried anything yet."

"No. Neither one of us has time for a relationship right now. He's very busy at work."

"But not too busy to find time to spend with you, right?"

"I'm the only one in town, besides his sister and his secretary, who's near his age."

"Sure. You do realize that there are a thousand people in the town, not a hundred, right? And just how old is he anyway?"

"He's thirty-six."

"See, you're not his age. He's got eleven years on you. When he was getting his driver's license, you were still eating paste. What about that secretary of his? Didn't you say she looked like a model?"

"Yeah, I've seen her a few times. She's definitely got a thing for Carter. But I don't think she's his type. Doesn't seem very bright. Although she is blonde, so maybe Carter will end up with her after all."

"But you don't really care who he dates, right?" Denny was being sarcastic, something he wasn't very good at.

"I honestly don't," I said truthfully, "but I think he's got too much sense to date his bimbo secretary. But either way, I don't really care."

"Alright. I believe you. I promise I won't try to push you and Carter together. But I can't say the same thing for James. You know he'll never let it drop. It'll be his only source of entertainment all weekend."

He'll be able to watch you and Emily fight, I thought but didn't say out loud.

"I'm making it your responsibility to keep James in line," I said firmly. "Think of it as your fee for staying at the cottage this weekend. And Emily, too." Just the thought of Emily sent chills up and down my spine. "You can make sure they both behave. And so help me God, if James starts pestering Carter about me, I'm holding you responsible."

"Sounds fair," he said laughing. "I've got to go, but I'll see you tomorrow."

"Bye."

After I hung up the phone, I thought about what Denny had said about Carter. True, Carter had been out here a lot. But he'd brought Alex with him a couple of times. If he was hoping to be more than just friends, he wouldn't have brought his sister along with him. And he always brought Mr. Smith. The dog was great. He stuck with me the whole time they were at my place. It was like I had a large yellow shadow.

I probably would have gone crazy alone out here for the last two weeks if they hadn't been around. More than a little crazy. Picture Jack Nicholson in 'The Shining' and multiply it by a factor of ten. In the city, I didn't have a problem living alone. Every time I stepped out of my apartment I'd see people. Most of them strangers, some of them really strange (like the guy down on Bloor who sings along to a karaoke machine all day). But they were people just the same.

Living at the cottage, I could go a long time without seeing or even hearing another human. Each morning after I woke up, I went for a run down the road leading into town. I didn't see a single car, except for the few times I'd bumped into Carter.

And what about Carter?

He hadn't once brought up my fantastic display of clumsiness at *Patrick's*, something that I really appreciated. He'd helped me paint the cottage the previous week after I mentioned that it needed to be done. It was nice to have company, and the painting kept me busy. We had worked on it in the late afternoons when he got off work. Then one of us would make dinner.

Actually, he made dinner every night except the first evening. I tried to cook a frozen lasagna and nearly set the kitchen on fire. After that he wouldn't let me near anything involving flame or heat.

After the painting was done, he helped me fix up the deck. He also came out to mow the lawn and rake the leaves. It was nice having him out here, but that was just because we were friends.

And if he drove out here six out of seven mornings with coffee, it was just because he had business in the area or wanted to let the dog stretch his legs. He might have been concerned that I'd burn down the entire side of the lake one morning if I had to make my own coffee.

Was I just kidding myself? Was he just doing this because he'd been friends with my father, or did he have other reasons? He didn't have any interest in me. He couldn't. It was too ridiculous. And regardless of what Carter felt, I knew I would never be interested in him that way.

Besides, I definitely wasn't his type. His sister had clearly indicated that Carter preferred his women tall and blond, neither of which description fit me.

But maybe I was just projecting my feelings on him. Just because I didn't want a relationship didn't mean that Carter felt the same. And the fact that I seemed to be extra clumsy whenever Carter was around definitely didn't mean anything.

It was all incredibly frustrating. I really wished Denny hadn't brought the idea up. I wouldn't have even thought about this if it hadn't been for him.

It was always hard to be friends with men. Straight men, anyway. This was why I loved James so much: his phone calls and attention never meant more than friendship. Plus, he always told me I was gorgeous and had great taste in clothes.

I tried to think about things logically. Carter had never mentioned anything or tried anything when he was over in the evenings, so obviously he wasn't interested in me. He never asked me out alone (if we went anywhere in town, Alex was there too), and he always left my place right after dinner. I knew I had nothing to worry about. I was too short and had the wrong hair colour. Which was a good thing. It meant we could be friends without anything screwing it up.

Trying to think about something (anything) other than Carter, I picked up my laptop with a sigh and went out to sit on the deck. But it was useless. I don't know why I even took my computer with me. I'd had absolutely no success with my writing during the past two weeks. The change of scenery hadn't been as inspiring as James had insisted it would be. No new ideas. Not a single one. It was hard to believe it, but I was even more discouraged than I had been before moving out into the middle of nowhere. I would have been better off staying in Toronto.

Things had been different for me when I wrote my first (and potentially only) novel. Or maybe I had been different. I was certainly younger and less jaded when I wrote it. I was twenty-one when I started and I was full of ideas that were just begging to be put down onto paper. It had actually been fun to sit at my desk writing. The words flew out of my head faster than I could type. I felt like I would explode if I didn't get them down.

I wrote day and night, sitting in my room in the apartment Sebastian and I shared. The apartment was a dump, that's for sure. Cockroaches were the least of our problems, but nothing bothered me while I was working (although I did remember to always tuck the cuffs of my pants into my socks). I forgot to eat and sleep. Sebastian would bring me plates of food that would sit mostly uneaten on my desk. I never even noticed when he entered or left the room. Food just seemed to appear on my desk at various times during the day. I think I lost ten pounds during that time. Sebastian and Denny were worried that I was anorexic. They didn't understand that I just couldn't be bothered to eat. It took too much time out of my day. I honestly didn't even notice that time was passing.

When I finished after writing for three weeks straight, I wasn't sure if I'd ever get it published. But Sebastian convinced me that it would. He was the one who sent it to the literary agents without me even knowing. And it did get published, even though it took several submissions and painful rejection letters before it saw print. But it was done.

But after that I hadn't felt that same need to write. No matter whether I was in Toronto or in the middle of nowhere at the cottage, I just couldn't break through my writer's block. It was incredibly depressing. I was twenty-five, and I was utterly and completely washed up. Soon I'd be sixty, telling people that once I'd written a book. And they'd smile patronizingly and nod, not really caring or believing.

I put my laptop back in my office with a discouraged sigh (if I hadn't put it safely away I was pretty sure I would have chucked the computer in the lake). I was bored and annoyed, and I needed something to divert my attention. Carter and I had finished all the painting. I was completely unpacked. The cottage had been cleaned, top to bottom, including vacuuming and windows. I had even bought groceries for the weekend. I still had a lot of time to kill before my guests arrived on Friday and nothing to do until then. I looked around my office for anything that would interest me.

The trunk that I'd found a few weeks earlier was still sitting in the middle of the room. I hadn't yet gotten around to opening it, and my curiosity was getting the better of me. Something had stopped me from opening it earlier. Part of me (the large vocal part) kept insisting that I didn't want to learn anything about my father or his family. But now boredom was outweighing my dislike for my father. Now was the perfect time to see what was inside. And I couldn't come up with any more reasons to avoid opening it.

I looked closely at the big old padlock. It looked pretty weak, but looks could be deceiving. I pulled firmly on it to see if it would open easily. I quickly realized that it was going to require more skill than I possessed to pick the lock, and I knew I couldn't just break it off with my bare hands. Smashing it was the only solution. I went down to the tool shed, found a hammer and brought it back up to the trunk. After a few swings I broke the lock and was able to open the trunk and take a look inside.

I could tell that the trunk hadn't been opened in a long time from the musty smell. The trunk wasn't filled with money, jewelry or even a dead body (the three most prevalent ideas in my head). The trunk was full of clothes, letters, books, old toys and pictures. It was kind of anticlimactic, but I decided to go through the contents anyway. I started pulling things out and piling them on the floor around me.

The trunk seemed to have stuff from different eras. It was like I was doing some bizarre archeological dig. I did my best to sort the contents into chronological piles on the floor. This was kind of difficult, since inside the trunk everything was jumbled together. There were toys that looked like they were from the sixties next to records from the eighties. I found some baby clothes that were definitely from the late seventies. There was a *Charlie's Angels* t-shirt that looked like it was for a two-year-old. I said a silent prayer in hopes that it hadn't belonged to me. I didn't know if I could survive the embarrassment of being a childhood *Angel's* fan. I put the shirt down and continued my search.

Beneath that was an old hot wheels version of the General Lee. This brought to mind an old memory of Sebastian and me playing Dukes of Hazard. Of course, I was three or four and he had been eleven, so it probably hadn't been much fun for him, but it was my favourite game. I remembered trying to convince my mother to have the doors of our car welded shut. My mother looked at me like I was crazy. She told me to stop annoying her and went back to her drink.

The unintentional memory of my mother took away some of the pleasure of my trip down memory lane. Putting down the toy, I picked up an old photo album from the floor and began to flip through it. I immediately recognized some of the people in the pictures. There were pictures of my mother from the early '60s holding a baby that must have been Maxine. Even then my mother had a cigarette sticking out of her mouth and a beer bottle in her other hand. My mother was thin and very pretty; with her long hair, she looked quite a bit like Maxine. She also looked very young. She was probably in her early twenties when the picture was taken, judging by the fact that Maxine was only about a year old. I imagined Maxine dodging the ashes and the cigarette smoke, much as I had done as a child. Flipping through the album I saw pictures of my father with Maxine, neither one of them looking very happy. The pictures showed my sister's childhood, and many of them appeared to have been taken at the cottage; I recognized the building in the background of several shots.

Sebastian joined the family album when Maxine was a sullen-looking seven-year old. And my mother still had a cigarette in her mouth. Hadn't anyone ever told her about the danger of smoking around kids, I thought? I wonder if that had anything to do with the fact that I couldn't stand the smell of smoke. I was probably assaulted with it in the womb.

At the sight of my brother in the pictures, I felt a lump in my throat. His familiar smile, the mischievous look in his eyes. Even as a child, it wasn't hard to see the man he became. The pictures were a reminder to me of just how much I missed him. It had been two years since he'd died, and I still had problems believing it was true. I still wanted to call him every time something good happened, or if I heard a funny story, or if I just needed someone to talk to. It was always difficult when I remembered that it was impossible to talk to him any more.

I put the album down and closed my eyes for a minute. I was not going to cry. I took a few deep breaths before opening my eyes again. Regaining my composure, I continued looking at the old pictures.

Then I began to recognize some of my own baby pictures. There weren't too many of them, but that wasn't really very surprising. By the time the third kid rolls around I'm sure a baby isn't very exciting. But it was still interesting to actually see some of my baby pictures. I hadn't seen many when I was living with my mom. Maxine wasn't in any of the shots. She had been away at boarding school when I was born, and I don't remember her being around much until after our father left.

One picture in particular caught my eye. I looked about three or four years old, and I had a huge smile on my face. I was being held by my father who was standing on the end of a dock. He also was smiling as he looked at me. We both looked very happy.

I closed the album quickly and put it back in the bottom of the trunk. I didn't feel like going through any of the rest of the contents that day. The fact that my father kept the album and the other things made me think that maybe he had actually cared about us. But he kept it locked away in the back of a closet, as if trying to shut the memories out of his life. I didn't feel any better about my father after I shut the trunk and left the room. And I certainly wasn't any closer to figuring out what kind of man my father had been.

Chapter Six

Friday morning on the May long weekend dawned bright and warm. The weather was beautiful, and I woke up in a good mood, which was immediately ruined when I remembered that Denny was bringing Emily up for the weekend.

James, Denny and Emily arrived early Friday afternoon at my place. I had done very little that morning and had been waiting anxiously for them to arrive. It was hot, but thankfully not too humid. And the black flies weren't too bad (I was told by every person in the town this was very strange, since the black flies are always bad in May. I merely smiled and nodded as I was told that few black flies meant short summers in one store and long summers in the next. I didn't know a black fly from a dragonfly.). If it had been a humid day with swarms of black flies, I probably would have killed Emily ten minutes after she stepped out of the car.

Emily had had her usual sour expression on her face when they pulled into the drive. I felt my shoulders sag at the prospect of four Emily-filled days. This is going to be a fun weekend, I thought wryly. I found out later from James what was wrong with Emily. Apparently, she wasn't too happy about leaving the baby for the weekend with Denny's parents. James told me that she and Denny had been arguing about it for most of the drive. I was glad they hadn't brought the little monster. I liked kids okay, but I doubted that I could spend a weekend with a baby without going a little crazy.

Emily's presence threw a dark cloud over the whole night. Denny had brought steaks up to the cottage for dinner, which he offered to cook. I'm pretty sure he only wanted to cook as a reason to get away from Emily for a while, and I was furious that he had left James and me to fend for ourselves. He was definitely in my bad books.

While Denny cooked the rest of us sat out on the deck, awkwardly trying to make conversation. It was like being at the dentist's without the fun of getting your teeth scraped.

I couldn't think of any way to start a conversation with Emily, so I turned to James.

"How was the drive?" I asked him. Traffic seemed like a safe topic.

"Not too bad. It was a little busy near Barrie, but otherwise it was fine. Wouldn't you agree, Emily?" James was smiling, trying valiantly to save the evening.

Emily barely nodded in agreement. I could feel her glaring at me. It was going to be a wonderful weekend if she was already mad at me.

"That's great," I said to James. "I know the traffic can be pretty bad on a long weekend." This was an incredibly stupid conversation. I really wanted to ask James about Denny and Emily's fight, but with her sitting right there, I couldn't.

"Yes," James agreed. "It's a good thing we left as early as we did."

"If you'd left any later, it probably would have taken you much longer." God, this was awkward. This was why I hated Emily. Or at least one of the reasons why I hated her. She always made me feel like an idiot because I had to force conversation around her.

Denny finally appeared with the steaks and headed towards the barbeque. Thank God, I thought.

"Hey Denny, need a hand?" James jumped up and ran to the grill before I could stop him. The bastard. I thought about running after him, but I couldn't do that in front of Emily without being completely obvious. So instead I sat there on the deck across from Emily, playing with my drink. The silence was painful. I couldn't think of a single thing to say to her.

I lifted my half-full beer to my lips and swallowed the entire contents. It was my only escape.

"I'm going to get another drink," I said to Emily as I stood up. "Would you like anything?"

"No thanks," she replied coldly. "I'm still drinking mine. I don't really feel the need to get drunk like an eighteen-year-old anymore, but if you do, go right ahead."

"Bitch," I said under my breath as I turned to enter the house.

"What did you say?" Emily shrieked at me.

"Nothing."

"You're lying. You called me a bitch, you little whore."

At that point, just before I could break my beer bottle over her head, Denny jumped in between Emily and me.

"Honey," he said to her in a sweet tone. "Why don't you help me with the steaks? That way we can make sure yours is done enough." He flashed me an apologetic smile before leading her to the grill.

James followed me inside. I grabbed a beer from the fridge and took a long swig.

"I swear to God I'm going to kill her," I said to James. "She's not going to survive the weekend. Hell, she's not even going to survive tonight. Is 'Justifiable Homicide' a valid defense in Canada?"

"I don't know, but it's a good thing that you know a lawyer. If she keeps acting as pleasant as this for the rest of the weekend, I'll probably help you dispose of the body. Keep in mind that I had to drive up here with them. I've already seen two hours of 'the Emily and Denny Show,' and it wasn't pretty."

I smiled at James and patted his arm fondly before returning outside. I sat on the opposite end of the deck to Emily. I had cooled down a little, but not enough to actually stomach her presence. The steaks were finally finished, and the four of us sat down to an incredibly awkward and silent meal.

Right after dinner we all went to bed.

I woke at what was unfortunately becoming my usual time: 9:00 AM. It was a beautiful, sunny morning. My room was flooded with light. I pulled a pillow over my face, but it didn't work. Despite nearly suffocating me, the pillow did little to block out the light. The light may have been annoying, but it was the noise from the room beside me that wouldn't allow me to get back to sleep. I could hear Denny and Emily arguing in their room, loud enough to wake the dead. I hadn't even had a cup of coffee yet, and they were already reenacting World War II.

"You're always taking her side," I heard Emily yell at him. It didn't take a genius to realize that they were talking about me.

I slowly got out of bed and went out into the hall. Part of me wanted to able to hear what they were saying a little clearer.

"I'm not taking her side," Denny yelled back. "You're just acting crazy as usual. Kerri was nice enough to invite us here this weekend. Where do you get off calling her a whore?"

"I know you're still sleeping with her," she shouted.

I flinched when I heard something smash against the wall. I didn't think there was anything valuable in that room. At least I hoped not. If the two of them ever came here again I'd have to remember to remove all breakable objects from Emily's reach. But I really doubted I'd ever be crazy enough to invite her again.

"Christ, Emily!" Denny shouted.

"Get the hell out of here!" Emily screamed.

I quickly dashed down the stairs as I heard the door open, trying to avoid an awkward confrontation with Denny in the hall. I didn't want him to know I'd been listening. It would embarrass him. Unfortunately, I was a little slow, and he saw me.

"Kerri," he called as I attempted to sneak out onto the deck.

"Yeah?" I said to him.

"Sorry about that," he said sheepishly. "I'll pay for the mirror." He looked really upset, and my heart went out to him.

"Don't worry about it. It's not really my stuff anyway. I hated my father, remember? It was his mirror. And I was up already. What's wrong with Emily?"

"Where do I start? It's just the usual today." I knew what he meant. She was mad at him because of me, as always.

"I don't know why you put up with it," I said softly, placing my hand on his arm in a comforting gesture.

Denny shrugged off my hand. "You'd better not. I don't want to give Emily any more reason to freak out."

"Good idea," I said with a laugh. Denny gave me a tiny smile before turning to go back and talk to Emily.

I went out on the deck. James was already outside with a cup of coffee in his hand.

"Is the battle over?" James asked as he looked up at me.

"Temporary cease fire," I replied, sitting down next to him. I took a section of the newspaper from James and leaned back in my lounge to enjoy the morning sunshine. It really was a beautiful morning, and it was promising to be a very warm afternoon. The water was sparkling, and already there were boats on the lake. It was quite a change from a week earlier when I had been the only one around. Suddenly the cottages were being opened, and the lake was getting crowded. Carter was right: the lake was starting to resemble rush hour traffic.

James and I had a lovely brunch in the sun on the back deck (which James, of course, cooked), while Denny and Emily took their battle away from us when they went for a walk. I made sure to enjoy the peace and quiet while they were gone. Why the hell had I wanted guests in the first place? The silence during the week was starting to look attractive.

I was hoping Emily might get lost in the bush or maybe even fall into an open well. Maybe she'd even get eaten by a bear. If the spring bear hunt had been called off, why couldn't I benefit from it? But I wasn't that lucky. Both Denny and Emily turned up shortly after noon, each with an angry look on his or her face. So much for my peaceful afternoon. I immediately felt sorry for Denny. He had his faults but he didn't deserve to be stuck with Emily for the rest of his life. Days like these made me feel slightly less guilty about Denny's wandering eye.

By one in the afternoon we were all so sick of each other's company that we were glad to head over to Carter and Alex's party. I'd had more than enough of Emily. It would be nice for her to have more people to bitch at.

"That's a lovely outfit," Emily sneered at me as we piled into the car. I looked down at what I was wearing. Immediately, I felt defensive. Her tone was remarkably like my mother's. There was nothing wrong with my outfit: I was wearing a light summer dress, sandals and I had a cardigan sweater with me in case the afternoon turned cool. The dress was form fitting at the body and loose around my legs. Emily was just jealous because of the way Denny was looking at me. I elbowed him in warning. I really didn't want Emily glaring at me all afternoon.

"Thanks," I said to her with a grin, purposely misinterpreting her tone.

"Any word on the article?" James asked, valiantly trying to change the subject. I gave him a smile of thanks.

"Actually, yes," I said. "The editor called me on Friday morning and said that he loved it. He also told me that he wanted to see more articles. I'll send one in every Thursday morning to be published in Friday's paper."

"Congratulations!" Denny said, patting me on the shoulder. "That's great news. I know you need the money."

"Yeah," I agreed. "I didn't know how I'd be able to pay my rent this fall without a steady pay cheque this summer. I was going to have to crash on James' couch for a couple of months." I think I saw James actually shudder at the thought.

"Have you ever considered getting a job?" Emily said nastily.

This coming from the woman whose sole ambition in life was to marry well. I felt my face getting warm with anger.

"Kerri has a job," Denny said in a cold voice. Shit. Why did they always have to fight about me? "She's doing exactly what she wants to do with her life. How many people can honestly say that?"

"Oh God," James whispered to me. "Round four. How much further to Carter's?"

"About five minutes," I whispered back to him. "Just turn on the radio to drown them out."

We spent the rest of the drive listening to loud music on the radio. I could see Denny and Emily arguing with each other in the rear view mirror. I didn't think I could stand it if they fought all night at the party.

Carter's house was near the outskirts of town on the lake. He had a small house on a large strip of property with a dock stretching out onto the water. His house was actually very cute. I had been expecting a grubby bachelor pad (like Denny'd had before he got married), and the place seemed far too nice for a single guy. My bet was that the ex-wife had picked it out, and Carter had ended up with it in the divorce.

It was a perfect place for a party. The neighbours weren't close enough to be bothered by any noise. However, judging by the crowd, the neighbours had probably been invited too.

The driveway was already completely full, and there were six or seven cars parked on the side of the road. There were even a couple of boats tied to the dock. I wondered how many people Carter had invited. At least Emily would have enough to distract her, I thought. Or I could get lost in the crowd and not have to spend any time with her.

We followed the sound of the party around to the back of the house. The yard was already covered with people, most of whom I'd never seen before. As soon as we stepped into the yard, Mr. Smith came bounding over to us with Alex behind him.

Mr. Smith was so excited to see me that he nearly knocked me over.

"Who does the dog belong to?" Denny asked, scratching Mr. Smith behind the ears.

"This is Mr. Smith," I said to him. "He's Carter's dog."

Mr. Smith looked at James and Emily suspiciously. After taking a quick sniff of Emily's leg, he quickly came back to me. I liked him even more.

"I'm glad you guys could make it today," Alex said to us as she approached. "Carter's over near the barbeque if you wanted to go and join him, Kerri."

I'd been here less than five minutes, and already someone was pushing Carter on me. It was going to be a really long day.

"I'm sure she will," Denny said, looking at Alex in a way that I could tell Emily wouldn't like. Luckily for him (and for Alex's safety) Emily was too busy focusing all her hatred on me and ignored Alex completely.

"Alex," I said, trying to diffuse the situation, while at the same time continuing to shower Mr. Smith with affection. "Have you met Denny's wife, Emily?" It would be a good idea to remind Alex that Denny was married, I thought. She was looking at him in a way that most women did. I didn't want to see Alex added to Denny's discard pile.

Denny shot me a dirty look and then turned the charm back on in Alex's direction. Let him dig his own grave, I thought to myself. That was the last time I'd try to help him. Some men should never get married.

Feeling the need for a drink, but not wanting to be left alone, I grabbed James and dragged him over to the coolers. Mr. Smith trailed after us. I handed James a beer and grabbed one for myself as well. I had no desire to socialize. I wanted to crawl into the darkest corner and stay there until the party was over. Everyone was staring at me, and I was sure they all knew that I was Peter Shepherd's daughter. James, on the other hand, was anxious to abandon me. The story of my life.

"There are some incredible looking guys here," he said looking around. "Do you think they're all straight?"

"Probably. We're not in Kansas any more, Toto."

"Maybe I should just make sure."

"Don't you dare leave me," I said to him, clutching his arm. "I'll never forgive you if you leave me all alone."

"You're a big girl," he said, eyeing up a tall, tanned blonde guy as he grabbed another drink. "I think I'll go and introduce myself."

"No!" I exclaimed, grabbing at his sweater in vain. I was too slow, and he slipped through my grasp. God damn it! Why did I consider these people to be my friends? Denny can't be around women without acting like an ass and deserting me, and James can't be around men without acting like an ass and deserting me. The only man I could rely on was Mr. Smith, who was still sitting obediently at my feet. In fact, I think he was actually asleep. I needed to find some female friends fast.

"Who are you hiding from?" a voice close behind me said.

I turned and saw a tall, somewhat good-looking guy standing next to me with a fake smile on his face. I groaned inwardly. It was a truth universally known: no matter how many men in attendance at a party, the biggest jerk would gravitate towards me immediately. This guy looked like a cross between a used car salesman and a game show host. James was going to get a serious talking to when the party was over.

"I'm not hiding," I said, looking for an escape route. "I just wanted to be close to the drink table." Please leave, my eyes screamed at him.

"A girl after my own heart," the man replied, flashing me another thousand-watt grin. "Here. Let me get you another drink."

Wow. A man who could open a cooler. Be still my heart. Why wouldn't he go away?

"Thanks, but I'm fine." I held my beer can up and gave it a little shake so he could see that it was only half empty.

"Well, finish 'er up, and I'll get you a new one."

Oh, for the love of God! I thought. Couldn't he take a hint? I was putting out my best 'stay the hell away from me' vibes. What did a girl have to do to get someone to leave her alone?

It was at that moment that Carter strolled over. I felt relief wash over me at the thought of being rescued. Even though a large part of me was rebelling against the need to be rescued, this guy was such a jerk that I probably wouldn't have cared if Carter had appeared on a white horse with a sword in his hand.

"Hi, Martin," he said, extending a hand to Mr. Obnoxious. "I see you've met my friend Kerrigan."

"Oh," Martin said, turning back to me. "*You're* Kerrigan. Alex told me about you. I'm sorry to disturb you. Carter, I'll talk to you later." He walked off, but not before giving Carter a knowing wink. Why do I put up with men? Now I was annoyed at Carter for coming over.

"Sorry," Carter said, looking sincere. "I didn't realize you were being trapped by Martin until my sister pointed it out to me. He's an ass, but he's harmless … I think. I'm sorry that Mr. Smith didn't do anything to stop him. I thought I'd trained him better than that. He's supposed to attack Martin on sight."

"I'm fine," I said. "Martin wasn't too annoying."

"I didn't even realize that you were here yet. How come you didn't come over and say hello?" He looked down at me with a serious expression in his clear blue eyes.

"You seemed to be busy with the barbecue. I didn't want to disturb you in your manly pursuit of burning meat over coals."

"That's understandable."

"Plus there are so many other people here, I figured you'd have enough company without me bothering you."

"You wouldn't have been bothering me," he said. "I was waiting for you most of the afternoon."

"So who was that jackass?" I asked, trying to change the subject.

"Martin Booker," Carter replied, taking a swig of beer. "He grew up down the street from Alex and me. He is a total ass and has been his entire life. My parents make me invite him to this party every year. In fact, my mom used to make me invite him to my birthday parties when we were kids. I hated it. But what can a kid do?"

"It's nice that you're still so tied to the apron strings," I said. "Nothing is more attractive than a mama's boy."

"I'm glad you approve," he said with a goofy grin, "because I want you to meet my parents." He looked at my stunned expression. "It's not really that bad. They're nice people. You don't need the deer-in-the-headlights expression. Come on."

"That's okay," I said, getting slightly nervous. "I'm not really a very social person. You can tell them that I said hello." I did *not* want to meet his parents. Carter was definitely getting the wrong idea about how I felt about him.

"Don't be ridiculous," he said, grabbing me by the hand and steering me away from the drinks and towards the house. "Besides, I already told them I was going to bring you over. They're both very excited to meet you."

Great, I thought, a feeling of panic washing over me. I get to meet his parents. We're not even a couple. We're not even *close* to being a couple. I don't even like him that way. He's not my type. I like blonde guys. All these arguments kept flying through my head as we approached his parents.

We stopped walking when we reached a middle-aged couple. The man was tall, with slightly graying dark hair. He was very distinguished looking, and I could see a great deal of him in Carter. The woman was impeccably dressed and looked too young to be Carter's mother. She was eyeing me with distaste. I felt six years old.

"Mom, Dad," Carter said. They turned around to face their son. "I'd like you both to meet Kerrigan Shepherd."

"You must be Pete's daughter," Carter's father said, extending his hand to me. "I'm very pleased to meet you, Miss Shepherd. I knew your father when I was a boy."

"Please, call me Kerri." This was a nightmare. Not only did I have to meet his parents, but now I was going to be forced to talk about my father.

"He was older than me, of course," Dr. Stevens continued. "He was actually a good friend of my father's. In fact, Peter was the best man at my parents' wedding. It's so nice to have another generation of Shepherds here in New Ferndale."

"Kerri actually doesn't like talking about her father too much, Dad," Carter said.

"Oh, I'm sorry," Dr. Stevens apologized sincerely. "I wasn't thinking."

"That's okay, Dr. Stevens," I replied.

"It must be hard for you. His death was very sudden, although he hadn't been well for some time," Dr. Stevens continued.

I wasn't sure what to say about that. Didn't Dr. Stevens realize that I hadn't seen my father since I was eight?

"If you ever want to talk about your father," he added, "please give me a call. Like I said, I knew Peter for a long time."

"Thank you." He was nice, but I doubted I'd ever take him up on the offer.

"How do you like the cottage?" Carter's mother asked, changing the subject.

"It's a beautiful spot, Mrs. Stevens," I replied. "If I could just get used to the sounds at night I'm sure I'd be able to sleep better."

"Well, I don't see how anyone can live in Toronto," she replied. Her voice was cold and I could tell she didn't like me. I wasn't sure why. I'd never even laid eyes on her before today. Maybe she'd spoken to Emily. Or my mother. "All those sirens all night long. You'll get used to the country in no time."

"I'm sure I will," I replied.

"You brought some friends with you, didn't you?" Mrs. Stevens added. "Is that blonde fellow your boyfriend?"

She gestured over to where James was talking to Denny and Emily. "No, James isn't my boyfriend," I said. "He's just a friend."

"I see." She seemed disappointed. I didn't understand it at first, but then it hit me. She wanted James and me to be a couple so that I wouldn't date her son. I was really starting to dislike this woman. Even though I wasn't interested in Carter, I thought that I might start dating him out of spite.

I looked over at Carter to see if he was reading the situation the same way I was. Fortunately, we seemed to be on the same wavelength. I could see he was uncomfortable with how his mother was acting.

"I think I should introduce Kerri to some other people here at the party," he said, turning me away from his parents. "I'll see both of you later this afternoon."

"It was nice meeting the both of you," I called over my shoulder.

"Sorry about that," he said as soon as we were out of earshot of his parents. He was kind of cute when he was embarrassed.

"I don't think your mother likes me very much," I said.

"It's not entirely your fault," he said. "I forgot that she's never cared much for your family. My mom's family has lived in New Ferndale for four generations. Her grandmother worked for the Shepherd family in the summers. I guess it kind of rubs her the wrong way that her grandmother was involved in domestic service."

"Great," I said sarcastically. "It would have been nice to have known that before facing the firing squad."

"Also, I don't think she likes the fact that you're a writer. She doesn't really consider that to be a real job."

"This is getting better and better."

"And she mentioned that she didn't like how you dressed."

"What's wrong with the way I'm dressed?" I asked, getting a little defensive.

"There's nothing wrong with the way you're dressed today," he said. "And I didn't say that I thought you were dressed funny. Mom saw you the day of your father's will reading. You weren't exactly dressed for a funeral."

I groaned. I just *knew* that day would come back and haunt me. Maxine was right. I hated the fact that Maxine was right.

Why did I even care what Carter's mother thought of me?

That thought was bugging me most of all.

Alex appeared at that moment, diverting me from all these troubling thoughts.

"I have to steal Carter," she said to me. "We're having a barbeque emergency. Apparently we've run out of propane."

"Alex, I thought it was your job to make sure we had enough," Carter said.

"No," she replied, "it was my job to make sure we had enough food. You were supposed to get the propane."

"Fine. I'll run over to the gas station and get some more," Carter said. He turned to me. "Want to come along for the ride?"

"As thrilling as that sounds, I think I'll have to pass. I'm going to grab another drink and find where James is hiding." I wasn't some infatuated teenager eager to go for a drive with him.

I watched Alex and Carter head off together and then went over to the drink table. I grabbed another beer and scanned the crowd for James. I couldn't see him (since I'm not very tall), so I decided to wander through the crowd and look for him somewhere on the lawn. As I made my way through the groups of people scattered about the lawn, trying my best to avoid another run-in with Martin, I heard something that caught my attention.

"I don't know what Carter sees in her," a female voice said. I quickly recognized it as coming from Mrs. Stevens. And she sounded incredibly annoyed.

"She's a very pretty girl," Carter's father said. I began to warm up to him slightly (I was assuming that I was the topic of their conversation).

"I don't know about that," Mrs. Stevens replied. "She'd be much more attractive if she did something with her hair and stopped dressing like a tramp."

"Helen!"

"Don't 'Helen' me, Brian. You didn't see her that day. And what kind of a name is Kerrigan, anyway? It sounds like a type of sweater."

That's cardigan, I thought angrily.

"Don't you think you're being a little harsh?" Dr Stevens asked.

"I don't think so. It's terrible that the Shepherds have sunk to this level. And she claims to be a writer. That's just a nice term for being unemployed."

I had had more than enough of this. Now I knew why you weren't supposed to listen to other people's conversations. Twice in the same day I'd overheard people insulting me. It was not good for my ego. I pushed my way past them and headed down to the dock with my beer in my hand. I knew that it wasn't exactly the best manners to let them know I had overheard, but I was too mad to care.

Mr. Smith followed me onto the dock and lay down next to me with his head in my lap. I had sat there for about thirty minutes, watching the sun begin to set, before someone sat down next to me. It was Carter.

"I'm really very sorry about my mother," he began. "She was fond of my wife and can't understand why we're not still married with four or five children by now."

"You told her the truth about your wife, right?"

"Yeah, but my mom is very old fashioned and refuses to believe that Marlie is a lesbian," he smiled at me. "But I really am sorry about my mother."

"What are you talking about?" I asked, turning to look at him.

"My dad told me that you might have overheard some things that my mother had said. He thought I should come down here and do a little damage control."

"I'm fine," I said. "I've been called worse things than a tramp by my own mother."

"Really," Carter said. He raised an eyebrow at me.

"And if your mother would like to learn some really colourful insults for me, she should talk to Denny's wife. Emily's been bitching at me since they got here yesterday."

"Doesn't it bother you?"

"I've got thick skin," I said, staring out onto the water. "I try not to care what other people think about me. It takes too much energy to be constantly worried about everyone else."

"That's a good way to be. Who taught you that?"

"My brother," I replied.

"He was right."

"Yeah, but sometimes I forget, and I just want to haul off and deck somebody."

"Well, I'm glad you didn't hit my mother. She can be a pain in the ass, but she's still my mother."

We sat in silence for a while, watching as some water skiers attempted to make use of the last little bit of sunlight. It was kind of nice. The silence wasn't awkward but strangely comforting. It was nice to sit with someone without needing to force conversation.

"How's the unpacking going?" Carter asked me after a few minutes.

"Not too bad. I'm pretty much settled in."

"Have you found anything interesting in the house? I'm assuming that you've done a little exploring."

I nodded. "I found an old *Dukes of Hazard* car that I think used to be mine. I have a vague memory of playing with it with my brother."

"Big *Dukes of Hazard* fan?"

"Yup. I used to want to be Bo Duke when I grew up."

"You do realize that Bo was a guy, right?"

"I was four. It didn't really matter to me back then. Before that I wanted to be an owl."

"I'm sorry that it didn't work out for you."

"I don't know. I've been seriously thinking about getting my car doors welded shut and painting the whole thing bright orange."

"Maybe you could get a pair of Daisy Duke shorts."

"They'd look better on you."

"Thanks," he said. "I'm glad you noticed that I have such lovely legs."

"I'm sure you'd cause quite the commotion in the office if you came to town in cutoffs."

"I think it might violate my own dress code."

He stretched his legs lazily out in front of him.

"Tell me something about you that no one else knows," I asked Carter after a couple of minutes.

"What sort of thing?"

"Anything."

Carter thought for a moment. "When I was eight, I was terrified of the woman who babysat for Alex and me. I mean really terrified. She used to put kids in the closet for 'time out' when they were bad and keep them there for hours at a time. I'm still a little claustrophobic because of it. I used to make myself throw up before my mom took us there, just so she'd keep me at home with her."

"And you didn't tell your mom?"

Carter shook his head. "No. She stopped taking us there and found someone else to look after us."

"That's awful."

"Your turn. Tell me something that you've never told anyone."

"I've seen *Mamma Mia* fifteen times."

He looked at me. "That's it?"

"It's a pretty serious addiction."

"I tell you a traumatic story from my childhood, and you tell me that you're obsessed with a musical about ABBA?"

"It's not *about* ABBA," I said firmly. "It integrates the music of ABBA into a story."

"Still."

"It's a brilliant musical."

"I get it." He paused. "I made mine up."

"What?"

He grinned at me sheepishly. "I read it in a book once. No one ever put me in a closet. Well, except the time Alex locked me in the closet. But that doesn't count."

"I told you something very serious and personal," I said.

"The fact that you've seen *Mamma Mia* fifteen times doesn't count as personal information," he insisted. "It's just a little crazy."

"Shut up."

We sat together for a few minutes before I spoke again. "Do you like living in such a small town?"

He nodded. "I lived in Toronto for university, and I hated it. I like living in a place where I can walk down the middle of the street without getting killed by a taxi. And I like being close to my family.

"I decided that I could never live in the city," he continued. "When I was a kid my dad took me to my uncle's office in downtown Toronto. His office was on the twentieth floor of this huge building. It was amazing: you could see the CN tower from his window. I was impressed." He looked at me. "Alright, I was eight years old and easily impressed. I remember that we stayed until it was dark, and I looked out at all those lights in all those windows and realized how many people lived there. It just made me realize how insignificant everything really was. I knew I could never be one of those people. It was just so anonymous, so cold and sterile. And so I decided to stay here, and have my law practice in a small town. I could probably make more money in Toronto, but I'd never be happy."

"You were eight and using the word 'insignificant'?"

"Okay, maybe I didn't actually think that," he said, grinning. "But my point is I can't live in the city, because it stinks."

"Toronto doesn't stink."

"Yes, it does."

"Hamilton stinks. Toronto smells fine."

"Maybe if you've been living there your entire life you become accustomed to the foul odor. Personally, I hold my nose when I enter the city."

"That's ridiculous," I said, taking a final swig from my beer can.

"What about you?" he asked. "Did you ever think of living outside of Toronto? I mean, as a writer you can pretty much live wherever you want."

"I never wanted to live anywhere else. Well, for a while I wanted to live in New York City and then Paris, but Toronto is still pretty nice."

"Do your mom and sister live in the city?"

"Mom lives in Scarborough and Maxine lives in Mississauga."

"Do you see them often?"

"No."

I could tell he was waiting for me to elaborate. I just sat there and stared at the water.

"Why not?" he asked when I didn't say anything.

"My mom and I don't get along very well. Neither do Maxine and I, as I'm sure you noticed at the will reading."

"What's the problem?"

"God, you're nosey today."

"I'm sorry," he said, not looking the least bit sorry. "What's the problem?"

I sighed. "Fine," I said. "Maxine was fifteen when I was born and Sebastian was eight. My parents weren't expecting to have any more children so they were a little surprised when I came along. My mother wasn't particularly nice to me, and I don't remember my father being around much. Sebastian was the only one I had. My dad left when I was eight. That would have made Maxine twenty-three and Sebastian about sixteen. As the perfect daughter, Maxine felt like she had to step in and take over the role as the head of the household. My mother was more than happy to hand Maxine this role. Maxine came in and all of a sudden there was someone who was acting like an authority figure. Up till then I'd pretty much done whatever I'd wanted. Suddenly there was someone telling me to brush my teeth and go to bed and do my homework. I hated it, and I hated her. And she didn't exactly like me either.

"Mom took off with some guy who she married immediately after the divorce from my dad was final. He wasn't interested in being a parent, so that left Maxine. Mom moved out with the new guy so Maxine came back home permanently, got a job and spent her time looking after me. She hated every minute of it, and let me know that I was keeping her from living the life she'd wanted. At least that was my impression of the whole thing. I'd never really known Maxine before my father left. She was away at boarding school when I was born, and she hadn't even seen me until I was three. And then, until I was eight, I only ever saw her at Christmas. She was a stranger to me when she moved back in, and I found it hard to be raised by someone I hardly even knew. I'm sure I didn't exactly make things easy on her. Looking back on it now, it must have been horrible for her. She was only twenty-three, and she had to look after two kids. I don't think I would have done it if our places had been reversed."

I paused and looked at him. "I didn't mean for this to turn into a speech."

"I'm really interested," he insisted. "Please. Go on."

I looked at him to see if he was serious before starting again. "When Mom and the new guy split after a year, she didn't bother to move back home. Maxine was an adult, Sebastian was pretty much grown up, and I was fine, so Mom kept on acting like a teenager. She didn't invite any of us to her third wedding, which didn't really bother me because I wouldn't have gone anyway.

"Then Sebastian left home two years later for university, and I went with him. I'd managed to get a scholarship to a private school in Toronto that was a short bus ride from our apartment. I was ten, and Sebastian was eighteen. I don't think Maxine has forgiven me for picking Sebastian over her." I remember the look in her eyes when I told her I didn't want to stay with her. There was pain but also something underneath that I took for relief.

"Sebastian was my best friend," I continued. "Maxine was finally able to act her age and immediately found a husband and had a kid. She has a daughter who'd be fifteen or sixteen by now.

"Sebastian and Denny were close friends all through high school and university. They were in the same program at U of T, although Sebastian didn't actually want to be an accountant. He was more interested in the marketing side of business. After he graduated, he got a job at a pharmaceutical company and made enough money that he was able to help me pay for university."

"What happened to him?" Carter asked cautiously.

I took a deep breath. I hated this part. "Car accident." Why did I lie?

"I'm sorry," Carter said, putting his arm around me. It was strangely comforting so I didn't shrug it off immediately. "It must have been hard for you."

"I miss him a lot," I admitted. "It's been two years, but it still feels like yesterday." I felt an incredible loneliness sweep over me. I leaned into Carter's arm, glad that he was there with me. It was more comforting than I wanted to admit.

"You're amazing," Carter said to me.

"What are you talking about?" I asked, looking up at him.

"You're independent. You've had a crappy childhood, but you seem pretty well adjusted."

I looked at him like he was crazy.

"And you're beautiful."

I wasn't expecting that. I looked up at him to see if he was kidding. Apparently, he wasn't. He leaned forward to kiss me.

My first reaction was to push him away. This was Carter. He was just a friend. I wasn't looking for a relationship with anyone, and if I was, I certainly wouldn't be interested in him.

But for some reason I couldn't push him away. I felt myself lean into the kiss, throwing my arms around his neck and running my fingers through his hair.

Oh God, I thought somewhere deep in my subconscious. What was I getting myself into?

Chapter Seven

Denny, Emily and James went back to the city on the Monday after Carter's party, leaving me alone once again at the cottage. I was thankful for the peace and quiet (I was especially glad to see Emily leave), but I was also a little lonely. I felt a sense of isolation coming on as they drove away Monday evening. I'd gotten used to having them around, and not just because they were keeping me company. Guests were a great excuse for doing little or no work. I had spent three guilt-free days without writing a single word. This was as opposed to the many unproductive days I'd had before they'd arrived, which had always left me feeling a little guilty. And then, once they'd left, I still had all the cleaning up to do from the weekend. When I was procrastinating, I never minded doing housework.

But it was nice to have the place to myself again. To be completely honest, it was just nice to have Emily out of the house. She had ignored me Sunday and Monday, which had been very nice, allowing me to enjoy at least some of the weekend with my friends. But she was still there, silently ruining the weekend. And Denny didn't seem to have enjoyed himself, and I was sure Emily would spend at least part of their drive back to the city yelling at him.

Despite my best efforts to really drag out the housework, by Wednesday I knew that had to get back to my real work. And not just on my non-existent novel. I still hadn't started my next article. I only had until Thursday to send it in. Less than twenty-four hours to come up with a half-decent idea and write the article. I wasn't panicking yet, but I was coming pretty close.

Maybe Emily was right to say that I should get a real job. The main problem with that idea was that I didn't know what exactly I could do. I wasn't really qualified to do anything, but I figured (probably somewhat optimistically) something would probably turn up. I had a university degree in English. I was sure Wendy's was eagerly waiting for me to apply. Or maybe McDonalds. But I probably wasn't even qualified to work there.

I paced the floor, starting at seven in the morning, for more than an hour, trying to come up with an idea for the article. Why the hell had I even agreed to write the stupid articles in the first place? I thought angrily. Apparently, I'd even lost the ability to work well under pressure.

I finally decided on a topic for my article after rejecting several earlier (horrible) ideas (such as the best way to kill a bat with a tennis racket or a commentary on why mental institutions were always located within a two hour hike of summer camps). It was going to be on small town bakeries. I knew it wasn't a great idea, but it was all I could think of at 8:30 on a Wednesday morning with a deadline looming before me. And with my stomach growling loudly all I could think about was food. I desperately wanted some donuts. I could turn this into a really pathetic series of articles if I wrote everything while I was hungry, I thought.

I was on my way out of the house at nine in the morning when the phone rang. I was awake, but no one knew that. No one I knew would call me this early. I was still the girl who slept till eleven on weekdays. I thought maybe it was James or Denny or even my agent nagging me for some pages or possibly someone from town who I was skillfully trying to avoid. Unfortunately, I was wrong.

The biggest problem with having call answer as opposed to a traditional answering machine was that I couldn't screen calls very efficiently. I made a mental note to get call display. That way I wouldn't be surprised by unwanted callers.

"Hello," I said warily as I answered the phone.

"Hello, Kerrigan."

It was Maxine.

Shit, shit, shit.

"Oh, hi Max," I said, forcing a cheerful tone.

"Don't call me that." She sounded annoyed. Less than thirty seconds into the call and I already managed to piss her off. It must be a new record. I'd have to call the good people at Guinness after I hung up.

"Why not? It never used to bother you."

"I'm not eighteen any more, Kerrigan. And yes, it did bother me."

"Sorry. Hello, Maxine. My name is Kerri. Is that better?"

Maxine sighed. "Don't be a smart ass, Kerri."

"Did you just call me to insult me, or does this conversation have a point?"

"Yes, it has a point. It's Mom's birthday next week. It might be nice for you to give her a call."

"Why?"

"Because she's your mother, that's why."

"Have you met our mother? She's not a very nice person, in case you've forgotten."

"Honestly, Kerri, if my daughter ever treated me the way you treat Mom, I don't know what I'd do."

"I don't think you treat Tina the way Mom treated me."

Maxine didn't have a reply for that.

"Besides," I continued. "You always acted more like my mother than she did."

"And you never call me either. Don't you ever miss having a family?"

"We can never get our family back the way it was. What we've got is a mockery of the word family. Dysfunctional doesn't even begin to describe it."

"So you don't even want to have anything to do with any of us," Maxine said angrily. "Fine. Goodbye, Kerri. I guess I'll see you the next time someone dies."

She hung up. I couldn't believe that she had hung up and left me with only the dial tone to yell at.

I was annoyed. That was just like Maxine to call, get me pissed off and then hang up before I could really get into a good fight with her.

Shrugging off my annoyance, I drove into town to research my article.

I started in Mary's Bakery on Main Street, where I'd had coffee with James on the day of the will reading. There wasn't too much else on Main Street: the bakery, a small grocery store, a few shops, the liquor store and Carter's office were really all that the street boasted. *Patrick's* (the pub where I'd been spectacularly humiliated when I'd had dinner with Carter and Alex) was on a side street just off Main. Now that cottage season was fast approaching, I began to notice that all the little shops were starting to carry tacky souvenirs. They were busier than they had been a week earlier, full of people I hadn't seen before.

Alex was in the bakery when I arrived. She was talking to another customer as she paid for a cup of coffee. My first instinct was to turn around and leave, but I was too late. She had already spotted me. That was the problem with red hair.

Or maybe it was just a problem with small towns. I could go anywhere I wanted in Toronto and not bump into a single person I knew. I loved the anonymity. I could go out and buy groceries at two in the morning looking like a complete and utter fool, and no one would bat an eye. I frequently grocery shopped in my pajamas and slippers. But here everyone knew who I was. They knew who my father had been, and they knew where I lived. I bet they even knew what had happened with Carter and me down at the dock. I didn't know how people could stand it.

"Kerri," Alex said to me as I came in. "I haven't seen you in days. How are you doing?"

I would have rather not talked to her. I hadn't seen any of them (meaning Carter or Alex) since the party on the weekend, and I didn't want to think about what had happened on the dock with Carter. I was doing my best to wipe the memory entirely from my mind. It was turning out to be more difficult than I had originally thought, which was very frustrating. Maybe I should have just stayed at the cottage. There'd be less chance of running into him out there.

I hadn't been forced to talk to him about it yet. He hadn't called me since the weekend (which, to be perfectly honest, bugged me much more than I cared to admit). I thought I was safe venturing back into town. I guess I'd been wrong.

"I'm fine," I said to Alex, approaching the counter to place my order. I was also making mental notes on the place to include in my article (actually, that's not really true; I was looking at the chocolate croissants and wondering if I should buy a half dozen of them). If I could get in and out as quickly as possible, maybe I could avoid any awkward conversations with Alex, I thought. I decided not to volunteer any information and just answer her questions as quickly and simply as possible.

"How are your friends doing?" she asked, far too casually. Her face coloured slightly and I realized immediately that she was talking about Denny. I knew that this could mean trouble. I was going to have to call him that evening and remind him for the millionth time that he was married. I liked Alex, despite my unfortunate incident with her brother. Someone was going to have to warn her that Denny was bad news. I knew this from personal experience.

"My friends are fine. They all went back to the city on Monday. Emily and Denny were anxious to get back to their baby." I tried to emphasize the fact that Denny was indeed a married man, even if he wasn't happily married.

"That's nice," Alex said distractedly as she paid for her coffee. "When are they coming back to visit you?"

I was definitely going to yell at Denny. I didn't want to see him lead Alex on. If things continued this way (and followed Denny's usual pattern), Alex would be a wreck by the middle of the summer. And then she'd hate me for introducing her to Denny.

"I'm not sure," I said honestly, "but I bet they'll be here a lot this summer. They can't pass up a free place to stay outside of the city. Maybe next time Denny and Emily will bring their baby." That was the last thing I wanted (the thought of Emily and the baby at my place for even a minute made me slightly nauseous), but maybe it would jolt Alex into reality.

"He's a cute little baby," I continued. "And Denny and Emily just adore him."

"So how come you've been avoiding Carter?"

The change in topic was so fast it caught me by surprise. I jumped, bumping my knee hard against the glass display case.

"Sorry," I said sheepishly to the man behind the counter as I rubbed my knee. "What are you talking about? I haven't been avoiding anyone. I've been very busy."

I wondered how believable that sounded. It sounded pretty lame to me.

"I'm glad to hear you haven't been avoiding him," Alex said with a grin, "since he's right over there."

She gestured to a spot behind the counter where Carter was in discussion with one of the clerks.

Shit. Why hadn't I seen him when I came in? It's not like this place was huge. There should be a law that people I'm trying to avoid should be forced to wear little bells around their necks. Of course, I wasn't avoiding Carter.

As soon as Alex pointed at him, Carter turned and grinned at me. Oh God, I thought. He's coming over. Shit, shit, shit! I started to panic, realizing that I had little hope of escape.

He looked good. Okay, to be perfectly honest, he looked great. He's not your type, the voice in my head kept screaming at me. He was dressed in a blue button-up shirt that matched his eyes (I was angry with myself for noticing) and a pair of khaki pants.

"I've got to go," I said quickly to Alex as I hurried backwards towards the door. I managed to only bump into two people on my way. "I've just remembered that I left the oven and the iron on. I'll tell Denny you said hello."

I bolted out the door. Smooth, I thought to myself. That didn't look obvious at all. My face was flushed with embarrassment. I hurried over to my car, berating myself mentally as I walked. As I went, I realized that I'd left the bakery without even buying anything. Chicken, a voice in my head said.

"Kerri!" Carter's voice called from behind me. "Slow down."

Maybe if I walk faster and ignore him he'll go back into the bakery, I thought. If I pretend I can't hear him, he'll give up and go away.

No such luck. He caught up with me at my car.

"It's not fair," I said fumbling for my keys. "I have short legs and can't walk as fast as you."

"Kerri, we need to talk."

He placed a hand on my arm. He was standing far too close to me. It was making me slightly nervous for some reason.

"Okay," I said. I looked up at him and forced a smile. "Hello. Now we've talked. Can I go?"

"No. We need to talk about Saturday."

"What about Saturday?" I said, not wanting to talk about what he wanted to talk about. "You know, you should discourage your sister from going after Denny. He's really not good enough for her. And he's married."

"That's not what I meant, and you know it," he said, scowling at me. "Although, I will tell her to stay away from him. I didn't even realize there was anything going on between them."

"I don't know if there's anything going on with them yet," I said, happy to latch onto anything other than what happened on the dock. "But give it time."

"That's not what I wanted to talk to you about, Kerri. I want to talk about what happened between us on Saturday."

"Look, I'm perfectly happy to forget about Saturday," I said cheerfully. "Let's just pretend it never happened. Mistakes happen to everyone."

"I don't think it was a mistake," he said.

"You don't?" Then why didn't you call me?

"No I don't." He leaned in towards me. He was making me nervous. I hated the fact that he was making me feel like I was in high school again. "I wanted to kiss you from the moment we met."

"That's nice ..." I said, trying to break eye contact and get the hell out of there. Just open the car door and drive away, I said to myself. But it was like my legs just wouldn't move.

"I think we'd be great together. You just need to give us a chance."

"I don't have time for a relationship," I said, the butterflies in my stomach making me feel slightly nauseous. He really did have the nicest eyes …

"You're just making excuses," he said softly, lightly touching my face with his hand.

"No I'm not," I said. "I'm really very busy …"

Carter leaned in closer and kissed me. "Have dinner with me tonight."

"Okay," I said softly, my eyes still closed. My legs felt like they were going to buckle under me.

"Great," he said, standing upright and talking in his normal voice. "I'll come around to your place at seven."

Damn it! I thought as he walked away.

After my disturbing morning in town, I went home to try to work on my article. My mind was too busy with other things to give my article the full attention it deserved. I sat in front of the television with my laptop and wrote a rough draft (an incredibly rough draft), trying with little success to keep my mind off Carter and the upcoming evening. Every time I thought about it, I felt slightly nauseous.

I was being an idiot. I never should have agreed to have dinner with him. What the hell was wrong with me? Why hadn't I just told him that I only wanted to be friends? Was there some part of me that did want Carter to be more than a friend? It was so confusing, and I didn't have anyone to talk to about it. I was so frazzled I couldn't concentrate properly on work. Instead, I sat back and turned on the television.

The phone rang in the middle of the afternoon disrupting my TV watching. I answered nervously, hoping it wasn't Carter.

It wasn't Carter.

"Hello," I said cautiously.

"Is there something wrong?"

"Maxine," I said, not bothering to hide my surprise. "What's going on?"

"What do you mean?"

"I haven't heard from you in ages and suddenly you call me twice in one day. Something must be up."

"Not really," she began. She sounded a little strange. "I felt a little bad about the way we left things this morning."

I smiled to myself. "Don't worry about it." This was weird. Why was Maxine calling to apologize? Since my trip into town, I had almost forgotten about our morning phone call.

"It's just that I'm concerned about you," she continued as if I hadn't spoken. "You're always so remote. I don't even know what's going on with your life. I don't know if you're seeing someone or if you're engaged. I bet you could have even gotten married, and you wouldn't have told me. Tina hasn't seen you in years."

I was a little surprised. Maxine was acting loopy. I didn't know what the hell was going on with her.

"I'm not engaged," I said. "Or married. And I'm not seeing anyone." I didn't want to mention Carter. There wasn't anything to mention. "There's nothing going on in my life."

"How are you doing? Are you working? Have you been writing?"

"What's with all this sudden concern about me?" I was starting to get suspicious of her motives.

"It's not really sudden. I didn't have your phone number before, remember?"

"True." I had avoided giving out my phone number to avoid calls just like this one.

"Besides, we *are* supposed to be a family, despite what you said earlier. And one day you're going to regret shutting us all out like this."

I started to protest, but she cut me off.

"I'm serious, Kerri. You might disagree with me now, but in a few years, you may have kids of your own. You wouldn't want them to go off and cut you out of their lives."

"Yeah, but you're my sister. Don't you think that Mom should be the one calling me about this?"

"You know Mom would never do that."

I did. Mom had never been affectionate or sentimental when I was a kid. She would certainly never call me and try to get back into my life.

"Look, I've got to go." I looked at my watch. It was almost 5:30 and I needed to get ready before Carter came over.

"Think about what I said, Kerrigan," Maxine said. "I'll call you again later."

I was a nervous wreck by 6:55. I had changed my clothes about fifteen times. I couldn't figure out what was wrong with me. I had cleaned the kitchen and the living room. I had even tried writing, without success (not that I was surprised). Nothing could distract me from the feeling of impending doom. I was convinced that I was about to ruin a perfectly good, platonic friendship just because he had eyes that were an amazing shade of blue and was a good kisser. I really hated myself sometimes. And I hated Carter. I hated how he made me feel off-balance and out of control. I hadn't felt this confused since I was sixteen and Billy Thompson's parents had gone out of town for the weekend.

Promptly at seven, there was a knock at the door. I walked over to open it, trying valiantly to dispel my last lingering feelings of doom. Carter stood on the stoop, dressed in a shirt and tie, carrying flowers and a bag of groceries with a big grin on his face.

"Since I invited myself over, I figured the least I could do is cook for you," he said, passing me the flowers. He stepped inside and carried the groceries into the kitchen.

"The very least," I said, trying to find something to put the flowers in (I settled for an old whisky bottle). "I really had no idea what we were going to eat. All I have is Cheerios." I had been too preoccupied with the ramifications of Carter coming over to even consider dinner. I didn't even have any milk to go along with the Cheerios.

"We can have that if you'd like," he said grinning. "Or I can cook some pasta for us. I make a great spaghetti sauce."

"You can decide," I said.

"Spaghetti it is." He started rummaging around in the cupboards for (I assumed) the pots and pans he needed. "Do you know where I would find …"

"You shouldn't even finish that sentence," I said, raising a hand to cut him off. "I don't have a clue where anything is. And I probably wouldn't even know what you were talking about."

"I guess I'll just have to search for it."

He bent over and continued to search for whatever strange cooking implement he decided he needed.

I couldn't help but laugh at the sight of him digging for pots in the kitchen.

"What's so funny?" he asked, his face serious.

"You are."

"There's nothing funny about what I'm doing."

"It's funny from this angle."

"Thanks," he said. "I don't even have my apron on yet."

"You do *not* have an apron."

"I do," he said proudly. He reached into the bag and pulled out an apron. He tied it around his neck and then turned to face me.

"You've got to be kidding," I said when I saw it. "Are you sure you have a Y chromosome?"

The apron was white and said 'Barbeque King' on it. I covered my mouth to stop from laughing.

"Laugh it up," he said, "but I always cook the best when I'm wearing this apron." He paused and looked over at me. "By the way, you look amazing."

I felt myself turn red. I had spent far too much time getting ready for something I didn't even consider to be a date—much more time than I was willing to admit. After two hours of searching I'd finally decided to wear my black slip dress. Yes, I'd actually spent two hours looking at my clothes. I basically laid every possible outfit on my bed and tried to find something appropriate. I'd even managed to tame my hair in a satisfactory manner: smooth curls, no trace of frizz. I don't know why I'd spent so much time on my appearance. I wasn't interested in him. Honestly.

"Thank you," I said, trying to will my face to change back to its normal colour.

"So, what did you do today?" he asked, changing the topic when he saw how embarrassed I was. He was using some pots and pans I'd never even seen before to make spaghetti sauce. I didn't know that people still did that. The only sauce I'd ever seen before had come from a jar.

"I spent the day watching TV," I said with a sigh, reluctantly admitting that I hadn't done any work all day. "First, I watched some annoying talk shows before switching to Law & Order. I think I watched about five hours of it. Did you know that you can find Law & Order on at least one channel every hour? I think that much crime television can only have a bad effect on me. I keep thinking that the squirrels are out to get me."

"That could be an indication of some kind of psychosis."

"Maybe. But just because you think they're out to get you doesn't mean that they aren't."

"You seem to have a lot of time on your hands," he said. "Any luck with the novel?"

"Nope," I replied truthfully. "But I did manage to almost finish my article. I'm going to send it off to the editor tomorrow."

"That's good. Did you get it done between episodes?"

"Yes. And I also worked on it during commercials. Plus my sister called. Twice. Law & Order and two conversations with Maxine. It was an exceptionally busy day."

"It sounds that way. How is your sister? I didn't think you two talked much. You two didn't look like you got along very well."

"We don't," I admitted. I was still confused as to why she'd called. Maxine always was a little odd. But I didn't want to waste my evening thinking about my crazy family. "She's acting a little stranger than usual, which is saying a lot."

"Did you ask her if there was anything wrong?"

"Of course," I said a little defensively. "But she didn't say." Honestly, why was he so curious about my sister?

"Interesting."

"What do you mean? I can honestly say that nothing about Maxine is interesting. She has the most uninteresting life of anyone I know."

"I just think it's interesting that your sister has been calling you. Maybe she's trying to get back in touch with you."

"Yeah, that's just what I need," I said sarcastically.

"Why not? You don't talk to your mother and Maxine's your only sister. I would think you'd be happy to be in contact with your family again."

"Maybe you would, but my sister isn't Alex. Maxine is annoying and domineering."

"All sisters are annoying and domineering. That's part of being a family."

"Well, I don't need to have contact with my family to be annoyed," I said, shooting him a dirty look.

He laughed. "Fine. I'll stop bugging you about it. But maybe you should think about talking to your sister again."

"So what was your day like?" I wanted to change the subject.

"Paper work, clients. The usual. Not an especially interesting day. No episodes of *Law & Order,* unfortunately. But I did talk to my sister. Can you pass me the onions I brought?"

"Where did you put them?"

"In the fridge. They're next to an empty bottle of water, some mustard and baking soda. Sounds like you had a good lunch."

"I'm not really big on grocery shopping," I said as I rooted around in the refrigerator. "But for some reason I always have mustard. I don't even like mustard. I think that bottle may have come with the fridge." I passed him the bag of onions.

"Thank you."

"Do you need any help?"

"Nope. I think the food would be safer if you stay far away from it."

I shot him a dirty look before going to set the table. I also put some music on while he finished up. When we sat down to eat, the conversation turned to Carter and Alex's childhood.

"You two can't have gotten along when you were kids," I protested. "It's unnatural and kind of weird."

"We fought a bit when we were younger," he admitted. "Actually, we fought a lot." He lifted up his left arm and rolled down his sleeve. "See this scar?" I nodded. "I got this when I was nine, and Alex pushed me off the end of the dock. I broke my arm in three places and had to have a metal pin put in. It sets off all the metal detectors at the airport."

"Seriously?"

"No. I actually just cut it on a dock nail. Three stitches."

"It's very manly."

"I thought so. That's why I brought it up."

"Why'd she push you off the dock?"

"It might have been because I put a snake in her bed. Personally I think she overreacted."

"That's horrible! You deserved what you got."

"It was just a joke! We pulled them on each other all the time."

"What else did you do to your poor sister?"

"When Alex was eight and I was twelve, I snuck into her room with a black magic marker and drew a moustache and eye glasses on her face," he said somewhat proudly.

"You didn't."

He nodded.

"What did your parents do? Better yet, what did Alex do to you? I would have done more than just push you off the end of the dock."

"My mom grounded me for a month. No leaving the house except for school, hockey practice and church. Alex got me back by shaving off my eyebrows when I was fourteen."

I laughed. "Do you have any pictures?"

"Not on me, but I'm sure Alex would be more than happy to give you a copy. I think she's still handing them out to people."

"Anything else?"

"Alex once filled my baseball glove with crazy glue. I had that thing stuck to my hand for about a week."

"Was she grounded?"

Carter laughed. "My parents couldn't really do anything to her since she did it to me when she was thirty-one."

I had just taken a drink of wine and nearly started to choke.

"My mother was mortified," he continued. "I had to go to work with a baseball glove on my hand. I just pretended like nothing was wrong. I didn't want to give Alex the satisfaction of thinking she'd won. Mom was furious with her. She wouldn't talk to Alex for a month. Mom can't stand the fact that the whole town knows her children act like idiots."

"I don't blame her."

"It's just a little harmless fun," he insisted. "We're always trying to out do each other. Plus I think the people around here get a kick out of seeing what we'll do next."

"Whose turn is it?"

"We don't really take turns, but I haven't gotten her back for the glove yet," he said with a grin. "I haven't figured out what to do to her. But I promise you it will be good. Maybe something involving public nudity. Any suggestions?"

"I think you should stop before you kill each other."

"That wouldn't be any fun," he protested.

"Your mother's right. You're acting like children."

"So you're going to take my mother's side? That's really weird."

"Does your mother know you're here tonight?" I asked, remembering how much she had disliked me when we met at the party.

"I don't tell my mother everything," he replied, taking a drink and avoiding my question.

"I see. You're afraid of her. That's understandable. I'm afraid of my mother too. I'm pretty sure my mother wears a wig to cover up her devil horns."

"I'm not afraid of my mother," he said. "I just don't keep her up to date with everything in my life."

"So, if she had her way, who would you be having dinner with this evening?"

"Probably with the daughter of one of her friends," he replied. "She's constantly trying to fix me up with someone or other, but she has horrible taste in women."

"And your taste is better? Remember, you've been married once already."

"There's nothing wrong with my taste in women. My wife just happened to have better taste in women than I did. But the fact that I'm here with you is a sign that my taste is improving."

I blushed again. God damn him. I hated how easily he could make me turn bright red.

We ate quietly for a while. He was a terrific cook, and it was nice to have a real meal for a change that didn't come from a restaurant. Living alone, I was used to eating sandwiches and cereal for dinner (or a bag of microwave popcorn when I was really desperate). It was great having someone to cook for me.

"This is my favourite song," he said suddenly. "Want to dance?"

"I don't dance," I replied firmly.

"Sure you do. Everyone can dance."

"No, I really can't." I wasn't being coy. I really couldn't dance. Two left feet, no sense of rhythm, you name it. The point was I just don't dance.

"I do." He stood and gestured for me to join him. Reluctantly, I stood and took his hand.

"Is this song really your favourite?" I asked suspiciously. I wasn't sure if I'd even heard this song before.

"No," he admitted. "I just wanted to dance with you."

He put his arms around me and attempted to guide me to the beat of the music. I stepped on his feet. More than once. It was humiliating.

"Sorry," I said sheepishly when I stepped on his feet for what felt like the hundredth time. My face was warm with embarrassment.

"It's okay." He looked down at me and grinned. "Maybe you could take off your shoes, though. And you could let me lead."

"One of us is supposed to lead?"

"Yeah, and traditionally it's the guy."

"Whatever you say."

I kicked off my shoes and danced with him in my bare feet. Without my shoes on he towered over me. I had to look up to see his face. I felt kind of ridiculous. The cynic inside me kept shouting that this was idiotic. I wasn't sure if I should ignore it or not. He was sweet, and it was kind of nice to be alone with him.

"You're a great dancer," I said. I needed something to say in order to break up the mood. The atmosphere in the room was becoming dangerous.

"You're a horrible dancer," he replied. "For someone so tiny, you're not very light on your feet. I think you broke one of my toes."

"Thanks," I said sarcastically.

"But I don't think there's anyone I'd rather be dancing with right now."

He looked down at me again. The butterflies in my stomach started doing little flips. I was angry at myself for falling for such an incredibly cheesy line. Why did his eyes have to be so gorgeous? Blue and clear, with a trace of mischief. I was a sucker for blue eyes. I felt my knees go weak. He reached down and tilted my chin up towards him. Then he leaned down and kissed me.

The kiss was soft and wonderful. I felt my arms reach around his neck to pull him closer. All the warning bells were screaming in my head. But I ignored them. Finally, we parted.

"It's getting late," he said softly. "Do you want me to go?"

Here's your chance, I thought to myself. You can get away scott-free.

"I want you to stay," I said. I took him by the hand and led him upstairs.

Chapter Eight

I woke up the next morning to the sound of the shower turning on. Looking at my clock, I saw that it was shortly before 9:00 AM. I was confused. Why was the shower on if I was still in bed?

Immediately memories of the previous night came back to me in a rush. It was like a bad dream—sort of. I kept hoping that it hadn't actually happened, that I hadn't ruined a perfectly good friendship by jumping into bed with Carter. I was incredibly embarrassed. I wasn't usually that forward. What was I going to do? He was going to be finished his shower in a couple of minutes. I had to figure out what to do before he came back. I needed someone to talk to. Picking up the phone, I dialed Denny's number without really thinking.

"Dennis Wells speaking."

"Hi Denny," I said, whispering into the phone. I didn't want Carter to hear me.

"Something must be wrong," he said. "It's not even nine in the morning. Why are you awake? And why are you whispering? Is there someone in the room?"

"I think I've done something stupid," I said, keeping one eye on the bathroom door. I wanted to be off the phone before Carter came out.

"What happened?" Denny sounded very concerned.

"Carter came over last night for dinner."

"And?"

"And he's in the shower right now."

There was silence on the other end of the phone.

"Denny? Are you still there?"

"Yes, I'm here. That's great." His voice sounded somewhat strangled.

Maybe I shouldn't have called him, I thought. It's generally not such a good idea to ask your ex-boyfriend for advice about your current flings. I think that's something they stress in those relationship books. But it wasn't my fault that my ex also happened to be one of my best friends. I sometimes forgot that Denny and I used to sleep together. It was times like these that I really wished I had some female friends. Or even that I could talk to Maxine about it. What was I thinking? There was no way in hell I'd ever talk to my sister about my relationships. I didn't think I'd even ask her advice about what brand of toothpaste to buy, let alone advice about my love life. I could just imagine Maxine's face if I told her about this. Her head would probably explode. I'm pretty sure she thought that sex outside of marriage was a capital offense.

"I think we may have moved too fast," I said to Denny.

"I don't think so," Denny said. "You've been panting after each other for weeks now. It was bound to happen." His tone was harsh and cold.

"We weren't panting after each other," I said, getting annoyed with him. He had no right to act like a jerk.

"Whatever you say, Kerri."

"We weren't."

"Fine. So, are we still invited up on weekends, or has your place turned into a love nest? I mean, James and I don't want to intrude if you and Carter want to have sex all over the cottage."

"Shut up," I said as I hung up on him. I shouldn't have called him. I should have called James instead. At least James would be somewhat impartial. Come to think of it, James would be ecstatic. He'd want all the details, and I wasn't sure I could handle that, so calling James was definitely out. I could always call Alex, I thought. But then again she might be slightly biased towards her brother.

Just after I hung up the phone, Carter came out of the bathroom. He looked great. His hair was wet and slightly tousled and he had a little half-grin on his face.

"Good morning," he said as he came over to the bed and kissed me. I felt incredibly awkward and stiffened involuntarily at his touch. "I hope I didn't wake you."

"It's okay," I said, drawing the sheet tight around me. "I should get up anyway. I've got work to do today. I've got to finish my article by noon."

"Why don't I go downstairs and make us breakfast? I can bring it up to you, if you'd like."

"No thanks," I said. "I'm going to hop into the shower."

After Carter left the room I quickly ran into the bathroom and jumped into the shower. I stayed under the water much longer than usual in an attempt to avoid seeing Carter downstairs. It was a weekday, so he should have to go to work, right?

No such luck.

By the time I had gotten dressed and ventured downstairs, Carter had made breakfast for the both of us. Omelets (I didn't even know that I'd had any eggs). I sat down at the table and ate without talking. I could hear Carter rambling about the weather, work and any number of things that I couldn't focus on.

He put down his fork. "Alright. What's going on?" he asked.

"Nothing," I said innocently. "I'm just enjoying my breakfast."

The truth was that I was horrible with the morning after. But I wasn't usually this bad. It usually wasn't this awkward. Most of the other guys hadn't started out as friends, except for Denny. Maybe that was the problem. Maybe men and women could be either friends or lovers but not both. It was a horrible thought, and I tried to banish it from my mind immediately.

"That's a load of crap and you know it," he replied. "I could cut the tension in this room with a knife."

"I still don't know what you're talking about." I had started with denial and decided to stick with it.

"I think you do. I'm not going to let you give me the brush off."

"I'm sorry," I said honestly, putting down my fork. "It's just that I'm not very good at this. The whole 'relationship' thing. I have a horrible track record. I'm afraid we're ruining our friendship and you and Alex are the only people I know here. After I've screwed this up neither one of you will talk to me any more."

"I think you're probably exaggerating."

"No, I'm not. I've never had a single relationship that went well."

"Not every relationship is doomed from the beginning."

"Don't say I didn't warn you. Maybe you should get out before you waste too much time."

"That's okay," he said. "I think you're worth the effort."

"I might not be." I was pretty sure that I wasn't.

"I'll take the risk," he said. He smiled at me as he stood. "I've got to get into the office. But I'm coming back here tonight with dinner. We can talk more about this tonight."

"Fine," I said. He kissed me before he left. I didn't back away from him, but it took a lot of will power not to.

I watched him walk to his car. What was wrong with me? I thought. Why did I always try to push the good ones away and let the bad ones take advantage of me? What did I have against commitment? Why couldn't I let myself get close to anyone?

I spent the morning sifting through the wreckage of my past relationships. My life was a psychologist's dream. I'm sure they'd tell me I had abandonment issues. You didn't have to be a doctor to realize that being abandoned first by my father and then (for all intents and purposes) by my mother and finally to have my brother die had left me an emotional wreck. Anyone who tried to love me had to tread carefully, or they'd be taken out by a landmine.

It all began with Denny. He wasn't my first but he was my first love. He wanted a commitment, and I bolted for the hills. I literally ran away. We'd had a huge fight, and I just up and left the country without a word to him before I went. I spent the summer before university backpacking through Europe with some guy I met in Paris. Denny didn't know we were broken up until I sent a letter to my brother three weeks after I'd left. It was a horrible thing for me to do to him. I don't know why he still talks to me. If our positions were reversed I would never have forgiven him.

Then there was Andrew. I met him when I was in my first year of university. Blonde hair and incredibly sweet, as soon as he started to suggest living together, I sent him packing.

I didn't let either of them hurt me, but I'm pretty sure I caused them a lot of pain. That was my greatest skill: get in and out as fast as possible without getting hurt. And I kept getting better and better at it as I got older.

The list kept growing. It was incredibly depressing. It wasn't that there were a lot of guys on the list; it was just that the entire exercise was very painful. Why did I have such a hard time with commitment? Wasn't it supposed to be men that didn't want to be chained down? It wasn't that I wanted to be with a different guy every night. What was wrong with me?

Maybe just the fact that I was aware of my problem meant that I could avoid it this time. But part of me kept insisting that any relationship I was in would be doomed before it started.

Incredibly disheartened by the entire event, I attempted to finish my article. It certainly wasn't my best work, but at least I had it finished and emailed off to the editor by noon. I made myself a quick lunch and went out onto the deck with my laptop.

Distracted by other matters it hardly even bothered me that I couldn't get any work done.

At around 1:30 I heard a car pull into the driveway. I felt my mouth grow dry. I was terrified that it was Carter, and I didn't know what to do. I wasn't ready to talk to him yet. Nervously, I walked around to the side of the house.

A silver Volvo station wagon was parked in the driveway. I didn't recognize it. I did, however, recognize the driver.

"Maxine," I said in surprise as my sister stepped out of the car. "What the hell are you doing here?"

"Hello to you too, Kerrigan," she said as she walked around to the back of the car and opened the trunk.

"Hello. Why are you here?" I wasn't in any mood for games. And I certainly wasn't in any mood to deal with my sister.

"To be perfectly frank," she said, taking two very large suitcases out of her trunk, "I've left Steven, and I need a place to stay."

I was shocked. "What?"

"You heard me. Grab a bag."

Stunned, I did as she asked. I had carried a bag into the main room before I could speak again.

"Why did you come here and not to Mom's?"

She looked slightly amused.

"Really, Kerrigan, do you think I could stay with her? I don't think I could stand all her smoking and drinking. Plus she probably has some guy living with her and she wouldn't want me there."

I needed to sit down. To have Maxine say something bad about our mother was tantamount to sacrilege.

"Don't look so alarmed," she said, laughing. "It will be a good chance for us to get reacquainted."

It was on the tip of my tongue to tell her that I didn't want to get reacquainted and she couldn't stay with me. Instead, I chickened out and asked her how long she'd be here.

"For awhile," she said absently, looking around. "I'm not really sure. You don't mind, do you?"

"No," I lied. "But what about Tina?"

"She's away at school right now, and then she's going to summer camp. She'll probably come here at some point for a visit."

"How is she taking it?" I asked, ignoring the fact that Maxine mentioned the word 'summer', seeming to imply that she'd be staying with me for months. "I assume you told her?"

"What?" she asked absently.

"About leaving Steven."

"Oh. Yes, of course I told her. She's taking it fine." Her tone made me think that she didn't want to talk about it.

Fine. If she didn't want to talk about it, I didn't care. There'd be plenty of time ...

Suddenly the reality of the situation dawned on me.

"You're staying here," I said stupidly.

"Yes, Kerrigan." She was speaking slowly as if to a child. "I really didn't have any place else to go."

"What about Steven? Couldn't you two have worked things out between you? Maybe if you call him, tell him you'd made a mistake ..."

"No." There was no indecision in her voice.

I thought back to the few times I'd met Steven. He was about ten years older than Maxine, and I'd always thought he was a jackass. I pretty much hated him, and I could never figure out what Maxine saw in him. I assumed it was his good job, and the fact that he'd be a good father. Steven didn't strike me as the type of man to inspire strong emotions of any kind. Maxine was only twenty-five when they'd married, and I remembered how happy she'd seemed. Tina was born a year later (which would make her about fourteen now, I realized). Steven always seemed boring but harmless. He had a good job and made a ton of money. I couldn't understand why Maxine would leave him. It didn't make any sense. He didn't seem interesting enough to have an affair, so it must have been some other reason.

"Fine," I said. "I guess you can stay here for a while."

"Great," she said smiling. "I'm going to take my bags up to one of the rooms and then we can sit down and talk."

Suddenly I wished that it had been Carter's car. This was going to be a nightmare.

I watched Maxine head up the stairs with her luggage. She still looked good for a woman in her forties. In fact, if I didn't know her age I would have guessed she was somewhere nearer to thirty. Her hair, which had no sign of grey, was a darker shade of red than mine. Her eyes were clear green and actually quite striking. She was still fairly thin, and I guessed from the ease with which she carried her luggage that she probably exercised regularly (which was more than I could say about myself). I wondered absently if perhaps Maxine had been the one to have an affair. I immediately banished the thought from my mind. Not Saint Maxine.

"I took the room at the end of the hall," she said as she came back down the stairs. "It used to be mine when I was a kid."

"Really?" I was surprised.

She nodded.

"We came here every summer when I was little. I think I probably spent every summer here from birth until I was fifteen. You used to come here too until you were about five or six. But I'm sure you remember that."

I didn't. I'm sure Maxine saw the surprise on my face, and so I explained to her.

"I didn't know that. Mom never mentioned it to me."

"I guess I shouldn't be surprised," Maxine said. "Mom isn't much for living in the past."

"No, she isn't," I agreed. "The only family photo album I've ever seen is here in an old trunk."

"Really?" Maxine said, sounding interested.

"Yeah. It was in a trunk full of a lot of old stuff. You should take a look at it. I think most of the stuff in the trunk is probably yours. Or maybe Sebastian's."

"Thanks. I will."

The afternoon passed kind of awkwardly. I spent most of the day staring at my computer on the ground floor while Maxine was upstairs doing God knows what. I was tempted to go up and see what she was doing (I had this nagging feeling that she was going through my stuff), but I resisted and tried to focus on my work. I still didn't know what to say to Maxine, but I was dying to ask her about her and Steven. And, I wanted to know how long she was staying. How long would we be able to live together without one of us killing the other?

After a few hours curiosity finally got the better of me. I went upstairs and into her room. I knocked lightly on the door to get her attention.

"Maxine," I said. "Aren't you going to be missing work if you stay here?"

"I work from home," she replied, turning back to her unpacking.

"What do you do?"

"I do illustrations for children's books."

"Really?"

Maxine nodded.

"That's very cool," I said sincerely. "I had no idea you were artistic. Are you working on anything now?"

"Yeah. My materials are over there." She gestured to a few unopened bags in the corner. "I can show you what I'm working on once I've unpacked."

I came into the room and sat on the bed. She had taken the room that I had been using for my office. I wasn't just gaining a sister. I was losing an office. I made a mental note to move my desk out to give her some extra space. Then I thought better of it; if I kept the room cramped and uncomfortable, maybe she wouldn't want to stay for long.

"You brought a lot of stuff," I pointed out to her as she unpacked.

"I don't know how long I'm going to be here, Kerri," she said with a sigh. "I wanted to be prepared."

I watched as she started to unpack her art materials. She had quite a lot of stuff, and I realized that it was going to take up a lot of space in the room.

"We could probably find some space for this stuff downstairs," I suggested. "And you'd probably have more light in the main room."

"Thanks," she said with a smile. "Did you want to see what I'm working on?"

I nodded and went over to her. She opened her portfolio and passed it to me. I was really impressed. Maxine had talent (at least in my opinion).

"What's the story about?" I asked her as I flipped through the book.

"It's about a toy bear that gets separated from his owner while they're on vacation," she replied.

"Do you do a lot of these?"

"I've been getting more and more in the past few years. When Tina started school I started doing it a bit more seriously. There are a few writers that I work with. Usually on books for kids aged three to five."

"I can't even draw a stick figure," I admitted. "These are great."

"Thanks," she said, sounding pleased. She paused for a moment. "You know, I'd love to read some of your stuff. If you're working on anything, or have anything finished …"

This was really weird. Maxine and I were talking, and we weren't fighting. This had never, ever happened before.

And it was freaking me out.

I had a few options. I could make a quick escape. I could talk to Maxine and finally come to terms with all our issues. Or I could pick a fight.

I, of course, chose the third option.

"Just because you're going to stay here doesn't mean we have to be all buddy-buddy," I said in a nasty tone. "I haven't written anything that you'd want to read."

"Kerri …"

"I'm serious, Maxine. Just drop it."

"Fine." She turned back to her unpacking.

Feeling a little guilty for being a bitch, I left the room and went back downstairs.

Promptly at seven that evening, Carter pulled into the driveway. I wasn't even nervous, because since Maxine had arrived I'd forgotten all about him. At least there was one good thing to come from Maxine's sudden appearance. Carter looked very cute carrying paper bags full of takeout when I opened the door.

"I brought burgers," he said as he came in, smiling at me.

"Good," I said. "I'm starved. There's hardly any food in this place. But there's a problem."

"What kind of a problem? You're not just giving me the brush off, are you?"

"No, but keep it up, and I will." I scowled at him. "My sister's here."

"That must be her car I saw outside," he replied. "I thought maybe you had some guy over."

"Just Maxine."

"How come she's here? I know you two don't get along very well. Is there something wrong with your mom?"

"I'll give you the short version, since she's probably going to come down here at any moment. She needed a place to stay because she left her husband. This is one of the first signs of the coming Apocalypse."

"Wow. How long were they married?"

"Fifteen years. And they have a daughter."

"Do you know what happened?"

I shook my head. "She hasn't told me yet. And yes, I did ask her."

"Kerrigan, did I hear someone at the door?" Maxine came down the stairs. She raised an eyebrow at me when she saw Carter.

I blushed. "Maxine, this is Carter Stevens."

"The lawyer," she said.

"Nice to see you again, Mrs …"

Maxine interrupted him. "It's Maxine. And I'm sorry that I've ruined your date."

"It's not a date," I said quickly.

"I've got tons of food," Carter said, lifting up the bags to show her. "You should join us for dinner. After all, as Kerri said, it's not a date."

I winced slightly at the tone of his voice. But I silently hoped that Maxine would agree to dinner and allow Carter and me to put off talking about last night.

"Sure," she said looking at me. "As long as Kerri doesn't mind …"

"Please. Carter brought the food, and he made the offer."

We sat down at the table to eat, making awkward conversation.

"How did your writing go today?" Carter asked me.

"I sent my article off and tried to think about next week's edition."

"What article?" Maxine asked.

I told her about the articles I'd been working on.

"How about your novel?" Carter asked. "Did you make any progress there?"

"Yes," I lied, my mouth full of French fries. "I got a couple of ideas down."

"That's great," he said. I couldn't tell if he believed me or not, and I suddenly felt terribly guilty about lying.

"Carter, are you related to Leslie Stevens?" Maxine asked suddenly. "I remember a little Stevens boy from when I used to come here as a kid."

"Yeah," Carter said awkwardly. "I know Leslie."

"What ever happened to him?" Maxine asked. "I remember he had a younger sister named Alex, I think."

I looked at Carter. "Do you have a brother?" I was pretty sure that he hadn't mentioned any siblings other than Alex.

"No brother." He looked very embarrassed. "Leslie's actually my first name."

"I thought you looked familiar when we first met," Maxine said.

"Your name is Leslie?" I said, stunned. I tried not to laugh.

"I haven't gone by Leslie since I was ten," he protested.

"Your name is Leslie?"

"Yes, Abigail. My name is Leslie."

"Point taken," I said, subdued. I turned to Maxine. "So you knew Carter when you were younger."

Maxine nodded. "I even babysat Carter and his sister when I was thirteen. I only did it once though."

"Why?" I asked.

"The Stevens' never wanted me back," she replied.
"What did you do?"
"It wasn't her fault," Carter interjected. "I think it was my fault. And Alex's. It was mostly Alex's fault. We weren't always well behaved when our parents were out."
"It's big of you to admit that," Maxine said with a laugh. "Even if it is twenty-seven years too late."
"Alright," I said firmly. "What the hell happened?"
Maxine looked at Carter.
He sighed.
"I chased Alex into the bathroom where she locked the door behind her. Then I took the key and broke it in the lock."
"I had to call the fire department to get her out," Maxine finished. "Mr. and Mrs. Stevens pulled into the driveway just as the fire truck was pulling out."
I nearly choked on a French fry as I laughed.
"I thought Mrs. Stevens was going to kill me," Maxine added. "She used to give me dirty looks when ever she saw me in town."
"No wonder she can't stand me," I said.
After we finished eating Carter went home. He said he couldn't stay because he needed to change his clothes and see a client first thing in the morning, but I think at least part of it had to do with Maxine. I was a little relieved.
"What's going on?" Maxine asked after Carter had left.
"Nothing."
"Right."
"It's nothing," I insisted.
"It looked like something."
I sighed. "It's complicated."
"Do you want to talk about it?"
"Not really."
"He seems nice. And he's very good-looking."
"Maybe you should date him," I said angrily.
"Not my type," she said, choosing to ignore my tone. "Plus, I make it a rule to never date anyone I used to baby-sit. And he seemed much more interested in you."
"Christ," I snapped at her. "Yes, he's perfect. Everyone keeps telling me that. I just don't want a relationship right now."
"Fine. I didn't realize it was such a sensitive subject."
"Look, I'm going to bed. I'll see you in the morning."

I walked upstairs with Maxine watching me.

Denny and James arrived Friday afternoon. Emily stayed at home with the baby because he'd come down with some sort of an infection. I had mixed feelings about Emily's absence. A large part of me was happy she wasn't coming because I couldn't stand her. Unfortunately, there would be no one to keep Denny in line for the weekend. James was useless when it came to keeping tabs on Denny. I knew it was going to be my job to keep him away from Alex.

After my big revelation to Denny the other day, I think he was coming in part to protect his territory. It was a guy thing. Despite the fact that Denny and I hadn't dated in seven years (I didn't want to think about the affair), he was still jealous and protective of me. I didn't know if part of him was trying to take Sebastian's place. All I knew was that he was going to drive me nuts.

When I went out to meet their car, Maxine was sitting down on the dock. She was going to be a great distraction all weekend.

"Maxine's here," was the first thing I said when they stepped out of the car.

"What?" James asked, looking confused. "Why would she be here?"

"She left her husband, and now she's living here. With me."

"That's crazy," Denny said.

"I know."

"What are you going to do?" He asked, following me into the cottage.

"What am I going to do about what?"

"About Maxine."

"Nothing."

"You mean you're just going to let her move in with you? That will be nice. Two old spinster sisters living together. You should get a cat. I promise I'll visit you in the mental institution once you go insane."

"First of all," I said, punching him hard in the arm, "Maxine's not a spinster, she's separated. Second, I hate cats, and third, I'm not old."

"Fine. So, where is he?" Denny asked looking around.

"James?" I asked innocently. "I think he's still out by the car."

"You know who I'm talking about," Denny said. "Where is Carter? Has he been staying here?"

"Leave the poor girl alone, Dennis," James said as he entered.

"I'm not bothering Kerri," Denny said innocently. "I'm just looking out for her. They've only known each other for about a month. I just thought it was a little early for him to move in."

This coming from the guy who got engaged after knowing a woman three weeks.

"I think it's sweet," James said as he put groceries away in the fridge. "Carter is a great guy, and I think he's perfect for Kerri. You're just jealous."

"I'm not jealous," Denny protested. "I just don't want to see her acting like a little idiot over some small-town lawyer. He seems like a nice guy, but we don't really know too much about him."

"Compared to some of the men Kerri's dated, Carter's a down right saint."

"What is that supposed to mean?" Denny asked in an annoyed tone.

"Will you two knock it off?" I asked. "Neither of you will survive the weekend if you keep this up. I have a lot of property where I can bury bodies. Carter isn't staying here. Okay, so he's stayed here once. And only once. He's not moving in."

"Who's moving in?" Maxine asked coming into the kitchen.

"Carter," James replied for me. "That terribly handsome lawyer who's madly in love with Kerri. I'm James, by the way. I was at the will reading with Kerri, but she didn't feel the need to introduce us." He extended his hand to Maxine.

"Nice to meet you. Hello, Dennis." Maxine's tone cooled noticeably as she turned to Denny.

"Hi."

"Where's your wife?" she asked him.

"At home with our son," Denny replied somewhat sheepishly.

"It's nice that you're still able to get away on weekends," Maxine said sarcastically.

Denny blushed.

"So, why are we talking about Carter? Is he here?" Maxine asked changing the subject and looking around.

"No, he's at work right now," I replied. "But he and Alex are coming here for dinner tonight."

"Excellent," James said, smiling. "We can make sure that Carter's intentions towards Kerri are honourable. Or at least more honourable than Denny ever was."

"I think I'll call them and ask them not to come," I said quickly, reaching for the phone. It had been a horrible mistake to invite Denny and James up for the weekend. These people were going to embarrass me and drive Carter nuts all evening. Far better to take the easy way out and cancel our dinner plans. And I knew it would be a good idea for Denny to stay away from Alex.

"They're probably already on their way over here," James said, looking at his watch. "It would be rude to call them now and make them turn around and go home."

"Fine," I said, resigned to my fate of being humiliated all night. "Just promise me you'll behave yourselves tonight."

"Don't be ridiculous," Denny said. "Of course we won't behave. But Alex and Carter should definitely come to dinner anyway."

"You're just interested in seeing Alex. Keep in mind that you're married," I reminded him. "How is the baby?" Maxine was watching the scene with amusement.

"Fine," he said. "All he has is a cold. He has a little cold, and Emily goes off the deep end. She's driving me crazy." He sounded incredibly frustrated. I would have felt sorry for him if he hadn't been aggravating me so much.

"I honestly don't know why you married her," James said, shaking his head.

"I do," Denny said, looking at me.

Maxine raised an eyebrow.

"Yes, we all know why you married Emily." I could feel my anger rising. "You married Emily in some pathetic attempt to make me jealous, since you claim I have commitment issues."

"That's very interesting," a voice behind me said. I turned around, feeling myself go very red. It was Carter followed by Alex and Mr. Smith.

Mr. Smith came bounding over to me with an excited look on his face. I bent down to pet him in order to cover my embarrassment.

"Hello, you two," James gushed, rushing up to them and giving each of them a big crushing hug. "We've heard all about you and Kerri," he said to Carter. "We couldn't be happier. Well, *I* couldn't be happier. I'm not so sure about Denny. If I were you, I wouldn't be alone with him for a while."

My God, I'm going to kill him.

"Thanks," Carter said, looking confused.

"Ignore him," Denny said to Carter (while staring at Alex the entire time). "James is full of shit."

"No I'm not. I'm just happy that Kerri is happy. Unlike you, Dennis, I actually like seeing her in a relationship."

Why doesn't the floor ever open up and swallow me whole?

"What did I miss?" Carter whispered to me. He looked very confused.

"Nothing," I said. "James thinks he's being funny."

"I thought maybe we were getting married, and no one remembered to tell me."

"No, I just made the mistake of having friends."

"I don't think Kerri is enjoying this discussion," Carter said. "So let's talk about something else. How was the traffic on the way here?"

"Horrible," Denny said. "I don't know why people come up north every weekend if they have to fight traffic."

"You won't have to worry about that any more," I grumbled. "You won't be coming here again."

"Aw, you don't really mean that," Denny said, grinning at me. "Please can I come back and stay with you? I promise to behave myself."

I sighed. "You know I can never say no to you."

Carter raised his eyebrows at me.

"I'll keep that in mind," Denny said, winking at me.

"That's not what I meant," I said in frustration. This day was not going well. I should have stayed in bed.

"Carter," James chimed in, turning to face Carter. "Kerri isn't really that kind of girl. I know for a fact that she's said no to Denny several times."

"I hate you both," I grumbled under my breath. Honestly, the only one I could trust not to embarrass me was the dog.

"Why don't we eat something," Carter said.

I smiled him at him gratefully.

"Maxine," Carter said, turning to her. "This is my sister Alex. Although I'm pretty sure you'll remember her."

"Nice to meet you again," Maxine said to her as she sat down at the table. "I haven't seen you since the firemen got you out of the bathroom."

"I'd forgotten about that," Alex said with a laugh. "It was terribly traumatic. I don't know that I'll ever really get over it."

"What are you talking about?" Denny asked.

"Carter trapped me in the bathroom when Maxine was babysitting," Alex explained. "Maxine had to call the fire department to get me out."

"That must have been awful for you," Denny said in a flirtatious tone.

I shook my head and went into the kitchen. I didn't think I could stomach watching Denny flirt with Alex. Instead, I unpacked the food that James had brought from the city and set it on the table.

We all sat down at the table for dinner. The food was from my favourite deli near Yonge and Eglinton. Tasting it made me feel homesick. I had to stop myself from jumping in the car and immediately driving back to Toronto.

"How's the city been since I've been gone?" I wistfully asked James.

"Well, it misses you terribly, but strangely enough everything is still running without you."

"Maybe I should come back for awhile. Just to make sure everything is still where I left it."

"My couch is always available," James offered half heartedly. The last thing James wanted was for me to stay at his place. He was convinced that I would cramp his style.

"I'd say you could stay at my place, but I don't think Emily would like it," Denny chimed in.

"I think you should stay with James," Carter said firmly.

"Why?" I asked.

"Because you'd be more likely to spend the whole night on the couch if you stayed at James' place," Alex piped up helpfully.

"Gee, I'm glad that everyone thinks I'm a whore," I grumbled. I looked at Carter angrily.

"That's not what I meant," Carter said quickly, trying to dig himself out of a hole. "I just don't trust Denny."

"I never trusted Denny either," Maxine added. I shot her a dirty look, but she ignored me. "I heard stories from Sebastian," she said by way of an explanation. "But I do think Kerri is trustworthy."

"At least you're honest," Denny said with a lecherous grin. Maxine shook her head at him but laughed.

"Although this is a lovely topic of conversation," I began, "can we please talk about something else? Something that doesn't involve me."

"Okay," Denny began, looking at Alex. "What do you guys do for fun around here?"

"Well, there's always the pig races," Carter said deadpan with a thick Southern accent. "And on really exciting nights, we often go cow-tipping." Something in his tone told me that he didn't really like Denny. I hoped this wouldn't become a problem.

I wasn't the only one who sensed the tension. Alex chimed in to lighten the mood.

"Carter's just being a jerk," Alex said, grinning at Denny. "Actually, we were thinking that this weekend might be a good time to go to *Patrick's* for karaoke."

"Who's Patrick?" James asked.

"*Patrick's* is a pub in town," I explained to him. "Apparently it's quite the spot in the summer."

"It definitely is," Carter agreed, nodding.

"But didn't Karaoke go out of style years ago?" I continued.

"Maybe in the big city, but up here in the sticks it's still going strong," Carter replied with a grin.

"I don't know if I'm up for karaoke," Denny said nervously. I smiled at him. Denny couldn't carry a tune. In fact, Denny was one of those guys who sang only one note and sang it badly. When we were dating, he used to sing in the shower. It was one of the reasons I knew I wasn't destined to spend my life with him. I couldn't see myself listening to him sing every morning. He sounded like a drowning bear.

Maybe karaoke wouldn't be such a bad idea. Any opportunity to see Denny humiliated should be cherished. But then I saw the expression on his face.

"You don't have to sing," I said to him, feeling a slight twinge of pity for him.

"Actually, you do," Carter said.

"What?"

"If you're new to the bar, you have to sing," Alex said. "It's a *Patrick's* tradition."

"It's kind of like hazing without all the legal ramifications," Carter added.

"Oh my God," Denny said under his breath. He had turned a sickly shade of white, and he looked like he might puke. If he got this nervous just talking about it, it would be worth the pain of karaoke just to see him humiliated.

"Well, that counts me out," I said smugly. "I've already been there once."

"Doesn't matter," Carter replied. "You've never been there for karaoke night."

"That doesn't seem fair."

"I don't make the rules," Carter said. "I just enforce them."

"We'd love to go," James said. "And we'll all sing."

"Great," Alex said grinning. "I can't wait to hear all of you."

"You'll take that back as soon as Denny opens his mouth," I warned her with a laugh.

"Laugh it up, Red," Denny scowled at me.

I stuck my tongue out at him.

We finished eating and moved out onto the deck to enjoy the evening. It was warm and peaceful. I sat next to Carter, his arm comfortably draped over the back of my chair.

In fact, I was so comfortable I started to get a little uneasy. He was so nice—too nice for me. And he was also good-looking and sweet. Why was he interested in me? I couldn't figure out why he was still hanging around. We'd already slept together, so he wasn't waiting for that. It was very confusing. I knew that there had to be something seriously wrong with him, something that I hadn't discovered yet (like a basement full of corpses or webbed toes).

I saw Maxine look over at me. I could tell she was reading my thoughts as if I was broadcasting them across my face. It pissed me off. She had a concerned look on her face. I looked away and tried not to think about it. What right did she have to read my mind?

Alex and Carter left to head back into town shortly after midnight. I was reluctant to see Carter leave (another thing that pissed me off), but I wasn't prepared to let him stay over with Maxine, Denny and James in the house. I ushered Carter and Alex out before going up to bed alone.

Saturday morning dawned warm and sunny. The sun woke me up before 7:00 AM, but I refused to get out of bed. I retreated under the protection of my duvet. I laid around in my bed until a decent hour (ten-ish), before heading downstairs in my swimsuit, looking forward to a day of being completely lazy. I didn't have to worry about work, and I wasn't going to even think about my novel for the entire weekend.

James and Denny were already up. They were deep in discussion about baseball or basketball or some other sport I didn't care anything about. Being a good friend, James always played along when Denny wanted to talk about sports. I was pretty sure that James really only knew about tennis. At least I knew I'd never catch them discussing the women they'd slept with. Denny handed me a cup of coffee when he saw me come down the stairs.

"She's awake," Denny said. "It's amazing."

"What's amazing?" I asked between sips of coffee, my tone barely civil. I really hated when people started talking to me before I was fully awake.

"I didn't think you even knew there was an AM."

"Thanks."

"So, what are the plans for today?" James asked.

"Sunbathing, followed by swimming and sunbathing," I replied.

"Excellent ideas. Planning to do any work?" James asked. He had to say it. I knew I was pushing my luck by hoping to avoid thinking about work.

"How can I work when I've got house guests? Miss Manners says I must be a good hostess and spend my day entertaining you. And by entertaining you, I mean ignore you completely and let you do whatever you want."

"Miss Manners would be impressed," James said. "Maxine's already outside, in case you were wondering."

I wasn't, but I stepped out onto the deck to join her anyway. She looked up when I came outside.

"Hi," she said, looking at me from beneath her sunglasses.

"Hi." I sat down on a lounge. "Nice day."

"Yeah it is. What's going on with you?"

"What do you mean?" I didn't have any idea what she was talking about.

"You seem to be intent on ruining your relationship with Carter. I just want to figure out why."

I see.

"There is no relationship," I said.

"There could be. He's a nice guy, and I can tell that he really likes you."

"I don't want to get into this," I said with a sigh as I slouched down in my chair. "It's too early in the morning to discuss my love life. Besides, why do you care so much?"

"I just worry that it's my fault."

"What?" I asked, sitting up to look at her.

"I think it could be my fault that you can't seem to have a real relationship."

"That's crazy," I said. "Besides, why would it be your fault?"

"No reason, I guess," she said quickly.

I raised my eyebrows at her. Maxine was going loopy. First she shows up out of the blue and now she wants to discuss things that have absolutely nothing to do with her.

"Are you out here to sunbathe or to talk?" She asked with a frown.

"Fine. I'll shut up."

"Kerri, I'm sorry. I just …"

I raised my hand to stop her. "Don't worry about it, Maxine. I didn't really want to talk to anyone. I'm going to enjoy the sun."

I put my headphones on and turned on my iPod to block her out.

I spent the entire day being lazy. It was wonderful. I swam, read magazines and even napped out on the deck. When it came time to get ready to go out, one look in the mirror made me regret ever setting foot outside.

There on my nose were three new freckles. I yelled for James to take a look.

"I can't see anything," he said, squinting at my nose. "Are you sure you're not imagining it?"

"No," I said sulkily. "There are three new spots. They're huge and ugly, and I don't think I'll be going out tonight." I was very sensitive about freckles. I'd been lucky enough not to have too many, but still I should have been more careful.

"I thought I was a diva," he said. "Maybe you should invest in some sunscreen."

"Or a hat," Denny chimed in from outside the bathroom door.

"No one asked you for your opinion," I yelled back at him.

"Okay. I'll just call Carter and tell him you can't go out tonight."

"Fine," I grumbled. "I'll go out. But if anyone comments on my freckles, I'll kill them."

I wasn't sure how people dressed to go out for an evening in a small town pub. The one and only time I'd been out there hadn't been many people there. But according to Carter, Saturdays were usually a busy night. I threw on some casual clothing; something I thought would be suitable for a pub—low-riding dark denim jeans and a tight red tank top. My tattoo was showing and I decided to wear my hair loose and crazy.

"Have fun," Maxine said as James, Denny and I went to the door. I was impressed that she glanced at my tattoo without commenting. Maxine was definitely mellowing in her old age.

"Are you sure you won't come with us?" James asked. I had to stop myself from elbowing him. The last thing I wanted was my sister tagging along with us.

"Thanks, but I can't," she replied, much to my relief. "I'm expecting a call. Maybe I'll see you later tonight."

"I wonder who's going to call," James said to me as we got into the car.

"Huh?" I said, preoccupied. I was looking at my reflection in the rear-view mirror to see if my freckles were noticeable.

"Who is Maxine expecting a call from?"

"Probably just her daughter Tina," I replied, not really interested.

"I bet it's from a boyfriend," James said.

"Maxine doesn't have a boyfriend," I replied firmly.

"I wouldn't be so quick to dismiss the idea, Kerri," Denny said. "Maxine's very attractive."

"So now you've got a thing for my sister?"

"No," he replied. "I'm just saying that a lot of men would find her attractive."

"I really don't want to discuss my sister this evening, okay?" I especially didn't want the mental image of Maxine with some guy.

We managed to find a parking spot on the street in front of the bar. I was surprised at how busy the place was. Carter had said it would be packed, but I thought he had been exaggerating. Apparently, he hadn't.

The place was full (I assumed) of weekend cottagers, mostly people I'd never seen before in town. I liked it. It reminded me a little of home. Carter and Alex were waiting at the bar and waved when they saw us. I waved back and the three of us walked over (or actually, we pushed our way through the crowd to reach them).

There were a lot of women hanging around Carter. A lot of women of various ages. I wasn't sure how I felt about that. I wasn't jealous, but it was mildly annoying to see the guy I was sort of dating surrounded by desperate females. It wasn't jealousy that made me want to claw the eyes out of the blonde woman practically throwing herself at Carter. And it wasn't jealousy that made me practically run over to him and put an arm around him.

"Where'd all these people come from?" Denny asked when we were finally able to reach them.

"We had them shipped in today just for you," Carter said. I could practically hear Carter calling Denny a jackass in his sarcastic tone. "We wanted to make a good impression. We'll be returning them tomorrow morning." He leaned over to kiss me.

The expressions on the faces of the nearby women were very satisfying. Half of them looked like they wanted to strangle me, and the other half just turned on their heels and left.

"This is nothing," Alex yelled to be heard over the music. The karaoke had already begun and some guy was doing a very bad, very loud rendition of 'Benny and the Jets'. "You should see this place on long weekends. It's a zoo."

"What do you call this?" I asked her as someone bumped into me on their way to the bar. I stumbled into Carter.

"I'd call this a slow night," she replied.

"Now I remember why I hate karaoke bars," Denny whispered in my ear as the singer grew even louder and more off key.

"No. You hate karaoke bars because you can't sing," I whispered back to him with a laugh.

I looked over at Carter. He had an annoyed look on his face. I couldn't figure out why at first, but then I realized that Denny was standing too close to me and had a hand on my waist. For some twisted reason, I was pleased at Carter's reaction.

He took a step closer to where I was standing, glaring at Denny's hand which was still on my waist.

"You look great," Carter yelled to me over the loud music.

"Thanks," I said. "Didn't Mr. Smith want to come tonight?"

"Sadly, I had to tell him the truth about you and me, and he's taking it rather badly. In fact, he hasn't spoken to me for days."

"Maybe I should talk to him," I said.

"That would probably be a good idea," Carter replied. "The poor guy doesn't seem to have any of his old spunk. He doesn't even try to bite the mailman anymore." He smiled at me and then gestured towards the bar. "Do you want anything to drink?"

"Rum and coke," Denny said, grinning. Carter shot him a dirty look.

"I'll have a beer," I said, elbowing Denny. Carter looked ready to kill him.

"I don't think Carter likes Denny very much," James said to me after Carter left to get the drinks.

"I think it's because I told him to warn Alex about Denny," I replied.

"I think it's more likely because you and Denny have a history," James said back to me. "And Denny has his hands on you. Carter is definitely smitten with you."

"What are you, an eighty-year-old woman? No one uses 'smitten' anymore."

"Okay, he digs you. He's hot for you. He wants what you've got. Better?"

"Give it a rest, '70s boy."

"I'm just never sure what terms to use when talking about hetero-love. The whole thing creeps me out." James gave a little shudder to further illustrate how he felt.

"Do you have a point?"

"I'm getting to it," James said with a grin. "He can tell that Denny still has lingering feelings for you. He's just not sure about your feelings for Denny. He's jealous. It's very simple."

"I'm glad you haven't given up your hobby of analyzing my relationships."

"Just be careful. Carter's a great guy, but he's still a guy. He'll only take so much before he'll pack it in."

Carter arrived with the drinks just then, putting an end to any further discussion of the subject. He handed Denny his drink, passed me a beer and steered me towards an empty table, leaving Denny, James and Alex at the bar.

"I thought we might be able to talk better over here," he said to me by way of an explanation. It wasn't any quieter at the table. The only difference was that we weren't with Denny.

"Don't you think it was kind of rude of us to take off like that?"

"I don't think they care," he said, gesturing back towards the group. Denny and Alex were laughing together and James was off talking to some blonde guy. Some friends, I thought. They probably hadn't even noticed that we'd left.

Finally, the Elton John-wannabe stepped off the stage and the MC picked up the microphone.

"Wonderful," he said, clapping. Very few people in the audience joined him. The guy really had been horrible. "That was Cameron from Markham. Don't give up your day job, buddy." Several people laughed, and Cameron turned bright red. "Now get ready for our next victim. This lovely young lady hails from the big smoke. She's a writer staying here for the summer, but this will be her first appearance here at *Patrick's*. Please welcome to the stage Miss Kerri Shepherd."

"What the hell?" I whispered to Carter as people in the bar burst into encouraging applause.

Carter grinned at me while he clapped. "I took the liberty of providing the MC with all of your names."

I stared at him in disbelief. "I am *not* drunk enough to get up there."

"Come on, don't be shy," the announcer said, scanning the crowd.

Everyone started chanting my name while clapping. I thought of slipping under the table but it was too late. Before I knew it I was standing and walking up to the stage. I shot Carter a dirty look as the microphone was placed in my hands. He was a dead man when I got back to my seat.

"What do you want to sing?" the announcer asked me.

"I don't know," I hissed at him covering the microphone with my hands.

"Pick something quick," he said back. He wasn't very friendly up close.

"Something by ABBA."

I looked out into the crowd while waiting for the music to start. It felt like hours before I heard anything. Denny raised his glass to me and winked. I could see that he had his hand on Alex's thigh.

Finally the music began. I felt a great relief when I recognized the tune. Then I remembered that I had to sing along to it and nearly threw up.

"'You can dance, you can jive ...'" I heard myself singing along to 'Dancing Queen'. At least it was a song that I knew. My face was scarlet, and I was going to kill Carter when I got back to the table.

Finally, after what felt like hours, the song finished. The crowd burst into applause (I'm sure they were glad to have me off the stage), and the MC took back the microphone. Thank God. I tried to run off the stage but the MC threw an arm around my shoulder and wouldn't let me leave.

"Let's hear it for Kerri!" he said. The crowd applauded again. "Should she come back again?"

There were cheers and a few whistles from the audience.

"Well, my dear," the MC said, again stopping me from leaving. "You've now been officially welcomed to New Ferndale. We've got a parting gift for you." He handed me a bag, and I rushed off the stage.

"Now we'd like you get re-acquainted with an old friend," the announcer continued. "Here's everybody's favourite bar maid, Cecilia, singing one of Patsy Kline's greatest hits."

I made my way back to the table as the woman began singing 'Crazy'. She was pretty good. Much, much better than I had been. I was glad that I didn't have to follow her. Thank God the guy who'd gone before me had been horrible.

"That was great," Carter said, trying to kiss me. I shrugged him off and punched him in the shoulder. "Ow! What was that for?"

"You must not know Kerri very well," Denny said as he and Alex sauntered up to the table. "Kerri doesn't like making a public spectacle of herself. You'll be sleeping alone for a while until that temper of hers cools down."

"I thought you were great," Alex said.

"Definitely," Carter agreed, rubbing his arm.

"I didn't hit you that hard, you big baby."

"Sure you did. For a little thing you pack quite a punch. Why are you so mad?"

"It was embarrassing," I said.

"So what?" Carter said. "Everyone here does it. It's goofy, but it's a tradition around here. No one cares if you're horrible. It's fun. The guy before you was terrible, but he comes in here every week and does another Elton John number."

"You could have at least given me a few minutes to prepare," I said pouting.

"I'm sorry," Carter said. "But if I had warned you, you would have snuck out the back door."

"She definitely would have done that," Denny agreed, laughing.

Carter glared at him. He didn't seem to like the fact that Denny knew everything about me. Every time Denny opened his mouth, Carter got more and more annoyed. One of these days, he was going to punch Denny in the face.

"I wouldn't laugh too hard," Carter said. "I gave the announcer your name too."

Denny turned white. Carter smiled smugly.

"So, do you forgive me?" Carter asked with a grin. "Or do I have to get a restraining order against you?"

"You're safe for now," I said in a warning tone. "But watch your step."

"I'll be careful," he replied leaning in to kiss me. This time I let him.

"Thank you, Cecilia," the announcer said as the woman finished her song. "Next on the list is one of our home-grown boys. Carter Stevens."

Carter grinned at me and bounded up onto the stage. He looked like a big kid. All the people in the audience went wild. Especially the women. I noticed a large group of them move closer to the stage.

"Carter's a big ham," Alex said to me. "He does this all the time. They love him here. Especially the women." She gestured over to a group of women who looked like they were going to see Elvis perform.

"Oh give me a break," I said, rolling my eyes.

"The ladies love him," Alex said. "Apparently he's quite a good catch. He gets this response all the time."

"Good to know."

"You'll have to be careful, Kerri," Denny said to me. "Looks like you've got some competition for Carter's affection."

"I don't think she has to worry," Alex replied.

"Carter's got a special request tonight," The announcer continued. "He'd like to dedicate this song to a special someone in the audience. Kerri, this one's for you."

I shook my head at Carter as he winked at me. He was loving every minute of this. It was ridiculous. A couple of those women looked like they were going to burst into hysterics any minute.

I recognized the song immediately. 'Sweet Caroline'.

"Neil Diamond is one of his favourites," Alex whispered to me.

"Of course he is," I replied. Carter really did seem like a Neil Diamond-kind of guy.

Carter was good. The crowd loved him, and he seemed to thrive on it.

"Does he always sing Neil Diamond?" I asked Alex.

He flashed me a big grin just before launching into the chorus.

"No," Alex replied. "He only sings Neil Diamond when he's in love."

Chapter Nine

By mid June I was lying to everyone about my writing. I'd even begun lying convincingly to myself. Despite my claims to the contrary I still hadn't made any progress with my novel. I was growing increasingly more frustrated with every passing day. The only writing I'd been able to successfully do was for my column.

And I usually waited until the last minute before writing it. I was pretty sure that I was going to get a call from the editor any day telling me that the column had been cancelled.

The weeks had gone by quickly. Maxine and I did our best to stay out of each other's way, and I was surprised at how well we were getting along. She wasn't nearly as annoying as I remembered from when I was a kid.

Of course, we weren't in as close quarters as we were when I was little. In our old apartment, we were practically tripping over each other. Here at the cottage, if (and when) she started bugging me, I could head into town, go down onto the dock or even hide out in my room pretending to work. Most days Maxine spent her time working on her illustrations, but sometimes she'd take her car and leave for a couple of hours and wouldn't tell me where she'd been. Or the phone would ring, and she'd dash off into her room with the portable. I never asked her what was going on and the suspense was almost killing me. The only reason I didn't just come out and ask her was because I didn't want to get into any personal conversations with her.

I was sitting out on the deck enjoying yet another wonderfully warm summer day when the phone rang. Maxine was off on one of her morning excursions. I darted inside to get it.

It was the editor of the paper where my column was being published. Immediately, my stomach clenched, and I felt like I was going to throw up.

"Hello, Kerrigan," he said to me. "I hope I'm not disturbing you."

"Not at all," I replied nervously. I crossed my fingers in the hope that this call wasn't to cancel my column. The money I was saving this summer was going to pay my rent in the fall. If he cancelled the column, I was going to be broke. I couldn't picture myself living at the cottage in the fall with my sister. The thought made me shudder.

"I just wanted to let you know how much I'm enjoying your column."

I sighed in relief. "That's great," I said, feeling much better. "I thought you were firing me."

"Firing you," he laughed. "Not at all. In fact, the reason I'm calling is that your column has been so well received, we want to offer you a full-time, year round job writing a syndicated Canadian tourism column."

I was slightly stunned. I wasn't sure if I had heard him correctly. This is great, I told myself, reining in my excitement. I was suddenly imagining myself traveling around the world, writing about exciting and exotic locations. And I'd be traveling on someone else's budget.

"Can I get back to you about this?" I said, my voice sounding slightly strangled even to my ears. I didn't want to let him know how excited I was. It could ruin my ability to get a good contract. Maybe I should talk to Carter about contract negotiations, I thought to myself.

"Certainly," he replied. "But don't leave us hanging for too long. We want to get going on this. Then we're going to want to get you back to Toronto for some publicity shots. And we'll discuss your first location. We were thinking somewhere out east."

Publicity shots? What was he going to do with those?

"I'll get back to you shortly," I promised.

I was ecstatic. This was the first true writing success I'd had in a long time. I didn't know who I should tell first!

I called James to tell him the good news. He'd been the one to take the brunt of my complaining when I couldn't write a word. I knew he'd be just as excited as I was. It was only fitting that I call him first.

Unfortunately, he wasn't home. Disappointed, I left him a brief message asking him to call me back. Next I called Denny. He sounded distracted and quickly brushed me off. I didn't even get a chance to tell him about the column. Must be having problems at home, I thought to myself. I was getting annoyed. Here I was with huge exciting news, and none of my friends were able to celebrate with me.

I needed more friends: my list of people to call consisted of two names. It was totally pathetic. I even started to wish that Maxine hadn't gone out that morning. At least then I would have been able to tell her.

Then I remembered Carter.

I got dressed quickly and headed into town. I thought I'd take Carter out for lunch to celebrate. I didn't bother to call first. I just assumed he'd make time for me.

When I reached his office, Carter's secretary, Miss Durand, didn't seem too pleased to see me.

I wasn't going to let her sour disposition ruin my good mood. I knew that the only reason she hated me was because I was dating Carter. I was in such a good mood, I almost felt sorry for her (of course her long legs, perfect figure and overall model-like appearance actually made that impossible).

"Can you tell Carter that I'm here?" I asked her, using my cheeriest voice and ignoring the dirty looks she kept throwing me.

"I'm afraid he's with a client right now, Miss Shepherd," she said with thinly veiled hostility.

"Tell him that I'm waiting in the coffee shop for him," I replied. "And let him know that it's important."

She shot me a look that expressed her disdain loudly. I smiled back at her and walked across the street. As I entered the coffee shop, Carter's parents were exiting.

Oh great.

"Kerrigan," Dr. Stevens said to me. He smiled and I actually felt that it was sincere. "It's nice to see you again. Isn't it, dear?"

Mrs. Stevens smiled coldly at me. "How are you doing?"

I felt like telling her that I was sleeping with her son. That would wipe the smug smile off her face. Of course, I didn't tell her that. If I had, I'm sure she would have reached out and grabbed me by the neck. She really was a terrifying woman.

"I'm fine, thank you both." I was in such a good mood that even Carter's stuck-up mother couldn't bring me down. "How are you both doing? I haven't seen you since Carter's party on the May long weekend."

"We've been good," his father replied. I could tell he was embarrassed for his wife's behaviour. "Carter has told us that you two are dating. We both think it's wonderful."

Mrs. Stevens forced a smile. I could tell what she thought about Carter dating me, and it was anything but wonderful. I suddenly felt overjoyed to be dating Carter.

"Your son is great," I said, enjoying her discomfort. I know I'm sadistic ... "You both must be very proud of him."

"Yes, we are," Mrs. Stevens said. "And we love him very much. We don't want to see him get hurt."

What was she getting at?

"I don't want to see that either," I replied cautiously.

"I'm glad we're in agreement," she said. I practically got frostbite from the tone of her voice.

"In agreement about what?" Carter said as he walked up behind me, putting an arm around my waist.

"They're in agreement that you're a great guy," his father said to him.

"Is that all? I could have told you that," he said, kissing his mom on the cheek. "Hi, Mom. Dad."

"We should be going," Mrs. Stevens said.

"You and Kerrigan should drop by for dinner one evening this week," his father said as they left.

"Sorry about that," Carter said, kissing me after they were gone. "If I'd known you were in front of the firing squad, I would have ditched my client."

"Were you afraid to kiss me in front of your mommy?" I teased him.

"Of course not," he said seriously. "I just didn't want her to have a stroke in the middle of down town."

"Aren't you just the perfect son!"

"That's what I've been telling her for years," he said as we entered the coffee shop. "So what's the big news? Not that I'm not glad to see you in the middle of the day."

"I got a great offer today from my editor," I began, too excited to drag out the suspense. "He wants me to write a year-long, syndicated column. It's going to be a travel column and they want me to start soon."

"That's great," Carter said, not sounding too enthusiastic.

Maybe I hadn't clearly indicated just how great this really was.

"It *is* great," I replied emphatically. "It means I'll have a steady pay check for as long as the column runs. And it means national exposure. A syndicated column is great."

"I didn't realize you wanted to be a columnist. I thought you were a novelist, not a travel reporter."

"I can be both," I replied defensively.

"How well is that going for you this summer, trying to do both?"

"I'm doing fine, thank you very much. Besides, it's not really any of your business." I was getting annoyed at him. He was supposed to be happy for me without question. That was how it worked.

"I'm only saying this because I care for you," he replied, looking serious. He gently grabbed my hand. I shook myself free.

"You don't have any idea what it's like to be a writer," I said, my voice growing louder. "You're a lawyer. You don't know what it's like to wonder where your next pay check will be coming from. A steady job is a good thing. I can write a novel any time."

"You should do what you want," he said, remaining frustratingly calm. I hated arguing with someone who wouldn't lose his temper. "I just think that tying yourself down to the column is a mistake. I think it's holding you back."

"I think you should mind your own business."

Carter stood. "Fine. I guess we'll talk about this later when you've calmed down a little." He left the shop.

I was fuming. I really hated it when someone else got the last word in a fight. I stormed out of the coffee shop, all eyes on me.

I hated this stupid town. Everyone knew him and me. I'm sure they all knew everything about our relationship.

The drive back to the cottage did nothing to cool me off. Maxine's car was still not there. She was useless as a sister and a roommate. Once I got inside, I noticed that the message light was flashing on my phone. James had returned my call. Eager for someone to vent my frustrations on, I called him back.

I quickly explained the situation to him.

"You're on my side, right?" I asked him. "You think the column is a great idea, don't you?"

I needed validation.

"Carter might be right, sweetie," he said cautiously.

I exploded. "Why can't any of you be happy for me? This is my life, and now I'm getting a chance to be paid for doing something that I love. You'd think my closest friends would be excited about this."

"Anything that makes you happy will make me happy," he replied. "But you're a novelist, Kerri. I can't see you being content with a column. You don't even like writing the column this summer. Imagine what it would be like doing it full-time. In a few months you'd start to get restless. Carter knows you better than you're willing to admit."

"I can't deal with you right now," I said to him. "I'll have to call you back later."

I hung up and paced the front room. I couldn't believe these people. Why wouldn't they see that this was a good thing? All I wanted was one person to say exactly what I wanted them to. If only Denny had been free to talk. He would have agreed with me.

Somewhere in the back of my mind a little voice was telling me that I was being unreasonable. I did my best to ignore it. When I was unreasonable, I wanted to be completely unreasonable. I never did anything half-assed.

A knock at the door jolted me back to my senses. I went to answer it. Carter was standing there. One look at his face and all my earlier anger came rushing back to me. In fact, since talking to James, I was even angrier than before. And since Carter was there, he was going to take the brunt of it.

"Look, Kerri ..." he began as he stepped in the room.

"What the hell do you want?" I yelled at him.

He looked surprised at my tone but shook it off and continued as if I hadn't spoken.

"We need to talk."

"No, we don't," I said, crossing my arms combatively over my chest. "You need to get out of here. I'm not in the mood to be patronized right now."

"I don't patronize you," he said.

"Sure you do," I replied. "Saint Carter the lawyer slumming it with an unemployed writer. The real reason you don't think the column is a good idea is because you can't bear to let mommy dearest know that you're dating someone that doesn't have a high-powered career."

"You're acting crazy," he said, looking slightly hurt. "Why should I care what you do for a living?"

"Exactly. Let me be concerned with what I do."

"I'm just trying to give you an honest opinion."

I laughed bitterly. "An honest opinion?"

"Yeah."

"Right. You just want to control my life so I can live up to your standards."

"What are you talking about?"

"You've been embarrassed about me since we met. I'm sorry I'm not as well-bred as you are. Maybe your mother was right about me."

"What is wrong with you?" he asked loudly, sounding very frustrated.

"There's nothing wrong with me," I shouted back.

"Then why are you acting insane?"

"Why are you even here?"

"I'm just worried about you," he said.

"You don't need to be," I replied. "It's not like I want you here and I definitely don't need you here."

"I thought we were in a relationship," he said. "I care about you, Kerri. And I can't understand why you're acting like this."

"Look, Carter, I don't know how they work things here in Hick-ville, but where I come from, sex and an occasional dinner together don't necessarily indicate a relationship. If that was the case, I'd still be in a relationship with Denny."

Whoops. I didn't mean that. I immediately realized I'd made a mistake.

"I see," he said quietly, his jaw clenched.

"I don't mean right now," I said. My little slip only served to make me angrier. "I'm not sleeping with Denny right now, you idiot. He can only handle one affair at a time, and right now he's sleeping with your sister."

Why was I saying this? I didn't even know for sure that Denny was sleeping with Alex. I was deliberately trying to hurt Carter.

"What do you think about that?" I continued smugly. "Your little sister is sleeping with a married man who has no intention of leaving his wife."

"I think you're lying about us," he said, taking a step towards me. "I know you feel more than you're letting on."

He reached out to take me by the hand. I took a step back, avoiding his touch.

"You're delusional," I said with a cruel laugh. "There never was anything more."

"I don't believe you," he said firmly.

"Believe me. I don't feel anything for you. You're kidding yourself if you think otherwise."

"Right. I'm not Denny."

"No, you're not. He knew when to leave."

"Maybe you should give him a call. I'm sure he'll rush right over."

"You don't know what the hell you're talking about."

"I know you."

"No, you don't. I've known you for a couple of months. That's it."

"It's long enough."

"You don't know a thing about me. You knew my father and thought you'd try to weasel into my life. It doesn't work that way. I don't do relationships."

"What are you talking about?"

"I never had any thoughts about having a relationship with you," I continued. "You're not my type."

"What was I to you?" he asked, his voice angry and loud. "Was this just some sort of a way for you to kill time? Was this a game with you? Your sister was right. I've never met anyone as incredibly selfish and self-centered as you. You're like a child who needs to be the centre of attention wherever you go. Especially male attention."

I could see the anger and hurt in his eyes.

"I think I'd like you to leave now." My voice was completely calm. I had my hand on the back of the couch for support. I was sure if I let go, I'd hit the floor.

"Fine," he said. Carter turned and left the cottage. "I'll give Denny a call tonight and tell him to rush on over. You're going to need someone to help fill the time." I heard the front door slam behind him and then heard his car drive up the road.

It was only when I was sure he was gone that I let go. I fell to the floor in a heap and started to cry.

Chapter Ten

It was mid-July. I'd been avoiding town as much as possible ever since I'd ended things with Carter, and we were getting dangerously low on food. I wouldn't even let Maxine go into town. In fact I didn't even want her to leave the house. I didn't want to be alone, even for the hour it would take for her to get supplies. I'd been eating cereal without milk for the last two days. Despite her concern, I could tell that Maxine was getting annoyed with me. I wouldn't even call the grocery store to get them to deliver.

Denny and James both bumped their vacations up by a few weeks in order to spend time with me. I was sure Maxine had called them and asked them to come. They were convinced that I was depressed. I wasn't. Honestly. I just felt like sleeping late most days and sitting around in my pajamas.

I spent most days lying in bed. Maxine kept insisting that I eat, which was probably a good idea.

I couldn't work either. My articles were getting shorter and shorter, written based on my memories of things I'd seen in town. I was sure that the editor was going to call and fire me any day, and I didn't even care.

I didn't understand what was wrong with me. Usually after a break-up I craved chocolate and other comfort foods. I could channel my disappointment and anger into my work. This was different. I had no appetite and no energy.

And I was really mad at myself. Every time the phone rang I kept expecting it to be him. I kept imagining that I heard his car coming up the drive. I was jumpy, and I was driving Maxine nuts.

"You can call him, you know," she said one day in frustration.

"I don't know what you're talking about."

"Carter. You can call him. You don't have to just sit here and mope all day."

"I'm not moping," I insisted. "And I don't want to have anything to do with him."

"Yes, you do. You miss him."

"No, I don't," I said. "I've just been really lazy lately. I think maybe I've got the flu."

"Right. Then what's with the music?"

"You know I'm an ABBA fan," I said. "There's nothing strange about listening to music."

"You've been listening to the same song for two weeks straight. It's starting to drive me slightly nuts."

It was on the tip of my tongue to tell her that no one had invited her to stay, but maybe she had a point. And I was worried that if I said anything, she'd leave, and I'd be alone again. Maybe I *was* acting like a ridiculous little idiot. But I liked 'Winner Takes it All'. There was nothing odd about a person listening to their favourite song over and over. The fact that the song was about a couple that had broken up was just a coincidence

Thankfully, when Denny and James arrived on Friday evening they brought tons of food. Maxine took it from them gratefully.

"Thank God," I said as I went outside to help them bring in the groceries. "I was getting a little sick of dry corn pops."

"You could go into town and buy groceries," James said. "There's no law against that. Or you could let Maxine go for you."

"Yeah, but I don't want to run into anyone," I replied.

"God, Kerri. You look like shit," Denny said in shock as he looked at me.

"Thanks," I replied.

"No seriously," he continued. "You look like you've been dragged backwards through a bush. When was the last time you had a shower and changed out of that robe?"

"A couple of days ago," I lied. I couldn't remember the last time I'd actually gotten dressed. The days were starting to blur together. Maxine shot me a dirty look.

"First thing you're doing is having a shower," James said. "Then we're going to burn that robe. It needs to be put out of its misery."

"Thank God," Maxine sighed. "I'm pretty sure that robe has been getting up at night and walking around by itself. I was afraid I was going to bump into it in the hall."

"I'm so lucky to have such a supportive sister and friends," I said sarcastically.

"Yes, you are," James said cheerfully. "But you really should go inside and change."

"Why?"

"We've got company coming for dinner."

"Who?" I asked, feeling an incredible sense of dread.

"Alex," Denny replied nervously.

"No way," I said firmly. "Definitely not. I don't think that's a good idea. Alex is not on my list of people to see right now."

"I think it's a great idea," Maxine disagreed. "You need to start seeing people again. And Alex is as good a place to start as any."

"I see people all the time," I replied. "I'm seeing three of you right now, aren't I?"

"Well, we've already invited her," James said, "and unless you want to seem incredibly rude, she's coming."

"I don't have a problem being rude," I protested.

"Well, I do," Maxine said firmly. "We're not cancelling. So unless you want Alex telling Carter that you look like something a cat puked up, you should have shower."

"Fine," I said, completely exasperated with them. They weren't going to give in and I just didn't have the energy to fight them any more. "I'll go and have a shower."

The water seemed to reinvigorate me. I'd been feeling rather tired the past few weeks, even though I'd been sleeping more than usual. It probably was the flu.

Maybe they were right. I needed to get dressed. The sight of my ratty old housecoat strengthened my reserve to put on some clean clothes and put my best foot forward.

By the time I was out of the shower and dressed, Alex had arrived. She was sitting out on the deck with Denny, James and Maxine. I stopped at the top of the stairs and watched the four of them talk for a while. It was like I was frozen. I couldn't make it any further down the stairs. I thought that I should just turn around and go back to bed. Unfortunately, Maxine looked up and saw me. She waved at me and gestured for me to move forward. Taking a deep breath, I went out to join them.

I wasn't looking forward to seeing Alex. In fact, there was only one person I was dreading more.

But strangely enough the sun didn't explode and the world didn't stop spinning just because I saw my ex-boyfriend's sister. Alex looked up at me and smiled when I stepped out onto the deck.

"Well look who's alive again," James said when he saw me. "You look much better than you did twenty minutes ago."

"Thanks," I said sarcastically. I sat down next to Maxine and tried to pretend that Alex wasn't there. "You can always count on your friends to tell you when you look hideous."

"We only do it for your own good, Kerri," Denny said. "We knew that you didn't want Alex to go back to Carter and tell him that you looked like crap."

At the mention of Carter's name, I felt my cheeks grow hot. I looked over to Alex to see her reaction.

She very politely pretended not to notice my embarrassment. I knew there was a reason why I liked her. "Don't worry. I'll tell him you looked great," Alex said in a comforting tone. "I brought someone who wanted to see you."

She gestured towards the dock.

"Mr. Smith!" When I called out to him he came bounding up onto the deck. He jumped up in excitement when he saw me.

I sat down on the deck next to him, petting him. He laid his head on my lap. I really was happy to see him.

"How come you've got Mr. Smith?" I asked Alex.

"He'd been acting a little strange lately," Alex said. "He was driving Carter nuts. I didn't tell him that I was bringing Mr. Smith here."

I read between the lines to understand that she didn't tell Carter that she was coming here either.

"So how's Carter taking the big break-up?" James asked. I was going to kill him. The man had no tact.

"He's been in a really bad mood for the past couple of weeks," Alex said frankly. "But I think he's getting over it. He went out with his secretary the other night."

Maxine put her hand on my shoulder to keep me from reacting.

It felt like someone punched me in the stomach. I *knew* he was interested in her. I knew it from the first time we met. How could he not be? She was tall, blonde and gorgeous. What did it matter that she was an idiot and had no personality? He obviously didn't care about that sort of thing. Like all men, it only mattered what she looked like. And I knew he and I were finished. I really didn't blame him. I should be glad that he's moved on, I thought. Of course, that didn't stop me from being furious with him.

"That's nice," I said, practically choking on rage. I only hoped that my face wasn't red. I felt Maxine's hand tighten on my shoulder. "I'm sure they're very happy together." I only hoped that I didn't sound too bitter.

"Well, my parents are happy about it," Alex said, seemingly oblivious to my feelings on the matter. "They've always wanted them together. But it's a little early to be buying a wedding present. They've only been on one date."

Isn't that perfect. I was so glad that his mother would be happy.

"So," Maxine said, trying to change the subject for me. "Anybody like a drink?"

"I'd love one," I said, standing up. "In fact, I'll help you get them."

I stood and went into the kitchen with Maxine following behind me after taking everyone's drink orders.

"How are you doing?" she asked as I got out the alcohol. I got out lots of alcohol.

I poured myself a big shot of tequila and drank it immediately.

"That good," Maxine answered herself. "Be careful."

"What do you mean?" I asked, taking another shot.

"Don't drink too much. You'll probably regret it tomorrow morning."

"Don't be ridiculous," I said, heading back outside.

Unfortunately, she was right. The rest of the evening passed in a blur of alcohol. I woke up the next morning with a horrible headache, unable to remember anything from the night before.

James and Denny went into town the next day to buy more groceries. Leave it to two men to only bring enough food to last one night. Specifically, they went to buy more alcohol, since I'd managed to drink pretty much everything we had the previous night.

I hadn't been that hung-over since my first year of university. Last night, drinking a ton of booze had seemed like a good idea. I realized my mistake after spending half the morning throwing up. Alex was going to be able to tell Carter that I had acted like an idiot. I only hoped she'd be able to restrain herself.

Maxine came into my room at around 11:30. I wasn't asleep, but I was hiding under my duvet. The knock on my door nearly killed me. My head was pounding so hard that I hoped Maxine was coming to kill me.

"How are you feeling?" She asked in a voice that sounded incredibly loud.

"I'm okay," I lied.

She raised an eyebrow at me.

"Okay, I'm not fine. My head hurts, I've thrown up more times than I can count and the room was spinning all night."

"Did the alcohol help at all?"

"Not really," I admitted grudgingly. I hated being wrong.

"Drink this," she said passing me a glass.

I eyed it suspiciously from the safety of my duvet.

"It's just water," she said. "You're dehydrated."

"Thanks." I took the glass from her and tried to drink it. "You should have made me a Prairie Oyster. They're supposed to be good for a hang over. It's …"

"I know what a Prairie Oyster is," Maxine interrupted. "The last thing you need is more alcohol in your system. It's still seeping out of your pores. You smell like a distillery."

"I know," I groaned as I tried to sit up. "I don't think I'm ever drinking again." Famous last words.

"Then why did you send Denny and James out to get more alcohol?"

"It never hurts to have a fully loaded bar," I replied with a shrug.

"Well, I just wanted to check on you before I head out. I thought I should make sure you were still alive. Alex went back into town with Denny and James, so you'll be on your own for awhile."

"I didn't even realize that she'd stayed here last night."

"After you passed out, we decided that Alex should stay. I thought it would be a good idea to have a doctor around in case you had alcohol poisoning. She left the dog here when she went back into town. She said she'd be back to pick him up this evening."

Great, I thought happily. At least I'd have Mr. Smith to cheer me up today.

"Okay, I'm getting out of bed soon," I said. "Where are you going?"

"Out," she said cryptically, leaving my room without shutting the door behind her.

Mr. Smith came running in through the open door. He jumped on the bed and lay down next to me. I curled up next to him and fell asleep for another half hour.

Eventually, I managed to get out of bed. Once I was fully conscious, I drank nearly a gallon of water before the room stopped spinning. Feeling almost completely human again, I decided to go for a swim. Slathering myself in sunscreen, I threw on a large-brimmed hat and ventured out into the mid-day heat. I headed down to the dock with Mr. Smith tagging along behind me.

Standing on the dock looking into the water made me re-think my decision to enter the lake. I stood there for a few moments, trying to determine if my head would actually explode on contact with the water. I was pretty sure that it would.

Mr. Smith looked at me hopefully. I could tell he was really anxious to get in the water.

"Hi there," a voice called.

Had Mr. Smith learned to talk?

I looked up. A guy on the neighbouring dock waved at me.

I wasn't in the mood to talk to anyone. My head hurt, I felt nauseous and I was sure I looked like an idiot. Mr. Smith sat at my feet whining, echoing my sentiments.

"Hello," the guy said again.

"Hi," I replied. He seemed like the kind of person who wouldn't give up until they got an answer.

"So have you made up your mind?" he asked.

"About what?"

"Are you going in or not?"

"I don't know," I said. "I think it's still too early in the day to go into cardiac arrest from the cold water."

He laughed. "It's really not that cold," he said. "I was in this morning, and it's practically tepid. I'm pretty sure your dog wants to go in."

"I think I'll have to take your word for it," I replied, backing away from the edge of the dock. "I'm going to pass for now." I turned to the dog. "But you can still go in, Mr. Smith." I picked up a stick and threw it into the lake.

Mr. Smith eagerly dove into the water to fetch it.

The guy grinned at me and started to walk over to my dock. He was tall, with blond hair. I couldn't tell what colour his eyes were because he was wearing sunglasses. He was definitely very attractive. I began to feel my hangover disappear.

"I'm Duncan MacDonald," he said, extending his hand to me with a smile.

"Kerrigan Shepherd," I replied, shaking his hand.

"Kerrigan's a great name."

"My friends usually call me Kerri."

"You've never been here before, have you Kerri," he said. "Because I'm sure I'd have remembered you."

A cheesy pick-up line, I thought to myself. Less than five minutes in. My opinion of Duncan slipped a little. Cheesy pick-up lines were always annoying, and even more so when I was fighting a hang over. But he was still cute, so I could probably forgive him.

"Oh, God," he said sheepishly, "I didn't mean that to sound like it did. I only meant that since I've been coming up here, I've never seen anyone out on the dock except an old man who didn't like me very much. He used to yell at me every time I had friends over for a barbeque."

I grinned at him. Maybe he wasn't hopeless. "Yes, actually I am new to the lake."

"Are you the new owner? I guess the old guy finally kicked it."

"Yes," I replied, not wanting to tell him that I inherited the place.

"I own the place next door," he said, gesturing to his place. "My friends and I come up every year from New York. I'm here until mid-August. How long are you here this summer?"

"I'm actually living here right now," I replied.

"Are you here with your family? Husband and kids?"

I smiled at him. "My sister's been staying with me for awhile. But no husband and no kids."

"Great," he said with a grin. "Since we're neighbours, why don't you come over for a barbeque this afternoon?"

Mr. Smith chose this moment to rush up on shore, drop the stick at my feet and then shake every drop of water off his body and onto Duncan and me.

"Mr. Smith!" I said, shrieking at the water. It was colder than I had expected. I was glad I'd decided not to go in.

Mr. Smith looked up at me with his big brown eyes.

"Your dog's name is Mr. Smith?" Duncan asked, looking confused.

"Yes, but he's not actually my dog, he's ..." How do I explain that the dog belongs to an ex-boyfriend? "He belongs to a friend." That seemed like a safe explanation.

"He seems like a great dog."

"He is," I said, petting Mr. Smith's wet head.

"So, how about it? Do you want to come to my barbeque?"

He was definitely flirting with me, and it did wonders for my otherwise fragile ego.

"I've got friends staying with me," I said, "otherwise I'd say yes. They're in town right now buying groceries."

I didn't know if I was ready to socialize with strangers, despite how nice he seemed.

"They're invited too, of course."

He smiled at me again. He really was cute. And suddenly the thought of Carter and his secretary made me reconsider. If he could date someone else, I could certainly go to a stupid barbeque.

"Great. We'll come." I flashed him a big smile.

"I should head back to my place," he said, "but you and your friends should come by in a couple of hours."

"Okay."

"And you don't need to bring anything. We've got tons of food."

When I got back to the cottage, Denny and James had returned. Along with groceries, they'd brought Alex.

"Hello," I said. "Don't you ever work?" I asked her.

"Not today," Alex replied with a grin. "It's Saturday." She shifted her eyes over to Denny. Oh no, I thought. I'd seen that look before. She'd fallen for him, hook, line and sinker. I was going to have to tell Denny to be careful with her. I really liked Alex. I'd broken up with her brother, and she was still being nice to me. But if Denny did her any damage, I doubt she'd talk to me any more. "Actually, I'm here for Mr. Smith. Carter wants him back."

"Why does he have to go?" I didn't want Mr. Smith to leave. I'd never had a dog of my own, and I'd grown strangely attached to Mr. Smith.

"The dog does belong to Carter," Alex said. "And he still thinks Mr. Smith's been with me the whole time."

"Fine. But you don't have to take him right now," I protested. "You guys can stick around here today."

"And do what?" Denny asked. "You haven't exactly been the most cheerful person lately. Are we going to spend an exciting afternoon watching you mope or helping you get drunk? We did that last night, and I'd like to actually have some fun on my vacation."

My friends wanted to ditch me. My sister had abandoned me. And I was supposed to be the one who needed cheering up.

"You can always go home," I said cheerfully.

Denny raised an eyebrow at me.

"Why are you suddenly in such a good mood?" he asked. "What's going on?"

"Well, I just thought that since we're all here, we might as well go to a party this afternoon," I said.

"What are you talking about?" Denny asked.

"I just met one of the neighbours, and we've been invited over for a barbeque. It sounded like it might be fun, so I told him we'd come over."

"A party with the New York boys," Alex said, not sounding too pleased.

"You've met them?" I asked her.

"I've seen them around," she replied. "They're all young, good looking and rich."

"Well, I don't know about all of them, but the owner was pretty cute," I said.

James looked smug while Denny looked annoyed.

"What's going on with you two?" I asked.

"We had a bet on how long it would take you to find a rebound guy," James said. "My money was on July, while Mr. Negative here said you'd wait until the first of August. But I told him our little Kerri always bounced back fast after a break-up. She's a fast mover, I said."

"What are you talking about?" I asked.

"Every time you end a relationship, you get a rebound guy," James said in a matter-of-fact tone, "and usually the rebound guy is Denny."

Denny turned bright red. I snuck a look at Alex, who was trying desperately not to laugh.

"I'm pleased to see that you've chosen a new rebound guy," Alex said.

"I hate you guys," I grumbled.

"The truth may hurt, but it's still the truth," James said

"Look, Duncan is not a rebound guy," I said. "He's just the next-door neighbour. I have no intention of getting involved with him. And I'm not on the rebound."

"Fine," James said in a tone that definitely indicated that he didn't believe me.

"What's fine?" Maxine asked, coming into the cottage.

"We left Kerri alone for about three hours, and she's already met a new guy," Denny explained to her.

I threw my hands up in frustration.

Maxine raised an eyebrow.

"Really?" she said. "Maybe we should have forced you out of the housecoat earlier."

"We've all been invited next door for a barbeque," I said trying to ignore all of them. "All of us. Not just me. It's a party."

"Yeah, but the guy only spoke to you," Alex pointed out. "He's never even seen the rest of us."

"Okay, you've got me. We've actually been having a torrid affair, and now I want it out in the open."

"A torrid affair?" James said. "You don't really strike me as the type."

"Thanks a lot," I replied.

"I really picked the wrong time to come home," Maxine said, shaking her head.

"Yeah," I agreed. "Where were you?"

"Out," she said absently. Then she turned to Alex. "Alex, you're a doctor. Do you mind if I ask you a question?"

"Not at all," Alex replied.

The rest of us looked at Maxine in anticipation.

"In private," Maxine said emphatically.

Denny, James and I went out onto the deck reluctantly.

"What's that all about?" James asked me as soon as we got outside.

"How should I know?" I replied with a shrug.

"Well," Denny said, "you are her sister. Don't you talk about anything?"

"Not really," I admitted. "How long have you known me? Have I ever talked to Maxine? This is the longest I've been with her since I was ten. Plus, I've been busy. She probably just wants to talk to Alex about me and Carter and doesn't want us to hear."

"Right, Kerri," Denny said sarcastically, "since everything is always about you."

"Not everything," I said sulkily. "But I think this is. It's the only explanation that makes sense. She's been harping about Carter for a while now."

"Alright then, where has she been going?" Denny asked.

"I bet she's been talking to a lawyer about her divorce," I said, suddenly realizing that this was actually a very likely explanation. "In fact, I bet that's what all the phone calls have been about." I was impressed by my powers of deduction.

"You're probably right," James admitted. "But I still don't think Maxine's talking to Alex about you."

"Why not?"

"She hasn't been looking too well lately," he said. "And I heard someone up this morning being sick."

"That was probably just me," I said. "Remember how much I drank last night?"

James seemed to accept that explanation, but what he said struck a chord with me. Had Maxine started to look ill? Was I so wrapped up in my own life that I didn't even notice that my sister was sick? What kind of person was I?

I suddenly felt slightly ill myself. What if she really was sick? What if that was actually why she'd come to stay with me? Maybe Maxine was dying and this was her way of tying up loose ends. It dawned on me that I was actually starting to like my sister. I was starting to rely on her being around. I didn't know how I'd be able to stand watching another sibling die. Once was already too much.

I looked up when Alex and Maxine stepped out onto the deck. I carefully studied my sister's face. She didn't look sick. I was sure she had been talking to Alex about me. I felt an unreasonable amount of relief, despite my annoyance at her interference.

Of course, Sebastian hadn't really looked sick until the end, I reminded myself. Maybe what Sebastian had was genetic.

I stepped towards Maxine as Alex went to talk with Denny and James.

"Are you alright?" I asked her quietly.

She looked down at me, her eyes sparkling with amusement. "I'm fine Kerri," she said. "Why do you ask?"

I didn't want to explain my thoughts about her dying. It seemed silly.

"Well, you were talking to a doctor," I began.

Maxine cut me off with a wave of her hand.

"I'm fine," she said firmly. "I was just asking Alex for some advice about something."

She had been talking about me.

"Can you tell me about it?"

"Not right now," she replied. "But I might tell you later."

I gave up. I knew she wasn't going to tell me anything and Alex certainly wouldn't volunteer any information. I was going to have to be content with my conviction that she was talking about me.

We went next door to Duncan's cottage later in the afternoon. His cottage was huge; at least twice the size of mine. He was sitting out on the back deck with his friends. When he saw us approach, he jumped to his feet. He was just as cute as I had remembered him. I could sense Denny and James grinning at each other.

"Kerrigan," he said. "I'm so glad you could come. I want you to meet my friends. Charlie, Dave, Tony and Glen."

I nodded hello to them and then introduced my friends to them. Duncan's friends looked to be around his age, and all four were fairly good-looking. Alex had been right about them. Unfortunately, they seemed to be perfectly aware that they were good-looking. They all seemed very interested in Alex, which really seemed to annoy Denny. Strangely enough they also seemed interested in Maxine, which I could tell she found amusing. I don't think any of them was over thirty-five years-old—far too young for Maxine. None of them paid any attention to me, which I found a little depressing.

The five of us (Maxine, James, Denny, Alex and I) found seats on the deck. Charlie got up and passed a beer to me.

"Duncan warned us that you were off-limits," he said to me with a knowing grin. He seemed a little drunk even though it wasn't even four in the afternoon yet.

"Leave the girl alone," Duncan said as he pulled a chair up next to mine. He shot Charlie a dirty look. Charlie pretended to be offended before heading back over to Alex and more alcohol.

"Sorry," Duncan apologized. "My friends are Neanderthals. Especially when they've been drinking."

"He wasn't bothering me," I said.

"I'm glad," he said with a grin. "But he would have if he had hung around much longer. He's really bothering your friend." He gestured to Alex who wasn't doing very well covering her annoyance. Duncan continued. "So tell me. What is it that you do that allows you to stay up here all summer?"

"I'm a writer," I said, waiting for his reaction.

"Really?" He seemed impressed. I couldn't tell if it was an act or not. "What kind of writer?"

"Mostly fiction," I replied. "But I've been doing some freelance articles lately."

"What have you written?"

"Right now, I write a travel column that is possibly going syndicated." Talking about the article only served to remind me about my fight with Carter. I pushed the memory down and continued. "I wrote a novel a couple of years back as well. But the column and the freelance stuff pay better and give me a lot of freedom." I immediately went on the defensive and felt the need to justify myself.

"What was your book called?" He was giving me his undivided attention.

"*Musings on Life*," I said. "It's pretty obscure, so don't feel bad that you've never heard of it."

Few people had actually heard of it. I think fewer than twenty people had even read it.

"I haven't read it," he admitted. "But I'd love to. Where can I get a copy?"

"I don't think you'll be able to find it in any stores," I said. "I can lend you a copy, if you'd like. But don't feel obligated to read it."

"Don't be ridiculous. I'd love to read it. I can't wait." He smiled at me, his clear green eyes shining.

I felt very pleased with myself. Here I was, the object of attention of a rich, handsome, obviously intelligent man. Carter could do whatever he wanted with his slut of a secretary. I didn't care.

Then why did I keep thinking of him, a voice in the back of my head chimed in cheerfully. I tried to banish that thought from my head but it didn't work.

Instead, I turned all my attention back to Duncan. He was still talking about my book.

"I can't believe you wrote a novel," he was saying. "I've never met an author before. At least, I don't think I have. Was it difficult? What's the book about?"

"It's ..." I struggled for words to describe it. "It's probably easier if you just read it. It's kind of a coming-of-age story about a girl and her relationship with her mother."

"Autobiographical?"

"No," I said shaking my head. "At least, not intentionally."

"I'm really very impressed. I'm sure you must get told that all the time."

"Not really," I said. "Not too many people actually read the book. Some people thought it was depressing."

"Well, I can't wait to read it," he said emphatically.

I wondered if he was being honest or just telling me what I wanted to hear. Right then, I didn't really care.

"And you must have been very young when it was published," he continued. "That alone is impressive. I know how hard it is to be taken seriously when you're young. When I started my company ..."

I looked over to see how the others were fairing, allowing my attention to Duncan drift for a moment. He didn't seem to notice and continued talking. Alex looked irritated and was at the center of Duncan's friends. Denny kept trying to push his way closer to her, but he kept getting blocked. Duncan's friends appeared to be working as a team to keep Denny away from Alex. It was actually very effective, and I was impressed. Emily should consider hiring them to follow Denny around twenty-four-hours-a-day, I thought. James appeared to be talking about sports to Tony. This amused me to no end, since the only sport James really enjoyed was tennis, and Tony didn't seem to be a tennis kind of guy. Maxine seemed to be fighting off the advances of Glen. She looked annoyed but didn't seem to need any assistance. It would do her good to be hit on by a good-looking younger man. A meaningless fling might help her get over Steven and her crumbling marriage.

I finally tuned back to what Duncan was saying. I had no idea what I'd missed but he didn't notice.

"... and so I bought this place three years ago for a song. I've spent the last couple of summers fixing it up."

"It's very nice," I said vaguely, not really focusing on what he was saying. What was I complimenting?

"It should be," he replied firmly. "I've put enough money into it. But thankfully the US dollar is so strong right now that everything I buy up here is practically half price."

"That's great for you."

"It is, isn't it?"

"So, what do you do?" I asked him. I really should join into our conversation, I thought. I hoped that he hadn't told me about his job when I wasn't paying attention.

Please don't be a lawyer.

"I'm in the high-tech industry. Luckily, I wasn't hurt when all those IT companies went bankrupt. I owned my own computer software company. We were bought out by IBM a few years ago. I made a killing. Now I'm working as a consultant."

"That's very interesting." It really wasn't, but what else was I supposed to say?

"It really is, isn't it? Not that I need to work," he continued in the same boastful tone. "I just can't imagine being retired at thirty-six. I think I'll work until I'm forty and then spend my life traveling around the world."

I could see Denny out of the corner of my eye. He was listening to our conversation and rolling his eyes at everything Duncan said. I wanted to shoot Denny a dirty look but there was no way to safely do this without Duncan seeing. All I could do was turn my full attention back to Duncan.

"... and then I bought the Sea-doos to go along with it," Duncan was saying.

Okay, so he was a little boring and a bit conceited. But not everyone I meet has to be a great conversationalist, I told myself.

The conversation was even more boring over dinner. I felt really awkward. Duncan seemed to be overly interested in everything I had to say, and I was conscious of Denny sitting nearby listening to the whole thing. I felt like he was laughing at me. Duncan was turning out to be incredibly dull. But maybe I was just being too critical. I tried my best to be interested.

A few hours later and we were still in pretty much the same seats. I could tell that Maxine, Denny, James and Alex were all very eager to leave. And Duncan's friends didn't appear to be having any more fun than we were. Dave and Glen stood and stretched suddenly.

"Alright, Dunc," Glen said. "We've had enough."

"We want to head into town to go to the bar," Dave added. The other guys nodded in agreement.

"Kerri, do you and your friends want to join us?" Duncan asked me.

I really didn't want to. It was actually one of the last things I wanted to do. It was right up there with going to the dentist or having to sit through a Yanni concert. I didn't want to risk running into Carter. I knew it was stupid, especially since I was completely over him (and there wasn't anything to get over, I kept reminding myself). But I wasn't sure what I'd do to his secretary.

"I think I'd rather just stay in tonight," I replied casually.

Maxine shot me a sympathetic look that showed she understood why.

"You guys go," Duncan said to his friends. "I think I'll stay here with Kerri."

"You don't have to do that," I said quickly.

"I want to."

I was touched. He seemed like such a nice, normal guy. Even if he was slightly boring and a little self-centered.

Denny looked over at Alex. "I think I'm going to give Alex a lift back into town," he said. I knew what he was really saying.

"Don't forget Mr. Smith," she added.

"Fine. I'm going to give Alex and Mr. Smith a ride back into town," Denny corrected himself.

"Why is the dog going with you?" Duncan asked. "Is it your dog?"

"No," Alex said. "He's my brother's dog."

Duncan raised his eyebrows and looked like he wanted to ask more questions. Thankfully, he didn't. I wasn't in the mood to discuss Carter.

"I've got to make a phone call," Maxine said, standing to head back over to the cottage. "I'll see you shortly, Kerri."

James, however, surprised me. "I think I'll tag along with the boys," he said.

"Really?"

He nodded. "It might be fun."

"Okay," I said to him.

"I'll get a ride back out here later," James added. "Or maybe I'll just stay at Alex's with Denny."

Denny shot him an incredibly dirty look.

I sat on the deck with Duncan and watched the others leave.

"Why don't we go for a boat ride," Duncan said to me after everyone else had left. "I can show you my new Star Craft."

"Sure," I said. We walked down to the dock, and he helped me into the boat.

It was a beautiful night for a boat ride. The water was calm, and the night breeze was balmy. It would have been a perfect evening if only Duncan could have talked about something interesting. The guy was turning out to have no personality. He kept talking about his boat and his cottage and his money. After about ten minutes, I tuned him out and enjoyed staring at the stars. We stayed out for an hour before heading back into shore. I was a little sad to see the dock. I'd had great evening, even though Duncan was boring. It wasn't bad for a first date. But it wasn't really a first date, I reminded myself. I was just getting to know my neighbour. I wasn't even sure if Duncan was date material. He was cute, rich and seemed to like me. I would have to be crazy to pass on him. Except he was boring, self-centered and kind of conceited, a voice in my head added.

But if Carter could date his secretary, I could date my neighbour.

"Do you have any plans tomorrow?" Duncan asked as he walked me to my cottage.

"Not really," I said. "Although I should try and do some work."

"Great. I'm going to teach you how to water ski."

I didn't know how to water ski, but it was annoying that he just assumed I wouldn't know.

He leaned over and kissed me lightly on the cheek when we reached the door. It was kind of sweet.

"I'll see you tomorrow at eleven for water skiing lessons."

I watched him walk back over to his place before entering the cottage. It was the first time in several weeks that I felt a sense of happiness entering the house.

That is, until I actually got inside. The place was quiet, dark and empty. Maxine had already gone to bed. I was disappointed. I had assumed she was going to wait up to ask me about my evening. Something about it made me feel lonely. I realized I had become dependent on Maxine and the thought depressed me even more. The house felt almost as empty as it had my first night there. Turning on all the lights, I went upstairs and climbed into bed.

Chapter Eleven

I awoke the next morning just after dawn to the sounds of birds chirping cheerfully outside my window. I hadn't slept well, tossing and turning through most of the night. I woke up feeling exhausted and irritated. Stupid birds, I thought. Why did they always have to greet the morning right next to my head? It was like they purposely tried to stop me from sleeping. I was convinced that the birds had a conspiracy against me. I was going to get them back someday.

Was this a sign that I was going nuts? Thinking that the birds were out to get me?

I jumped out of bed and threw the window open.

"Shut up!" I screamed. "Shut up! Shut up! Shut up!"

I slammed the window shut and jumped back into bed. I tried in vain to get back to sleep but I was too angry. I pulled my pillow over my head and tried to block out the birds. It didn't work. The birds wouldn't be quiet. I finally decided that I probably should get out of bed.

I sat up and tried to think rationally. A few deep breaths and I stopped feeling homicidal. Maybe I should take up yoga, I thought.

Since I was wide awake at an ungodly hour, I decided I should try to make the most of it. An early morning swim was just what I needed to kick start my day, I thought. This was only because we were completely out of coffee and any other products that contained caffeine. Why did Denny and James remember to buy three cases of beer, Twinkies and salsa but forget coffee? We didn't even have any coffee-flavoured ice cream. The cold lake water should be enough to clear my head, I thought. I pulled on my bathing suit and headed for the stairs.

On my way down the stairs, I saw Denny. He was just entering the cottage and he was tiptoeing around so as not to make any noise. He looked very nervous and had a guilty expression on his face.

"Late night?" I said loudly to him. I was standing on the stairs with my arms crossed over my chest.

He jumped. I was still on the stairs, and he hadn't seen me as he came in.

"Jesus Christ," he exclaimed, clutching his chest. "Are you trying to give me a heart attack?"

"So where were you all night?"

"What are you, my mother?"

"No. And I'm certainly not your wife."

He cringed at the word wife.

"Before I dropped Alex off, we stopped in at the pub for a drink. I didn't think it was right for me to drive back out here, so I spent the night on her couch." His story sounded rehearsed and I wasn't going to let him get away with it.

I raised an eyebrow at him.

"Scout's honour," he said. "I was a perfect gentleman."

Right.

"I'm sure you were," I said sarcastically. "Keep in mind how well I know you."

He looked sheepish.

"Not that I'm trying to change the subject, but I saw Carter last night."

"Really," I said with what I hoped was indifference. My face felt hot, and I had butterflies in my stomach. I hated that just the mention of his name caused this.

"He was out with his new girlfriend. She's a real bimbo."

"That's nice," I replied, trying to sound as casual as possible.

"I just thought you'd want to know," he continued. "He may have been out with another woman, but he looked miserable."

Suddenly, I felt slightly cheered up.

"Really?"

Denny nodded. "Of course, it might have just been the fact that he saw that I was out with his sister. I don't think he likes me very much."

"Of course not," I said, venting some of my anger at Carter onto Denny. "Is he supposed to like the married guy who's sleeping with his little sister?"

"If you're going to put it that way ..."

"What other way can I put it?" I asked him. "I don't think there's anything you can do that would make Carter like you. Except maybe go back in time and not sleep with Alex."

"You're just full of helpful suggestions today," he said sarcastically. "It must be because you're up so early."

"What do you mean up early? I've been sitting here all night waiting up for you. I was out of my mind with worry."

"Sorry. Next time I'll call."

"You'd better, mister. As long as you're living under my roof you'll do as I say."

"Wow. Was your mom like that, or are you just channeling Emily?"

"No. My mom was more like 'shut the hell up, I've got a hangover' and 'why can't you kids eat somewhere else'. She did teach me how to hide cigarette burns on furniture. That's one thing you'll never learn from Martha Stewart."

Denny laughed as he made his way past me and into his room.

Promptly at eleven, Duncan arrived at my door as promised. He was dressed in his bathing suit and was holding a life jacket.

"Ready?" he asked with a grin.

"As ready as I'll ever be," I replied nervously. I grabbed my towel and followed him to his boat.

Two hours later, I found that I had muscles in places that I'd never even known about. I had never been in so much pain before. My legs wouldn't cooperate as I tried to get out of the boat, and I couldn't lift my arms above shoulder height. With Duncan's assistance I struggled to walk back up to the deck where James was out sunbathing. I felt like I had been pulled behind wild horses all morning. I was sure that my arms were a couple of inches longer than they had been when I had started my day. None of my sweaters were going to fit me any more.

"How did it go?" James asked me from behind his sunglasses.

"Wonderful," I said with a grimace as I climbed the steps onto the porch. "I think I stayed up for about five seconds."

"She wasn't that bad," Duncan replied with a laugh. "Near the end you managed to get up almost every time."

"And now every muscle in my body is killing me," I replied, stretching my arms. "Plus, I think I swallowed half the lake." The whole experience was like being pulled underwater by a motor boat, which was actually a pretty accurate description of my water skiing ability.

"If you're not too sore, do you want to come with me into town for a bit?" Duncan asked me. "I want to get some groceries, and I'd love some company."

"Sure," I replied. James raised an eyebrow at me. "Just give me five minutes to change."

When Duncan left, I turned to James.

"What's the big deal?" I asked him.

"Yesterday, you wouldn't even have thought about going into town."

"Yeah, that was yesterday."

"You're finally heading out into the rest of the world," James replied. "I'm impressed. Never underestimate the power of the rebound guy."

"First of all, Duncan is a friend, and that's it. Second, I'm not on the rebound. To be on the rebound implies that I was emotionally involved with someone. And I wasn't."

"Right."

"Of course I'm right. There was nothing between Carter and me. We were just killing time together. I was bored, he was there. That's all that it was. He obviously has had a thing for his secretary for a while now. It's great that they've finally gotten together. I wish them the best." I didn't think my voice sounded too bitter.

"He really did a number on you, didn't he?" James said. "Or rather, you did a number on yourself."

I shook my head and limped inside to change.

Or I went inside with the intention of changing.

I was distracted by the sight of Maxine talking to some guy in the driveway.

'Talking' wasn't exactly what they were doing.

'Making out' was a better description.

I was stunned. Forgetting that I was only wearing my bathing suit, I ran outside.

"What the hell is going on?" I yelled.

Maxine broke away from the guy with a guilty look on her face.

"I didn't hear you," Maxine said.

"What are you doing?" I asked. "You're a married woman." Part of me couldn't believe what I was saying. I kept remembering the number of times I'd slept with Denny since he got married. I'd never thought about marriage as any sort of restriction on my behaviour. But this was about Maxine, not me.

The guy looked at Maxine with a raised eyebrow.

"Kerri, this is Jack," Maxine said. She had stepped away from him a bit but was still holding his hand.

"I'm very happy to meet you," Jack said with a huge smile on his face. "Finally. I've heard so much about you."

"I've never heard anything about you," I said bluntly.

He kept smiling. "That's understandable," he said.

I just stared at him with a shocked expression on my face.

He was of average height with thick, light-brown, curly hair. His hair was graying slightly around the temples, and I guessed he was in his early to mid forties. He was a nice looking man and seemed very happy.

"Jack's going to be staying here for a few days," Maxine said. She must have noticed a funny look on my face because she continued. "That's alright with you, isn't it?"

I nodded in agreement before turning to go back inside. I was in a daze. James was just coming in from the deck and noticed my stunned expression.

"What's wrong?" he asked me.

"The end of the world is coming," I said. "Maxine has a boyfriend."

I ran upstairs as quickly as I could with my muscles screaming at me. After changing into the first clean clothing I could find, I ran back outside just as Duncan pulled into the driveway.

"We're going to have a little chat when I get back," I said firmly to Maxine as I ran by her and jumped into Duncan's car.

"Who's the guy with your sister?" Duncan asked as I got in.

"I don't have a clue," I replied.

Duncan parked out in front of the grocery store. He had a small, flashy sports car that he parked diagonally across two spots. I looked around for any familiar vehicles, but I didn't see anything. It seemed safe to go inside.

"I just need to get a few things," he said, pulling out his list. "Actually, it seems that I have to pick up a lot of things. Five guys eat a lot of food."

"That's why I always make my guests bring their own food," I replied. "I haven't been to town in weeks."

"You'll turn into a regular hermit," he replied. "Aren't most great writers hermits?"

"I'm not sure," I said with a laugh. "I think a lot of them were alcoholics too." I was easily on my way to being one myself.

I grabbed a cart and followed Duncan around the store. He was actually a pleasure to shop with. He was funny, and he didn't talk about himself for almost an entire minute while we were inside. It was a welcome change.

We were headed to the check-out counter when Duncan stopped.

"I forgot to get milk," he said. "I'll be right back."

As I watched him walk away, I saw Carter. Oh shit. I felt my face go red and my heart start to beat faster. There were butterflies in my stomach. A knot in my throat was preventing me from swallowing. I looked around quickly. Nowhere to hide. I thought about hiding under the cart, but it was too late. He'd seen me and was walking over. Crap.

"Hi," he said awkwardly.

"Hi." He looked great.

"So, buying groceries?"

"I'm with a friend." Actually, he looked amazing.

"I haven't seen you in town for a while."

"I've been busy." What a lie. But I wasn't going to let him know that I'd been staying at home in my housecoat and pajamas for the last two weeks while he had been out on the town with his secretary.

Had his eyes always been that blue?

"Yeah, Alex told me that your friends were visiting again."

"How is Alex?" Why was I asking this? I saw her last night!

"She's good."

"That's nice."

"Yes."

"How's Mr. Smith?" I asked after a moment of incredibly awkward silence.

"He's okay. I think he's been a little depressed lately though."

Then we both spoke at the same time.

"I hear you're ..."

"I'm glad to see ..."

We both laughed nervously.

"You first," he said to me.

"No, you go first."

"I'm glad to see you again," he said softly. "You should come by sometime."

Great. It's the 'I hope we can still be friends' speech. Usually I was the one giving it. I felt my body grow tense.

"I'd like to, but as I said, I'm really very busy." I kept my tone as cold and impersonal as I could. I looked at my watch. "I'm late. I've got to go."

I started to leave. Then I felt his hand on my arm. His touch was electric. I got goose bumps all over my body. God damn him.

"Don't go," he said quietly. "We need to …"

At that moment we were interrupted by Duncan.

Shit.

"What's going on?" Duncan asked, looking from one of us to the other.

I know I had a guilty look on my face.

"Duncan, this is my friend Carter." I didn't think it was possible for my face to turn any redder, but I'm sure it did.

Duncan extended his hand with a smile. "Nice to meet you."

I saw Carter's jaw clench. He didn't shake Duncan's hand.

"Hello."

"Kerri and I were just heading back out to the lake," Duncan said, clueless to the fact that I wanted to sink into the floor and Carter looked like he wanted to punch him. "Why don't you come out later and join us for a drink?"

Oh God, why was Duncan using 'us'? There was no 'us'.

"Thanks, but I'm really busy," Carter said, shooting me a dirty look. At least, I think he shot me a dirty look. I was too busy studying my shoes to be sure.

"Another time," Duncan replied cheerfully.

I looked up to see Carter head deeper into the store.

"He seems like a nice guy," Duncan said obliviously.

"Yeah," I said, suddenly not feeling too well. "He's Alex's brother."

"I thought he looked familiar," Duncan said.

"Can we go home now?" I asked him.

"Sure," he replied, sounding confused. "What's wrong?"

"I'm getting a migraine," I lied.

"We'll go right now."

When I got back to the cottage, James and Denny had both gone out somewhere. I was glad, because I really didn't feel like talking to either of them. I didn't feel like talking to anyone.

I went straight upstairs to my room and lay down on the bed with all the lights off.

About five minutes later there was a knock on my door. I didn't reply. The door opened a crack and Maxine popped her head inside.

"Can I come in?" she asked quietly.

"No," I replied, burying my head under the covers even though it was sweltering hot in my room.

Maxine ignored me, came inside and sat on the bed.

"What's wrong?"

"Nothing."

"There is something wrong with you."

"You're crazy," I said from underneath the blankets.

Maxine ripped the blankets off my head. "I can hardly hear you under there."

"Fine," I said sitting up. "If you must know I ran into Carter when I was out."

"Now I understand. The first run in after a break-up is always bad."

"Yes. Who's the guy?"

"What?" Maxine was caught off-guard by my quick change in the topic of conversation.

"The guy. The one you were making out with earlier."

Maxine smiled. "Jack."

"Does he have a last name, or is he like Cher?"

"McKay," she replied. "His name is Jack McKay."

"Who is he?" I insisted. "Did you have an affair? Is that why you and Steven are separated?"

"He's someone I care a great deal about," Maxine said, her face growing red.

This was fun. Finally, Maxine was the one in the hot seat. And she was actually answering my questions.

"How long have you known him?"

Maxine sighed.

"I've known him since I was fourteen," she said. She must have noticed the surprised look on my face because she continued. "He was my first love. Actually, he was probably my only love. We dated until I was fifteen. Jack was seventeen."

"What happened?" I was intrigued. "If you were in love with him, why would you break up?"

Maxine wouldn't meet my eyes. "My parents didn't like Jack," she said. "Mom didn't think that Jack's family was good enough, which was completely ridiculous. Dad felt that we were too young to be so seriously involved. Jack's parents felt the same way. So I was shipped off to private school in Switzerland, and he was sent to private school in the States."

"Did you keep in touch?"

"For a while we did," she admitted, "but it was hard. We were so far apart, and we were both so young ... we just lost touch. Then suddenly we ran into each other. All the old feelings came back for both of us. It was like we'd never been apart."

"When was that?"

"Huh?"

"When did you two meet up again?"

"Oh. About a year and a half ago."

That didn't make sense. If they'd met up more than a year ago, why would Maxine have stayed with Steven until a couple of months ago?

I said as much to Maxine.

"There's something that you're not telling me," I added.

"I don't know what you're talking about," she replied, still not meeting my eye.

I didn't believe her, but I wasn't in any mood to press the point.

"Fine," I said, my voice tight. "So he's staying with you?"

"Yes."

"For how long?"

"A few days," she replied. "He has to get back to work."

"What does he do?"

"He's a lawyer," she said with a funny half-smile.

Great. Another lawyer.

"I really want you to get to know him," she continued. "I know he really wants to get to know you."

"Why? Why should he care about me?"

"Because I've told him all about you," she explained. "He's just interested in getting to know my family."

"Has he met Mom yet?"

"Not since we were in high school."

"What about Tina?"

"Yes, he's met Tina. He's very fond of her, and she likes him too."

How would Maxine's daughter have met this guy if the day she left Steven she came to stay with me? It wasn't making any sense. Maxine was obviously not telling me the whole story.

"Will you join us for dinner?" she was asking me. "Denny and James are both out so it will give us time to talk."

"Fine," I said reluctantly. "But I'm staying up here until it's time to eat."

I pulled the duvet back over my head as she left the room.

At dinner time I made my way downstairs. Maxine and Jack were both in the kitchen and from the sound of their laughter, it seemed like they were having a great time. I was a little reluctant to interrupt.

Maxine saw me coming down the stairs. I couldn't remember when I'd seen her so happy before. She gave me a big smile when she saw me.

"Hello," she said. "Perfect timing."

"Do you need any help?" I asked.

"Nope," Jack said, placing a salad on the table and then giving Maxine a light kiss on the cheek. "Just sit down and enjoy."

During dinner Jack seemed intent on finding out absolutely everything about me. He kept asking me question after question. It was kind of irritating at first, but I realized that he seemed honestly interested in everything I said. He wanted to know about my book, my columns, where I'd lived in Toronto. He asked me about my school, my childhood and about past boyfriends. It was starting to resemble the Spanish Inquisition. But it wasn't difficult to like Jack and not just for Maxine's sake. He was charming, funny and nice and definitely seemed to be madly in love with my sister.

"What about you?" I asked him finally. "What's your story?"

"What do you want to know?" he asked with a smile.

"It's my turn to interrogate you," I replied.

Jack seemed amused. "It's not too interesting," he began. "I went to school, became a lawyer. Married the daughter of a family friend and had three kids. Jessica, Zack and Sam are thirteen, eleven and ten. I was divorced about four years ago, and I share custody of the kids with my ex-wife. Actually, they live with me most of the time, but they're with their mother right now. I have a picture if you want to see."

He looked so eager that I couldn't refuse. He passed me a picture that he had in his wallet.

The two boys had brown curly hair and blue eyes like their father. The girl, who was the eldest, had long, blond, curly hair and blue eyes.

I passed the picture back to Jack. "They're all very nice looking." I didn't know what I was supposed to say. I was never very good at complimenting people's children.

Jack didn't seem to notice my awkwardness.

"They're really smart too," he said proudly. "Sam's even something of a writer. I can't wait to tell him that I've met an actual author."

"I'm not much of an author," I said self-deprecatingly. "Authors generally write something."

"Still blocked?" Maxine asked sympathetically.

I nodded in frustration. "It's driving me nuts. I'm seriously considering giving up and getting a job."

"Don't give up yet," Jack said seriously. "I'm sure you'll think of something to write about."

Usually, comments like that nearly pushed me over the edge. But there was something in Jack's tone that actually made his words seem comforting.

"Thanks," I said honestly.

We sat around talking for hours before Maxine and Jack stood up to go to bed. Watching them head up the stairs together, I felt a surge of happiness for Maxine. I also had never felt so lonely in my life.

I spent the next day wearing my bathrobe while sitting on my bed with my laptop. I was still feeling miserable. But I was also strangely productive. It was as if my despondency had finally motivated me to write.

In the middle of the afternoon, there was a quiet knock on my bedroom door.

"Come in," I said, not looking up from the screen.

It was James. He had ice cream. People who had ice cream were always allowed in my room.

"Hi sweetie," he said handing me the tub. It was cookie dough. My favourite flavour. "What's going on?"

"Nothing," I said, taking a big spoonful. "I'm just working." This time I was being honest.

"You're all red and puffy," he replied. "There must be something wrong."

"I ran into Carter yesterday in town," I said in a tone I hoped was light an airy.

"You need to talk to him."

"I don't," I said firmly. "There's nothing to talk about."

"You know that I love you, right?" I nodded. James continued. "I only want what's best for you. You've only had a few relationships in your life, and none of them have ended well. You've never been able to even talk to any of the guys after you break-up. It's like they just fall off the face of the planet. Denny is the exception—although I'm not sure that I'd say that the relationship is healthy. One thing your relationships have had in common is that you sabotage them all once they start to get serious."

"That's not true!" I exclaimed. But I knew he was right. I've always been great at ending relationships.

"You have problems trusting people," he continued. "And I know you have good reasons not to trust anyone. If I had your childhood, I'd probably be the same way."

"I trust lots of people."

"No, you don't." He held out a hand and began counting off my flaws on his fingers. "You only trust Denny and me because we've known you too long. And you've tried multiple times to push us away. You really only have two close friends. You don't trust your sister. You don't even know your niece. You don't like to form serious attachments. You're afraid that if you get too close to someone, they'll leave you like your dad, your mom and Sebastian did. You don't want to give anyone a chance to hurt you. But you waited too long this time, didn't you?"

I didn't reply.

"You cared a lot more for Carter than you're willing to let on."

I still didn't reply.

James continued. "And, if what Alex says is true, you really did a number on Carter."

"Thanks," I said sarcastically. "If I'm such an awful person, I don't know why you and Denny even try to be friends with me."

"You're a wonderful person," James said giving me a hug. "You're like a pineapple."

"A pineapple." I had no idea what he was getting at.

"Yeah. Once you get past the crusty exterior, you're really very sweet."

I started to laugh. It was incredibly stupid. It didn't even deserve a laugh. Then I started crying. I hated crying. I wasn't the crying sort of person. I was a tough-as-nails, independent, modern woman. But lately I'd been crying like a little girl. It was starting to get on my own nerves, so I could just imagine what it was like for everyone else.

"Sweetie, you need to talk to him." James had a very serious look on his face.

"It's too late," I said. "Besides, I wasn't crying about him." That was mostly true.

James gave me another hug. "I'll let you get back to your writing."

"James," I called to him as he started to close the door.

"Yes?"

"I turned down the columnist job," I said to him. "And I think I may have an idea for my novel."

James came back, kissed me on the forehead and then left me to my work.

Chapter Twelve

By the end of July, I'd stopped wearing my housecoat throughout the day. Only at night and after showers. I was feeling pretty good about myself. There were several reasons for this and one of them was Duncan.

James had been right about me and how I pushed people away. I wanted to change. I wanted to let people in. I had learned my lesson, and I was not going to ruin things with Duncan.

Over the last couple of weeks, Jack had been back and forth staying with Maxine on the weekends. At first, I wasn't too happy with the idea of yet another person staying with us, but then I started getting used to him. I was really growing quite fond of him. I liked him a lot better than I ever liked Maxine's ex-husband Steven. Jack made Maxine happier than I'd ever seen her. She looked younger and walked around the house with a huge grin on her face constantly. My sister was a totally different person than I remembered from when I was a kid.

I liked Jack so much that I told him he should bring his kids up sometime in August. I wasn't sure what had come over me. I just blurted it out before I knew what I was doing. Maxine looked so happy when I made the offer I thought she would explode.

In a little while, the cottage would be crammed full of kids, I realized. I was more than a little worried about it. I couldn't take back the invitation without offending Jack and hurting Maxine. She was so set on us playing 'happy family'. But I didn't know how I was supposed to act around children. I'd never babysat for kids when I was younger. I hadn't really spent much time around them. This was going to be a very interesting visit.

Spending time with Duncan managed to keep my mind off other things. His friends had gone back home to New York for a while. Duncan wasn't really sure when they'd be back. It appeared he was the only one of them capable of taking months at a time off from work. When I asked him how long he was planning on staying at the cottage, he said he didn't really know. He hinted that I had a lot to do with the fact he was still around.

I was flattered. Duncan was a nice guy, and we'd been spending quite a bit of time together during the past couple of weeks. He'd take me water skiing (I still didn't really like it, but at least I was on my feet more often than not) or for boat rides, and we had dinner together at least three times a week. It was nice to have someone to spend time with, especially with Maxine so preoccupied with Jack. Duncan wasn't the most interesting guy I'd ever known, but he was nice. We hadn't slept together yet, and it seemed like neither one of us was ready to take the relationship to the next level. Or, more likely, I wasn't ready to take it to the next level, and he was being very patient and tolerant. I liked that about him. Plus, he was cute and had a Sea-doo. What can I say? Sometimes I'm shallow.

"You're going out with him again?" Maxine said as I was leaving.

I nodded. "And I don't want to hear anything from you about it."

She raised her hands in surrender. Maxine had never made any attempt to hide her dislike of Duncan.

"Fine, "she said. "But I don't like him."

"You don't have to."

"That's good. Since I don't."

"I get it. You don't like him. Well, I didn't like Steven."

"I didn't either," she said with a laugh. "That's why I left him."

"I thought Jack was why you left him."

"Only part of the reason," she said seriously. "I was never happy with Steven. The only good thing to come out of that relationship was Tina."

"How is she?" I asked her, changing the subject.

"Fine. She's at camp right now."

"Right. I forgot."

"She may come up here near the end of the summer," she continued.

"Does she know that Jack has kids?"

"Yes, and they get along perfectly. Jack's daughter Jessica is only a year younger than Tina."

I wondered if they actually got along or if it was just wishful thinking on Maxine's part. And I still couldn't figure out exactly how and when Tina had ever met Jack and his kids. Maxine wasn't telling me everything, but I didn't have time to get right into it then.

"I've got to go," I said looking at my watch. "I probably won't be out too late."

"Alright," Maxine said. "We'll talk more when you get back. We can continue our discussion about Duncan then."

I went next door, and Duncan met me with a kiss.

"Hi, gorgeous," he said, stepping back to let me inside.

Yet another reason to like him.

I followed him into the sitting room and sat down on the couch.

"How was your day?" I asked him as he got us each a glass of wine.

"Lousy," he said. "I kept hoping that you would come outside and join me for a boat ride or go waterskiing, but instead you stayed indoors all day and left me to fend for myself."

"I'm sorry," I said with a laugh. He was pouting like a four-year-old. "I was on a roll with my writing this afternoon. The words were just flying onto the page. I swear I think this book is writing itself. I think I'm finally over my writer's block." I was really excited about this and wanted to share it with someone other than Maxine.

"That's nice," he said, looking slightly uninterested. "I think I might go fishing tomorrow. Want to come?"

"I don't have a fishing license."

"Neither do I." He shrugged. "Come anyway."

"I can't." He was starting to get on my nerves. "I've got work to do."

"Yeah, but you can do that any time," he protested. "The weather will only be nice for a couple more months. You should be taking advantage of it, not hiding yourself away inside. Plus you should spend time with me while my friends aren't around. Who knows how much longer we'll be alone."

"I really need to work on this now while the ideas are fresh in my head," I explained. He was behaving like a child, and it was getting on my nerves. "If I wait for a couple of months, I may never be able to finish it."

"Then you'd just have to get another idea."

He said this like it was just a matter of pulling an idea out of thin air. I clenched my teeth to stop myself from replying angrily.

"It's a little harder than that."

"Well, I think you need a break," he said. Then he changed the subject abruptly. "My friends called today to say they're coming up this weekend. They'll be here Friday. I hope you can take time away from your busy schedule to go out with us." I ignored the sarcasm in his tone.

"We'll have to make it a group outing," I said. "Denny is coming up for the weekend too."

"Oh." His tone was a little annoyed.

"What's wrong?"

"Does Denny have to come up every weekend?" he asked. "I mean, all he does is monopolize your time and hang out with Alex. I don't know why you spend so much time with him. I think he has a thing for you. How long have you known him?"

I hadn't told Duncan about my history with Denny. It was never an easy subject to bring up and since they weren't too fond of each other, Duncan and I had never discussed it. I didn't know how much I wanted to get into at the moment. Duncan was acting childishly, and I knew he wouldn't like what I had to say.

"I've known Denny for years, and we're just good friends," I explained in a tone I hoped wouldn't invite more questions.

He opened his mouth to say something, but then he closed it again quickly. I could tell he wanted to ask more, but he wasn't going to say anything. He was only interested in talking about things that had to do with him.

The conversation kind of lagged after that. I was starting to realize that we didn't have much to say to each other. We sat in near silence for a couple of minutes before Duncan spoke.

"Hey, do you want to go into town and go to the bar?" He seemed kind of restless.

It was a week night. Should be safe. "Sure." I certainly didn't want to spend the rest of the evening sitting with Duncan and listening to him breathe.

We drove into town and parked in front of *Patrick's*. Despite the fact that it was a Wednesday, the place was packed. There must be a lot of vacationers, I thought as I looked around the bar. I managed to find us a table with only a little difficulty while Duncan went to the bar to get us some drinks.

I looked slowly around the room for familiar faces. I didn't want to get caught off-guard like at the grocery store. I realized suddenly that a great many of the people were familiar. I knew I had been living in this town too long if I was able to recognize the locals. Then suddenly I recognized one person in particular. Shit, I thought. At a table nearby, Carter and his new girlfriend were having a beer. I hadn't seen his vehicle out front, but I should have expected them to be here. They had probably walked over together after work. I started to back away from them but I bumped into a table, knocking a pitcher of beer onto the floor.

"I'm really sorry," I mumbled to the people at the table. "I'll get you another pitcher."

I spun around to order the beer. And I collided with a waitress carrying a tray of drinks.

I was not having a good night.

My face was bright red. Everyone in the pub was staring at me. There was no way that Carter hadn't seen me.

Humiliated beyond belief, I sat down at an empty table and tried to sink into the floor.

"Hello."

I looked up and saw Charlotte, Carter's date, standing next to my chair. She was taller and blonder than I remembered her. She was even better-looking than when I had first met her. No wonder Carter was madly in love with her. I noticed most of the men in the pub were staring at Charlotte. She had an extremely smug look on her face. She had won, and she wanted me to know it. I forced my lips to smile and tried not to jump up and strangle her. Carter was standing behind her, looking serious. Charlotte grabbed his hand possessively.

"Hi," I said, wishing that I wasn't sitting alone.

"We saw that you were alone, and I wanted to invite you over to our table," Charlotte said. "Your friends must not be staying with you right now. It's a shame you had to come by yourself."

"I'm not alone," I said firmly. "Duncan is just over there getting our drinks." I pointed to Duncan who was talking to the bartender.

"That's nice," Charlotte said, the smug smile on her face fading slightly. If I was alone her victory in landing Carter would be twice as sweet. The fact that I had a date put a cramp in her plans. "Well, we should head back to our table before someone else takes it, shouldn't we Carter?"

Carter still hadn't said anything to me. And he still wasn't smiling.

"Nice to see you," he said finally as he left. His tone was extremely cold.

Duncan arrived back at the table right as they turned to leave. "Hi," he said to Carter.

Carter said nothing in reply. Instead, he bumped Duncan with his shoulder, spilling the drinks slightly.

"What the hell was that all about?" Duncan asked, looking back at Carter and wiping his hands with a napkin.

"They just came over to say hello," I said.

"That guy is a jerk. I'll admit that his girlfriend is hot, but he's a complete asshole."

I looked over at their table. Charlotte was laughing at something that Carter was whispering to her. I moved a little closer to Duncan, and he put his arm around me.

Carter moved closer to Charlotte.

I didn't think I'd win this fight. I was pretty sure Carter and Charlotte were going to start kissing any second, and I didn't think I could stand it. I had a pretty light gag-reflex.

"Why don't we go now?" I suggested to Duncan.

"I don't want to go yet," he replied, hardly even looking at me. He was staring at some bimbo who was walking past our table.

"Why don't you join her," I said sarcastically.

"Huh?" he turned back to me, looking confused.

He grinned. "Jealous?"

I wasn't jealous, but I didn't want him drooling over other women when we were out in public.

I didn't bother to reply.

This seemed to be the right answer. It made him think that his conduct was bothering me much more than it was. Duncan laughed and moved closer to me. He leaned over and started kissing me on the neck, which I found incredibly irritating. But I wanted to put on a good show for anyone watching, so I pretended to enjoy it.

I looked up when I saw Carter and Charlotte leaving the bar. I had won the first round. My satisfaction lasted until I saw the door swing shut behind them. I realized that they were going home together. I felt like I had been kicked in the stomach.

All I wanted to do was crawl home and hide in bed.

But I was with Duncan. And Duncan actually wanted to be with *me*. I forced myself to remember that and tried to give him the attention he deserved.

Duncan and I stayed a couple of hours longer, and then he drove me home. He left me at my doorstep with a kiss.

On Friday afternoon when Denny arrived, I was in a foul mood. Maxine was gone. She had left earlier in the day after deciding to spend the weekend with

Jack at his place. Unfortunately, the time alone was not helping me with my writing. I was still progressing with my novel, but it was slowing down. I was worried that the writer's block was coming back.

Duncan had been bugging me non-stop to spend more time with him. He was like a little kid begging for his parent's attention. I wasn't used to being the emotionally mature person in the relationship, and it was taking a lot out of me.

All-in-all, Denny was in for an unpleasant arrival.

"So," he said, throwing his bag down in the hallway when he entered. "What are the big plans for the weekend?"

"Duncan's coming for dinner tonight," I said. "And I told him that we'd go out with him and his friends this weekend."

"Oh." Denny didn't sound very enthusiastic. He sat down on the couch with a sigh.

"What's wrong?"

"I don't like him," Denny said. "And I don't really like his friends either. I think you should get back with Carter."

"Gee, I haven't heard that before."

"I'm serious," he replied. "Carter was much better for you than this Duncan guy."

"What's wrong with you?" I asked in a frustrated tone. "First, you're telling me not to get involved with Carter. And then, when I break it off with him, you want me to date him again. What's really going on here?"

"There's nothing going on," he said seriously. "I was wrong. I shouldn't have said anything against Carter. I guess maybe I was a little jealous at first. But Duncan seriously is a jerk. You don't have good judgment when it comes to men. You need James and me to look out for you."

That was it. I'd had just about enough of everyone telling me what to do.

"I'm sick of you, Maxine and James always putting Duncan down," I yelled at him. "I'm an adult. I can take care of myself."

"I just can't see why you like him, that's all," he replied calmly. "And quit yelling."

"I'm sorry that you don't like him, but I do. He's nice. And I'm not yelling. I'm just trying to speak loud enough to get through to you."

"He's a jerk."

"He's not a jerk. You don't even know him!"

"Neither do you."

"You haven't even tried to get to know him. Every time he's around, you practically ignore him."

"He's just really, really boring. I don't have anything to say to the guy. And I can't imagine what you two would even talk about."

"What right do you have to tell me who I can and can't date?"

"I'm not telling you who to date," Denny protested. "Well, maybe I am telling you who to date. But I've got your best interests at heart. I'm just looking out for you."

"The way you looked out for me when I was eighteen?" I was angry and grasping at ways to hurt him.

"That's not fair, Kerrigan," Denny said. "Things were different. We were different. It was seven years ago."

"How do you think my brother felt when his best friend started sleeping with his little sister? Even if it was a long time ago, it still hurt him. You were his best friend, and I was just a kid."

"You weren't a kid."

"I was. And Sebastian wanted to kill you. The only reason he didn't was because I told him not to. But he spent the rest of his life hating you." I didn't know if that was true or not, but I knew it would hurt Denny to hear it.

"Sebastian knew that I loved you," Denny said. "I'll always love you, Kerri. That's why I'm looking out for you."

"You're one of the reasons I'm so fucked up," I continued. I couldn't believe I was saying this. My brain was screaming at me, telling me to shut up. But I wouldn't listen. "And now the only reason you want me to get back together with Carter is so that you can continue screwing his sister without feeling so guilty."

"That's not true, Kerri," he said angrily. "You don't know a single thing that's going on with me right now. You're too self-involved to notice. You've been this way ever since Sebastian died. Even before he died you were like this. You're like a child, always needing to be the centre of attention. You love having all the men fawning all over you. That's the only reason you keep me around. You need to have someone around who's willing to play your little games. Someone who'll jump to your side whenever you call. But that's not me anymore, kiddo. You're going to have to find someone else to be your bitch."

"That's not true," I yelled. "I've never treated you like that!"

"It is true. You don't care about your mother. You don't care about your sister. You don't care about your friends, and you've only got two of them. The only thing that you care about is yourself. You're not the only one who lost Sebastian. You weren't the only one who loved him. The only reason you keep bringing up Sebastian is because it turns you into the poor bereaved little girl, abandoned by everyone. I bet you've even started to believe that line you tell everyone about his death. But I know the truth."

"I don't know what they hell you're talking about."

"Yes, you do. I've heard you tell people that he died in a car accident. I guess it makes you look better if it was quick and didn't involve you at all. You weren't there when he died. I was. He was in so much pain. He was so tired. All he wanted to do was rest. And you wouldn't let him. You made him feel like a coward for dying."

"Shut up," I said quietly.

"I won't. I've been quiet for too long. He died peacefully, not screaming in pain like he would have if you'd gotten your way."

"That's not true. I wanted him to fight. He was young and strong. He could have beaten it. But he gave in."

"He forgave you in the end," Denny said. "He wanted to make sure that you were okay. He asked me to look out for you. But I'm finished."

"Good. Get the hell out."

He picked up his bags and left.

Chapter Thirteen

I spent a horrible weekend alone. Denny's words had bothered me more than I wanted to admit. I wanted to stay angry with him. But I couldn't. I had never wanted to face the truth about Sebastian's death. Denny knew that. Everything he said was true.

I didn't tell James what had happened. He would have been understanding and sweet but it wouldn't have been fair to make him choose sides. And I was a little worried about whose side he'd pick.

Tuesday morning Duncan came by to let me know he'd be out of town most of the day. He was driving up to the airport to pick up his friends. It turned out that they hadn't been able to come up for the weekend. One of them (Glen or Tony, I wasn't really listening when Duncan mentioned it) found out at the last minute that he had to work so all four of them changed their plans.

"I'll be back in the evening," Duncan said. "I'll come by and see you then."

"That'll be great," I replied. I was happy to have the company since Maxine was still out of town. She and Jack were staying in the city until Friday when they would be coming up with his kids.

"I'd like to stay with you tonight," he said.

"Oh."

"Don't you think we've known each other long enough?"

"Yes," I said cautiously. "But what about your friends?"

"They'll be on their own. There are four of them after all. They'll probably just go into town and get drunk. They won't even notice that I'm not there."

"Yeah, but …" I didn't really have another excuse.

"I've got to go," he said, looking at his watch. "We can talk about this later."

I watched him leave with a slight feeling of dread. He wanted to stay the night. Well, with Maxine out of town and no one else staying with me, it seemed like a fine time to have Duncan over. And we had known each other for a couple of weeks. Plus, I had no doubt at all that Carter and Charlotte were sleeping together. Logically, it was time for Duncan and me to move forward.

The problem was that I didn't know how I felt about Duncan. He was nice enough, but I wasn't sure if I liked him that way. I didn't feel anything when he kissed me. He was really very self-centered, and when we talked, I had to force myself not to tune him out. But we had had some fun together, and I often enjoyed his company. We'd have to talk when he got back.

I spent the morning swimming and then settled into working on my novel on the patio. I was engrossed in writing when Alex came around to the back deck. I hadn't even heard her car pull up in the driveway. That was a good sign. It meant that I was really focused on my work.

"Hi," I said, looking up. I looked around to see if she'd brought Mr. Smith with her. I didn't see him anywhere.

"How's it going?" she asked casually, sitting down next to me.

"Good," I said. I closed my laptop and set it on the picnic table. "I'm going to get myself a drink. Do you want an iced tea?"

"That'd be great," she replied.

I went inside to get the drinks. I had a feeling that I knew why she was here. And I wasn't in any mood to talk about Denny.

I handed Alex her drink. "Beautiful weather we've been having."

"Yes," she agreed. "It's been a great July. Great for tourism."

"I'm sure." This was ridiculous. We were sitting on my porch drinking iced tea and dancing around the real reason for her visit. But I wasn't going to be the one to bring it up.

Alex finally got to the point. "Denny was a little upset the other night."

"I wasn't too happy myself," I replied. "Denny and I have been friends for a long time."

"I know. He said the same thing."

"Did he tell you what the fight was about? Did he tell you what he said to me?"

"No, he didn't. Whatever happened was between the two of you. It's not my place to interfere."

"I don't know why he won't talk to me," I continued. "He usually calls me every day. I haven't spoken to him since last Friday." When Denny had left that night, I wasn't sure I ever wanted to see him again. But looking at the fight several days later, I had a clearer view of the situation. Although I didn't really want to admit it, it had been mostly my fault. I had practically picked a fight with Denny that evening. And I missed him. I missed not talking to him every day.

"I think you're going to have to call him," Alex said. "You need to be the one to bridge the gap."

"What about him?" I asked. "He had a part in the fight too, you know." I didn't want to tell her that the whole thing began with me defending Duncan. And I didn't want her to know the truth about my brother.

"I'm sure he did. And he's too stubborn to admit it to himself. But you two have too much history to ruin your friendship over something so insignificant."

I didn't know how insignificant it was. We'd both said some horrible things, things that must have been in the back of both of our minds for a long time.

"I just wish he'd call," I said. "Every time I call him at work, he hangs up on me. And he's never home anymore. I've called his place a million times, and I can't reach him." I didn't tell her that Emily always hung up when she heard my voice. That fact was a little embarrassing.

"That's because he's moved out," Alex said.

"What!" I wasn't sure if I'd heard her correctly.

"He's moved out. He's moving in with me."

"Denny is moving out of the city? He's leaving Emily?" I couldn't believe it. I'd seen Denny and his many different women before. None were serious. I'd just assumed Alex was the same. I assumed Denny would break it off with her when things got too serious. Why hadn't I seen this coming?

"Yes."

I didn't know what to say. I still wasn't sure if I believed her. "That's great for you two," I said. It sounded stupid and a little forced.

"I think so," Alex agreed. "He's going for joint custody of the baby, and I think he'll get it. Emily knows that their marriage has been over for a long time. He thinks she's actually relieved that it's finally happened."

She's probably just relieved that he's not moving in with me, I thought darkly.

Denny had been right. I hadn't been paying attention to him.

"Can you let Denny know that I'm sorry?" I asked her. "And tell him that I really want to talk to him."

"I'll try," Alex said. She got up to leave. "It was nice to see you again. Thanks for the iced tea."

"You're welcome," I said. Then I spoke before my brain could tell me to shut up. "How's Carter doing?" I cringed inwardly. I'm sure I sounded like a bitter ex-girlfriend.

"He's good. He seems to be getting pretty involved with Charlotte." She gave me a sympathetic smile.

"Good for him. That's great for both of them. I've been getting close to Duncan." I put on a big grin, trying to make it sound like things were terrific. "He really is a great guy."

"You know," she continued, "despite everything that had happened, I still hoped that you and Carter would get back together."

"Really?"

She nodded. "He seemed so in love with you. And you seemed like a great couple. But I guess things work out for the best. He's really happy with Charlotte, and I guess the two of them were meant to be together. Whatever makes my brother happy is fine with me. Even if I don't really like Charlotte that much."

Great. So now I was the person who made Carter realize that his true love had been in front of his eyes all the time. It wasn't a good feeling.

"I'm happy for him," I said, honestly trying to feel happy for him but not really succeeding. "I'm happy for both of them."

"I'll tell him you said that," she said with a smile as she left.

After Alex was gone, I struggled to get back to my writing. I also struggled not to curl up into a ball in my housecoat on the couch. I was becoming quite pathetic.

I thought about Denny and Alex. It was truly amazing. I hoped (very honestly) that they would be happy together. I liked her much better than Emily. But a tiny part of me felt like I was losing something, something very important. I had never really considered Emily as a part of Denny's life, despite their marriage and child. Alex was different. It was like she was taking a spot in Denny's life that had up to then belonged to me.

After a few hours of moping, I managed to get back to work. I stopped in the early evening to have a shower before Duncan came over.

Duncan came by at nine. His friends were settled in next door, and he arrived with a bottle of wine and some flowers. I smiled when I saw him. But the sight of him didn't make my stomach flip, and I didn't feel a tingle at his touch.

I went and got some wine glasses while he put the flowers in water for me. I looked at him objectively. He was handsome, nice and rich. What did Carter have that Duncan doesn't? I asked myself. A sense of humour and a personality, my mind replied.

We sat close together on the couch. Duncan had one arm draped comfortably over my shoulder. We sat without talking much, as if neither one of us knew what to say.

"How was the drive?" I asked him, attempting to make small-talk. I couldn't stand the awkward silence any longer. I thought I'd let him start talking about himself. It was his favourite subject.

"Too much traffic," he said. "I can't believe how many people drive to and from the city each day from up north. It's ridiculous. Plus, their plane was late. And then I had to find parking at the airport. I'm just glad to be here with you right now."

He put one hand on my knee. He leaned in and started kissing me. It was nice. I started kissing him back. His lips moved over my face to my ear, something that really irritated me. I had a thing about my ears. I guided him back to my lips.

Gently, he laid me down on the couch. I decided that this was actually going to happen. I decided to turn off my brain and just go with the situation. Things were going great when the phone rang.

"Ignore it," Duncan murmured.

"I can't," I said. "It might be Denny."

I pushed him off me gently and reached for the phone. It was James.

"What did you do?" he asked immediately.

"What do you mean?"

"To poor, innocent Denny," he replied. "The boy is a wreck. Worse than the last time you broke up with him."

"I'm taking care of it," I said, hanging up.

I turned back to Duncan. He had an impatient look on his face.

"I'm sorry," I said. "Can we continue?"

I took the lead and started kissing him again. He immediately responded. His hands were all over me. It was like kissing an octopus. He had just started to take off my top when the phone rang again.

"Just unplug it," he said angrily.

"I can't. I really need to talk to Denny," I said as I answered the phone. I could hear Duncan mumbling to himself in an annoyed tone.

"Hello," I said into the receiver.

"Hi."

It wasn't Denny.

It was Carter.

I moved away from Duncan and sat up straightening my top.

"Hi."

Duncan put his hand back on my knee. I quickly pushed it off.

"How are you doing?" Carter asked, his voice incredibly calm.

How could he be so calm? "Fine. What do you want?" I'm sure I sounded in near hysterics. Of all the God damned times he could have called, he had to pick now.

"I miss you."

I was silent. It wasn't that I didn't know what to say, it was just that I couldn't breathe. Duncan, on the other hand, wasn't having this same problem.

"Who is it?" he asked loudly. It was like he was deliberately trying to be overheard. Come to think of it, he probably was.

Carter definitely heard him. I felt the tension through the line. His voice lost all its softness and immediately became cold and hard. "I'm sorry for interrupting. I shouldn't have called. I won't make that mistake again." He hung up before I could explain.

I was flustered. My face felt flushed. I didn't know what to do. Duncan put his arms around me. I shrugged him off. I didn't want him to touch me. In fact, I didn't even want him near me. I wanted to be alone. I needed to be alone.

"What's with you?" he asked angrily. "One minute you're all over me and the next you don't want me to touch you."

"I'm sorry."

"You're just a tease," he continued, growing even angrier. "You're nothing but a God damned tease. You've been leading me on. We've been together for a couple of weeks now, and we haven't slept together yet. It's getting ridiculous. You know, this is the longest I've stuck around with anyone before sex."

"I'm sorry I wasted your time," I replied angrily.

"Me too," he said, storming out and slamming the door viciously behind him.

I didn't care. He was acting like a complete and total asshole, and I didn't care at all. I realized then that Duncan didn't mean a thing to me. I felt nothing as I watched him walk away. Well, not exactly nothing. I felt relief and satisfaction at seeing him finally leave.

Chapter Fourteen

Maxine and Jack returned early Friday afternoon with his three kids. I had spent the entire morning attempting to kid-proof the cottage. I didn't even know what that meant. At first, I thought about covering all the electrical outlets and getting rid of any cleaning solvents, but then I figured that a ten-year-old probably wouldn't stick his fingers in an electrical outlet. Instead, I got rid of (actually I just hid) all the alcohol and put my stuff away so they wouldn't touch anything. Then I spent the rest of the morning waiting in terror for them to arrive.

I walked out to the driveway when I heard the car pull up. Maxine looked at me critically when she stepped out of the car. I could tell Maxine sensed that there was something up with me, but she didn't say anything. She just smiled hello and started getting the bags out of the trunk.

"Kerri," Jack said as he got out of the car. "I'd like you to meet my daughter Jessica and my sons Zack and Sam."

"Hi," I said to them with a smile, suppressing my growing feelings of terror. Kids can sense fear, right? Or was that dogs?

The boys looked at me shyly but smiled. They were both smaller versions of their father. Jessica grinned at me. Maybe I didn't need to be afraid.

"Hi," she said. "I'm Jess. You've got great hair."

I laughed. "I was thinking the same thing about you. Maybe you can give me some advice on how to manage the frizz."

Jess shook her head. "No clue. I'm thinking about letting mine turn into dreadlocks." She tossed her long blond curls over her shoulder.

"No, you aren't," Jack said firmly as he unloaded the trunk. "Remember the rule."

"No doing crazy things to your hair until you're sixteen," Jess recited, rolling her eyes.

"Dreadlocks aren't a good idea anyway," I said to her. "You'd have to shave your head to get rid of them."

"That was another option," she replied.

I liked her immediately. At thirteen, she was about my height, and her fashion sense appealed to me. There was nothing girly about her. She was wearing cargo capris and a tank top. She carried herself with a confidence that I rarely saw in women twice her age.

"I'll show you guys to your rooms," I said to the kids as I grabbed a bag. They followed me inside. The boys seemed to consider me as an authority figure, which struck me as slightly ridiculous.

"This place is great," Sam said in awe. "It's huge. Dad said you were a writer, but he didn't say you were rich."

I'm not," I said. "In fact, usually I can hardly pay the rent on my apartment in Toronto. I inherited this place from my father."

"But …" Zack began, looking confused or concerned. Jess hit him before he could say anything else.

"It's very nice," she said, her tone indicating that there would be no more discussion on the subject. I had heard that tone a lot from my older siblings while growing up, especially from Maxine. I guess all older sisters act alike.

I led the three of them upstairs. I gave the boys the room overlooking the back, the one with bunk beds. They both loved it immediately. Or at least that's what they told me. I think they were still a little too afraid of me to tell me what they actually thought.

I gave Jess the room on the main level, the one that James had been using on the weekends.

"This can be your room," I said to Jess. "I may have a friend coming up from the city next weekend, and if that happens you can stay with me in my room."

"Is it your boyfriend?" she asked, looking interested.

"No," I replied, laughing as I thought about James. "He's just a friend."

"Right. Maxine said you were dating the guy next door."

"Not anymore. Just how much has my sister said about me?"

"Enough," Jess replied.

I was going to have to have a talk with Maxine about keeping her mouth shut.

I left Jess to unpack. I turned to head out onto the deck before a thought struck me, and I went back to ask Jess a question.

I knocked lightly on the door before stepping back into the room. She had her back to me but looked up at the sound.

"Can I ask you something?" I asked her.

"Sure," she replied turning her back to look at her suitcase. She was concentrating on putting her stuff away.

"What do you think of Maxine?"

"She's great." She sounded surprised that I would ask.

"You're okay with the fact that she's with your father?"

She looked up from her luggage. "Why shouldn't I be? My parents divorced years ago. I'm glad he's found someone nice."

I looked at her, my disbelief showing on my face.

"Besides," she continued, turning her focus back to unpacking. "I think the whole thing is really romantic, don't you?"

"I guess." I couldn't believe that a thirteen-year-old was so well adjusted.

I wasn't going to let the subject drop. She was only thirteen for Christ's sake. She's got to have at least a few deeply-rooted issues that I could dig up.

"I just remember when my parents split up," I added. "It was difficult."

"Yeah, but your mom wasn't really the best parent, was she?"

I looked at her in surprise.

"Maxine told us," she explained quickly.

Great. I'd love to know what Maxine *hasn't* been blabbing about, I thought.

"I mean," she continued kind of awkwardly. "At least both my parents continued to act like parents. Their divorce wasn't like your parents' divorce."

"Okay," I said turning to leave.

"Wait," she called. "I didn't mean to sound so nosey. I've just been really anxious to meet you."

"Really? Why?"

"It'll be like having a big sister," she grinned. "All I've got are two annoying, little brothers."

I left the room feeling quite pleased with myself. Maxine was in the kitchen with Jack, so I went in there instead of going out onto the deck.

"What's up?" she asked as I came in. She looked up briefly when I came in before turning back to putting the food away.

"Nothing much," I replied. I turned to Jack. "Your kids seem great."

"They are. I don't know how they turned out so great. I'm glad you like them." Jack looked very pleased.

"You looked like something was up when we arrived," Maxine insisted.

"Oh yeah." It had totally slipped my mind. "Duncan and I split up." The thing with Duncan didn't bother me at all. I'd tell her about my fight with Denny later. I was still hoping to patch things up with him soon.

"Really?" Maxine was smiling. "I mean, I'm terribly sorry." She forced a sympathetic expression on her face.

"I'm not. He really was a jerk. I'll give you the details later."

"I notice you're not back in the housecoat, so you must not be too devastated."

"Did I miss something?" Jack said, looking from one of us to the other.

"Yes," we said at the same time.

"It's not really important," I said.

"I'll fill you in later," Maxine added.

I shot her a dirty look.

Before I could say anything, Sam and Zack came bursting into the kitchen. Both were in their swimming trunks and were carrying towels.

"What's up, guys?" Jack asked them.

"Can we go swimming?" Sam asked.

"Not right now, Sam," Jack replied ruffling Sam's hair. "I want to put some stuff away first."

They both looked like they'd just seen someone kick a puppy.

Something had to be done. I couldn't stand to see anyone look that disappointed. "I can swim with them," I said before I had a chance to think things through.

Sam smiled. "Really?" He sounded very excited.

"Yeah. I'll just get my swimsuit on and see if Jess wants to come too," I said. Then I looked at Jack. "If that's okay with you."

"Be my guest," he replied. "That will give Maxine and me time to get everything ready for dinner. But are you sure you want to do this?"

"Sure," I said with more confidence than I felt. "I'm positive everything will be perfectly fine." I hoped. Oh, God. What if one of them drowned? What if they swam out into the channel and got hit by a boat? Maybe this wasn't such a good idea.

I think Jack must have seen the terrified look on my face because he spoke again with a laugh. "Don't worry. They can swim. And Jessica has been taking life saving classes. Everything will be okay."

I spent the rest of the afternoon swimming with the kids. Jack was right; they could swim. I eventually got over my terror every time they jumped into the water and began to have a good time. We had a blast. It was a lot of fun having people around to swim with.

I was floating on my back staring up at the sun when Jessica swam up and tapped me on the shoulder.

"That guy over there keeps staring at you," Jess said to me quietly, gesturing over to Duncan's cottage.

I looked where she was pointing and saw Duncan sitting with his friends on the dock. Jessica was right. He was staring at all four of us and giving me a dirty look.

"He's just being a jerk," I replied to her, looking away.

"Ex-boyfriend?" she asked in a knowing tone.

I laughed.

"Had a lot of those?" I asked her.

"A few," she admitted. "Guys can be such assholes sometimes."

"Are thirteen-year-olds supposed to swear?"

She shot me a withering look. "Are you trying to sound like an old person? 'cause you're succeeding."

I laughed and splashed her. She splashed me back. It turned into a mini water fight before Zack ended it by canon-balling the two of us.

Jess swam off in pursuit. I took the opportunity to get out of the water and sit on the dock to watch them swim.

The kids stayed in the water for hours. I didn't know how they could stay in for so long. I had only been in for forty-five minutes, but I was freezing. I had a feeling that Sam and Zack would have stayed in the water until they were completely blue. After they dried off, we went back up to the cottage.

"How was the water?" Maxine asked as we came in. "Zachary, Samuel please don't track any water on the floors."

"It was great," Jessica said, toweling her hair.

"Really warm," Zack added, carefully drying his feet and shaking with cold at the same time.

"Dinner's not for a few hours," Jack said, "and we need a few things from the grocery store."

"Give me the list, and I'll go get it." I was feeling charitable and selfless. I had turned over a new leaf. I was a whole new Kerri; a Kerri who thought of others and wasn't completely self-centered. "Jess, want to come with me?"

"Sure," she said with a grin.

"We'll take Maxine's car," I said.

"Really," Maxine said dryly.

"You don't mind, do you?" I asked with a winning smile. "After all, I am doing you a favour."

"What's wrong with your car?" Maxine asked.

"Nothing. Except it's a piece of crap, and I don't think Jack would like me driving his only daughter around in a death trap."

"Fine," Maxine said with a sigh. "You've made your point. Here are the keys."

Jess and I both went inside to change. We jumped into Maxine's car, and I drove towards town.

It really was a nice car. I could understand why Maxine didn't want me driving it.

I looked at Jess out of the corner of my eye.

"Have you been to New Ferndale before?" I asked her.

"We drove through on the way out here today, but we didn't stop," she replied. "Can you show me around before we go to the store?" She put her right foot up on the dashboard.

Maxine would freak out.

I ignored it.

"Sure," I said. "But there's really not too much in the town."

"Can we take a look around anyway?" she asked.

"Okay."

I parked in front of the grocery store.

"Where do you want to go?"

"Give me the tour," she said, throwing on her sunglasses.

It didn't take long to show her all the highlights of the town. Of course we avoided a certain law office (I didn't think a thirteen-year-old would be too interested in lawyers, even if her dad was one).

"Is that it?" she asked. "Isn't there a movie theatre or an arcade?"

"It's not a big town," I said. "We're lucky that we can rent movies from the convenience store. And I think there's a gym somewhere on one of the side streets. Other than that, you've seen just about everything. The only place left is the bakery. Should we get something for desert?"

"Okay."

We walked into the bakery. Mary, the owner, was behind the counter and recognized me immediately. She looked at us with a big smile on her face.

"Miss Shepherd," she said. "I haven't seen you in a while."

"I haven't been in town for a while," I replied. "How's business been?"

"We're having a record year. Thanks at least in part to your article. I've posted it up behind the counter." She gestured to a framed newspaper clipping.

I blushed. No one had ever framed anything I'd written before. My mom never even put anything I wrote or drew on the fridge when I was a little kid.

"Thanks, Mary," I said sheepishly.

"So what would you like? You and your sister pick whatever you want. On the house."

"She's not my sister," I said. "She's …" my sister's boyfriend's daughter was too complicated. "She's a friend of the family."

"Really?" Mary seemed surprised. "Anyway, what would you like?"

Jessica picked out a pie, and I tried to pay. Mary wouldn't let me, saying it was payment for the free advertising I had given her.

"That was weird," I said to Jess as I put the pie in the car.

"What was weird?" Jess asked.

"That she thought we were sisters."

"Yeah. Weird. Are we going to the grocery store now?"

"Sure."

The store was fairly empty. It didn't take us long to find everything on Jack's list and get in line to pay. I was looking at the tabloid magazines when I heard my name.

"Hi Kerri."

It was Alex.

"Hi."

"I'm not here with Denny," she said quickly. I guess she could tell that I wasn't in the mood for a confrontation. "I'm here with Carter." She gestured over her shoulder.

It might have been better if she had been with Denny.

"Okay." Great. What was I supposed to say?

"Where's Duncan?" She was looking around as Carter came up next to her.

"Hi," he said to me.

I made a mental note never to enter this grocery store again. I wasn't having much luck here.

Jess cleared her throat. In all the excitement I had forgotten all about her.

I turned to face her. "Oh, yeah. Jess, this is Carter and Alex."

"Hi," Jess said shyly. She was staring at Carter with puppy-dog admiration. What was it with this guy?

"Hi," Alex replied.

"You must be Maxine's daughter," Carter said.

"Actually, no," Jess said. "Maxine's dating my dad."

Carter looked confused.

"It's the hair," Alex explained. "Except for the colour, you two have the same hair. And eyes."

"Just a coincidence," I said.

"Well …" Carter said awkwardly.

"Yeah, we have to go too," I said with a smile.

He grinned at me.

"Tell Denny to call me," I said to Alex.

"I'll try," she said as they left.

I paid for the groceries and ushered Jessica out to the car. She seemed to be much more interested in watching Carter shop.

"Who was that?" she asked, looking back over her shoulder.

"Alex and Carter Stevens. He's a lawyer, and she's a doctor. They're friends of mine."

"Are they married?"

"No. They're brother and sister."

"That guy was so hot," she gushed. "And he kept staring at you."

"I must have had something on my face."

"There's nothing on your face. He couldn't keep his eyes off you."

"He was waiting for me to do something stupid, like I usually do when I'm around him. I'm surprised I didn't knock over a magazine rack."

"You're lying," she insisted. "Is there something going on between you two?"

"No."

"But there used to be, right?"

"Sort of …" I didn't want to talk about it with a thirteen-year-old I'd just met.

"I knew it," she said smugly. "What happened?"

"Nothing really happened."

"Something must have happened if you two are no longer together," she insisted.

This really wasn't something I wanted to talk about.

"Honestly, it was nothing. It just wasn't meant to be. He's dating someone else," a bimbo, I thought but didn't say, "and he's much happier with her. He and I are just friends."

Jess gave me a funny look. "He's still in love with you. Even I can tell that, and I'm just a kid."

"You're crazy," I said. Time to change the subject. "It's funny that two different people thought we look alike." I laughed. "Must be the hair."

"Yeah," she said dismissively. "But that guy—Carter was his name?—You should get back together with him. It's so romantic. You should call him and tell him that you're still in love with him. And then he'll tell you that he's still in love with you. It's perfect."

I sighed. I wasn't going to win this battle, so I gave up. I blocked her out for the rest of the drive, which wasn't easy, since she wouldn't stop talking.

Jess jumped out of the car with the groceries when we stopped in front of the cottage. I followed her inside, where the lovely conversation from the car was continuing in the kitchen.

"We saw Kerri's ex-boyfriend in town," Jess was saying to Maxine when I walked in. "The cute lawyer. Not the guy next door."

"Great," I said sarcastically. "We're still talking about this. Let me know when we're done."

"Kerri doesn't like to talk about Carter," Maxine explained as if I wasn't in the room.

"I see," Jess said. "She's in denial."

Christ. Now a thirteen-year-old was psychoanalyzing my behaviour. I definitely didn't need this. I was seconds away from kicking them all out of the cottage. After all, it was mine. I was being nice enough to let these people stay here. I didn't have to put up with this kind of abuse. So much for the new Kerri. I wanted to be selfish and childish again.

Maxine could sense my impatience because she changed the subject.

"Tina called while you guys were out," she said.

"How is she?" Jess asked, grabbing a carrot stick from a tray.

"She hates camp, and she's leaving," Maxine replied. "I told her she could come here. That's alright, isn't it Kerri?"

Another guest. Just what I wanted. But what could I say?

I was going to have to build a few extra rooms onto the place.

"Sure. When is she coming?"

"She's catching a bus tomorrow," Maxine said. "But the bus doesn't come all the way to New Ferndale. Can you drive to Orillia to pick her up?"

Perfect. Now they wanted me to be their errand girl. All I had to do was tell Maxine no. Instead, I opened my mouth and heard myself say:

"Okay. What time does her bus come in?"

"Noon."

As a result of my idiotic agreement to do Maxine's bidding, I was on the road by eleven the next morning. Maxine let me use her car again, since I was doing her a favour. And because I was in her car, not my own, I drove about twenty over the speed limit with the stereo blasting. Maxine's car had a great sound system. I pressed play on my ABBA CD and sang along at the top of my lungs the entire way to Orillia. I was driving alone since Jess was still asleep when I left and neither of the boys wanted to come with me.

I pulled into the bus terminal ten minutes after Tina's bus had arrived. There weren't too many people around so it was easy to notice a pissed off teenager.

I recognized her immediately even though I hadn't seen her in a couple of years. She looked exactly like Maxine, except for the nose ring.

"Hi Tina," I said as I got out of the car.

She stood and tipped her sunglasses down to look at me. At fourteen, Tina was already taller than me and had long, perfectly straight, dark red hair down to the middle of her back. Her eyes were the same colour of green as Maxine's. She was a very beautiful fourteen-year-old, who looked more like eighteen.

I could tell that Maxine was up for a rough couple of years with this one.

"Took you long enough," she said in an annoyed tone.

"Nice to see you too," I said back. "You're too tall."

"You're just too short," she said with a grin. "But I guess I shouldn't be mean to the person who's rescuing me from that hell they call summer camp."

"Maxine said you liked camp."

"Yeah, well Maxine's been too busy to notice that I'm almost fifteen, not eight."

"I bet the nose ring helps."

"Mom doesn't actually know about it yet. I'm hoping to surprise her. What do you think?"

"I think it's great, but Maxine's probably going to freak out."

"That's the reaction I'm hoping for," she said with a grin.

"So what exactly happened at that summer camp?" I asked as I threw her bag into the trunk. We both got into the car. "Why did you want to leave?"

"I can't believe Mom's letting you drive her car," she said in disbelief. She shrugged. "I wanted to get out of there right from the start. It was horrible. They treat us all like children. I didn't have any place better to go at first, so I stuck it out for a while. Mom's been staying with you in the middle of nowhere. It sounded even more boring than camp. I certainly wasn't going to live with Dad and his twenty-three-year-old slut. Then Mom and Jack and his kids started staying with you guys, so I thought I'd come and see Jess. So I gathered up my gear and left."

Her father was dating a twenty-three-year-old? Why hadn't Maxine mentioned that?

"That's it?"

She grinned. "Mostly. Well actually they sort of kicked me out. But I was planning on leaving anyway."

"They kicked you out."

"Yup."

"Why?"

"Because I'm a badass," she said with a laugh. "They don't think I set a good example for the younger campers."

"What did you do?"

"It's a long story."

"It's a long drive. Give me the Coles notes version."

"Can we turn down the music?" she asked, reaching for the stereo. "Seriously, who listens to ABBA?"

"Watch what you say about ABBA, or you might find yourself walking to the cottage." I glared at her as I slapped her hand away from the volume dial. "Now spill the details."

She sighed. "I got caught smoking. I got caught breaking into the dining hall after hours. I got caught hotwiring one of the camp vehicles. Oh, and I got caught making out with one of the junior counselors. He's sixteen and really cute. But he's acting a little annoying now. Too clingy. I'm going to have to kick him to the curb soon."

"You smoke?"

"Only for shock value," she said. "It's a cry for help." She looked at me with a fake expression of innocence.

I swatted her in the arm.

"You seem to get caught a lot," I said to her. "You're not a very good badass."

"You should hear about the stuff I did that they didn't catch me doing," she said happily. "I only let them catch me at the little things. But you'd better not tell Mom any of this. 'Cause I'm pretty sure you were ten times worse than I ever was."

"All I did was get a tattoo," I insisted. "But I won't tell Maxine anything."

"You promise?"

I nodded. "But won't the camp call and tell her anyway?"

"No. I told them my mom was dead and that I was being raised by my aunt who liked to lock me in the closet every day. I even changed the phone number in my file one time when I broke into the office."

"One time?"

"Yeah. It's pretty easy to break in if you know how to pick a lock."

"I'm so glad to hear that you've opted for a life of crime. I'll come and visit you in prison."

She looked at me closely.

"What?" I asked her.

"It's just good to see you again," she said. I raised an eyebrow at her. I wasn't sure if she was making fun of me or not.

"I'm serious," she insisted. "It's been at least a couple of years."

"Since Sebastian's funeral," I added. "You were at least a foot shorter and you definitely didn't have anything pierced."

"Anything exciting happen to you in the last two years?" she asked.

"Not really. I've just been working."

"Yeah, I've seen your articles. Mom always sends them to me."

Really? That was interesting. Maxine had never let me know that she read my stuff. It was definitely surprising to find out she'd sent it on to Tina. This summer had been full of surprises.

"I even read your book," she was saying. "It wasn't bad."

"Gee, thanks."

"You're welcome. No wonder Grandma's been pissed at you so long."

"What are you talking about?"

"Oh, come on," she said, shaking her head. "The main character's mother was obviously Grandma. Anyone could see that. She was an ultra-controlling harpy. If that isn't Grandma, I don't know what is."

I hadn't intended it that way, but she was probably right.

"It wasn't intentional," I protested. "I never even noticed."

"Well I guess you're supposed to write what you know. And Grandma would provide enough for several books."

"Do you think she would notice herself? I don't think Mom's even read my book."

Tina looked at me. "Of course Mom's read your book. She's the one who gave it to me."

"Not Maxine. My mother."

"Now you're just being thick," Tina said in an annoyed tone. "I know. I've known for years. You don't have to protect me. I'm not a little kid, you know."

"What are you talking about?" She was acting crazy.

Tina sighed in frustration. "Grandma's not your mother. Maxine is. Everybody knows that. You don't have to pretend any more."

I hardly heard a word Tina said on the rest of the drive. My face was red with suppressed anger. I was thinking about what she said. It wasn't true. It couldn't be true.

What the hell was going on?

Chapter Fifteen

My face still felt flushed when we entered the cottage. I followed Tina inside without saying a word.

"Hi Jess, Mom," Tina said as she came in with her bag, completely oblivious to the distress she'd caused me. She tossed her bag on the floor. "I've got a bag full of laundry for you."

"Hi," Maxine called back from the kitchen. "Jess, can you show Tina to your room? The two of you will have to share."

"Sure."

"And then you can show Tina where the washing machine is."

Tina rolled her eyes at Maxine as the two girls left the room. I turned and went into the kitchen to confront Maxine. I had never been angrier in my life, but I didn't know what to say.

"Kerri, thanks for …" she began. She stopped when she saw the fury in my face. "My God. What's wrong?"

"Is it true?" I said in a harsh whisper.

"Is what true?" Maxine looked incredibly confused. "What are you talking about?"

"Just something that Tina and I were discussing on our drive over here," I said, actually remaining calm. "It seems that I've been lied to my whole God damned life."

Maxine turned white. "What do you mean?" Her voice was hardly more than a whisper. It was like she knew what was coming next.

I snapped. "Who the fuck are my parents?" I screamed. "Tell me the truth! I think I deserve to know the truth. If you've been lying to me for the last twenty-five years, I think that it's time that I knew."

Maxine looked like she was going to faint. I didn't care.

"So, it is true. You got yourself knocked up at fifteen and then gave me to your own parents to raise. Even though you'd already seen first hand just how crappy they were at being parents. Then you took off for three years so as to not have anything to do with me."

Maxine looked up at me. There were tears in her eyes, and she looked like I had hit her.

"No," she said quietly. "That's not entirely true. Yes, I got pregnant at fifteen. But I wanted to keep the baby. You. Jack and I thought we were ready. Our parents didn't agree. They might have been right. But it wasn't their decision to make. I was stupid enough to actually think they would let us decide on our own."

She laughed bitterly before continuing.

"His parents shipped him off as soon as they found out. I didn't even know where he went. My parents kept me locked up so that none of the neighbours would know I was pregnant. Mom said that I had disgraced the family. But she was doing a good job of that on her own. Mom started drinking more and more. I *never* would have given her my child."

She struggled to suppress a sob. "They told me that the baby had been put up for adoption. I stayed in the hospital for a week before being sent to Switzerland. I didn't even know if I'd had a boy or a girl. The doctor felt that I wouldn't get attached to the baby if I never held it.

"I was so mad at my parents, I never wanted to see them again. I stayed at school for all the holidays and summer vacations. I only came home after graduation when I was eighteen."

She finally looked me in the eyes.

"Imagine my surprise when I returned home and found out that I had a three-year-old sister that I'd never even heard of. You were so shy, and you would hardly even look at me. But as soon as I saw you I knew. You have Jack's eyes, you know? I was furious. I told Mom I was going to take you away. You were mine.

"She just laughed at me. She said that legally you belonged to her. Even though she drank all the time and neglected you, I still couldn't take you. I was eighteen with only a high school education, no money and no job. She told me that no court would ever give me custody. And you wouldn't have come voluntarily even if they had. It made me sick. I couldn't look at you without pain."

I was shocked. I couldn't say anything.

"I'm sorry," she said quietly. Then she laughed lightly with the same bitterness as before. "I know that doesn't mean anything, but I really am sorry."

"I'm sorry too," I said to her, keeping all emotion out of my voice. "I'm sorry that you felt you couldn't tell me the truth."

"I wanted to," she said. "Every day I wanted to. But when you were little, I thought you'd be happier not knowing. And when you were older, you were always so angry with me. It never seemed like a good time. And I guess I'm just a coward."

"Did Sebastian know?"

"I don't know. I don't think so. He was only eight when you were born. I'm pretty sure he believed what Mom and Dad told him."

I was relieved. I would have hated to find out that Sebastian had been lying to me too. But it was also horrible to think that he had died without knowing the truth. I didn't know if I should believe her or not.

"Are you okay with this?" Maxine said.

"I don't know," I said honestly. "It's going to take some time to get used to."

"I realize that. And we'll give you all the time you need." She paused. "I know this is hard for you, but this summer has been wonderful for me. We've finally been able to get to know each other. When I saw you at Dad's will reading, you were so ... distant. And I can't help feeling that it's all my fault."

"What are you talking about?"

"You and Carter. Your problems with commitment. It's my fault. If I'd told you back when you were a child that I was your mother, maybe we would have had a real relationship. Maybe you wouldn't have felt abandoned by everyone."

"It's not your fault, Maxine." I sighed. "At least, it's not entirely your fault. Maybe things *would* have been different if I'd know when I was a kid. But I didn't. And what happened with Carter and me was ... well, it was my fault."

"I'm so sorry, Kerri. You'll never know how sorry I am."

I paced the kitchen, still not really believing what I'd heard. Then I thought of something.

"So, I guess Tina is actually my sister, not my niece. Well, half-sibling anyway."

Maxine nodded. "And Jessica, Sam and Zack too."

I hadn't even considered that. Suddenly, things made sense. Jess really did look like me. No wonder people had thought she was Maxine's daughter at first.

I needed to sit down. I was too stunned to process any additional information.

"I have four half-siblings," I said. It was kind of overwhelming. Not just kind of. Absolutely and totally overwhelming.

Maxine looked like she had something to add.

"What?" I asked her. "Please don't tell me I've got some more hidden away somewhere. I don't think I can take any more surprises."

"No. But you will be getting a full sibling in about five months."

"What?"

I realized what had been going on with Maxine this summer. She wasn't sick. She was pregnant.

"That's what you were talking to Alex about." It was a statement, not a question.

Maxine nodded.

"But you can't be pregnant," I protested.

"Why not?"

"Because you're so old." It was the only thing I could think of.

"I'm not that old. I'm only forty-one."

"Do the others know?"

"Yes," she said. "We were waiting to tell you. Actually, I was waiting. Jack wanted me to tell you a long time ago."

That would have been nice, I thought to myself.

"What about you and Jack?" I wasn't prepared to call him my father. "Obviously you and Steven split more than a month ago."

"You're right. Steven and I split a little over a year ago. The divorce was final two weeks ago, and Jack and I are going to get married in the fall." She grinned. "We thought it was only fitting to get married while I was pregnant, since that was what we had originally planned to do twenty-five years ago."

"But why did you lie to me?" I asked her, feeling tears choking my voice. It was just too much to absorb in one sitting. "How do you think that makes me feel? Especially since I'm obviously the last one to know about everything." I felt like throwing a tantrum like a little kid, and for once I had a legitimate reason to act like one.

"I'm sorry. I wish you hadn't found out this way. I wanted to tell you myself. Tina knew that she wasn't supposed to say anything."

"Yeah, well maybe I thought I was helping."

I turned and saw Tina standing at the door of the kitchen, her arms crossed over her chest.

"I mean, you were never going to tell her," she continued, "so someone had to."

"I was going to tell her," Maxine insisted firmly.

"When?" Tina asked. "Probably after the baby graduated from college. I was just speeding things up a little."

"It could have been handled a little bit more delicately," Maxine said wryly.

Tina shrugged her shoulders. "Yeah, well, it's done now. Everyone knows the truth." She looked very satisfied with herself.

I turned all my rage onto Tina. I couldn't stand the sight of her standing there looking so pleased with herself. All the crappy things I was feeling were her fault.

"What are you looking so smug about?" I shouted at her.

"Nothing," she replied. "I just think that maybe you should have been able to figure it out on your own."

"How? How exactly was I supposed to figure it out?"

"Tina, please don't butt in any more," Maxine said impatiently. "It's none of your business."

"But Mom," Tina protested.

"I'm serious," Maxine said. "Please go outside for a while before Kerri gets really angry and kicks your ass. Which I wouldn't stop, because you deserve it, I might add."

Tina made a face before leaving.

Maxine turned back to me.

"Are you going to be okay with this?"

"I don't know. It's a lot to take in all at once." I was shocked, stunned and angry, and I didn't want to talk about it any more.

"I know. And I really am sorry." She looked at me. She reached out as if to grab my hand and then stopped herself. "What are you going to do?"

"I need to go out for a while," I said, turning my back to Maxine. I needed to get away from her before I did or said something I really regretted.

"Where are you going?"

"I'm not sure."

"When will you be back?"

"I don't know. Just because you're my biological mother doesn't mean you can start sticking your nose into my life." I didn't owe her an explanation for anything, and I certainly wasn't going to let her start keeping tabs on me.

I left the cottage and got into my car. It was like I was having an out-of-body experience. I felt like I was floating, looking down on myself driving. I probably shouldn't have even been behind the wheel. I was driving fast and erratically. I didn't realize where I was headed until I reached the house. I parked my car on the street and turned off the ignition. I sat there for a couple of minutes before getting out of the car, walking quickly up the drive and knocking on the door.

Carter opened the door with a confused look on his face. I could tell that I was the last person he was expecting to see. In fact, he looked like he was expecting someone else.

"Kerri? What's going on?"

"Hi, I'm sorry to bother you," I began. "I should go." Then I burst into tears.

He quickly ushered me into the house. After he shut the door behind me he put his arms around me. I was sobbing uncontrollably, and Carter being nice to me didn't help any.

"What's wrong?" he asked looking concerned.

I needed to tell someone, and he was the first person I thought of.

"I'm sorry," I said sniffling and stepping away from him. "I just needed someone to talk to."

"What's wrong?" he repeated. He had a very serious expression on his face. "You can tell me anything."

"I just found out that Maxine is my mother."

He looked at me with a stunned expression. "Let's sit down."

He led me over to the couch, and we sat down, keeping a safe distance from each other. It was oddly familiar, yet it made me feel incredibly alone. I tried my best to shake the feeling.

"What happened?"

"Short story, Maxine got pregnant at fifteen and her parents ended up taking custody of the baby. Me." Once I managed to stop bawling like a little baby, I was amazed at how calm I sounded.

"And you just found this out now?"

I nodded. "My niece ... I mean my sister Tina intentionally let it slip today. She thought I should know."

"Do you know, I mean ..." he looked very uncomfortable.

"Do I know who my father is?" I finished for him.

He nodded.

"Yeah. His name is Jack, and he and Maxine are getting married in the fall." I paused. "And she's pregnant."

"How are you doing? I mean, that's a lot to absorb in one day."

"Aside from my entire universe being shattered beyond recognition, I'm okay."

I felt surprisingly better after talking to him. I looked into his eyes and could see his concern for me reflected in them. And I suddenly felt the need to come clean about everything.

"I lied to you," I blurted out suddenly.

"What?"

"I lied to you."

"About what?"

"About my brother. How he died."

Carter didn't say anything. I continued anyway.

"It wasn't a car accident. He had cancer. He was sick for a long time, and then he died. I told him that he had to fight it. I told him that he couldn't give in. He tried everything; chemo, radiation. Nothing worked. There was an experimental treatment that I wanted him to try, but he wouldn't. I was so angry with him. I told him he was giving up. We had a horrible fight, and then he died. He had been in horrible pain, and I wouldn't let him rest. The last time I saw him we fought."

"It wasn't your fault he died."

"I know, but it was my fault that he was in pain for so long. Denny knew that Sebastian wanted to go. But I wouldn't let him."

"I'm sure your brother knew how you felt," Carter insisted. "He knew that you didn't want him to die. He knew that you loved him."

"Maybe, but it doesn't make things any better. And I don't know why I lied to you about it. Why I lie to everyone. It's easier to pretend that Sebastian died in an accident. Something quick. I think I was even starting to believe it myself, until Denny called me on it."

"Is that why the two of you are fighting?"

"It's one of the reasons. The main reason is because of how horribly I've treated everyone. I've been acting like a spoiled idiot my entire life."

I sighed and sank back into the couch.

"I'm sure you haven't been that bad," he said, patting my hand in a somewhat condescending manner.

I shook my head. "No. I was. I am. I'm horrible. Looking back on everything, my whole life I've only thought about myself. Denny was right. You were right. If

I hadn't been so self-involved I might have been able to figure things out. I should have known the truth about Maxine."

"How could you have been expected to know that Maxine was your mother? If no one had told you, you probably never would have known."

"Are you saying I'm not very observant?" I raised an eyebrow at him.

He laughed. "Well, you're not exactly Sherlock Holmes."

I grabbed a cushion from the couch and chucked it at him. It hit him square in the head.

He lunged at me, tickling me under the ribs. I was incredibly ticklish, and he knew it.

Suddenly, we were kissing. I didn't know how it happened. I wasn't sure which one of us started it. I curled my fingers in his hair, not wanting the kiss to end. I felt his hands moving slowly over my body.

It felt right. It felt perfect. I never wanted to let go of him.

And then there was the sound of the front door opening. Carter was off me so fast, I thought maybe I'd imagined the whole thing. I sat up and straightened my clothes.

"Carter, there's someone's car out front," Charlotte said as she came into the room.

Carter stood quickly and kissed her.

"Hi sweetie," he said to her. "Kerri just dropped by to talk."

I jumped up with a forced smile on my face. "And I was just leaving. Carter, thanks for listening. Charlotte, it was nice to see you again."

I left the two of them standing in the living room staring after me. I walked out to my car, reaching slowly into my purse for my keys.

This was the point in the story where Carter was supposed to come running out of the house, grab my hand to stop me from getting into the car and sweep me into his arms. I hated myself for wanting him to do it.

But I hated him even more for not doing it.

Chapter Sixteen

I didn't go home that night. I didn't want to see any of the people staying in my house. James was in Toronto, and Denny still wasn't talking to me. I didn't have any place to go, so I didn't go anywhere. I spent the time driving around town and all the side roads. At around five in the morning, I pulled back into the driveway and quietly crept into the house.

"Where were you?"

I jumped. I wasn't expecting anyone to be up. That was why I had waited until five in the morning to come home.

"Christ, Maxine!" I said. "What the hell are you doing? It's almost dawn. Why are you still up?"

"I was worried about you," she said. She was sitting on the couch in her housecoat. "Where were you?"

"I was out." I wasn't about to start explaining myself to her.

"You could have called."

"Just because you tell me you're my mother doesn't mean I have to start acting any differently."

"Oh."

I looked at her. She looked tired and hurt.

With a sigh, I told her about my visit to Carter. "After I left his place, I just spent the night driving around. And now I'm really too tired to talk anymore. I'm going to bed."

"Kerri," Maxine said to me as I turned to go upstairs.

"Yeah?"

"Are we okay?"

"We're fine. I'm just still a little confused. I need a little more time to think about this on my own. Then I'm sure we'll be the perfect family."

I went into my room and crawled into bed without turning on the light or changing into my pajamas. I was physically and mentally exhausted. All I wanted to do was sleep for the next twenty-four hours. I was lying down with my eyes shut when I heard the door open.

"I said I need some space, Maxine."

"It's Tina."

I opened my eyes. Tina was standing at the foot of my bed.

"What do you want?"

"I'm really sorry about yesterday," she said. I looked at her closely in the sunlight that was just beginning to brighten the room. It looked like she'd been crying. "I just wanted you to know the truth." She sniffed. She wasn't as tough as she wanted everyone to think. Either that or she was just trying to scam me into not killing her. I was so tired I didn't care.

"I forgive you," I said as I yawned.

"Really?"

"Just don't do it again." I closed my eyes again, hoping she would get the hint and leave.

"Kerri?"

"What now?"

"Can I sleep here with you? Jess snores and talks in her sleep."

I moved over to one side of the bed, and she jumped in next to me.

It was nearly two in the afternoon when I woke up. I was stiff and kind of grumpy. Tina was lying on my right arm, leaving me with no feeling in it at all. I tried to pull my arm out from under her without success. Then I tried to push her off me. She quickly rolled over and punched me in the eye.

"Ow!" I yelled, smacking her on the top of the head.

"What's going on?" she mumbled sleepily.

"You punched me in the eye," I yelled at her. I jumped out of bed to look in the mirror. The eye was already red and puffy. "I think you've given me a black eye."

Tina sat up. "Sorry."

"Plus I think my arm is dead from where you've been lying on it."

"It was obviously on my side of the bed then," she insisted with a yawn.

I turned back to the mirror after scowling at her.

"Let me take a look at it," she sighed as she climbed out of bed. She came over to me and looked down into my eye. "It's not that bad, you big baby."

"I'm the baby?" I said.

"I hardly touched you, and you're acting all crazy."

"Okay. That's it. You're going down."

"Do you want to stand on this chair? Then maybe you'll be able to reach me."

I dove at her, knocking her back onto the bed. I picked up the nearest pillow and hit her with it. She hit me with the other one. I managed to pin her down by sitting on her. Then I started tickling her.

"Stop, please," she pleaded in between her laughter.

"Who's the baby?"

"I am," she said, her voiced muffled slightly by the pillow.

The door swung open. Maxine stood in the doorway with her arms crossed.

"What's going on here?" she said. "It sounded like you were killing each other."

"Tina punched me!"

"In my sleep!"

"So now you're attempting to squish her," Maxine said dryly.

I rolled off Tina.

"Are you two planning to sleep all day?" Maxine asked. "It's already after two."

"I'm getting up now," I said. "But first I'm having a shower."

After I got dressed, I went downstairs. Everyone was outside on the deck, so I joined them. It was strange. Two days earlier I hadn't even met Jack's kids, and then suddenly I find out I'm related to all of them. I didn't know how to deal with it. Should I bring it up or ignore it? Should I go back inside or should I stay and talk to everyone? Sam made the decision for me.

"Hi, Kerri," Sam said as I stepped outside. "Nice black eye. What happened?"

I glared at Tina. "A word of advice for all of you. Tina is extremely dangerous and shouldn't be messed with. I'm sure someday she'll be behind bars where she belongs but until then be very, very careful."

Tina punched me in the arm.

"See what I mean?" I said to the boys.

"How are you doing today?" Jack asked cautiously.

I was really sick of people asking me that.

"I'm fine, aside from a black eye."

"I mean after yesterday," Jack insisted.

"With the big news? I guess I'm okay. It's strange, but I suppose I'll get used to it eventually."

We spent the rest of Sunday enjoying the warm weather. Aside from the fact that Maxine and Jack kept staring at me to make sure I was okay, the day wasn't too bad. I didn't know what I should be feeling. Part of me knew I should still be furious with Maxine and Jack for lying to me for so long. But another part of me seemed to be calmly accepting the news.

If I could have stopped thinking about kissing Carter and fighting with Denny, it would have been a perfect day.

I woke up Monday morning, resolved to patch things up with Denny. I dialed Alex's number, unsure if I'd be able to reach him there so late on a weekday. I didn't have a clue as to where he was. Alex had told me he'd left Emily, but I didn't know if he was staying in the city or if he'd moved in with Alex already. Denny never kept his cell phone on, making it difficult to get in touch with him. And I'd already left dozens of messages on his office voicemail. Alex really was my only option.

"Hi, Alex," I said when she answered. "It's Kerri. Thanks for not hanging up at the sound of my voice. You wouldn't happen to have Denny there, would you?"

"He's right here," she said. "I'll get him.

"Hello." He sounded angry. I knew Alex had pretty much forced him to talk to me. That didn't exactly fill me with confidence.

I started talking right away so that he could hear what I wanted to say before he hung up.

I tried to keep my tone light and friendly. "I've been calling you, but I didn't know where you were."

"You've found me."

"Can we meet somewhere to talk in person?" I was going to get him to forgive me even if I had to get on my hands and knees and beg.

"I don't know. I'm very busy." His voice sounded incredibly cold.

I forged on despite this. "Come on. You'll need to eat. It will only take an hour out of your day. I'll even pay."

"Right."

"No, seriously. Meet me for lunch at *Patrick's*." I was even willing to risk a run in with you-know-who in order to clear the air with Denny. That's just a sign of how desperate I was.

"Fine." He hung up. At least the dial tone sounded a little friendlier than the previous times he had hung up on me.

When I arrived at *Patrick's,* Denny was already there. He was sitting at a table near the bar with his arms crossed. He looked annoyed and nervous at the same time. When I saw him sitting there, I realized just how much I had missed him. I wanted to run over to the table and throw my arms around his neck. Instead, I walked calmly over to the table and handed him a gift-wrapped package.

"What's this?" he asked suspiciously.

"It's a peace offering," I replied. "I'm really, really sorry." I gave him what I hoped was a winning smile.

He opened the gift. It was a picture of Denny and me with Sebastian the year before he died. The three of us had gone to Mexico, and we were sitting on the beach. It was one of my favourite pictures.

He knew how much it meant to me.

"Kerri, I'm sorry too," he said, standing up and giving me a big bear hug.

"I know I've been awful since Sebastian died," I said. "I'm sorry. I guess I just don't want to open up and get hurt again. I've been an awful friend. I had to hear from Alex that you and Emily had split. I didn't even know what had been happening to you. You were going through a lot, and I wasn't any support."

"That's okay," he said. "I've known for a long time that you were an awful friend."

I took a swing at him.

"But I still love you," he added.

"I don't know what I'd do without you," I said truthfully, grabbing his hand. "I've been miserable not being able to talk to you. I haven't had anyone to bitch to in weeks."

"Well, now that it's a local call you can phone me any time."

"That reminds me. What are you going to do here anyway? Why are you here in the middle of the week? I was half expecting you to be in the city. Don't you work anymore?"

"I still had a lot of vacation time left, so I decided to stay here this week."

"Is Alex taking time off too?"

"She's working a couple of days, but she's off today."

"That's great. I think you make a great couple. I really like Alex. She's too good for you, you know."

"I know," he replied with a huge smile.

"Don't forget that."

He looked at me closely. "Kerri, why do you have a black eye?"

I sighed. "It's a long story."

"Tell me. What's been happening in your life lately? I want to know everything. James has been afraid to even mention your name to me. I think he expected me to act crazy if he brought you up."

"Poor James. He's had a rough time of it. He'll be ecstatic that we're talking again."

"Tell me what's going on."

"Well, I'm almost finished my novel."

"That's wonderful!" he said. "I didn't even know that you had started."

"Yeah. I've got to do some editing, and then I'll be done."

"I can't wait to read it," he said. "What's it about?"

"It's a secret. You'll have to wait and read it when it's finished."

"I'm so happy for you."

"Plus, my agent has gotten me an advance based on some of the chapters that I've sent in so far. Not a huge advance, but it's nice to have some money again. That's why I'm going to pay for lunch today. As long as you order something cheap."

"Can't you tell me what it's about?"

"Nope. Oh, and I'm not seeing Duncan anymore."

"That is great news."

"I also found out that Maxine's pregnant."

I was going to drag this out. It would be fun to see the look on his face when I told him.

"What? How old is she?"

"Well, she was fifteen when she had me, so that would make her almost forty-one."

"Forty-one isn't too old," he said. Then he realized what else I'd said. "What do you mean, 'had you'?"

"Oh, didn't I tell you? I found out that Maxine's not my sister. She's actually my mother."

Denny looked at me with his mouth hanging open.

"And her boyfriend, Jack, is my father," I continued in a very casual tone. "The baby will be my only full sibling."

"Are you telling me the truth?"

"Yeah. My other brothers and sisters are only my half-siblings. You should see how much Jack's daughter Jessica looks like me."

"No, about Maxine. She's your mother?"

"Yes."

"When did you find out? And why are you so calm about this?"

"I found out a couple of days ago. It's had some time to sink in." I grinned at him. "I definitely wasn't this calm when I first found out. Kind of makes you wish you hadn't been so pissed off at me, huh?"

He kept staring at me, open-mouthed with shock.

"I was really surprised to hear about you and Alex," I continued, changing the subject. "Surprised, but happy. Alex's great. I hope you two will be really happy."

"Yeah," he agreed, "she really is great. She's amazing. I guess she reminds me a bit of you without the emotional baggage."

"Thanks," I said sarcastically.

"You're welcome."

"What about work? Are you going to commute?"

"Actually, I'm transferring to the Barrie office. It's only a twenty minute drive from here. I think it will be much better than living in Toronto for the rest of my life. It's a smaller office and everyone seems great."

"This is serious. You're even moving for her."

"It's very serious. I really do love her."

I took his hand. "I can tell. And I know she loves you too."

Denny looked so happy I couldn't help smiling. I was glad he was so happy with Alex. Even if he was kind of a schmuck sometimes, he deserved it.

"Alex and I are meeting here for dinner tonight. You should join us."

"I don't want to intrude," I said. "Plus, I've got work to do."

"You've got to eat," he protested. "And I'm sure you don't have any food in that house of yours."

"Actually, now that I'm living with my whole family," the sound of that was ridiculous, "the fridge is fully stocked."

"You're loving this, aren't you?"

I nodded. "I guess it's just nice having a normal family. Once I got over the initial strangeness, that is."

"I'm happy for you," Denny said, squeezing my hand. "But you should still join us for dinner."

"Fine," I agreed at last. "I'll meet you here at seven."
I gave Denny a big hug before heading back to the cottage.

By the time I arrived back at *Patrick's* that night, Alex and Denny were already seated. I joined them and ordered a beer and a burger. There was live music, and the place was packed. I felt a little like a third wheel, but it was nice being out with Denny again.

"I'm glad you two are talking finally," Alex said. "I couldn't stand him moping around the house all day."

"I wasn't moping," Denny said.

"Dennis, you were acting like a little girl," Alex said seriously. "It was starting to grate on my nerves. If you two hadn't patched things up, I was going to have to send you back to your wife."

Denny grimaced. I couldn't tell if it was at the mention of his wife or at the thought of having to go back to her.

"Thanks," he said sarcastically.

"You're welcome," she replied, patting his hand affectionately.

The waiter brought our food. I took a big bite of my burger.

"I'm just glad that Denny's with someone who doesn't hate me," I said. "It will be nice to come and visit you without getting the cold shoulder."

Carter walked in with his girlfriend right at that moment.

"Speaking of the cold shoulder," I mumbled.

"Oh, shit," Alex said, dropping a French fry. "I'm so sorry. I didn't realize he'd be here. If I'd known, we would have gone somewhere else."

"They must eat here every night," I grumbled. "Considering how many times I've bumped into them here."

"I'm really sorry," Alex said again. "Do you want to leave? We could get our meals wrapped up and finish them at my place."

"Don't be silly," I said in a reassuring tone. "Carter and I are friends." I was impressed with how mature I was acting. "Besides, I don't think there's any place else in town where we could have gone." I wasn't really that concerned about seeing Carter.

However, I did slouch down in my chair so that he couldn't see me.

Unfortunately, he came over to the table anyway. I forgot that I was sitting with his sister.

"Hi Alex, Denny," he said when he came up. Then he saw me. "Kerri."

Charlotte was glaring at me angrily. I don't think she was pleased that I had been at his house the other day.

"Hi," I said back. I wasn't about to give him (or her) the privilege of seeing me act like an idiot. I would prove to all of them that I could keep it together. I wouldn't knock anything over, and I wouldn't bump into any of the staff. Carter had already seen me have a melt down, and I wanted to show him that I didn't care who he was out with.

But I didn't have to look at them.

"Nice to see you both," Alex said, her voice sounding strange. I couldn't tell what her facial expression was because I was concentrating on my food. It really was very interesting. I think she may have been laughing at me, but I wasn't sure.

I was pretty sure I could feel Carter's eyes on the top of my head. Of course, I could have just been imagining things. I had to stop being so paranoid and self-centered.

"Oh, look," Charlotte was saying. "There's a table right over there." She seemed to be very anxious to get away from us. Which suited me just fine. I was getting a pain in my neck from looking down.

"Great," Carter replied. "It was nice to see all of you."

I let out my breath. I hadn't even realized that I'd been holding it.

"I'm sorry, Kerri," Alex said.

"About what?" I asked, taking another bite of my burger.

"Nothing," Alex said.

"It didn't sound like Carter wanted to kill you, Denny," I said. "You two seemed to have made some progress."

"I thought Carter was going to kill him a few weeks ago," Alex admitted. "But since Denny left his wife, Carter has started being civil to him."

"It helps that your parents like me," Denny added.

"Wait a minute," I said. "You're married and dating their daughter, and they like you? Even Alex's mom?"

Denny nodded.

"That is *so* not fair," I grumbled.

Shortly after Carter and Charlotte sat down at their table, Duncan and his friends entered. This just wasn't going to be a good night for me, I thought. As soon as they saw us, Duncan made a bee-line for our table.

"Kerri," he said, looking sorrowful and drunk, "I'm so sorry. Can we go outside and talk?"

I stood up. The last thing I wanted was for him to make a scene. Not here. And he looked like he was ready to make a scene.

I followed him to the side of the room. I wasn't going to go outside alone with him.

"What do you want, Duncan?" I asked him firmly. I wasn't in any mood to talk with him so my tone was angry.

"I want you back," he said sorrowfully. He was really drunk. I could smell the alcohol on his breath and his speech was slightly slurred.

Good lord.

"That's too bad, Duncan," I said. "We're not getting back together."

"Why not?" he asked drunkenly, stepping closer to me.

"Because I'm not interested in you."

"Please, Kerri," he continued, his voice rising. "I'm in love with you. I'm sorry about the way I acted the other night."

"Look, Duncan," I said in a loud whisper. "You're not in love with me. You're a nice guy, but I'm just not interested in you that way. I just want us to be friends." I didn't even want that, but I really wanted to shut him up.

Suddenly, he grew very angry. He grabbed me firmly by the arm and pulled me closer to him. He absolutely reeked of alcohol.

"Let go of me," I said angrily, trying to pull out of his grasp. He was a lot stronger than me, and he wasn't ready to let go. I saw Denny jump to his feet.

"Maybe Alex's more your type," Duncan said nastily.

I rolled my eyes at him. "Yeah, that's original. Just because a woman doesn't want to sleep with you, you assume she's a lesbian. Did you ever think it might be because you're just not very interesting?"

Great idea, Kerri. Insult the jackass who's grabbing your arm. He tightened his grip. It was actually starting to hurt.

"Is he bothering you?" Carter's voice said behind me.

"Yes, he is, but I can handle it." I didn't need him to rescue me from this jerk.

"Get lost, asshole," Duncan said to Carter.

"Let go of her," Carter said to Duncan.

"Mind your own business," Duncan yelled back at him.

Every head in the bar turned to stare at us.

Then things really went out of control.

Carter shoved Duncan, knocking him into the table behind him. Duncan let go of my arm in order to take a swing at Carter. I stepped back to get out of their way (I already had one black eye and I didn't want another). Suddenly, punches started flying. Glass broke, people were screaming. Then the bartender was in the middle of the two of them, and Duncan and his friends were kicked out. It all happened so quickly that I couldn't exactly figure out what happened.

Charlotte ran to Carter, a look of concern plastered on her face.

Carter was looking at me. It was one of those moments of absolute clarity. I could read every emotion in his eyes. He felt nothing for me but friendship.

I realized I didn't want to be friends with him.

I was in love with him.

And that thought scared the crap out of me.

Chapter Seventeen

It was something I'd been putting off for too long. But finally I had the courage to do it. The drive to visit my mother—I'm sorry, my grandmother—was long and stressful. I left the cottage early in the morning, and I unfortunately got caught in the rush hour traffic around Toronto. It was a sign that I'd been away from the city for far too long. I didn't want to see her, but I needed to talk to her. I wanted to clear the air and make some sense of things.

Maxine had offered to go with me, so had Tina, but I needed to go alone. I needed to talk to the woman that I had thought was my mother and having Maxine and Tina there might make me less able to say what I needed to. But while I was driving, I started wishing that they were both with me.

When I pulled into the visitor's parking lot behind my moth ... grandmother's building, I froze. What was I doing? The woman had struck fear into my heart for as long as I could remember. There was no way in hell that I was going to willingly face her. I hadn't seen her in years. I should keep it that way. I could easily turn around and leave, pretend that I never came.

Instead, I got out of the car. I walked around to the front of the building and pressed the buzzer for Irene Shepherd. While waiting for her to answer and let me in, I looked around. The building was only five stories and was in desperate need of maintenance. The lobby smelled like alcohol and stale cigarettes. The smell of my childhood. I had to fight the urge to run back outside into the fresh air.

"Who is it?" a disembodied voice said through the speaker. She sounded pissed off, but then again, that was how she usually sounded. Ah, the memories.

"It's Kerri," I replied.

"Who? I don't know any 'Kerris'."

I sighed. "It's Abigail."

"What do you want?"

Isn't she nice? She hadn't seen me in over two years and this was the greeting I got.

"Can I come up?"

The only reply was the sound of the front door being unlocked. I walked up one flight of stairs and knocked on the door of apartment 206.

I could hear movement inside as someone looked through the peephole. This was followed by the sound of many locks being undone. Finally, the door opened.

"Hello, Abigail," she said to me. She stepped back to let me inside.

"Hello, Irene," I replied.

She looked at me with a critical eye. I could tell she was analyzing my hair, my clothes and my general appearance. For my part, I examined her. She was looking much older than her sixty-two years. Her hair was died a hideous shade of red, and her skin was a sickly yellow colour, as were the walls of her apartment. In her right hand was a cigarette, already forming a long ash at the tip. Her left hand held a glass of some sort of amber-coloured alcohol. She was just as I had remembered her.

"So you're calling me by my first name now?" she asked viciously. "In my day young people were taught to respect their elders, especially their mothers."

Only people who earn my respect get it from me, I thought. I didn't say anything like that of course.

"We both know you're not my mother," I blurted out before I could stop myself. I hadn't wanted to get into this right away. It just came out. So much for the incredibly cool confrontation scene I'd imagined on the drive down.

She laughed cruelly. "So Maxine finally told you, eh? I didn't think the girl would do it. She's got no backbone, never did have. Always led around by other people. So what does Steven have to say about Maxine's bastard child? You can bet she never told him about you."

"She and Steven are divorced," I said, trying valiantly to keep my temper. What I really wanted to do was knock her teeth in.

"Really?" she said, sounding surprised.

It was finally nice not to be the last person to hear about something.

"Yes. She moved out more than a year ago."

"Well, I can't imagine why she'd do that. The girl never did have any sense. Giving up her meal ticket after all these years. Where is she living? I can't imagine she's living with you. You couldn't stand her."

"She's been staying with me all summer," I said. "But she's getting married in the fall."

"To whom?"

"My father," I said with a smile. I hoped that would take the smug look off her face.

"I see. So she's marrying ... what was his name? I remember she was always with the eldest McKay boy. He was worthless, just like all the McKays. Never did a day's worth of honest labour in their lives. They just lived off of their inheritance. Old money gone bad." She paused to take a long drag from her cigarette and a drink from her glass. "But I doubt she really knows who your father actually is. Maxine was a little whore, getting pregnant at fifteen like that. And she was always one for slumming. Something you resemble her a great deal in, if I'm not mistaken."

"I don't know what you're talking about."

"Don't play Miss Innocent with me, young lady. I knew all about your relationship with that friend of Sebastian's. The pedophile should have been arrested for dating you. It was disgusting. He was always hanging off you like a bad suit. Sebastian hated it. He told me so. But since you weren't really my daughter, there wasn't anything I could do."

"Sebastian never would have told you anything," I snapped at her. "The only reason he talked to you at all was because he was such a decent person. He was a much better person than the rest of us. You did everything in your power to fuck us all up. I don't know how Sebastian managed to be the wonderful person that he was."

"Abigail, don't swear in front of me."

"And since when did we become too good to associate with certain people?" I continued. "I don't remember us being any better than anyone else. And look at you now. You're one step below white trash."

"That's because you were too young to remember what things were like before your father left." She paused. "I should say your grandfather."

"I remember him," I said.

"Yes, but you didn't know him before you were born. He was a happy man then, content with his children. We had money and the respect of our friends. And it was family money, not like some of the new money today." She took another drink. "The children had everything. They were spoiled. Certainly Maxine was. One day she comes to us, pregnant, defiantly claiming she's going to have the baby. Her father was heartbroken. We wanted her to have an abortion but she refused. She said she wanted to raise her bastard child on her own. That is, until she saw you. She wanted to put you up for adoption and go back to acting like a wild teenager. But we decided to raise Maxine's child ourselves. At least then we could prevent a scandal."

Maxine's version was more credible, and I didn't want to believe a word she said. But it still hurt.

"So what happened to all this money that was around before I was born?" I asked her. I wanted to find holes in her story, and I definitely wanted to take her down a peg.

"Your fa ... grandfather took it when he left."

I remembered being eight years old and living with Maxine and Sebastian in a tiny apartment in a not-too-nice part of the city. And I realized that Irene had probably been receiving child support payments, drinking a large part of them, using it for herself and only sending us money when she felt like it. I wondered how Maxine had managed it, only twenty-three and looking after two kids, one of whom was her own daughter who could hardly stand her. I felt like shit. I was lucky Maxine even spoke to me. At twenty-five, I could hardly support myself. Maxine had had two people who relied on her completely when she had been my age.

"I don't believe you," I said bluntly to Irene. "I think you drank all the money. Your ex-husbands probably got some of it. Thankfully, my grandfather had enough sense or enough distrust of you to put money away for Sebastian's education."

She narrowed her eyes at me.

"You always were a horrid child," she said. "No wonder you turned out the way you did."

"How would you know what I was like when I was a kid? You were never around. And I think I've turned out fine." While you've turned into a decrepit old bat, I thought. My restraint really was amazing. I was imagining my fingers wrapped tightly around her bony neck.

"This is the thanks I get for taking in Maxine's bastard child? For feeding and clothing you? For giving you a home? You ungrateful little bitch."

"You never did a single thing for me my entire life," I said to her. "You deserve everything you get."

"Get out of my house," she yelled at me. If her glass had been empty, I think she would have thrown it at me (she would never waste a drop of booze).

"Gladly," I said to her as I headed for the door. I turned back to her before leaving. "And for Christ's sake stop drinking. It's not even noon."

Maxine was standing in the kitchen when I returned to the cottage. I was physically and emotionally drained. I walked over to her and gave her a big hug.

"Was it horrible?" she asked me.

"Yes." I stepped back from her. "I'm pretty sure I'm out of her will."

"Did you tell her that you know the truth?"

"Yeah. She only had nasty things to say about all of us." I gave Maxine a kiss on the cheek.

She looked at me in surprise. "What was that for?"

"I'm just glad that I'm not as closely related to the old witch as I had thought." Maxine laughed. "And I'm sorry about how I treated you my entire life. I was awful to you. You gave up everything to look after Sebastian and me, and I was an ungrateful little brat. I promise to try and be a better daughter than I was a sister.

"And you wouldn't believe her, but she tried to pin all the blame for your father leaving on me," I continued, hoping Maxine would contradict me. She didn't disappoint.

"That's ridiculous," she said angrily. "He loved you more than any of us. It was her that drove him away. He wasn't strong enough to stand up to her or to take you and Sebastian with him. He was just a small man who was pushed past his breaking point. But you definitely weren't the reason he left."

"Thanks," I said, "but you don't need to worry. I didn't believe much of what she said anyway. It was only eleven in the morning, and the woman was already drunk."

"That's sad," she said. "I bet she's a very lonely person. I should probably go and visit her."

For some reason I knew she was going to say that. Maxine was very susceptible to guilt.

"Don't," I said, putting a restraining hand on her arm. "She doesn't deserve it."

"But she's my mother."

"I've seen sea turtles that were better mothers than her," I replied. "She's not worth the effort."

"How are you feeling about everything?" She asked, looking at me closely.

"I'm good, except for the fact that people keep asking me that."

"Seriously."

"I've never been so happy to find out that I was your illegitimate daughter after talking to Irene."

Maxine pulled me into a big hug. Suddenly, she was sobbing. I wasn't sure what I had done, and I didn't know what to do.

"Is everything okay?" Jack asked as he came into the kitchen. He looked very concerned.

Maxine turned and fell into his arms. She was practically in hysterics.

Jack looked at me in confusion. I shrugged.

"Don't look at me. I swear I didn't do anything. I was just being nice."

"It's just hormones," Maxine said sniffling. "I'm so happy." She burst into tears again.

"I can handle this," Jack said to me. "I've dealt with pregnant women before."

"I leave her in your capable hands," I replied.

"Alright, sweetie," Jack said. "I bought you some cookie dough ice cream. Will that help?"

Maxine nodded.

I smiled at them as I left the kitchen. I was doing a lot of that lately. Smiling. It was kind of cheesy. I shook off my annoyance at myself and walked into the living room. Tina and Jess were sitting on the couch in the living room watching TV. I flopped down between them.

"What's going on?" I asked them.

"Not much," Tina said, hardly taking her eyes off the screen. "The weather's too shitty to do anything outside."

I smacked her on the back of the head.

"What the hell was that for?" she yelled, rubbing her head.

"You shouldn't swear," I said to her.

"Why the hell not?" she demanded.

"Because there's going to be a baby around here soon," I said. "I don't want its first words to make a sailor blush."

"The baby's not going to be born for a while, and then it'll be at least twelve months more before it can talk."

"Yes, but now that I'm your sister, it's my job to make sure you act properly."

"Will you two be quiet?" Jess said angrily. "I'm trying to watch TV."
"It's the *Young & the Restless*," Tina whispered to me. "Very important."
Jess shot us each a dirty look.
"We should be quiet now."

The rest of the week passed in a blur. There were so many people around. I didn't have a minute to myself the entire time. But it was actually fun. Suddenly, it was Sunday afternoon and my guests were heading back to the city. All of them, that is, except Tina. Since she'd run away from summer camp, she claimed she didn't have anything better to do than to stay with me. I didn't mind—I was glad to have the company, and I was starting to like Tina. It would be nice to have the time to get to know her better.

Plus, if they'd all left, I think the place would have been a little too quiet. I had gotten used to having other people around.

"You'll call every day?" Maxine said to Tina as they packed up the car.

"Yes, Mother," Tina replied.

"And you'll make sure Tina behaves herself?" Maxine asked me.

"Yes, Mother," I echoed Tina. "But I doubt I'll have much success. If she misbehaves, I'll make sure the police escort her back to your place."

"Remember that chicken should be white inside before you eat it," Maxine continued. "And cook ground beef all the way through to prevent e.coli infection."

"Maxine," I said exasperated. "I've lived on my own before. I'm not going to kill Tina. Unless she pisses me off. Then I'll probably just drown her in the lake."

"I wish I was staying too," Jess said sulkily.

"You can't," Jack said shutting the trunk of his car. "You're working at the tennis club next week."

"I know," she replied.

"And then you have to go to your mother's," he continued.

"I know," she said again. "But it's still not fair."

"You can come up another time," I said to her. "And Tina and I will be back in the city in a couple of weeks."

I hugged everyone good bye and then turned to Tina after the cars left.

"So what's the plan?" I said to her.

"I say we head into town, buy some beer and get sloshed," she said eagerly.

I raised an eyebrow at her.

"Or we could have dinner and go to bed early like good little school girls," she amended.

"Why don't I call Denny and Alex and see if they've got plans for tonight?" I suggested. "Maybe we can do some sort of a group activity."

It turned out that Alex and Denny did in fact have plans for the evening. But they were more than willing to include Tina and me. A great band (or at least, Alex said they were great, I'd never heard of them) was playing at *Patrick's* that evening and they were planning on going to the show. After I got confirmation from Alex that an underage person like Tina would be able to attend, I told them we'd love to join them.

"And," I said to Tina as we drove into town that evening, "you get to wear a lovely arm band that tells the world you're not nineteen yet. It serves two purposes. To stop you from getting served alcohol and to keep the sleazy older men from trying to pick you up."

Even though Tina was only fourteen, she looked at least four years older. It was terrifying. I was going to have to keep an eye on her. Maxine would kill me if Tina got into any real trouble.

"Thanks," she said sarcastically.

"Well, I've got to look out for my little sister," I said innocently. "We wouldn't want you to get off on the wrong track when you're so young."

"Mom's told me what you were like when you were my age, and I know all about her when she was fifteen, so I don't think it's fair that I'm being punished because you two were delinquents."

"I beg your pardon, Miss I-got-kicked-out-of-summer-camp? I may have been a delinquent, and Maxine may have been a little easy, but neither one of us were on the way to becoming felons. I would have left you at home tonight, but I was afraid you'd sell all my stuff on the black market."

"I'm glad you think so highly of me," she said sullenly.

"I do. It's very impressive that you're planning on being a career criminal."

"You're so very funny," she said sarcastically.

The street in front of the bar was crowded by the time we arrived. I had to park a couple of blocks away. Luckily, we were still able to get a table when we got inside. Tina put on her wristband only slightly reluctantly. At fourteen, I didn't think she'd had many opportunities to be inside a pub (at least I hoped not), so this was something of a treat for her.

I wasn't sure how Maxine would feel about it. I realized that I had forgotten to ask Maxine if it would be alright.

"Do you think Maxine will mind that I brought you here?" I asked Tina.

"Probably," Tina replied. "If you want, I don't have to tell her."

"No, you can tell her. But make sure you emphasize the fact that you were wearing an arm band, and I didn't let you out of my sight all evening."

Denny and Alex came in and joined us at our table. I introduced both of them to Tina.

"I actually think we've met before," Denny said to her. "You were younger then. At Sebastian's funeral. You probably don't remember me."

"Sure I do," Tina said. "You were all over Kerri, and Mom didn't like you too much."

"Yeah," Denny said sheepishly. "That was me."

"If you see him all over Kerri again, let me know," Alex said.

"I wouldn't do that," Denny said.

"I know, honey," Alex said, patting his hand reassuringly. "You're sufficiently whipped not to do anything without consulting me first."

"May I please go to the bar and get you lovely ladies a drink?" He asked Alex.

"Sure," she replied. "Just don't talk to any strange women on your way there and come straight back again."

"Yes, ma'am." Denny saluted her before heading to the bar.

We all gave Denny our drink orders. I ordered a Coke so Tina wouldn't be the only one at our table not drinking alcohol.

"So is this band any good?" Tina asked Alex when Denny left.

"They're great," Alex said. "They play here a couple of times a year, but they also play all over the country."

"What type of music do they play?" Tina asked.

I tuned them out while the two of them launched into a discussion about music. Instead, I looked around the bar, astonished at the number of familiar faces I saw. This must be what it's like living in a small town, I thought. It wasn't as annoying as it had been a few weeks earlier. Everyone was fairly nice, and they were no longer treating me like a pariah for breaking up with Carter. I could almost see why someone would want to stay here all year long. Until I remembered that there was nowhere else to go and nothing to do. The winters would be unbearable.

My examination of the crowd came to an abrupt end when the band came on the stage. Alex had been right; they were fairly good. The Fighting Fish were a mix of punk and alternative. Just loud enough to partially deafen you for the rest of the evening. Tina loved them. She especially loved the drummer, and, from the way he kept staring at her, it looked like he was interested in her too. We weren't going to stick around after they were done.

We stayed in the pub until the band's last set at around midnight. I ushered Tina to her feet before the band was off the stage. I knew she wanted to talk to the drummer, but I was sure Maxine would have me killed if anything happened to Tina.

"That was great," I said to Alex as we stood to leave. "Thanks for letting us tag along. I hope we didn't ruin your date."

"Anytime," Alex said. "It was great to meet you Tina."

"You too," Tina said with a smile.

Denny shook his head. "I can't believe I didn't see it before."

"Didn't see what?" I asked him.

"The resemblance," he said. "You two look a lot alike. You're definitely sisters."

"It's the hair colour," Alex added. "And your eyes are the same shape."

"She looks more like Jess," Tina said. "They both have a ton of hair. They look like Chewbacca."

"Thanks," I said, scowling at her.

"I'm sorry that your father has such curly hair," Tina said with a shrug.

"And I'm sorry that you're going to be walking home," I replied to her.

Denny laughed and gave me a hug. "I'll talk to you later this week."

"Bye," I said, moving Tina towards the exit. "I need to get her out of here before the band gets packed up. That drummer was eyeing her up through their sets."

"I'll make sure he knows she's fourteen," Alex called out to us.

Tina and I went outside to find the car. It was dark and somewhat eerie. I always got a little jumpy walking in the dark here. It was much darker than in Toronto. There was a serious lack of street lights. Our car was parked a couple of blocks away, and I almost felt like running. I would have, but I was sure Tina would have made fun of me.

"Can I walk you back to your car?" a voice directly behind me said, making me jump.

I turned around quickly and bumped into Carter.

"Sorry," he said sheepishly. He was standing with Charlotte. She was holding his hand rather possessively. "I saw you two in the bar and thought maybe I'd walk you back to your car."

"I didn't even see you in there," I said to him. I tried not to blush. For the first time, I'd been in *Patrick's* without even thinking about Carter. But here he was. My heart started beating faster. I had to stop myself from knocking Charlotte onto her ass. I was going to be an adult, even if it killed me.

"Yeah, it was pretty crowded," he admitted. Charlotte was standing next to him, looking incredibly angry. It made her look old. "We were near the back."

"I'm Tina," Tina said, sticking her hand out to Carter. I could tell that she thought he was good looking. If there had been any light, I'm sure I would have seen her blush.

"Hi, Tina," he said with a grin.

"Tina's my sister," I explained. "She's Maxine's daughter."

Charlotte sighed impatiently. It was not an attractive sound.

"So, can I walk you two back to your car?" Carter asked.

"We're okay," I began. "We're just parked over …"

"Yes, please," Tina said sweetly. "It's awfully dark out."

Seriously, what was it with this guy? Why does he get this reaction from all the females in my family?

"Great," Carter said.

"I don't think they need anyone to walk with them," Charlotte said with a pout. "There are two of them."

"It will just take a second," Carter said in a slightly annoyed tone.

The four of us started walking towards where I had parked the car. Charlotte came along because she certainly wasn't going to leave Carter alone with me, even if my sister was acting as a chaperone. Charlotte and Tina walked ahead of Carter and me. I noticed that he had slowed his pace slightly so we could talk without being overheard.

"How are you doing?" he asked me.

"Great." Except I'm in love with you, and you've moved on. "How about you?"

"I'm fine. Tina seems nice. She looks a lot like Maxine."

"She's great," I said honestly. "I can't believe she's only fourteen."

"Fourteen!" Carter exclaimed. "When I was that age, girls didn't look like her. There were a ton of guys in the bar that kept talking about her. I'm going to have to spread the word that she's only a kid."

"I would appreciate it if you would," I said to him. "So would Maxine. The women in my family don't seem to have the best judgment when we're in our teens."

Carter laughed. "What did you do?"

"Oh, I'm not telling you."

"Come on, tell."

"No way. I'll just say that all records were expunged, and no one was charged with anything."

"Really."

"That's all I'm saying."

We were silent for a little while.

"Can you and I be friends now?" he asked me when we were in sight of the car.

"Of course we're friends."

"So you won't avoid me every time you see me in town?"

"I haven't been avoiding you."

"Yes, you have."

"Well, maybe just a little," I admitted sheepishly. "But this stupid town is so small it was kind of difficult."

"That is very true," he replied with a laugh. "Fifteen minutes after I split from my wife, the whole town knew she was a lesbian. It was great for my ego."

"I'm sure it was."

"And after you and I broke up, everyone was sure it was for the same reason. It was good that you started dating that jerk."

"I'm glad I could help."

"So seriously, we're friends again? No more looking for places to hide when you see me in the grocery store?"

"I promise." I crossed my heart with two fingers.

"Great," he smiled at me. I felt butterflies in my stomach, and my heart was pounding so loud I was sure he'd be able to hear it.

"Well, here we are," I said forcing a cheerful tone when we reached the car. "Thanks for the escort."

"No problem, ma'am," he said with a bow in a Southern accent. Then he grabbed my hand and kissed the top of it. He looked at me with a grin.

I was pretty sure that my heart had stopped beating.

As Tina and I got into the car, I watched Carter and Charlotte walk away. I could tell that she was arguing with him about something. Good, I thought. I didn't like her.

I kept thinking about Carter as I tried to sleep that night. I was glad that we could be civil to each other, but I didn't want to be friends with him. Unfortunately, there was nothing I could do about it.

Chapter Eighteen

My book was finished by the second week in August. I couldn't believe how fast I had been able to write it. And I was actually happy with the final result. It was much better than my first book. At least this story had a happy ending. Printing out the final copy felt like a weight had been lifted from my shoulders. Even if no one ever read it, I was still happy.

"Finished?" Tina asked as I came downstairs carrying a stack of paper.
"Yes. Finally."
"How long did it take you?"
"About a month. But that was after two years of not writing anything."
"When can I read it?" she asked.
"You can read it today, if you want. I'll print you off a copy when I get back."
"Where are you going?"
"I have to send a copy to my agent, so I'm going into town. Do you want to come?"
"No, thanks. I think I'll stay here and get a suntan before we have to go back to the city."

"Suit yourself," I said picking my keys off the table. "I'll see you when I get back. Stay away from the lake while I'm gone."

She scowled at me. "I'm not a child."

"I know you're not a child. I just don't want to come back and find you floating face down in the water."

"Fine," she grumbled. "What time do you want to leave?"

Tina and I were heading back to Toronto. I had a lot of things to do that I couldn't do at the cottage. I needed to meet with my agent. I needed to find an apartment. Tina had to start getting ready to go back to school. And there wasn't any reason for me to stay at the cottage. I needed to get back into my real life again. I'd been putting it off for too long.

"I'd like to head out sometime this afternoon," I replied. "I still have a few things to pack before we go."

When I got to town, my first stop was the post office. I paid the extra money to have my manuscript sent express to my agent. It was very satisfying to send him a stack of papers. I hoped he'd be happy with the final result.

I had one more stop to make before Tina and I could leave. I had to drop by Carter's office. Now that we were friends again, I knew I had to stop by before leaving town.

When I entered his office, I immediately noticed that something was different. And it wasn't a subtle difference. Charlotte was no longer sitting behind the desk at reception. Carter probably didn't want his girlfriend to work for him. In Charlotte's place was a matronly-looking woman in her forties. She looked stern and very official. I liked her right away.

"Hello," I said to her. "Is Carter in?"

"May I have your name?"

"Kerrigan Shepherd," I said, "but I don't have an appointment. I just want to drop something off for him." I held up the package for her to see. "I can just leave it here with you if you'd like."

"I'll see if he's available." She picked up the phone and spoke quietly to him. "You can go right in."

I walked down the hall and handed him the package.

"What's this?" he asked, taking it from me. His desk was covered with files, and I could tell that I was interrupting him on a busy day.

"Just read it," I said. "I'm sorry to interrupt. You look busy."

"I am busy," he replied. "But that's okay. I needed to take a break anyway. Do you want to go get a coffee or something?"

I shook my head. "I've got to get back to the cottage. Tina's waiting for me. We're heading back to Toronto today."

"Oh."

"I wanted to let you know, since we're friends and all."

"Thanks." He looked down at the folder in his hands. "What's in the package?"

"My book. I wanted you to have a copy before it was published."

He looked pleased. "Thanks."

"You're welcome." I turned to leave his office.

"Kerri?"

I turned back to look at him.

"Yeah?"

"I'll give you a call when I've finished it."

"You don't have to," I said with a smile.

"No," he replied seriously. "I want to."

I knew this was the last time we'd see each other. I wouldn't be coming back. There was more that I wanted to say to him, but I couldn't find the words. I wanted to tell him that I was sorry. I wanted to tell him that I'd been an idiot.

I wanted to tell him that I loved him.

But I couldn't.

So instead I just smiled at him and left.

I left his office and walked back to my car. I opened the door and sat behind the wheel. After a few deep, calming breaths I was able to turn the key and start the engine. Even though it felt like my heart was breaking, I managed to drive back out to the cottage without crashing the car.

Tina was out on the deck in her bathing suit. I sat down on the lounge next to her with a sigh.

"You okay?" she asked, tipping her sunglasses down to look at me.

"If I had a dollar for every time someone asked me that ..." I grumbled.

"Sorry."

"I didn't mean to snap at you," I said. "I'm fine. I was just saying goodbye to some people in town."

"By 'some people', you mean Carter, don't you?"

I nodded. "It was a very civil goodbye."

"But you're going to come back here, aren't you? It's not like you're never going to see him again."

"I don't know, Tina. I don't think I'll ever come back. It would be too weird."

"You're an idiot."

"Thanks. Any specific reason why you're calling me an idiot?"

"If I was in love with someone, I'd tell them. I wouldn't run away."

"You don't know what you're talking about," I said, shaking my head at her. "You're just a kid."

"I'm not a kid," she insisted. "And I still say you're being an idiot."

"Have you packed yet?"

"Nice segue," she said. "Yeah, I've packed."

"Good. I'm going inside. Be ready to leave in an hour."

I went upstairs to pack my bags. I packed everything I could fit into two duffel bags. I was leaving behind my books and my desk, but I knew I could get Maxine and Jack to bring it to me later.

Tina came into my room as I was zipping up one of my bags. She flopped down on the bed and looked up at me.

"You ready to go?" she asked me.

"Almost. How about you?"

She nodded. "I hate to leave. I don't want to go back to the city. Are you sure we have to go?"

"Yeah, I have to go in person to talk with my agent. And you need to get ready to go back to school."

"School is still weeks away. Why don't I stay here by myself?"

"I'm sure Maxine would love that," I said sarcastically.

"Why not? I'm almost fifteen."

"And look what happened to Maxine when she was fifteen." I gestured to myself. "Claiming to be a mature almost-fifteen-year-old won't work as much of an argument with her."

"True."

"Come on. Let's get going before traffic gets too bad."

I grabbed both of my bags and carried them downstairs. We made sure that all the doors were securely locked before we went out to the car. Tina got into the passenger's seat while I stood staring at the cottage.

I knew I was doing the right thing by leaving. I knew it was time I moved on. But a large part of me wanted to stay.

With a sigh and a final glance at the lake, I started the car.

"Ready to go?" I asked Tina.

"As long as you don't choose the music, I'm ready."

"Too bad." I stuck my tongue out at her and put *ABBA Gold* in the CD player.

She groaned as the cheerful music started blaring out of the speakers. "You're going to kill me with this stuff."

"By the time we've reached Newmarket, you'll love it."

Less than two hours later, I pulled into Maxine and Jack's driveway. I got out of the car to help Tina with her bags.

Maxine opened the front door and practically ran out to meet us. She pulled Tina into a bone crushing hug before turning and doing the same to me.

"I'm glad you're both still alive," she said, putting an arm around Tina's shoulder and another around mine before leading us inside. She turned and looked at me. "Did you have a good drive? Did Tina behave herself? Did *you* behave yourself?"

I raised an eyebrow at her. "Which of those questions do you want me to answer first?"

"I behaved perfectly," Tina said. "The drive was fine, despite the ABBA music. Kerri behaved okay, but she's a bit of an idiot."

"Thanks," I said to her.

Tina continued as if I hadn't spoken. "She wouldn't tell Carter how she felt about him."

Jess came into the room at that moment. "Really? Kerri, you need to tell him that you love him."

I threw my hands up in frustration. "This isn't some romantic-comedy, where Hugh Grant comes bursting in at the last moment professing his undying love. This is real life. Sometimes relationships don't work out."

"Yeah, but ..." Jess started.

I cut her off. "Carter's moved on, and I'm going to as well." Eventually ...

"That's the spirit," Maxine said, putting her arm around my shoulder.

"Where's Jack?" I asked, eager to have something else to talk about.

"He took the boys to Canada's Wonderland," Jess said. She didn't look too impressed. "I had to work."

"Are you going to stay for dinner?" Maxine asked me.

I shook my head. "I'm going to get something to eat with James. I should probably head down there now, before traffic gets bad."

"Traffic is always bad downtown," Maxine reminded me. "You're going to have to get used to it again."

"I'm going to have to get used to a lot of things," I admitted. "I'll call you once I'm settled in."

"Good." Maxine smiled at me.

"How come you're not staying here with us?" Tina asked me she walked me back to my car.

"I'm going to stay with my friend James for a little while," I said to her. "Then I'm going to find my own place. I'll call you, and we'll get together soon."

She gave me a big hug.

"Okay," she said. "I love you."

"I love you too." Strangely, I had a lump in my throat. I was going to miss having Tina around.

As I pulled out of Maxine's driveway, I dialed James' number on my cell phone. He answered on the third ring.

"Am I still allowed to sleep on your couch?" I asked him.

"Of course, sweetie," he said to me, although he didn't sound as enthusiastic as I hoped he would. "It's just for a while, isn't it?"

"Yes, James. I'm not permanently moving in with you."

"I'm looking forward to having you stay with me."

"You are such a liar," I said laughing at him. "I'll see you in about a half an hour."

I drove to James' apartment building and pulled into the visitor's lot. The traffic was horrible. By the time I had reached James' building, my knuckles were white from clenching the steering wheel.

I hadn't wanted to impose on Jack and Maxine. I needed to find my own place and a sure way to do that was to spend time sleeping on a friend's couch. I needed no other motivation than James continually harping on me to get out.

"Hi, sweetie," James said when he let me into his condo. "Welcome to my home."

James had a great one-bedroom apartment on Lakeshore. His view was spectacular, and I knew he had paid a ton for it.

"How long are you staying?" James asked as I came in.

"Hopefully, not too long," I replied. "I'm going to start looking for my own place tomorrow."

"Great," he said, the relief evident in his voice. Then he quickly back tracked. "Not that I wouldn't love having you stay here indefinitely, but can you imagine the gossip if people found out I was living here with a woman?"

"I promise your reputation will not be harmed. I'll be out of here as soon as I find a decent place in my price range."

"And what exactly is your price range?"

"I'm not sure," I said with a grin. "I'll have to see how my agent likes my book before deciding. I'll probably have to find another job waiting tables." The thought made me shudder. I hated working in restaurants.

"Why don't you just move permanently into your house up north?"

"I can't stay there all winter," I said. "I'd go crazy up there all by myself. I've read 'The Shining'. I know what happens. I think I've gotten used to having other people around. If you think I'm bad now, imagine how crazy I'd be after spending the entire winter alone up north." I paused before continuing. "And I've decided not to keep the place. He wasn't my father. I'm giving it to Maxine. It really should be hers. Then the kids could enjoy it every summer. And as her first born, I would be the one to inherit it."

"That's big of you. You'll still get to go there in the summer but Maxine and Jack can take care of the property taxes and general maintenance."

"I don't think I'll be going up there again."

"Sweetie …"

I cut him off. "It was nice for this summer. But I've got to get back to the real world. *This* is the real world. Expensive apartments, traffic and me being alone again. It's time I got used to it."

"Why don't you …"

I didn't want any advice. "James, I'm fine. I'm excited about finding a new place."

I sat down on the couch and picked the newspaper up off the coffee table. With my feet up on the coffee table, I started to search for the classified section.

I looked up to the sound of James clearing his throat.

"Yes?" I asked.

"Your feet … my table … $6,000 …" he stammered.

I took that to mean that he wanted my feet off his coffee table.

"Sorry," I said as I removed my feet.

I shifted my gaze back to the classifieds, looking for the section advertising rentals. Fortunately, there seemed to be quite a few places listed.

"I've taken the liberty of marking out a few places you might want to look at," James said.

"So I see. And you've used different colours. Do they mean something?"

"Red means more expensive than your last place. Blue means it's not in a great neighbourhood and purple means that it's on the subway line. Green means cheap but in the suburbs. Orange means …"

I held up my hand to stop him. "I get it. There's a lot of red."

"Yeah. I think you should focus on the purple ones."

"You really want me out of here, don't you?"

"More than words can express."

I threw the newspaper at him.

"So what are our exciting plans for tonight?" James asked sitting down next to me. "Dancing till dawn? Drinking like we're eighteen again?"

"Actually, I'm kind of tired," I said sheepishly. "I don't think I can handle a late night. I want to get up early to look at apartments."

"So now you and Denny have both grown up and deserted me," James complained. "What am I supposed to do without you guys? I think I need to get some new friends."

"What are you going to do?"

"I'm going to go out without you," he said, standing up with a determined look on his face.

"Good for you."

"You can sleep in my room. I'll take the couch when I stumble in around dawn."

After a few phone calls, James discovered that he did have friends other than Denny and me who were more than willing to go out with him. I sat on his couch while he got ready, eating Chinese food and attempting to watch a really bad movie on TV. It took James at least three times longer than I usually took to get ready. But by the time he was finished he looked absolutely gorgeous.

"So?" he asked as he did a little twirl in front of me.

"You look great," I said truthfully.

"You don't," he said, scowling at me.

I was wearing an old McMaster t-shirt, a pair of boxer shorts and I had my hair up in a bun.

"You look like you're about fifteen," he continued. "Are you sure you won't change your mind and come with me?"

"As much as I'd love to spend the evening with you in a gay bar, I think I'll stay here and get some rest."

"But it will be fun! Lots of great music, tons of guys. I'm sure they'll even be playing some ABBA. It will help you take your mind off of your lawyer-friend."

"I'm not sitting at home pining over Carter," I said, scowling at him. "I'm honestly just tired."

"Fine. I'll bring you a glow stick." He paused. "And please, *please* don't spill anything on that couch."

My plan was to start searching for an apartment first thing in the morning. I woke up at eight without even having to set my alarm. I walked as quietly as I could into the kitchen to get some juice. James had passed out fully dressed on the couch, and I didn't want to wake him.

I took a glass out of the cupboard and set it on the counter silently. Then I poured myself a big glass of orange juice, took one sip and started to walk back towards the bedroom.

Unfortunately, I caught my foot on the edge of the rug and flung the glass against the wall. The glass shattered into a thousand pieces and orange juice was sprayed everywhere.

"Fuck!" I said loudly.

James was going to kill me.

I held my breath, waiting for him to scream at me. When nothing happened I crept over to the couch to look at him. He hadn't even moved.

I breathed a sigh of relief before I started to worry about him. Was it possible that he'd died of alcohol poisoning?

I knelt in front of him, trying to determine if he was still alive. His chest was rising and falling slowly, so I knew he was still breathing (and his incredibly foul breath was also a good indication of life).

But he was lying on his back, and I didn't want to leave the condo with him in that position. I was worried that he might choke on his own vomit.

I poked and prodded him, but he didn't move.

"James," I said softly. Nothing. "James!" I yelled.

Finally, he groaned and opened his eyes slightly.

"Shit," he mumbled.

"What's wrong?"

"I drank too much and came home with a woman."

"Ha, ha."

"Why are you waking me up?" he asked as he rolled onto his side. "It's still early."

"I didn't want you to choke on your own vomit and die."

"Like Mama Cass?"

"I think that was a ham sandwich."

"Whatever," he grumbled, turning away from me and facing the back of the couch.

Feeling confident that James wasn't going to die, I picked up a cloth from the kitchen and started to clean up my spilt juice. I carefully swept the broken glass into a plastic bag. I wasn't sure how I was going to tell James about the broken glass. It probably cost more than my car.

After I carefully hid the broken glass at the bottom of the garbage bin, I picked up the portable phone and went back into the bedroom. I sat down on the bed and dialed Maxine's number.

"Tina?" I asked when the phone was answered.

"Hi, Kerri," she replied.

"Want to help me look for an apartment?" I didn't feel like doing it alone, and James was in no shape to assist me. I wanted to have someone to bounce ideas off of.

"Sure."

"Ask Jess if she wants to come too."

"Jess!" I heard Tina shout. I don't think she even bothered to cover the phone. "Wanna go look at apartments with Kerri?" There were a few seconds of silence while she waited for Jess' answer. "We're both in."

"Thanks for screaming in my ear."

"Don't mention it," she said cheerfully.

"Can you get Jack or Maxine to drop you off at Yorkdale? I can meet you there, and we'll take the subway."

"We can take the subway downtown and meet you," she said.

"There's no way I'm letting you and Jess take the subway on your own," I said firmly. "And I'm sure there's no way Maxine would let you go on your own either."

Tina sighed. "Fine. We'll meet you at Yorkdale."

An hour later I met the girls at Yorkdale shopping center. Jess seemed to be more interested in shopping than in helping me look for a place to live, and only my promise of browsing in the afternoon would drag her out of the stores. I led the girls to the subway, and we headed back into the city. I was a little wary about having the girls with me on the subway, so I made sure to keep a close eye on them.

"You're staring," Tina said to me.

"No, I'm not," I said. "I'm just trying to make sure you don't get lost."

"Kerri, we're teenagers," Jess said indignantly.

"Exactly," I replied. "You're not to be trusted."

"We're not going to wander off and get lost," Tina said.

"I'm more concerned that you might try and steal someone's wallet. Keep your hands where I can see them."

Tina scowled at me and slouched down in her seat.

I had decided not to use my car for the apartment hunt. I wanted to find something on the subway line, since I was planning on selling the car. I couldn't really afford it now that I was back in Toronto. The insurance, gas and parking were going to bankrupt me. But selling it was probably going to be difficult. The car was such a piece of crap it would be easier to let it roll down a hill into the lake than find someone stupid enough to buy it.

While I sat across from Tina and Jess on the subway, I pulled out the rental list and gave it a quick scan. I didn't have any appointments, but I thought I'd see how many places we could look at anyway. When we reached the stop at Yonge and St. Clair, I ushered the girls out of the subway car (I really would have preferred to live further downtown but there was no way I could afford it).

It was a beautiful day. I felt surprisingly optimistic. I was really looking forward to finding a new place of my own.

Halfway through the morning, I remembered why I hated looking for a place to live in Toronto. All the good places were taken. All the ads in the paper were misleading. Quaint meant tiny. Rustic meant that the place was a dump. Fixer-upper meant that it should be condemned. It was hopeless.

I could tell by the look in both Tina and Jess' eyes that they were just as discouraged as I was.

The first place on our list was a bachelor apartment near St. Clair. The toilet was in the living room, and there was no shower. The second place was listed as a room in a shared apartment. The apartment itself was okay, but I was pretty sure that the occupants were members of a cult.

"I think you'd have to shave your head to live here," Jess said quietly to me while we were in the apartment.

"Shhh!" I hushed her.

"I don't know," Tina added. "Bald might be a good look for you. I just wouldn't drink any Kool-Aid if they offer it to you."

I had to pretend to cough in order to cover a laugh.

The third place was the worst yet.

"I think this place should be condemned," Jess said as we looked around.

"Shit!" Tina jumped. "Either I just saw a rat, or the cockroaches are wearing fur this year."

We gave up at around four in the afternoon and headed back to James' apartment. The girls wanted to see where I was staying, and we all needed to take a break. We were discouraged and exhausted.

I called Maxine from my cell phone and told her where we were. She said she'd have Jack pick the girls up, which meant I didn't have to take another long subway ride up to Yorkdale.

"What about something in this building?" Jess suggested tiredly, throwing herself onto the couch. I could just imagine James' reaction.

"Too expensive," I said as I grabbed some sodas from the fridge.

I didn't say anything as Jess put her feet up on James' precious coffee table.

"Don't you have any money?" Tina said in an exasperated tone. She took a drink from me and sat down next to Jess.

"Not really."

"How can you not have any money? You were living rent-free all summer."

"But I wasn't making that much either," I pointed out to her. "Especially after I stopped writing the column."

"But still."

"I have a little money saved up," I admitted. "But not enough for the rent in this building. I'd have to pay first and last months rent. I think some of the places here are renting for almost three grand a month."

"Then why don't you buy some place?" Tina asked, sounding exasperated with me. "It makes more sense then renting for the rest of your life."

"Again, I'd need money. I'd need at least 10% for a down payment."

"Borrow it from Mom," Tina said as she took a swig from her soda. "She'd totally lend it to you. You've got total guilt-leverage you can use."

"Yeah, but buying's a big deal," I explained. "You'll understand when you're my age."

"When I'm as old as you," Tina said, stressing the word 'old', "I'll definitely own my own place."

"I'm twenty-five, you jackass. I'm not old."

"Old enough to own your own place," Tina insisted.

"I'm not sure about real estate."

"Then move in with the creepy cult-peoples and change your name to Sister Moonshine," Tina said. "It's the best you're going to do."

"Maybe I'll just move in with Jack and Maxine," I said. "Then you two will have to share a room."

"No way am I sharing a room with Jess," Tina said firmly. "She snores."

"Yeah, well, you punch people in your sleep," I pointed out to her.

"You really should move in with us," Jess said sounding pleased. "I know Dad would love that. He really wants to get to know you better."

"I'll think about it," I said.

"I really think you should buy a place," Tina said firmly.

"I said I'll think about it."

Despite my protests, I turned to the condo section of the paper after Jess and Tina left. I was engrossed in the ads when James came in.

"Any luck?" he asked, sitting next to me on the couch.

"Yes. All bad," I said. "There's not a single decent place in the entire city. And they all want too much money, my first born and a phoenix feather for rent."

"What are you going to do?"

I knew he wanted me out ASAP but was being too polite at the moment to say it to my face. It wouldn't last.

"I thought you and I could get married," I said not looking up at his face. "Then we'd get the tax benefits of a married couple, and I could stay here with you indefinitely."

I looked up at him finally, an innocent expression on my face. He was looking incredibly pale.

"Don't worry," I said, patting his hand. "I was only kidding."

He sighed in relief.

"Seriously, though," I continued. "I took Jess and Tina with me today. The apartments we saw were awful. Tina suggested I buy a place, and I've started to think that she might be right."

"It's a good idea, but …" He didn't finish his thought.

"But what?"

"Well, don't get angry, but I was still hoping you'd end up moving to New Ferndale."

"I already told you I'm giving the cottage to Maxine. And I don't want to go back there."

"Not to the cottage. I was hoping you and Carter would get back together."

"It's not going to happen."

"Why not?"

I couldn't tell him that I knew from Carter's face that he didn't love me. It was a little humiliating.

So instead, I told a little lie.

"He and I talked before I left. We both decided that it would be best if we just stayed friends. In fact, I think he and Charlotte are getting quite serious."

James raised an eyebrow at me.

"I'm serious," I said. "You'll just have to put up with me for a little while longer."

The following week I went to see my agent. He was extremely happy to see me, which was a big change from the last time we'd met. The last two years, he hadn't been too happy with me. I didn't know why he kept me. In the past two years, I'd only written a handful of short stories, and he hadn't been able to get any of them published.

"Kerrigan, darling," he said as he kissed me on the cheek. "It's wonderful. Fabulous."

"I take it you liked the book."

"Like it! I love it! It's the best thing you've ever written. It's nothing like your first book." He paused. "Not that I didn't love your first book."

"It is different," I admitted.

"It has a happy ending. I've never seen you write anything with a happy ending. Something must have changed for you."

I shrugged. "It just seemed to work this time. Don't expect a happy ending on everything I write."

He laughed. "I know you too well for that. But this," he gestured to my manuscript, "was fabulous. I didn't have any trouble getting a publisher to accept your manuscript. They're going to rush the release date. It's going to be a best seller, I can just feel it."

"Great," I said, smiling so hard it felt like my face would split.

"The publishers want to send you on a media tour in January," he continued. "In fact, they've been in talks with their US parent company, and they're thinking about doing a huge North American release. They're going to try and get the book into one of those book clubs that all the talk show hosts have. You know what that means."

A book club could mean that sales would go through the roof. I was stunned.

"That's great," was all I could manage. I was glad I was already sitting down. I didn't think my legs would be able to hold me up.

"It's certainly something that people are going to adore. What made you write about a couple that reunites after twenty-five years of separation? Even I was crying at the end."

"I had a little help," I said. I told him the whole story about Maxine and Jack.

"That's marvelous," he exclaimed. "We can even tell people that it's based on a true story. Do you think your parents would be interested in doing some interviews?"

"I don't think so," I said quickly. I hadn't told Maxine and Jack yet that my book was loosely based on them. "I didn't stick to the facts too much, so it might be best not to talk about it being a true story."

"Fine." He really was in a great mood. "And the company wants to sign you to a three book deal. This could make you a house-hold name,"

"That's fabulous," I said. I knew I sounded like an idiot, but all I could do was gush. I was feeling a little light headed. "I've already started on my next book."

"Wonderful. Send me some chapters whenever you're ready. I'll have papers for you to sign by the end of the week."

I thanked him and left the office in a daze.

Stepping out onto the sidewalk, I felt very pleased. My first thought was to call Maxine. I pulled out my cell phone and dialed her number.

"Hello?" she said as she answered. She sounded rushed.

"Hi. It's Kerri." I launched into my story without giving her time to interrupt.

"That's fabulous," she said when I finished. "We'll have to celebrate. Come over for dinner tonight."

"Okay."

I was quite pleased with myself. Not only was I getting my book published but I actually had a family to celebrate with. I couldn't help but think that Sebastian would have been happy.

I was putting my cell phone back in my purse when I heard my name.

I turned and saw Carter running up to me.

"Hi," he said, catching his breath.

"What are you doing here?" I asked him, confused.

"James told me where you were," he said.

"Why did you go see James?"

"I called Maxine first, and she said you were staying with him."

Why didn't she warn me when I was on the phone with her? I was definitely going to ask her that when I went over for dinner.

"Why are you here? I thought you hated Toronto?"

"I do."

"I thought you said Toronto stank?"

"It does."

"Then why are you here?"

"I wanted to tell you that I read your book."

"Oh?"

"And I wanted you to know that I loved it. It was great."

"Thanks," I said. I didn't think I could manage anything else.

He looked at me like he had something more to say.

"Well, I just wanted you to know that. I guess I should go." He turned to leave.

He was walking away from me. I couldn't let him do it. And suddenly, I panicked.

"I love you," I blurted out.

I quickly covered my mouth with both hands. It was too late. He'd heard.

Carter turned around.

"What did you say?"

"Nothing," I lied.

"I heard you say something," he persisted.

I looked down at my feet. It was too late to take it back. "I said that I love you."

"Do you?"

"Yes." I kept my eyes on the sidewalk. "I was an idiot. I was scared. Scared that you would leave me like everyone else in my life. So I pushed you away. I'm not asking you for anything. I just wanted you to know."

He stepped forward and, placing a hand on my chin, he tilted my head to look up at him.

"What are you doing?" I asked him. I felt dizzy. My heart was beating out of control in my chest. Why wouldn't he say anything?

"I was just checking to make sure you weren't teasing me," he said. "I love you too."

And then he leaned in and kissed me. I pushed him back.

"What about Charlotte?"

"We're through. I ended it weeks ago. It wasn't fair for me to lead her on while I was in love with someone else." He kissed me again. Then he stepped back. "What about your crazy commitment problems? Are you going to freak out again?"

I grabbed him by his jacket and pulled him close. "We'll just have to wait and see."

Epilogue

"I can't get the dress to zip up," I said in frustration. I craned my neck to look at the back of the dress in the mirror.

"Maybe you should have gone to that final fitting last week," Carter said, stepping into the bathroom to help. I sucked in my breath as he pulled the zipper for me. He kissed me on the top of the head.

"Thanks," I said. The dress was so tight, I could hardly breathe. I was pretty sure the zipper would burst if I sat down. "But if the baby's born with a line across its head, don't blame me."

"I'm sure it's going to have too much hair for anyone to notice a line," he said with a grin as he tied his bow tie.

It was a beautiful day for a wedding. It was mid-June and the weather was fabulous. The day was warm but not too hot. But I was still going to be uncomfortable in the dress, which was more than a little too tight. Carter was right. I shouldn't have missed that final dress fitting. But as of a week ago, no one had been able to tell that I was pregnant. Then suddenly, at the beginning of the fourth month, it started to show. It was like I'd swallowed a balloon that was starting to inflate. And it was making my feet swell.

I stood sideways, looking at my profile in the mirror. "Maxine wasn't this big at five months," I grumbled, "and she had twins."

Lilly and Dermot had been born a month after Maxine and Jack's wedding, more than a year and a half earlier.

"I think you look wonderful," Carter said, putting his arms around me with his hands on my stomach.

"You're not exactly an unbiased observer," I said. But I did feel a little better.

Mr. Smith looked up at us from his spot on the floor. I swear that he raised an eyebrow.

"Just be glad we're not forcing you into a suit and tie," I said to the dog. I turned to face Carter. "Remind me why we're doing this?"

"Denny and Alex were nice enough to include us in their wedding party. So you've crammed yourself into that sea-foam green dress to be nice to my sister, and I've tied this bow tie to show my parents that I'm still a member of the Stevens' family."

"Even though you and I got married in Vegas without any of them there," I added for him. "I'm so glad we didn't have to go through all of this."

"It would be nice if my mother would speak to me."

"She's not mad that you eloped," I said. "She's angry about whom you eloped with. But she'll come around as soon as her first grandchild is born."

"I hope so."

I looked at my watch. "We'd better go. I'm already in Alex's bad books for missing that fitting. She'll kill me if we're late for the wedding."

We got to the church just as the rest of the wedding party arrived. As we walked towards them, Carter slipped his hand in mine. I felt the same tingling sensation I always did and smiled. I was happy and I loved him. Life was looking great. And we'd already agreed that if we had a boy we'd name him Sebastian.

978-0-595-44331-4
0-595-44331-1

Printed in the United States
83012LV00004B/16-27/A